"You stubborn wench! It's time to rid you of the notion that you're suitable to be a nun!"

Reyner had been standing over her; suddenly Alouette felt herself pulled to her feet and molded against his lean, powerfully muscled body. His implacable hand tangled in the hair at her nape, holding her still as his lips descended on hers.

It was a wild, hungry kiss, full of anger in the rough way his lips massaged hers, taunting her. It was a kiss full of passion and need, a kiss that demanded an answer. With a whimper, she gave in, leaning into him, feeling the hardness of his body and the evidence of his desire for her. As if in a dream, she felt him caress her neck, then follow its curve down her shoulder until his hand cupped the fullness of her breast. A fire began to smolder in the core of her being, a fire that had been only a spark earlier when he kissed her by the Rhône. She had to believe what he said; she would believe him . . .

"I love you, Alouette," he groaned, raising his head for a moment. "Please . . . let me just hold you. I won't hurt you . . . . . love, I promise . . ."

Laurie Grant
Love's Own Crown

POPULAR LIBRARY

An Imprint of Warner Books, Inc.

A Warner Communications Company

To Margaret Shoemaker,
"Trauma Cop Extraordinaire,"
Grant Emergency Room,
and of course, to Michael,
my own knight in shining armor

XXXVIII

First time he kissed me, he but only kissed
The fingers of this hand wherewith I write,
And ever since, it grew more clean and white,
Slow to world-greetings, quick with its "Oh, list"
When the angels speak. A ring of amethyst
I could not wear here, plainer to my sight,
Than that first kiss. The second passed in height
The first, and sought the forehead, and half missed,
Half falling on the hair. O beyond meed!
That was the chrism of love, which love's own crown,
With sanctifying sweetness, did precede.
The third upon my lips was folded down
In perfect, purple state; since when, indeed,
I have been proud and said, "My love, my own."

From *Sonnets From the Portuguese*
—Elizabeth Barrett Browning

ONE

"But *why*, Your Majesty, must I go on this crusade with you before entering the convent? It's such a long
journey, it could be *years* before I am able to take my
vows! Please, brother," Alouette entreated, lowering her
voice even though they were alone and dropping to her
knees before him, "there is *nothing* for me in this world. I
have been asking to enter Fontevrault since I was fourteen.
Please honor your word to me!"

Phillip Augustus, the young king of France, studied his
half sister's imploring face from his ornately carved
wooden throne, where he sat with the indolent grace of a
large, loose-limbed black cat, complete with narrowly slit-
ted, jade-green eyes.

By the Rood, she's beautiful, he thought to himself, his
eyes gleaming proudly as he gazed at her. His feeling of
guilt still tormented him every time he looked at her or
even thought of her, but this failing he kept secret even
from his personal chaplain. There were some things a Ca-
petian king could not do, and confessing that he had failed
in his chivalric duty to Alouette had been one of them.
Well, he would take care of her now.

Though it seemed the perfect means of protecting her for
a lifetime, he was loath to think of Alouette disappearing
behind convent walls, of her shining ebony tresses hacked
off, of her glorious clear voice raised only in plainsong
chants, of her limpid, luminous eyes concealed from him.

He answered her at last. "Surely, if you long to serve

God, you could do it equally well on crusade. Think of it, *ma soeur*." He allowed his voice to become soft and caressing as he called her sister, knowing it was a great honor to be acknowledged as a relative of the king, particularly if one were born on the wrong side of the blanket. "Think how your singing and lute playing will inspire the sore hearts of weary soldiers pledged to wrest Jerusalem from the Infidel. That, too, will be a service to Our Lord. And if you still wished to enter the convent, you could do so afterward, perhaps even in Rome, or Jerusalem itself!" he added persuasively, though he knew he would never allow her to live so far from him.

"What do you have against Fontevrault, my lord?"

At least she had not refused to come with him, he thought with relief. "Its situation in Plantagenet territory, of course. It is not fitting that a sister of Phillip Capet should be in residence where that she-wolf, Eleanor of Aquitaine, will some day retire!" His voice took on a snarling quality as he spoke of the woman who, had she remained wed to Louis, might have been his mother. "We have perfectly acceptable convents in the Ile de France—I might even found a new one for you and make you its first abbess."

Alouette sighed and made a graceful gesture of acquiescence. "Handing me an abbacy like a beribboned New Year's gift won't be necessary," she said. "I desire only to serve God as a humble *religieuse*." She stood, her slim, elegant fingers smoothing the folds of her mulberry sarcenet gown.

"I would rather bestow the gift of a rich husband upon you, Alouette," he countered. "You could look very high, you know—even a count would not scorn to marry a bastard of the House of Capet!"

He felt rather than saw her wince at his unnecessary cruelty. Though her parentage was an open secret between them, he knew he need not have referred aloud to the fact that her real sire was not Édouard de Chenevy, the obedient count whom Louis had ordered to marry Lisette. The lovely serving wench had become pregnant with his child while Queen Adela lay recovering from a miscarriage.

"We have been over this before, Your Majesty," Alouette replied stiffly. "My mind is made up. I wish to be a bride of Christ rather than of an earthly man." And striving unsuccessfully to conceal how hurt she felt at being called a bastard, she added, "Surely a lifetime of devotion and penance would make up for the stain of my illegitimacy."

Phillip cringed, ashamed despite himself for his thoughtlessness, but really, she should not feel such guilt. Her parentage was no sin of hers—not even the most ascetic monk would say so. Yet he himself had done nothing to elevate her position. And he was not sure he could have borne giving her to some complaisant noble, even with the advantages that such an alliance could bring, knowing that noble would gladly fill her belly with a brat a year, and brag of his children's royal blood. No, perhaps it was better that she be immured with women, her tall, slender figure swathed in black and white robes.

"Very well, Lady Alouette, the bargain is struck. You may enter a convent upon your return from the crusade. We depart in a fortnight for Vézélay, where we shall meet our fellow crusader, Richard, King of England, and combine our armies."

"By God, they've come at last! It's Phillip, only three days late, damn his fat French arse!" Richard Plantagenet cursed loudly, knowing that the procession was too far off for his words to be heard above the jingling of harness and the creak of leather. He vented his irritation upon a small circle of knights and barons standing in the courtyard of the shrine of St. Mary Magdalene. Shortly, a mass of thanksgiving would honor the coming together of the two great armies for the common goal of freeing the Holy Land. The English were assembled in the shadow cast by the statue of Jesus Christ which stood above the basilica. Its arms were poised in a gesture half-welcoming, half-threatening, not unlike Richard of England's own posture as he watched Phillip Augustus draw near.

The king of France rode a white palfrey caparisoned in cloth of gold, with multicolored jewels winking from the horse's headstall.

"Perhaps he was delayed by the necessity of mourning his wife, Your Grace," suggested a voice at Richard's right, in a tone neither timid nor censuring, merely offering an explanation that the king, already called "Coeur de Lion," might not have thought of. "I understand she died in childbirth only ten days ago."

Richard glanced over his shoulder, seeing that the speaker was Sir Reyner of Winslade. The king had to lower his eyes only slightly, for the Norman knight was just an inch or two shorter than his own lofty height. Reyner's deep brown eyes met Richard's evenly, with a look of respect but not servility.

"I suppose so," Richard grudgingly agreed, adding, "That she had to die on the very day the treaty between Phillip and me went into effect is at best unfortunate." His voice suggested that there had been something deliberately inconsiderate in Queen Margaret's choice of days to die. "Still, look at him. One could hardly tell he mourned a beloved wife—see his fat sly face!"

Reyner had to agree that the younger king's face was triumphant, rather than grieving. There was nothing of the bereaved widower in his haughty, regal manner when he dismounted and strode warily toward the Plantagenet's outstretched arms.

"Make sure that wolf doesn't disgrace us all by taking a hunk out of Phillip," Richard admonished in an undertone, but Reyner caught the twinkle in his king's eye that suggested he wouldn't blame the dog for doing just that. Despite his warning, Richard leaned down to ruffle the big animal's fur.

"Zeus won't attack, except by my command," Reyner assured his sovereign, glancing fondly down at the massive black and gray creature sitting on his haunches at Reyner's feet. In truth Zeus was only half wolf. His dam was a descendant of the huge mastiff Ami that had come from Aquitaine with Reyner's mother, Ysabeau de Ré, and been lured into the woods by the passionate mating call of the wolf.

Zeus began to growl, the sound rumbling from low in his throat, as the younger king approached Richard.

"Easy, boy," Reyner murmured, and the huge canine looked up, grinning as if to say, "I promise you I won't attack, but you must agree it's tempting."

Reyner wondered what was in King Phillip's mind as he greeted Richard, the man who had kept his sister, Princess Alais, dangling all these years, refusing to marry her or to part company with her dowry, the strategically important county of the Vexin.

If Phillip's blood ran hot at the thought of Alais's awkward position (some said more than awkward, in that Henry II had made her his mistress years ago), he gave no sign. He smiled graciously as the taller, English king gave a courtly welcoming speech to the French army, spread out behind Phillip among the clustered gray houses of the Burgundian countryside.

With a gesture Richard invited Phillip inside, where the bishop waited. Only a fraction of the crusading armies would be able to crowd into the basilica, but Reyner was confident of a place. He was one of the trusted inner circle about Richard, just as Reyner's father had been one of Henry II's intimates.

Even so, he nearly lost his place in the procession, so distracted was he by the sight of the girl dismounting from the matching white palfrey next to Phillip's.

What had caught his eye initially was her slight stumble as she apparently misjudged the lackey's waiting arms, perhaps because she was looking above the servant's head as she alighted. After that, however, he forgot the brief moment of clumsiness as he was captured by her beauty.

The girl was as slender as Phillip was corpulent. From his slightly elevated vantage point a few yards away, it appeared to Reyner that the top of her head would graze his chin if she were standing in front of him. (Good God! Why was *that* his first thought?) Once dismounted, she stood still, her chin turning slowly as if she were watching for someone, so he was able to study her at some length.

A sheer linen barbette and veil framed a heart-shaped face with high cheekbones and large eyes of brilliant cobalt blue, a delicately carved nose like that of an alabaster Madonna, set above lips as temptingly curved as a Magdalen's—before repentance. It was her mouth that kept the girl's face from being too remote and virginal and bespoke the promise of passion and fire beneath her composed exterior.

Who was she? he wondered. He looked about for someone to ask, but all his companions had long since vanished into the church's cool interior. He noted the scarlet fleur-de-lis embroidered on her palfrey's golden trappings, which matched the decoration on the French king's mount, and decided with a sinking feeling that she must be Phillip's mistress. As different from each other as they looked, Phillip and the girl could not possibly be related.

If she were the French king's mistress, it would be dangerous even to play the courtly lover with her, for he knew instinctively that Phillip Capet would not share the girl in such a traditional fashion. Holy Mary, the French girl could not belong to Phillip!

He saw her pluck nervously at the skirts of her azure silk gown as the moments lengthened and she still stood alone. He was just about to stride over and offer his services when a young *chevalier* appeared at her side and spoke briefly to her.

At once, the girl's face became animated with relief, though she did not turn to face the speaker. She took his arm, and walked with measured steps toward the church. Reyner watched with growing realization as he saw the young man carefully shepherd her up the steps and into the basilica. The unknown beauty was blind.

The fact did not diminish Reyner's dawning ardor. Now it was doubly important to get inside, preferably someplace where he could observe her and obtain some clue as to her identity.

"Stay, Zeus," he commanded the dog, and the massive canine sank obediently back to his haunches. Reyner knew he could come back in five minutes or five hours and the dog would still be waiting, resisting the enticements of other dogs, teasing cats, and men who would have liked to possess such an animal.

* * *

By the time Reyner had maneuvered his way through the crowd, it was too late to secure a place among the English court, but that suited his purpose. He found himself next to William des Barres, a French knight. From where he stood he could also see the girl, standing behind and to the left of Phillip.

"*Sieur* William," he whispered above the swelling anthem of the choir.

"Reyner!" whispered back the Frenchman, a smile of recognition lighting his face, for he and Reyner had fought side by side in Richard's recent rebellion against the aging Henry—an insurrection that had been supported by Phillip, who stood to gain when there was discord between Plantagenet father and son. "We are well met!"

But it was not of old times that Reyner wished to speak. "That woman there—behind Phillip, in the azure gown embroidered with fleur-de-lis. Who is she?"

"Ah, I see she has collected your heart, along with dozens of others," William answered with a sympathetic look, watching Reyner's earnest brown eyes. "Her name is Lady Alouette de Chenevy, *mon vieux.*"

"Alouette—Lark," Reyner translated, still watching the girl as she stood raptly listening to the pure clear tones of the choir.

"Yes, a very fitting name, for her voice is as lovely as her person. Ah, *mon ami*, wait until you hear her sing!" Des Barres's hands fluttered with Gallic expressiveness.

"She is coming on crusade?" Reyner asked in disbelief, for Richard had discouraged the bringing of wives and sweethearts. A part of him rejoiced that this was not the only time he would set eyes on her, while a cooler portion of his brain was surer than before that she was Phillip's mistress. "*What* is she, then?" he asked, a guarded look stealing over his handsome features.

"Officially, the daughter of Baron de Chenevy. But actually, the natural daughter of Louis Capet."

"King Louis had a b—...a love child?" muttered Reyner in disbelief, stumbling over the ugly word *bastard*, unable to apply it to the lovely female he saw fingering a pearl and onyx rosary. "I thought he was too much of a monk."

"He was a man," corrected the other knight, "and his monkish ways were much exaggerated by your Queen Eleanor to secure her divorce. Yes, it is common knowledge that Lady Alouette is half sister to King Phillip, though none speak of it, of course. But it is said that the king dotes on her, and insists that she come to Outremer to sing and play her lute for him."

Reyner smoothed back an errant lock of the tawny-gold hair that was a heritage from his Norman sire, Simon of Winslade, Earl of Hawkingham. His heart sang. The girl did not share Phillip Capet's bed!

"Has she been blind from birth, William? She does not have that shadowed look; her eyes are beautiful and clear, as if she could see."

"Nay, I have heard she was born with normal sight, and that she became ill sometime in childhood. When she emerged from the sickroom she was blind. Naturally, all the best physicians have examined her and tried various treatments, from bleeding to prayers. Phillip even called in a Jew, but she remains sightless. A pity, though perhaps Our Lord gave her musical talent in compensation."

"Perhaps," echoed Reyner, though he was not convinced it was a fair trade. "And is she betrothed to some Frenchman, then? The man with her, perhaps?" He was half afraid to hear the answer—to have his hopes dashed again. His expression betrayed more than he knew of his feelings.

"What has become of the dashing, devil-may-care bachelor knight in Richard's service?" teased des Barres. "When we rode together last it was a different wench every night for you. You swore marriage was not for you; only your older brother, as your father's heir, must breed legitimate sons for Hawkingham! You vowed to stay free to seduce a different noble's wife each month!"

"That was before I saw Alouette de Chenevy."

"Ah, *mon brave*, you are smitten," observed his companion. "No, she is not betrothed, and that is Henri de Chenevy, her stepbrother, at her side. It may interest you to know that she has been allowed to refuse the suitors Phillip has permitted near her, though there have been several. I have heard it said she wants to become a nun, and will be allowed to do so after the crusade."

"No, by God!" Reyner of Winslade made the vow loudly enough that several knights turned around to glare at him. The crosses on their surcoats, indicating their pledge to go on crusade, rippled as they moved. There were white crosses for the French, red for English, green for Flemings.

"Good luck then, Reyner, but have a care. As I have said, she is related to Phillip."

"I don't care if she's the sister of all twelve apostles," Reyner said recklessly, though he did trouble to lower his voice. "That one was not meant to be a nun."

"Ah, there I agree with you, Reyner," was William's final comment on the subject.

Reyner forced himself to look away from Alouette, thinking it a pity that she could not see the ornate splendor of the church. The altar of gray marble draped in red velvet was a fitting tribute to the female saint, whose remains, it was said, had been stolen from St. Maximen's in Provence, where legend had it the three Marys had come ashore following the Crucifixion. Each pillar of tiger-striped stone was a work of art in itself, with the capital of each column featuring flamelike carvings of azure, vermillion, and gold. St. Bernard had condemned such decoration, Reyner had heard, and as he looked more carefully he could see why the austere saint had been so disapproving. One capital featured jongleurs piping to the demon of lust, who was caressing a pair of naked breasts, while others had beasts and chimaeras chasing each other around the top. The decorations were a vivid feast for the eyes, however, and during the interminable mass, Reyner wished Alouette could see them also. He would have enjoyed watching her reaction to the pagan delights situated so incongruously in this holy place.

Throughout the tedious and repetitive service, hope sustained him that afterwards, somehow, he could contrive to meet her—to see if the voice matched the lovely face, to watch her respond to his own voice, even if she could not evaluate his features. At the very least he wanted to be near her, to breathe her essence. He was sure she would smell of lilies.

He was to be disappointed. As the combined armies of Christendom marched back out into the sunlight, buoyed by the blessing of the bishop on their holy enterprise, he saw Alouette de Chenevy whisked out a side exit by her brother.

Trying to change course in the milling throng was impossible, and he was carried along willy-nilly until he reached the dazzling sunlight outside. There he was detained by King Richard himself, who informed him that he was to take charge of guarding the English camp tonight.

"My men may as well learn now that I will not tolerate misbehavior in those dedicated to a holy cause. They are not to fight among themselves or with crusaders of other nations, and they are to stay within the encampment perimeter. I don't want to have to scour Vézelay when we leave, scraping Englishmen out of taverns and stews. Let them be warned that my penalties will be severe."

Reyner sighed heavily, summoning Zeus from his station at the foot of the steps with a snap of his fingers as the king went back to his conversation with the bishop. Guard duty. It meant he would miss the banquet Richard was giving tonight for Phillip and his retinue—an event he was sure Alouette de Chenevy would be attending. Perhaps she would even be asked to sing, and he would not be there to hear it. He would be out attempting a miracle—trying to make hundreds of Englishmen behave like the saints they were not.

TWO

Alouette de Chenevy, her hand holding lightly to her page's arm, walked carefully up the cobbled streets of Vézélay, feeling the early morning mist on her cheeks and the guilty pricking of her conscience.

She knew she should not disobey Phillip, who had ordered her not to leave the large townhouse, which he had commandeered from a prosperous burgher, unless he or Henri accompanied her. But her royal brother would be closeted with Richard Plantagenet all day, and Henri would be drilling with the French army until God knew when. She wanted to go to confession and mass now, while it was quiet and peaceful, to see if she could recapture that blissful sense of joy that had tantalized her so fleetingly yesterday.

When the choir had sung the *Te Deum*, and she had smelled the sweet incense, she had briefly felt a sense of peace and serenity that had been absent in the hectic hustle and bustle of traveling in the royal train. Even with the numerous auditory distractions that echoed in the high-ceilinged basilica—the coughs, the sighs and whispers, the rustle of clothing—she had felt happy, able to filter out the irrelevancies and concentrate on her prayers. But her absorption had been transitory, broken by a growing sense of unease—no, she thought, that was not precisely the word, for the feeling was not totally unpleasant. She had had the distinct feeling that someone was watching her. The sensation had caused an odd *frisson* of excitement to travel down her spine.

But surely that was a silly fancy, she told herself sternly, and one more fitting to a moon-kissed tavern wench than one who would be a bride of Christ. She should confess it, along with her ungratefulness to Phillip, before taking the sacraments.

"Lovely Alouette, who wouldn't stare at you? A man would be a fool not to!" Henri had said, making light of her question as he guided her to their lodging. He had always been devoted to her, as if he were in fact her brother, and she loved him. "But no, I noticed no one in particular. Most of us were busy wondering if Richard Plantagenet would be able to sit through the entire mass— the House of Anjou is said to be of the Devil, you know."

Phillip was being shaved by the royal barber when she mentioned her intention to go to mass.

"Why go out? My chaplain will be celebrating it here in a few minutes. You are welcome to be present," Phillip told her, not unkindly, "and you can make your confession to him, of course. But what could such a lovely innocent as yourself have to confess, *ma douce?*"

That I distrust you, brother, though I'm not sure why. And I resent you for keeping me from the convent. Aloud she said, "No, thank you, Your Majesty. I think I shall return to my chamber, after all. I seem to be getting a headache."

Not for anything in the world would she consider confessing to Father Ambrose, Phillip's chaplain. He was too thoroughly Phillip's creature. Whatever she confessed might well go straight to her half brother's ears. She avoided the chaplain's masses whenever possible, disliking the way his unctuous voice slid over the sacred Latin as rapidly as possible.

"But I need a lute string, Your Majesty. Might I go out later, with a page? I'm told there is a little shop in the square. I would go only there and right back, *mon frère*, I promise! I must have my music—it gets so boring, you see."

"When Henri or I can escort you," repeated Phillip. "If you could see, dear Alouette, you would know that the town is thronging with crusaders. They are mere sinful men, after all—even though they bear the cross on their shoulders. Many of them are drunk in the streets, and not one of them would know or care that you are the sister of the king of France. You would be too vulnerable with just a page as escort, my dear."

His patronizing tone rankled. *If you could see*. "I may be blind, but I am not deaf, my lord. I can hear the crowds, talking in a dozen tongues," she retorted with spirit. "All right, then, perhaps you are right. Delegate a pair of men-at-arms, then, if it pleases you."

"No. My men are needed at their duties. You seem dreadfully eager to be out for one who has a headache. Not meeting anyone, are you, *ma chère*?"

The injustice of his silky insinuation had stung her into an indignant denial, and she had fled to her chamber.

Perhaps Phillip had been right, she thought, as she was jostled yet again by a passing soldier. Stale wine fumes enveloped her as he careened drunkenly into Alouette's path, despite young Renart's efforts to steer her clear of him. She had not expected there to be many out this early, except for the townsfolk of Vézélay, for the banquet had lasted late. She had heard the roistering shouts of the crusaders through the wooden shutters at intervals all night. It seemed some of them were just seeking their beds now, however.

"*Alors, mes amis*, what have we here? A comely wench, dressed like a duchess, strolling right into our path! What ho, my fair? How much do ye charge for your favors?" They were French, but spoke a Paris gutter *patois* difficult for her to follow.

The acrid odor of unwashed bodies reached Alouette's nostrils even as she felt Renart stiffen and heard the hiss as he drew his short sword. She clutched the soft leather bag that held her lute.

"Make way, fellow, 'way for the demoiselle de Chenevy, sister of Phillip of France."

Alouette knew this was not a time when she should object to the mention of her powerful connection. She had foolishly placed herself in great danger and would claim kinship to the Virgin Mary if it would aid her.

"Sister of the King o' France? I've never heard of her— just Alais, that piece o' used goods Richard keeps shut away in Rouen. What kind o' fools d'ye take us for? Nay, she's just a higher-priced trull than ye think we have coin for, eh? All right, if that's the way ye treat fellow crusaders, we'll just take what we want. Here's yer payment, pup!"

There was the sound of a fist connecting solidly to bone and a muffled groan as Renart was wrenched away from her. She screamed then, retreating until she felt the solid barrier of a stone wall at her back. She was terrified. It had been madness, childish madness, to defy Phillip by sneaking out of the house against his order. And now she would pay the price of her disobedience—as Renart already had —unless the saints sent a miracle. The Lord had protected chaste women of old, hadn't He? Surely He would send an angel to guard her—surely He didn't mean for her to be ravished as she went to mass!

Suddenly the voice of Édouard de Chenevy, the kindly count she had known as father, echoed in her ear. "Our Lord gave you beauty, but never forget He also gave you wisdom. The Lord helps them that help themselves."

There was nowhere to run. She felt the rough projecting stones scraping her back; she could hear the ragged breathing of the three ruffians as they stood around her in a half-circle. Perhaps, she thought, cursing the handicap her blindness imposed, they were even signaling each other how and when to grab her. She wasn't sure if they were aware she was blind; but if not, it was best not to give them any advantage. Such men would not see it as a reason for mercy.

"Halt right there, gentlemen. Don't do something you may regret," she said, the quaver in her voice disappearing as she spoke. "I *am* the sister of His Majesty, the king of France. I am on my way to mass. Surely you realize God would punish you for such an evil deed if there was anything left of you after the king's justice was satisfied." She said it to gain time, rather than from any belief it would change their minds. As she spoke, her fingers reached inside the sack, grasping the neck of the lute.

"If scruples didn't stop us from cracking yon lad's skull, *chèrie*, it won't keep us from taking what we want from ye."

She groaned inwardly, wondering if Renart, a bright young lad who only moments before had been chattering excitedly about the Holy Land, was already dead. But she could not afford to be distracted just now. There would be time for horror and guilt later.

Abruptly Alouette snatched the lute from the bag, raising it by its slender neck high above her head and bringing it down with crashing force in the direction of the closest ruffian's breathing. The pear-shaped body of the stringed instrument connected with a satisfying thud on the head of the man, who cursed as he retreated out of range.

She wasted no time in triumph, however, for there were two others to deal with. Swinging sideways, she managed to strike one of them in the belly, judging by his grunt of pain. The third man sprang on her, however, wresting the lute from her grasp and bashing it against the wall with one hand while he seized her around the throat and held her in the crook of his elbow, tightening his hold until she gasped for air against the stench of his clothing.

"Feisty, eh? I like a spirited woman, sweetheart. Are ye so energetic in bed?"

He was apparently not interested in her answer, for he had clapped a filthy hand over her mouth. Alouette didn't hesitate, but seized the fleshy part of his palm with her teeth and bit down.

"Ow! Damn you, wench! You'll pay for that!" the smelly brute howled, boxing her ears until she sagged in his grasp. Flashing gold and crimson streaks exploded across her brain. "Look, Jacques! The bitch drew blood!"

"Mayhap we'll have to make her bleed—elsewhere," the other said with an evil chuckle. "And how 'bout if we carve *whore* on one lovely cheek? From then on there'd be no mistake!" He laid the flat of his blade against her cheek and she froze, fearing he would cut her if she moved or breathed.

"I wouldn't go further if I were you, scoundrels. Unhand her immediately, in the king's name," commanded a voice a few feet behind them. Alouette heard the hiss of a sword being unsheathed.

"King? Which king?" sneered one with defiant insolence. "There's two in town at the moment."

"You just want her for yerself," drunkenly accused the smelly fellow who held her pinioned. "Well, we saw this *putaine* first!"

"I speak for Richard, king of England, who has promised severe penalties to anyone committing such crimes as you're contemplating. Let her go now, and you might escape with just a flogging."

"A flogging, is it? For accosting a whore?" snorted one of them. "That's all she is! Perhaps you English believe that likely tale—!"

"They also assaulted my page!" Alouette cried out in the direction of her rescuer's voice. "He's lying somewhere near—he may be dead!"

"Sir Reyner of Winslade is my name, Lady Alouette. Do not fear—this rabble shall not harm you further." His voice was calm, reassuring, as if its owner knew no rush of fear at taking on three rough brigands by himself—for the one Alouette had bludgeoned with her lute had staggered back to join his fellows.

There was a clanging sound and a tinny clunk as the knight's sword knocked the shorter blade from a brigand's hand, then a howl as Sir Reyner scored his cheek.

"If King Richard allows you to live I want all men to know what you are," he growled.

Alouette could hear the second man scrambling away, gabbling in fear. Evidently he was impressed by the greater length of the knight's blade.

"Bring him back, Zeus," Sir Reyner said softly. Before Alouette had time to wonder who was being addressed, she heard the thudding of a large dog's paws.

Moments later, accompanied by snarling and snapping, the would-be rapist ran back, begging, "Call off that wolf! Please, my lord!"

"Hold him, Zeus." There was a yip in response, then a

low-pitched rumble of warning in the canine's throat as he held the two brigands at bay.

There remained only the brute holding Alouette.

"Now, fellow, will you surrender, face my sword—or shall I let Zeus loose?"

"You can't touch me—I have the girl! Anything you do will harm her!" His voice held great bravado and he clutched Alouette tighter, but now she could smell fear mixed with the rankness of his body.

"Using a woman as a shield, blackguard? What pretty chivalry is this?" her rescuer mocked.

"You have the blade and the beast, Englishman. The way I figures it, chivalry has naught to do with the likes of me."

Alouette could feel her captor trembling. He could neither continue holding her or run without her. And then she felt the knife blade on her throat. A low moan escaped her lips.

"Let me go, Sir Knight, and I'll let the woman free—at a safe distance, o' course. Make a move at me, you or that hound, and I'll make sure I slit her gullet first, no matter what you do. I'm not worth risking her pretty neck for, now, am I?"

They had reached a stalemate. Alouette was conscious of the brigand's shuddering breathing, his racing heart. Any moment now his fear might cause him to do something rash. Alouette forced herself to go limp and boneless, falling backward in a fake faint so that the man was forced to support her weight for a vital moment before he released her to the cobbles.

It was long enough. Instantly Reyner was upon him, his broadsword trained on his chest. "Mercy, my lord!" Alouette heard him cry out.

"That will be up to the king. Ho, the watch!"

His shout summoned the patrolling sergeants-at-arms, who led the miscreants away in chains, and carried with them the inert form of Renart. The page was still unconscious, but one of the sergeants deemed it likely he would waken soon with a fierce headache.

Alouette waited silently as the sounds of the captured

molesters being hustled away merged with the early morning noises of the city, then said at last: *"Chevalier? Are you still there?"* She knew he was; she could hear his slowing breaths, but why didn't he *say* something? It made her uneasy to be around people who did not speak, for she could not read their expressions.

"I? Yes, my lady." Reyner realized he had been standing there smiling at her, drinking in her loveliness, idiotically pleased at playing the hero for this woman. "Are you all right, Lady Alouette?"

"Yes . . . yes, I think so . . . just badly frightened. And you, my lord?" What a pleasant, caressing voice the English knight possessed—gravelly, rough-gentle, it wrapped itself in subtle folds around her consciousness, like warm velvet.

"Unscathed, my lady, and deeply humbled by the privilege of coming to the aid of one so fair."

"So it's true that King Richard's knights are as adept at courtly speeches as they are in deeds of arms," she riposted, fighting the flush she felt creeping up her neck. With difficulty she pulled herself back to serious matters. "I feel so guilty about Renart, my page. He would never have been injured, had I not been so disobedient!" Self-reproach welled up now with the tears that came spilling from her eyes, and she trembled with the fear that she had held in check as she realized what could have happened.

His hand seized hers, and it warmed her even through the linked-metal gauntlet. *"Chère damoiselle!* Please don't distress yourself! It is those vile men who have sinned, not you!"

Alouette was about to correct him, to say that he didn't understand. She had not even recovered from the tumult his touching her had provoked, when suddenly her other hand was being licked by a warm wet tongue, and she felt a large furry body against her, a wagging tail fanning her skirts.

She sprang backward. "What is that?" The terror in the brigands' voices when they had called the animal a wolf had brought back childhood memories of the hungry wolves howling at night outside the walls of Chateau de

Chenevy. She could feel by its weight as it pressed against her skirts that the beast was of massive size.

"Have no fear, Lady. Zeus is gentle as a lamb with the fair sex, though he is half wolf. Your sadness concerns him, as it does me. Easy, boy, you will overwhelm Lady Alouette with your affection."

In spite of herself, Alouette smiled and patted the furry head that nuzzled into her waist.

Sir Reyner evidently took that as encouragement, for he went on, "Your page will live to fight again, though he will doubtless curse himself when he wakens for his inability to protect you. Unfortunately, your lute did not fare so well. There's not much of it left. But how magnificently you fought with it! I came around the corner in time to see you swinging it like a Viking berserker!" He went on as if he did not mark her uncontrollable blush at the picture she must have presented. "And now, it seems to me that you have an obvious need for a new lute. Come with me, my lady. I know of a shop that sells such items."

He did not wait to ask permission, for perhaps she might have been able to find the words to drive him away. Alouette felt her hand placed securely on his mail-clad arm and he turned back in the direction of the square, his step sure, guiding her gently but firmly, knowing instinctively the right speed to walk. She heard the dog galloping ahead, barking merry encouragement.

"But . . . but how did you, one of King Richard's knights, know me? Were you at the banquet last night?" The thought of him sitting among the nobles, listening to her sing her repertoire of lays and caroles—and Bernard de Ventador's lovesongs!—set her pulse racing. Had he thought her voice pleasing?

"*Hélas*, I fear I had not the pleasure. King Richard set me to guarding the English camp, in hopes of preventing such incidents as the one that just occurred. I fear I was not wholly successful. There are as many English as any other nationality running drunk in the streets this morning. My liege lord will not be pleased."

"It sounds an impossible task, given the numbers of men," she said lightly. "But—"

"But I did not answer your question," he acknowledged. "I knew who you were, my lady, because I asked Sir William des Barres the identity of the beautiful young lady I glimpsed as she rode into Vézélay yesterday. I had tried to speak with you after the mass, but the crowd made it impossible."

So she *had* been watched in the church. They were *his* eyes that had rested on her. She had suspected as much for several minutes, but his confirmation gave her such an instant surge of pleasure that she was frightened. It must not be. She had dedicated herself to God. Not for her the love games, the light flirtations with which noble damsels amused themselves. And of course this Norman knight was after nothing more than that—unless, of course, he was brash enough to think of seducing the half sister of Phillip Capet, king of France.

Alouette banished the smile of joy that had begun to illumine her face and purposefully made her tone cool. "Mayhap you should have paid closer attention to the bishop saying mass, Sir Knight, and less to worldly things. 'Tis a holy errand you are about to embark upon, and a dangerous one."

It was like watching a glowing flame extinguished, he thought, as the dewy flush faded from her cheek by the effort of her will. He could almost see Alouette pull her thoughts back from the path of worldly pleasure. It was true, then. She did desire to enter the convent. Now that he had met her, he was more than ever determined to change her mind, if he could. But the task could not be rushed. And it need not be. Outremer was far away, and he could not imagine that they would reconquer Jerusalem in a fortnight. He would have months to persuade the beautiful French girl that she belonged in his arms rather than in a nunnery. At the thought he broke into a grin, which he was thankful she couldn't see.

"I am properly chastised, my lady," he said, his voice giving no hint that he was aught but completely sincere, "though I assure you that as I admire your beauty, I am grateful for Our Lord's infinite capacity to create lovely things."

This man would not be discouraged easily, but discourage him she must, Alouette realized. For of all the men who had ever approached her, he was the only one who had ever left her inwardly trembling, like the last leaf on a tree in the path of an approaching storm.

THREE

Ermengarde, the old woman who had been with Alouette since babyhood, had helped her charge escape the confines of the townhouse much earlier. She now waited at the back entrance to spirit her back to her chamber. She saw the strange knight kiss Alouette's hand before her young mistress snatched it back as if she'd touched a flame, and saw Alouette whirl around, clutching the leather lute bag. Ermengarde's ears were too old to pick up the terse words Alouette tossed over her shoulder, but even through her rheumy eyes Ermengarde discerned the heightened color on Alouette's cheeks. *Benedicite!* Not her lamb!

"I am here, Lady Alouette," she said, though the young woman had told her so often that such a statement was unnecessary. Ermengarde's asthmatic wheezing announced her presence without words. The old woman gave the unfamiliar knight a glare before shutting the door firmly, but his eyes were on Alouette, and he did not seem to notice her frosty regard.

Ermengarde and Alouette reached the privacy of Alouette's chamber without encountering anyone. "Does the king know I was gone?" she asked worriedly.

"Nay, I believe your secret's safe—though there *was* a commotion in the kitchen when the watch brought young Renart in. He looked frightful! I was so afraid for you, *chèrie*! What happened?" Her old eyes saw the smudges on her charge's silk gown now, the tiny rips and snags at the back, the missing wimple.

Alouette told her the story, omitting no detail, and began to weep anew as she castigated herself for the page's injuries.

The old woman enfolded her against her soft bosom, much as she had done when Alouette was a child. "I must at least share the blame, my lady. I should never have helped you to hoodwink the king. He'd have my head if he knew!"

"No one will harm you," Alouette reassured her old nurse. "I'll deny you had any part in my foolish adventure," she said, though a shadow passed across her face as she wondered what her brother might do to her if and when he found out.

"And who was that young *chevalier*, the one who saved ye?" Ermengarde inquired casually, noting again the blush that tinged the blind girl's cheeks.

"His name is Reyner de Winslade."

Amazing how differently the name is said, when one loves the owner of that name, Ermengarde thought with a pang of misgiving—for in that brief sentence Alouette had revealed an emotion she had not yet recognized in herself. She might never realize it, if Ermengarde were skillful. She had not come this far only to break her promise to Lisette, the former scullery wench who had caught King Louis's eye and who had bled to death following Alouette's delivery.

"Guard my babe, Ermengarde," the dying girl had pleaded with waning strength. "Never let her repeat my mistake. Give her to the holy nuns when she is of an age. If she knows no man's touch she will know no heartbreak . . ."

When Lisette had whispered these last words, Ermengarde had wept for her friend, once so saucy and lighthearted, with lustrous black, bouncing curls, who had had the misfortune to attract a royal lover. King Louis had repented his philandering soon after the queen had recovered, and piously renounced the scullery wench, marrying her off with a shudder as soon as her pregnancy was discovered. That she was incredibly fortunate for a woman of her station to be marrying a count, and a kindly one at that, was forgotten in Lisette's heartbreak over Louis's betrayal. She had thought the king would set her up in some luxurious apartments in the palace and continue to visit her and the royal love child. She made up her mind on the wedding journey to Chenevy Castle to die, and it surprised no one when she did, after giving birth to the babe.

Only Ermengarde knew of the deathbed promise she had made to Alouette's mother. No matter, she would keep the vow as if it had been witnessed by the bishop himself. She would mold the girl subtly, so that Alouette believed the desire to embrace the religious life came from within herself.

"I asked you what he looked like, Ermengarde," Alouette said, breaking into the old woman's remembrances.

"Who?"

"The English knight, of course! I know you saw him as he . . . escorted me to the door. Was he well-favored, or a beefy, red-faced lout, as Phillip describes King Richard and all Englishmen?"

"Why do you care, *ma petite*? You're going to be a nun, aren't you?" her tirewoman answered, a trifle sharply.

Alouette's face fell. "Yes, I am, Ermengarde. Nothing will alter my course, by the Rood. But I rely on you and others to be my eyes in this world. I would be curious no matter who had rescued me today. Is it wrong to ask about him?"

Ermengarde sounded contrite. "Of course not, my lady. Sometimes I forget you are not still a wee poppet at my knee." But what should she say? Should she admit that Sir Reyner was a veritable Adonis—tall and broad-shouldered, with a thick thatch of tawny-gold hair, eyes like warm honey, and a sensual, determined mouth below an arrogantly chiseled nose? No, and the Virgin would understand the necessity of the lie. She must not let her lamb wander away from her holy destiny into the path of temptation and destruction. Alouette would not suffer as Lisette had!

Uncomfortable with the lie, Ermengarde murmured, "I don't like to be lacking in charity, but truly, this English knight was ill-favored in the extreme. No doubt he was grateful that you are blind. Maidens probably run from the sight of him!"

Ermengarde was sure she had gone too far when she heard Alouette giggle. "Next you'll accuse him of being a Saracen!"

"Indeed, I'm sure the heathen Saracen has no more lustful glint in his eye than did that English knight. You stay far away from him, nursling," she commanded with the familiarity of an old retainer.

Alouette patted her shoulder fondly. "Don't fret yourself about that, Ermengarde. I seek no worldly lover, French *or* English. And I'm much more worried about my royal brother. Will he learn of Renart's injuries, do you think?" She felt her way to the settee and sat down, lifting the new lute from her bag and unconsciously fondling its fat, curved belly. It had a smoother finish than her old one had and sounded even mellower as she plucked the strings experimentally.

"I had a talk with that young jackanapes as soon as his eyelids flickered open," Ermengarde replied, "and he swore on the True Cross to say he got his cuts and bruises in a dicing quarrel." She stood with hands on stout hips, watching as her young mistress leaned over the instrument, midnight-colored tendrils straying down her cheeks.

"He swore on the holiest relic in Christendom to *lie* for me," Alouette murmured, her face troubled. "Ah, nurse, what a small sin this started out to be."

"You're too hard on yourself, *ma demoiselle*," the old woman insisted. "Likely His Majesty wouldn't notice a mark or two on a mere page. He has more important things to occupy his mind. If anyone has sinned, it's the king, for not allowing you to follow your holy vocation long ago." Ermengarde dared not say anything more negative about Phillip Capet. One never knew what chance remark might trigger a memory of things best forgotten.

* * *

Alouette did not encounter the English knight again during the three days the armies rested in Vézélay. For the most part, she stayed in her chamber, except when Henri was available to escort her to mass or to table. She needed the solitude for her prayers, she claimed, and hoped by this means to avoid her royal half brother as well, for fear he would discover her disobedience and its aftermath.

By the time she supped with him and his nobles on the evening of the third day, she had stopped jumping at every footfall outside her door. Apparently there would be no lasting consequences for her rash act.

In fact, Phillip had been busy hammering out an agreement with the English king that any booty won by crusaders of any nationality was to be shared equally by all.

"The English king is a fanatic fighter," Phillip crowed over his trencher to his assembled nobles, who were sharing the evening meal with him in the townhouse's hall. "Let the 'Lionheart' lead the foolhardy hotbloods into the fray! There will be more of *us* alive to reap the bounty for their efforts, eh, *mes amis*? Richard has already proven himself a fool, leaving his kingdom in the hands of that rascally brother of his, John Lackland, and that scoundrel minister, Longchamp. If anyone is to lose his life rescuing the Holy Sepulchre, *I* say let it be Richard! I will gladly bid his soul farewell as it floats to Heaven—or more likely, sinks to Hell—and then snatch Aquitaine and Normandy back into France. Taking them from King John would be child's play!"

Alouette, seated next to Henri de Chenevy down the high table from the king, was sickened by her half brother's deviousness and total lack of dedication to the cause of the crusade. They hadn't even left France, and already Phillip was scheming to reap the maximum material reward for the minimum participation, *and* to steal English territory if given the opportunity.

"Isn't the wine delicious?" chortled a throaty voice on the other side of Henri. Alouette wrinkled her nose as a wave of the musky perfume Lady Peronel favored struck her nostrils. Though Peronel was Phillip's mistress, she was flirting shamelessly with Henri. Alouette turned her face away from the offensive aroma, hoping Peronel would not deign to speak to her. It was an effort to remain civil to the opportunistic wench, who was the daughter of one of Phillip's sergeants-at-arms and no true "lady" at all.

Although Phillip dared not offend the proprieties by having his paramour seated by his side, sharing his trencher, no one in the hall was deceived. Alouette remembered with disgust that Queen Margaret had barely been laid in her tomb, the first queen to be interred in Notre Dame, when Phillip had taken this noisy, pushy woman to his bed. Peronel had immediately begun to lord it over the ladies' bower, and Alouette had fled to the chapel. She found comfort in her prayers for the departed queen. Margaret had always been kind to her, as if there were indeed no stain on her birth.

"My lords, we bid you good even," Phillip announced in dismissal, and benches creaked as the barons, counts, and knights struggled to their feet, groaning at the effort after having indulged too freely at the king's table.

"No, stay, Alouette—you also, sweet Peronel," Phillip said smoothly, when Alouette would have departed with Henri. "We would have you play for us before we retire."

"Your Majesty, I will have to send for my lute," Alouette began. "I did not know you would require my music to-night—"

"I took the liberty of having it brought to the hall," Phillip interrupted her, as he watched the last tipsy *chevalier* bow out of his presence.

"My lady, your instrument," said a voice at her ear, and Alouette was startled to recognize it as Renart's. *Sainte Vierge*, did the boy still bear the bruises of his beating? Would Phillip notice?

"Thank you, Renart," she said graciously, hoping her voice did not betray her inner nervousness. A tocsin of alarm began chiming in her mind, but she resolutely tuned the fine instrument and settled more comfortably on the backless bench.

"None of your austere hymns to Jerusalem," warned Phillip from the ornate, high-backed chair in the center of the dais. "Something about love, if it pleases you—for it would please me and my sweet lady here," he chuckled. He gathered up the plump armful that was his mistress and settled her on his lap.

Peronel snickered, knowing his actions had probably upset Lady Alouette. Haughty bitch—as if she were not a bastard! At least she, Peronel, had been legitimately born, though only by a matter of weeks.

> You towering winds that roll in from the sea,
> Buffeted by the winds incessantly,
> Bring some good tidings of my love to me,
> For his returning sail I never see.
> Ah, cruel fate,

"How swiftly joy and sorrow alternate—" Alouette sang in her pure, clear voice, resolutely divorcing herself from her audience.

"How lovely," Phillip said at the close of the plaintive love song, and clapped, the sound echoing like thunder in the near-deserted hall. "But Alouette, I noticed something while you sang—perhaps you could enlighten me! That instrument you play does not appear to be the same lute I gave you for your saint's day, unless someone has painted marguerites on it that were not there before, and changed the color of the ribbons. Is that what happened, *chère soeur*?"

His voice sounded completely surprised, but she knew him better than that. Her heart went cold within her as she sat waiting for him to coil and strike.

Actually, Phillip had known what had happened, since the hour of the incident in the streets, and had questioned the young page and the brigands remorselessly, threatening them with the loss of certain body parts if they did not tell the truth. Had Alouette been able to see, she would have noted the haunted look of pain in the page's eyes. The fingers the king's henchman had broken (it took two before he confessed all) in the course of the "inquiry" still hurt. But worse to the boy was the knowledge that the beauteous Lady Alouette might suffer for his cowardice.

Phillip had waited to see if Alouette's conscience would

compel her to confess her disobedience. When she did not, he was surprised. She had always been so open with him. He had bided his time, and now he would teach her a lesson.

She sighed. "Yes, *mon roi*, it is a new lute. The one you gave me . . . met with an accident of sorts. This one was purchased here in Vézélay." *By the Norman knight whose very voice turns my blood to liquid fire, whose one slightest touch troubles my dreams.*

"Of course it was, and how foolish of you to think I knew nothing of your stealing out of this building and nearly dishonoring the House of Capet by your foolishness!" Phillip rasped, dumping Peronel unceremoniously from his lap and striding to Alouette, his feet rustling in the brittle rushes. "I know all about the so-gallant Englishman who rescued you and purchased you another lute, dear Alouette. I have eyes everywhere." He spoke into her ear with chilling emphasis. "Now, sing some more, and do not think to cozen me again."

After a moment she continued, her voice shaky as she struggled against the tears of fear and resentment, doubly angry because she had heard Phillip's plump little concubine give a satisfied little "hmmmph" as Phillip finished his harangue. No doubt Peronel was smiling smugly at her humiliation.

Her fingers slipped on the strings again and again as she wondered if Phillip would curtail her freedom even more now. Somehow, the regimentation of convent life seemed like perfect freedom compared to playing the mouse to Phillip's cat.

And the knight, Reyner de Winslade—would he suffer for his chivalry to her? Surely Phillip knew the meeting had been accidental, didn't he?

There had been such an odd, discordant note to Phillip's voice, almost as if there was more than mere anger at her disobedience, with its dangerous consequences. Perhaps he did not approve because Sir Reyner was English. *Sainte Vierge*, the man had acted as anyone true to his knightly vows would have done!

But Alouette had been aware of the warm interest behind

the knight's words and touch. There had been more than mere chivalry in the way he had insisted on buying her the new lute, though the merchant had priced it dearly. And that kiss on the hand— When she thought of it, her hand still burned as if red-hot iron had touched her fingers!

She longed to ask for reassurance that Phillip would not effect reprisals against Sir Reyner, but she knew it would be a mistake to make him seem important to her. She knew he could not openly threaten an English knight for such an "offense." But as she had realized tonight after the conversation at the table, there was little King Phillip might not scruple to do, if it could be done secretly.

As she sang on, she recognized by the little chuckles, squeals, and panting breaths that Peronel was growing amorous. Indeed, she seemed to feel the lute music merely provided a background counterpoint to their love play.

"Your Majesty, I am fatigued," she said in a quiet, neutral tone. "Have I your leave to withdraw?"

There was no answer save the rustling of cloth as Phillip thrust his hand under Peronel's skirts. After a moment, Alouette stood and walked slowly and carefully out of the circle of flickering tallow candles, finding her way by memory.

She did not know that Phillip stared after her, one hand mechanically stroking Peronel, while his mind was still haunted by the guilt that had settled so heavily on him ever since that drunken night in Paris so many years ago. On the streets of Vézélay, Alouette again had been in danger and once again he had failed to protect her. He realized she did not deserve his anger, but the thought of one of *Richard's* knights rescuing her—and obviously impressing her with his gallantry—enraged him. Was the adoring little half sister, who used to stare at him with such admiration and worship, gone forever? He knew within himself that she was lost to him beyond all hope of recall. Very well. If Alouette could not love him, perhaps she could still be useful to him.

FOUR

Four days after the French arrived, the combined armies of Christendom moved out of Vézélay, hugging the valleys of the Massif Central whenever possible.

The announced plan was to journey to Lyon and ford the Rhône there, but Reyner wondered whether such a vast horde could travel anywhere successfully. After two days of foraging in the Burgundian countryside, there were already violent conflicts over the availability of food. Soldiers on the march were expected to obtain their own supplements to the meager fare provided, but that did not take into account the fact that they were supposed to be a peaceful army passing through friendly territory. The Burgundian peasants did not take kindly to the plague of crusaders trampling through their fields and vineyards, stealing their bread and livestock and raping their women.

The fact was that there was simply not enough food in Burgundy—or anywhere—to supply such a host. And if they couldn't live off such a green, peaceful country, how were the crusaders of England, France, and Flanders to survive together in the arid country of the hostile saracen? Already there had been a stabbing incident when possession of a stolen piglet was in dispute. Reyner did not know how they would ever reach the Holy Land with their sacred purpose intact.

He did not voice his misgivings to King Richard, riding just ahead of him. The huge blond Plantagenet radiated boundless energy, although he had consumed endless goblets of wine until the wee hours of the morning at another one of the interminable banquets held by the kings. These were chiefly attended by their inner circle of nobles—who for the most part ignored the fact that their men-at-arms had to steal food to quiet their bellies.

Reyner had quit the feast early, disappointed that none of the French nobility had chosen to attend. He had hoped to talk over old times with William des Barres. God-a-mercy! Did he even hope to fool *himself*? Why not admit that his first thought, upon hearing that Phillip's retinue had been invited, was that he would get to see Lady Alouette de Chenevy again?

Ever since the morning he had rescued her from the three would-be rapists, he had looked for her everywhere. As much as his duties to King Richard allowed, he and Zeus had patrolled the streets of Vézélay, searching for her. They had checked each shop. He had even begun to haunt the cathedral precincts at dawn, hoping to encounter her going to mass.

Sir Hubert, the fat old priest back at Hawkingham, would be pleased at my faithfulness, he had thought ironically as yet another mass ended without a glimpse of her fair face.

He had even thought of walking boldly up to the guarded entrance of Phillip's quarters in the town and requesting to see her, though she had indicated with icy reserve that she would not receive him. It was unlikely that King Phillip would permit such a visit, in any case. Perhaps he should not have kissed her hand before asking, though surely that was a mere courtesy from a knight to a lady?

Could her desire to be a nun really account for the sudden shift in her attitude, after her initial fervent gratitude and openness? She had allowed him to buy her the new lute, but her face had become shuttered, her manner guarded, and as they drew near to the French king's headquarters, Alouette had become almost furtive. She had insisted he take her to the back entrance, where an old harridan of a tirewoman was apparently waiting for her.

Zeus, who had watched his master and the beautiful female make their farewells, had cocked his head in puzzle-

ment at the sharp tones in which the female had addressed
Reyner. He had whined low in his throat, wagging his tail
as the door had slammed shut, gazing at Reyner as if expecting him to explain Alouette's behavior.

"You rather like her, don't you, fellow?" Reyner had
said, fondling the half-wolf's ears. "Nay, I can't tell you
why she's acting so oddly. All I know is that I love her, and
by my troth, she *will* be mine someday, vocation be
damned!"

He had a degree of respect for the holy priests and nuns
who spent their lives in prayer and service to the lowly.
The convent was a fine refuge for widows, tired of the
world's cares, or those young damsels truly more suited to
spending their lives on their knees. But surely God did not
call for such as Alouette to hack off the lovely ebony
tresses he'd glimpsed beneath her wimple, neatly braided
and coiled at the nape of her slender neck, or to clothe her
lissome body in harsh serge robes and kneel in endless
prayer? Most nuns did back-breaking labor; could tasks be
found suitable for one with her handicap? She would not be
able to spend her hours copying the magnificent illuminated manuscripts that adorned abbey libraries. But by
God, she could, even as a blind woman, be the chatelaine
of Winslade, supervising the many tasks that kept such a
castle running, greeting his guests and making lively conversation, loving her lord and the babes they would make
together.

A wave of longing swept over him as he pictured
presenting his French bride to his parents, Earl Simon and
Lady Ysabeau, at Hawkingham, after he and Alouette had
returned from Outremer.

He thought of the sacred shrines of England, such as
Canterbury and Walsingham, where miracles of healing
were said to take place. He had never needed such miracles, but had tolerantly listened to the tales of those who
claimed to be transformed by touching a saint's tomb or
beholding a holy relic. But how many more miracles must
take place in the wondrous Holy Land, a place Our Lord
had actually walked? Perhaps Alouette's sight might even
be restored! If blindness was what had convinced her that

the only fitting place for her was behind convent walls, then perhaps after the miracle, she would realize she was indeed destined to sleep in the arms of a beloved husband, rather than alone on an austere nun's pallet!

He laughed aloud at his own romantic fantasies as he stalked through the streets of Vézélay, always frustrated in his search for that one unforgettable face. So intent on his thoughts was he one afternoon that he had tripped over a French *chevalier* lounging at his ease on the steps outside St. Mary Magdalene.

"I beg your pardon, my lord. Clumsy of me—I was daydreaming, I fear. . ." Then his apology died away as he looked into a face that was like a blurred image of his brother Aimery.

"*Despardieux!* Are all the English so maladroit?" asked the French knight, an amused sneer souring the handsome features.

Reyner was aware he was staring. "Sir Reyner of Winslade at your service, *mon sieur*, and I repeat my apology," he said stiffly. The hackles had risen on Zeus's neck.

"Ah—the name explains your gaping mouth," the Frenchman declared. "Let me satisfy your curiosity as to the resemblance. I am Fulk, Sieur de Langres, and we are cousins, Sir Reyner; my father is Gervase of Hawkingham, who was foully deprived of his earldom by your father, his twin brother—with the assistance of the late Henry II, of course." He snorted and sat back to note the effect of his words.

So that was it. Reyner had of course grown up with the story of how his father had come to possess the earldom, though he was the secondborn twin. Gervase had plotted against Henry Plantagenet and kidnapped Simon's intended bride, Ysabeau de Ré, whom he planned to starve into submission. When Henry and Simon had used a ruse that allowed them to sneak inside the walls of his stronghold, Gervase had been beaten in a duel of swords and banished from England. Reyner had heard that Gervase had taken service with Louis of France, who had presumably granted him lands there; but Reyner had never met him during the campaigns with Richard, when much of the young nobility of France had fought at the English prince's side.

"Of course that is how you would have been told of it, Sir Fulk—I quite understand. However, that was long ago and none of my doing or yours. I hope we can go beyond that and be friends, cousin. After all, we will be on crusade for months—perhaps years. It would be good to have a kinsman among the French chivalry."

Fulk ignored the proffered hand and friendship. "You are not the eldest. Where is your brother, whom I am told I greatly resemble?"

"Aimery is in England, overseeing our father's demesne lands."

"He did not feel it was his obligation to take the cross?" Again, Fulk's lip curled.

"It was decided that I would go, as a younger son, and moreover, one who has not the responsibility of a wife and family," Reyner said evenly.

"Ah, the estimable Aimery hides at home behind a woman's skirts. *Eh bien*, I suppose it is good that someone cares for the lands. Someday they will belong to my father again, you know, and then to me."

Against his will Reyner felt himself being drawn into an argument. "They were reassigned to my father by royal decree, sir—a decree that Henry's son Richard would never change." He had backed away from the lounging figure, his hand straying toward his sword hilt. He could see the French knight was spoiling for a fight. Well, he'd not give it to him, unless it was unavoidable, for there'd be hell to pay from Richard for the pleasure.

Fulk had risen to his feet, his stance openly belligerent. "Richard will not make old bones—nor any heirs, if the rumors are true. When John is king—or Arthur of Brittany—then we will see which branch of the family possesses Hawkingham, Winslade, Lingfield, and Chawton," he boasted, eyes gleaming as his tongue rolled over the listing of lands held by the Earl of Hawkingham.

"I am sorry you feel that way," Reyner said coldly, "for you and yours are doomed to disappointment." He turned on his heel and snapped his fingers to Zeus, daring the Frenchman to attack after he had turned his back.

Thoughts of the unpleasant encounter with Cousin Fulk fled as Reyner and King Richard, riding together on the journey eastward, rounded an outcropping of rock and came upon the very object of Reyner's frustrated desire.

Alouette, clothed in a gown of peacock blue sarcenet with a barbette and veil of a lighter blue, was standing by her mount, clearly dismayed. By her side stood the king of France.

"Where is that irresponsible brother of yours?" Phillip fumed. "How could he have put you on a lame horse this morn?"

"Blanchefleur wasn't lame then," Alouette explained patiently. "I would have felt it in her gait. She probably picked up a stone on that rocky stretch we just passed."

"No doubt. Well, we'll just have to get you another mount when the baggage wains catch up. Father Ambrose, will you wait with Lady Alouette—ah, Richard, well met!" Phillip cried, looking up to see the English king.

"Indeed, Your Majesty," Richard replied, with ironic emphasis on Phillip's title, for he did in fact owe homage to Phillip for his continental lands. "Can we be of some assistance? You seem to have a problem, Lady Alouette." Richard addressed her easily, having been introduced to Phillip's beautiful troubador at the banquet in Vézélay.

"Yes, Your Grace, but do not trouble yourself over it. Another horse will be brought for me presently," Alouette said in that sweet, lilting voice Reyner had longed to hear again.

Reyner was already off his horse, examining the white palfrey's right foreleg and lifting it gently. He found a stone lodged against the shoe, just as Alouette had predicted.

"The stone is out, but the mare shouldn't bear any weight for a day or two—even so slight a weight as Lady Alouette," Reyner said. He looked up and was pleased to see a blush appear on her sun-kissed cheeks as she recognized his voice. "I would be honored to lead Hercules, my horse, while you ride."

"Nonsense, Reyner," Richard interjected, "your destrier can carry two. Let Lady Alouette ride pillion behind you, so that you're available to us."

Reyner could have knelt and kissed his liege lord's feet for the suggestion—a bolder one than he dared to make. The thought of having the winsome French girl clinging to his back as they rode was like a foretaste of heaven.

Although Phillip obviously would have preferred a solution that gave Reyner no contact with his half sister, Richard gave him no chance. "Good! That's solved! My lord, I had wanted to talk with you anyway. We've been trying to catch up all morning. The lady's safe with Reyner. I can vouch for him."

Reyner was hard-pressed not to grin. "As my king commands," he murmured as Phillip gave a grudging nod, "if it is agreeable to you, Lady Alouette. If not, I can walk Hercules as I offered before."

She nodded uncertainly, torn between courtesy and her desire to keep him at arm's length. "I should not wish to have you walk all day, in full mail, when we could both easily ride." Her voice was calm, distant, but he could detect the racing pulse in her throat.

Zeus barked his approval as Alouette seated herself on the broad rump of the great destrier and put her arms around Reyner's waist. It was a necessary precaution against falling off, but one that seemed unbearably intimate, even with the metal hauberk that covered Reyner from neck to knees.

Her arms tightened around Reyner as the tall horse moved forward in the wake of the kings' mounts. The lurching motion brought her into contact with the sun- and flesh-warmed links of metal on his back, and she drew in a shaky breath full of the mingled smells of man and horse. Riding pillion with Henri had never seemed so *physical* an act. She found that unless she kept her back rigidly straight, her breasts rubbed against Reyner's mid-back, a contact that made her pulse beat faster.

"It seems I am in your debt again, *mon chevalier*. I

thank you for coming to my aid," she said, speaking into his ear over the creak of leather and the clank of metal.

"No thanks are necessary, my lady."

They rode in silence for many miles, hearing the two kings' talk wash back at them, but hardly paying attention to it. They were much more conscious of the creak of Reyner's saddle, the birdsong from the trees, the sun on their faces—and each other.

"How is your new—"

"My new lute is—" Both laughed as they seized on the same safe topic.

"My new lute plays very well, thank you again."

"I would love to hear you play it."

"I am sure you will, somewhere along the way," she said noncommittally, thankful that his back was to her. It was easier to maintain her poise, knowing he could not easily look at her.

"And your page, how does he fare?"

"Renart has recovered well. He says the bruises are a delightful shade of green now." She heard him chuckle. "The three brigands—whatever happened to them?"

He wished she had not asked. "Hanged—at King Richard's order." Reyner felt her gasp. He would not tell her that he had been ordered to supervise the execution.

She drew a shuddering breath against his back, slumping against him. "They were shriven first?" she asked in a small voice.

Something warmed within him, glad that she could not bear to see human life spent so cheaply, even though the three had been bent on harming her. Many women would have laughed in satisfaction. "They were shriven," he assured her.

"God rest their souls." Her voice was thick with tears.

He was moved with pity for her tender heart. How would such a one survive the rigors of a crusade in which the taking of lives, although infidel ones, would doubtless become commonplace? She didn't belong here! What was Phillip thinking about, dragging her along?

"Who is your dragon of a gatekeeper?" he asked, more to get away from the depressing subject of the hangings than any desire to know. "The old woman who greeted you at the back door the other day," he added, as a glance over his shoulder showed him a puzzled face.

"Oh, Ermengarde! My tirewoman! My lord, your description of her is hardly kind!"

He saw he had succeeded admirably, and decided to tease her further to draw her out. "She looked as if she would as soon breathe fire out of her nostrils as continue to let me walk the earth."

"As a matter of fact, she was hardly complimentary of you, either, Sir Reyner," Alouette felt compelled to tell him.

Aha. He would have given much to know if Alouette had asked the old woman for a description of him. "Indeed? She did not tell you I was handsome and debonair, a credit to mankind in general and English knighthood in particular?"

The insufferable conceit of the man! "Indeed not! She said you were ugly, and that you were probably grateful that I couldn't see just how ugly..." She gasped again, embarrassed by her unthinking frankness.

He was pleased, rather than offended by her tart response. Such a one as she would never accept the passive role of the nun! Reyner laughed then, the rich, masculine sound coming from deep in his chest, echoing off her heart even as she demanded to know what was so amusing.

"Ha, ha—nothing! Nothing, I assure you! It is merely to resist being overcome by melancholy—a common enough frame of mind, you understand, in one so repellent as I. I had hoped..." Here he allowed an enormous sigh to shake his entire frame, knowing she would feel it.

"Hoped what, Sir Reyner?" she encouraged in a gentler tone.

"That Venus, the goddess of love, would preserve my awful secret, if only for a little while... that I could enjoy the pleasure of your favor until you, too, learned the dreadful truth and turned from me, like the others, in loathing..." He allowed another heavy sigh to ripple through his shoulders, then waited to see if she could resist the challenge to rise above the "other women."

"I promise you, what the world considers a handsome countenance matters naught to me—"

"Ah, Lady Alouette!" he interrupted with extravagant gratitude. "I knew you were the wisest of women, that my affection was well founded . . ." He watched carefully over his shoulder for her reaction.

"Stop, oh stop, I pray you!" she pled in distress. He had gone too far. "Sir Reyner, you must *not* continue this way! What I was *trying* to say was not that I was so exceptionally virtuous a woman, but that my goal is different from that of most others! I plan to enter the convent as soon as this crusade is over, my lord. That is why your features don't matter to me, and why you must not speak of my 'favor' as if we were playing at courtly love!"

There. The issue was out in the open between them, palpable and quivering.

She waited, bracing herself for the inevitable tide of protest she had heard before from her stepfather, Henri, Phillip, and almost every male she had ever encountered.

But he said nothing. As the minutes wore on, she began to feel more and more uneasy, and yes, a trifle *piqued*.

"Sir Reyner? Have I . . . offended you? Such was not my intent . . ."

"'Sdeath, my lady, it is I who must beg forgiveness for any offense! How unpleasant my gallantries must have been to one who has already dedicated herself to a higher calling. Forgive my bold words, Lady Alouette—they shall not trouble your ears again!"

Wasn't that exactly what she wanted to hear? Why then did she feel so—disappointed? Alouette was annoyed at her perverse reactions. Obviously she needed to spend more time in prayer and self-examination.

"Very well, then, your apology is accepted," she said, choosing her words carefully. "Now that we understand one another better, I would like to be friends. You saved me once, my lord, and have come to my aid again today. I do . . . like you, Sir Reyner."

He smiled as she unconsciously tightened her hold about his waist, unaware that he could feel her pounding heartbeat through the thin silk of her gown. *No, dear Alouette, you don't understand me at all, but you will, after you have begun to love me.* He suspected she didn't fully understand herself, either.

"Thank you, Lady Alouette. I should be honored to be your friend. Tell me, have you always wanted to be one of the holy sisters?"

Her response was enthusiastic. "Oh, yes. Ermengarde tells me that from the time I could lisp a few words, I attempted to say the Lord's Prayer and Hail Mary, and I would ask to touch the crucifix on the wall. I showed little interest in the dolls she would fashion for me, but would enact the lives of the saints with them."

Ermengarde again. He began to suspect the old servant of molding her charge's memories—but why?

"This Ermengarde—she has been with you a long time? Does your mother tell you such stories as well?"

Now it was her turn to sigh, but hers was guileless. "My mother died in giving me birth, Sir Reyner. Yes, Ermengarde has been with me all my life."

He murmured something sympathetic while his mind raced. He believed he was very close to some important truth about this beautiful young woman, but some inner voice warned him to tread cautiously. From this point on he asked only innocuous questions about her girlhood at Chateau de Chenevy, but as the miles passed underneath his destrier's mighty hooves, he listened carefully for what was left unsaid, until at last it was time to stop for the midday meal.

FIVE

Reyner was disappointed but not surprised when a spare mount was brought for Alouette at the end of the midday meal. He had seen the French king casting suspicious looks at him all morning.

"Ah, there you are, Count de Chenevy," Phillip greeted Henri as he brought over the bay mare. When Henri had been found by Renart the page and ordered to find a suitable lady's mount, Alouette's stepbrother had assumed that "Lady" Peronel had opted to ride, though normally she preferred her cushioned wagon.

"Where were you this morning?" Phillip asked pettishly. "Your sister's mare went lame, and she had to ride pillion with an English stranger! My thanks, Sir Reyner," he added dismissively to the tawny-haired knight. "You are free of your obligation now. We are grateful for your service. You would doubtless like to rejoin your own men." The French king's eyes were cold. He ignored Alouette's brother's stammered apology.

"It was my pleasure, Your Majesty, and my privilege," returned Reyner evenly, looking Phillip Capet in the eye, which was something few men dared do. "Lady Alouette, I will take my leave."

He smiled inwardly to see the blind girl color again where she sat at the makeshift trestle table that bore the remains of the noontime repast.

"I would add my thanks to His Majesty's—"

Alouette was interrupted by King Richard. "Nonsense,

my lord. Reyner always rides with me. His retinue will do very well with the other men-at-arms, as usual. I value his opinion, just as my sire trusted Reyner's father. He's a keen judge of the terrain, Phillip."

Richard was baiting Phillip with his condescending speech, taking advantage of their nine-year age difference. Reyner wondered if his king had gone too far. Calling King Phillip "my lord" was pure mockery, for Richard Plantagenet knew no true overlord on earth.

A glance at the English king revealed blue eyes dancing with deviltry. Reyner was under no illusions as to his position with his sovereign. He was a trusted vassal, but one of several. Richard wanted him at his side purely because Phillip did not, for whatever reason. It was a contest of wills.

"Very well, Richard," purred King Phillip. "If you prefer to have a mere *knight* as your attendant, who am I to object? Your preference for the lower ranks harks back to your father, as well. But his taste ran more to pretty *wenches*, I have heard."

The reference to Richard's rumored sexual perversion hung between them like a heavy black cloud, poisoning the air. Men around them cleared their throats uneasily and backed away, pretending intense interest in packing up and remounting for the remainder of the day's journey.

Reyner felt an initial surge of rage toward the French king for the slur upon his manhood, for his implication that he might be Richard's partner in sexual abberration. He forced himself to stifle the impulse to draw his sword. It would be madness for him, a mere knight, to draw steel on the king of France, especially for a patent lie. All men who knew him well knew he did not share Richard's alleged vice. Nor had Richard ever given him the least indication that he saw Reyner as anyone but a trusted vassal.

It was up to Richard, as king, to react to the insult made by another king. A quick glance at Coeur de Lion revealed the blond giant's face flushed with impotent fury. He dared not dignify Phillip's jab by even acknowledging it. Such a slander could compromise his ability to lead.

"You would do well to listen to some of *your* knights,

Phillip," said Richard at last, his eyes glittering like blue shards of ice. "They might well keep you from a *fatal* mistake."

"Mayhap I will, the next time I'm lacking good advice. I've always found my own counsel sufficient in the past," Phillip said. "Very well, we have tarried long enough. Henri, thank you for the palfrey, but I feel Alouette is fatigued from the stress of the morning's events. See that she reaches the carriage among the baggage wains, will you, where she can rest as we travel? No arguments, Lady Alouette. We can't have you falling ill."

It had been neatly done. If Richard persisted in keeping his knight near him, then Phillip would remove Alouette. Phillip knew perfectly well that Reyner wasn't one of Richard's "favorites." If the French king did not already know about his encounter with Alouette in Vézélay, he must have seen the way Reyner looked at her today. It was not the look of a man who preferred the love of men.

Reyner watched the conflict in Alouette's face, but knew there was nothing she could do. Any argument from her might further threaten Phillip's authority and come down on her innocent, lovely head. Punishment rather than thoughtfulness underlay Phillip's suggestion that Alouette could "rest" in the jolting, lurching carriage that shuddered with every rut. Such uncomfortable vehicles were the refuge only of those unable or too lazy to ride.

The cavalcade reached Lyon on July tenth, descending the foothills of the Massif Central in the drizzling rain that had dogged their steps since breaking camp that morning. The town was set on a plateau across the narrow old wooden bridge that spanned the Rhône; and though it was late in the day, the two kings were determined to spend the night in the town.

"Tired, *chère soeur*?" Phillip inquired in a kind voice as he brought his mount back to where the carriage waited with the baggage wains to cross the wide, gray river. He had insisted that Alouette ride in the carriage again today because of the inclement weather.

"Oh, yes, Your Majesty!" Alouette was quick to agree.

The roof of the carriage was leaky, and the dampness had eventually soaked through her gown and cloak. "I'm chilled to the bone. I doubt if I could be any wetter had I ridden my horse today. Why don't we just make camp here? I vow I could fall asleep as soon as my head touched a pillow!"

She forbore to say that her fatigue and headache were as much caused by the chatter of her tirewoman as the endless jolting of the uncomfortable conveyance. Ermengarde rode in the wheeled vehicle every day because of her age and was glad to have her mistress as a captive audience when Alouette could not ride. Alouette was secretly dismayed, but she supposed it was selfish of her—after all, it was an arduous journey for an old woman, and Ermengarde was making it simply for love of her.

"Nay, I'll be damned if Richard is going to enjoy the comforts of town while the French camp on the cold ground," Phillip said in answer to her plea. "And I really should confer with Richard one last time tonight—we part company on the morrow, you know. You'll be glad that you crossed tonight once we're over the river, Alouette." His reassurance sounded like an order.

The nobles and knights of all the nations traveled at the head of the procession, so they would cross first, followed by the French and Flemish men-at-arms. Alouette estimated that the crossing could take hours, so she settled herself down in the uncomfortable wagon to daydream, imagining the comfort of the goose down mattress and soft pillow that would surely be hers in Lyon. At least they weren't to be last! The English foot soldiers would bring up the rear.

"It will be such a blessing when we reach Genoa, where we can finally travel by ship," Ermengarde said. "Though I will rejoice to part company with the damned English. They are so loud, and they murder the French tongue!"

"Mmmm-hmmm," Alouette replied absentmindedly, only half-listening, wondering if she would have any further encounters with Reyner de Winslade before the armies divided in the morning.

The kings had finally realized the impracticality of trying to feed such a vast army on the march. At Lyon the host would divide, with the English journeying south to take ship at Marseilles, while the French and Flemings traveled the coastline as far as Genoa, where they would embark on ships bound for Sicily. The English would join them at Messina, Sicily, and all would sail for Outremer as a massive fleet.

Though she dreaded the idea of further overland travel, Alouette looked forward to the weeks the armies would be separated. During that time she would spend every spare moment in diligent prayer—perhaps she would fast—and emerge stronger, more devout of purpose, her heart totally armored against invasion by the English knight. By the time the armies came together at Messina, she would be resolute again, invulnerable to the temptation of his rich, caressing voice.

Mayhap she could even exert a positive influence on him. She had a vision of him joining one of the monastic military orders, the Templars or the Knights Hospitallers, because of her shining example—then spent the next several minutes rebuking herself for spiritual pride.

Putting any emotional distance between herself and the English knight on the march was difficult when Sir Reyner was always *there*. Accompanied by the half-wolf, Zeus, he had adopted the habit of riding alongside her and Henri, ostensibly because Richard usually rode with Phillip near her. Henri thoroughly liked the fellow!

"I don't understand why you're so cool to the *Sieur* de Winslade," Henri had said one evening after Reyner had gone to see to his men. "You admit he saved your life after you took that foolish walk in Vézélay. And he *is* a most amusing companion—for an Englishman, of course! I think he admires you, *ma soeur*," Henri had remarked in his bluff, kindly way.

"Him? Bah! How ridiculous! He spends all his time talking to you and *Sieur* William des Barres about old campaigns!" An edge of pique crept into her voice.

"It's too bad you can't see how his eyes light up when he greets you, Alouette," Henri teased. "I'm afraid des Barres and I, for all our worthy qualities, are being used as an excuse to approach you." He chuckled. "Perhaps—"

Alouette cut him off. "Now, Henri, I know what you're going to say, and pray do not. *Sieur* Reyner knows of my vocation—I have made it clear enough that even an Englishman can understand!"

Henri privately thought that the handsome Englishman looked like a very determined man, whom Alouette's holy protestations would only make more determined, but he knew when to hold his peace. His persistence would only make his sister more stubborn. He had better let the Englishman play the game of love at his own pace.

From his vantage point on the high bank of the river, Reyner watched in the drizzle as the last of the French army prepared to cross the Rhône on the ancient bridge. Concern furrowed his brow beneath the link-mail coif. He didn't like the flimsy appearance of the bridge, or the way it had creaked and shuddered with the impact of hundreds of crusaders' feet. Far too many of the mounted knights and foot soldiers had crowded onto the narrow span at once. He wished fervently that Alouette had already crossed, but the gaily painted wooden carriage in which she rode still stood among the baggage wains. He should be seeing to lodgings for his men, but he could not have left the river bank if his soul's salvation had depended on it—not while Alouette was still on the other side.

King Phillip, closely accompanied by his painted, chattering mistress, had clattered across nearly an hour before and was doubtless now comfortably ensconced in some confiscated hall.

Reyner had offered, before crossing himself, to take Alouette across on his destrier. She thanked him graciously but had nevertheless firmly refused.

"It would not be kind of me to leave my faithful servant," she had informed him. Ermengarde, seated inside the carriage, sent him a stony stare.

"I would be happy to help her across as well," he offered. "Hercules can easily carry both of you while I lead him."

"*Sainte Vierge!* I would die of fright, sitting on that huge beast's back!" Ermengarde had shrieked in exaggerated horror.

"Then you could walk across with us, surely," Reyner said with more calm than he felt, seeing defeat even before Ermengarde protested.

"Nay, I fear I could not—these old hips are stiff from the day's jolting. Doubtless I shall have to be lifted from this wagon when we are safe in town."

Alouette had shrugged, unsure whether she was relieved or irritated that Ermengarde's obstinance prevented her from accepting Reyner's offer. "You see, my lord, I am obligated to stay with her. If she did not love me so, she would not be traveling halfway across the world at her age, exposing herself to such exhausting conditions."

Brown eyes blazed with irritation as his gaze left Alouette's uplifted oval face with its sightless azure eyes and stared at the old woman's smug countenance. Triumph shone in the cloudy irises, and for a moment he wanted to throttle her.

A moment later, after saying farewell, he had been ashamed at his reaction and realized that the woman was merely afraid of losing her central place in her mistress's life. Perhaps Ermengarde planned to follow Alouette into the convent. Did the old woman think that he would forbid her to accompany Alouette to Winslade if she married him? Somehow, he had to transform this enemy into an ally.

There—the last wheeled vehicles, including Alouette's carriage, were starting onto the wooden structure. Once they were across, he could breathe more easily.

As the first warning shudder of the bridge shook the wagon, Ermengarde let out a long wail. Immediately, she grabbed the confused Alouette and held her to her vast bosom, interspersing shrieks with frightened cries to the saints to aid them.

"Ermengarde! What's amiss? Loose me!" Alouette cried.

"The bridge is breaking, my lady! We're all going to die! Oh! Oh!" Ermengarde screamed as the span sagged, then gave way. With an ear-splitting crash the ancient structure collapsed, tossing its terror-stricken animal and human occupants into the flowing dark waters below.

Reyner did not remember tossing off his coif, jumping down from Hercules' back, or pulling off his hauberk as he ran. The next thing he felt was the surprising shock of the Alps-fed water as he made a long arching dive. Zeus charged in, barking, right after him.

The middle of the river was a roiling confusion of beam fragments, thrashing animals, and struggling humans when Reyner reached the spot where he had seen the carriage sink. Narrowly avoiding the plunging hooves of an ox trapped in its harness, he submerged himself in the icy water. He pictured Alouette drowning in the water-filled carriage, unable to find her way out because of her blindness (not that vision was any help in these black depths), drowning in panicked terror. *Damn the tirewoman for causing Alouette to stay in the carriage!*

Ahead of him in the inky water he could just make out a struggling shape. The water had transformed the garments into formless draperies that served only to drag their wearer down. He had no idea if it was Alouette or not; the floating wimple obscured the face. He realized after he got his arms underneath the woman's and began to assist her toward the surface, that it was Ermengarde. God's blood! He could not, however, in simple human decency, let her go!

He surfaced, his lungs burning for lack of air. The woman had a stranglehold about his neck and shoulders that threatened to pull him under.

"My lady! Save my lady!" she sputtered.

"Then let me loose!" he shouted in her ear, but the old woman was too hysterical to hear. Frantically, he looked around for someone to deposit her with, all the while struggling to remain afloat despite Ermengarde's panicked thrashing. All around him horses were swimming toward the shore. A tumult of curses and whinnies split the air.

From out of nowhere, seemingly, Henri de Chenevy was beside him. Reyner thrust the tirewoman into his arms. Before any words could be exchanged, Reyner again dived beneath the water's surface.

There was nothing. Nothing! All who had been able to

save themselves had done so by now. He found the carriage, with a large jagged hole in its side from the submerged log it had struck. There was no one in it.

He had to have air, had to breathe. *Alouette!* his heart cried in despair as he propelled his body toward the failing light. As soon as he filled his lungs he would go down again, and again, and again, until he found her. He would not leave her in a watery grave.

As his tawny head broke the surface, the sound of cheers filled his ears. He looked across the water to see Zeus swimming strongly for the bank nearest the town, dragging a motionless form by the cloak. The woman's long black hair floated free of a wimple. *Alouette.* Was she alive, or had the valiant dog been too late? Reyner swam after them, his long, powerful arms cutting through the water.

Henri had made it to shore with the whimpering Ermengarde, so he was nearby to assist as the massive canine reached the mossy shallows with his burden. He had just pulled Alouette out of the water and stretched her out on the grassy bank when Reyner sloshed out of the water to join him.

Alouette was chalk-white, her bloodless lips parted. A lock of ebony hair was plastered to one alabaster cheek. A strand of green moss festooned the opposite ear. Her eyes were closed. Zeus lay beside her, alternately panting from his exertions and whining anxiously.

"She breathes, Reyner. God be praised!" Henri said, and Reyner sank to his knees in weak relief, taking the limp figure of Alouette into his arms. He murmured his own thanks to God and his brave dog all at once, then rained kisses onto the girl's cold face.

Alouette returned to consciousness coughing, hearing a voice—*his* voice—calling her name: "Alouette, Alouette, my love! Oh, thank God, thank God! Waken, my love, open your eyes!" She was being clutched against a hard form as wet as her own.

"Reyner?" she murmured in confusion, not remembering at first why she was wet and cold. Was she dreaming?

"My love, I thought I had lost you! I thought you were

drowned, and I would never have the chance to tell you how I— Oh, Alouette!"

A very warm pair of lips descended on hers, and she was being kissed—expertly, and with a thoroughness that left her breathless and trembling. It all came back to her now —the collapse of the bridge, the terror, the panicked feeling that she was about to die, never having shared love with this man who was now pouring all his heart and soul into his kiss. Her arms went about him of their own accord, her fingers curling into the dripping locks at the nape of his neck, her lips opening as naturally as if this were not the first such kiss she had ever experienced in her life.

Her blindness made it easy to believe that they were the only two beings on this grassy bank as she felt him stroke her hair, her cheek. . . . His lips left hers and she felt a sense of loss until she heard him whisper, "Alouette, I love you! *I love you!*" and his lips exultantly claimed hers again. There was a tingling in her breasts as if he already touched them, and she realized with shock that she wished him to do so.

"Reyner, please . . ." she began, color flooding her wan cheeks as she wondered how to request such a thing. Did a maiden *ask*, or did the man mystically know that her nipples were hard and ached to feel his hands on them?

He knew. With her soggy cloak shielding his actions from general view, his long, elegant fingers found the pebble-hard center of one breast, circling the sensitive areola and eliciting soft moans of ecstasy from her.

"Alouette, Alouette, sweetheart, surely you must see now that you were not meant for the convent, but to love me. You are *mine*, Alouette, and I want you to be my . . ."

"My lady, my lady! Saint Blandina be praised that you are redeemed from the arms of death, to be restored to God's service! We will make a pilgrimage in thanks! We will lay a wreath of lilies at the Holy Sepulchre in Jerusalem!" babbled the waterlogged Ermengarde, who had finally struggled to her feet, just in time to behold her young mistress in the arms of that English devil.

As if a second icy blast of river water had awakened her fully, Alouette struggled out of Reyner's embrace. She realized guiltily that she had not spared a thought for her tirewoman's survival. "Thanks be to Our Lady that you are safe, too, Ermengarde."

She looked like a child caught with a stolen comfit, thought Reyner in exasperation, damning the old servant to the nether regions yet again.

King Phillip, who had already disappeared into Lyon to capture the best accommodations for the French, knew nothing about the disaster that had cost the lives of three Englishmen and several horses and oxen—and trapped a significant portion of the English army on the wrong side of the river. He began to be concerned at Alouette's failure to appear, however, by the time the messenger rode into town with the news.

He was waiting at the entrance of the bishop's palace when they arrived, therefore, and saw Alouette being carried on the saddlebow of Reyner de Winslade's tall black destrier, resting against his chest in utter exhaustion. Her tirewoman sat lumpily on the mule which brayed in fright when it got too near the stallion and the mighty horse kicked out at it. Trotting merrily on the other side of the warhorse was that huge wolf the damned Englishman kept as a pet.

Phillip started forward, intending to take Alouette from the Englishman's arms and bear her away, but the wolf's growling stopped him. He looked at the bared teeth, then dueled with Sir Reyner's perceptive brown eyes before laughing self-consciously. He'd be damned if he'd *ask* the English knight to call off the animal.

"Bring her inside, my lord," Phillip said coolly. "There is a soft, warm bed awaiting you, Lady Alouette."

Reyner, marveling at Alouette's lightness, despite the heavy wet garments, carried her up a flight of stairs and into a well-lit chamber on the second floor of the bishop's palace. Here was no austere denial of comfort. An Oriental carpet covered the floor in a vivid swirl of crimson and gold. The bed had hangings of purple velvet and a coverlet of softest wool trimmed in vair and pulled back to display sheets of snowy white linen.

Alouette was deposited onto a chair nearby, still in her wet clothes. Ermengarde clucked excitedly in the background and, ignoring her own sodden state, sent a page in search of hot water and blankets for her mistress, for the chest containing her clothes lay at the bottom of the Rhône.

During the ride into Lyon, Reyner had found it impossible to talk any further of the things that were in his heart, thanks to the basilisk presence of the tirewoman. Nor was he to be allowed any further time now to do more than take his farewell of Alouette, he realized, noting that Phillip Capet was waiting to escort him out.

"Lady Alouette, if I do not see you again before the French army leaves, I trust we will meet again in Sicily," he said carefully, feeling the French king's eyes on his back as he knelt before her. There was so much more he wanted to say but dared not in her royal half brother's presence.

In the jewellike clarity of her cerulean eyes, Reyner saw the gleam of tears as she leaned forward, swathed in blankets. "I cannot thank you enough, my lord, for your heroic efforts and those of your brave dog . . ." She reached out a hand, palm down, and instantly Zeus was there enjoying her touch. Reyner had not even noticed the dog behind him, but he was amused now to see that Phillip kept a careful distance.

"I'm certain the *Sieur* de Winslade will have many duties to fulfill following this unfortunate accident, Alouette. We must not keep him," Phillip hinted broadly, locking eyes with Reyner.

"Yes, of course not. Go with God until we meet again in Sicily, my lord—you and your wonderful Zeus."

Reyner gazed at Alouette, trying to memorize her lovely alabaster features in the brief seconds that were left before they must part for weeks. He found it was an unnecessary labor of love, for her face had been etched in his soul since he first had seen her.

"Come, Zeus." He snapped his fingers for the dog, who still looked up adoringly at Alouette. Zeus had never ignored a command since puppyhood. Yet, as clearly as if the dog had spoken, he conveyed his wish that Reyner and

Alouette stay together, but if they must part, he wanted to remain with her.

Reyner stared at the dog in surprise. "Aren't you coming, Zeus?" He had always spoken to the dog as if it were human and fully capable of a reply.

Zeus gave a short bark, and wagged his tail, but made no move to follow his master.

"It seems you have made a conquest, my lady. Zeus wishes to remain at your side." Although he would miss the half-wolf's companionship, Reyner felt no sadness. Allowing Zeus to stay with her would be like leaving a part of himself with Alouette; and when she patted the dog, perhaps she would think of his master. She would be safer with Zeus protecting her, Reyner thought as he ruffled the beast's ears in affectionate farewell.

"Thank you. I will keep him for you until we meet in Messina," Alouette told him. "Don't worry, my lord, I will treat him well."

SIX

Richard Plantagenet, informed of the calamitous bridge collapse which had trapped his army on the opposite side of the river, stood on the high, grassy bank of the Rhône staring moodily at the ruined remains of the bridge and at the rest of his army, which milled helplessly about on the opposite bank.

"A thousand curses on that damnable bridge *and* Phillip Capet," he said in disgust as Reyner joined him. "D'you know what Fat Phillip offered to do to help me, Reyner? Exactly nothing. 'I am sure you agree it is useless for both our armies to remain in Lyon because of this unfortunate accident,'" he mimicked the French king in a mocking falsetto. "He's leaving for Genoa tomorrow—as if nothing has happened!" He struck a clenched fist into his extended palm—a fairly mild reaction for an Angevin. His father, Henry II, had been known to bite straw, roll on the ground, and foam at the mouth when crossed. The Plantagenets were, after all, descended from Melusine, the witch.

"I can imagine you are disappointed in the lack of assistance from your ally," Reyner said carefully, wary of the Plantagenet temper.

"'Disappointed' isn't the word I'd have chosen," Richard replied with a wry twist to his mouth, but a twinkle in his eyes revealed that he would soon turn his energies to a solution, rather than merely bewailing the problem. "Ah, what an ally I have, Reyner! I wonder whether to fear Saladin or Phillip more?"

"I don't believe you fear either of them, sire." It was not a courtier's flattery, just a simple fact, but it pleased the Plantagenet nevertheless.

"Quite so. I suspect the crusade would be better off if Phillip went home and left me his crusaders. Then I'd only have to worry about him menacing my borders at home, though, so perhaps I'm better off being able to keep an eye on the scoundrel. Did you see your little 'lark' safely dried off and put to bed?"

Surprised that his king was aware of such a small detail in the midst of his current predicament, Reyner managed a grin. "Yes, my lord."

"It was provident that you and your wolf could be the means of saving Phillip's natural sister. Maybe it will make partial amends for Alais," Richard said, referring to Phillip's sister, whom Richard refused to marry. "You're rather entranced by the blind girl, aren't you? Finally found one who isn't frightened by that ugly visage of yours, eh?" Richard teased.

Reyner took the jest in good part, for Richard had often jested with him about his handsomeness and its effect on women—from scullery wenches to barons' ladies.

"I do find her appealing," he admitted with a grin, but shrugged his shoulders. "I fear the lady will have none of me, however. She desires the religious life."

"Hmmmh! Well, you'll have a long journey in which to change her mind," Richard said, looking back at the river, but not before Reyner had surprised a look on his monarch's face—was it regret? His voice had resumed its jocular tenor when he spoke again, however. "Where is the heroic wolf? Perhaps I should knight him for his chivalrous act!"

There was every possibility that Richard was serious.

"I fear that will have to be deferred until Sicily, Your Grace. Zeus elected to stay at Lady Alouette's side."

"'Sdeath! This is looking interesting!" Richard gave him a final playful poke in the ribs, then turned his attention back to the dilemma at hand.

* * *

In the end, the king used Reyner's suggestion and lashed together a fleet of small boats, obtained by emptying the docks at Lyon and summoning all the river craft for several leagues up and down the Rhône. By this means the rest of the English army crossed to the opposite bank, which took less time than if they had been ferried across in small groups. Nevertheless, the accident cost them a precious three days.

> Who calls me greedy does not lie
> I hunger after love remote
> No joy within my grasp can vie
> With that of winning love remote . . .

Alouette, alone on the forecastle of the great galley, plucked her lute and sang the plaintive love song written by an earlier crusader. All the others were in the aftcastle, watching the Genoa harbor recede in the distance, exultant to be finally underway.

More than a month had passed since they had left Lyon for the remaining overland leg of the journey to the Italian port, where Phillip planned to hire the fleet that would take the French crusaders to Sicily, and from there to Palestine. In Genoa they had lost over a week while Phillip's commanders haggled over ships and Alouette's royal half brother lay ill of an unknown sickness. She suspected that at the heart of Phillip's malady lay his well-known fear of sailing, though he had deemed this partial journey by water to be less hazardous and time-consuming than a summer passage over the Alps. But at last Phillip had pronounced himself well enough to depart, spurred on, perhaps, by a brief visit from King Richard, who had been following the shore of Italy and had heard of the French king's illness.

The inevitable banquet had been planned for Richard's reception. Though this was only to be a brief, informal visit, it was a meeting Alouette had anticipated eagerly. Now she would be able to show Sir Reyner that she had regained control of her feelings. She would be cool, distant but friendly. There would be no trace of the impressionable young demoiselle who had grown giddy when he was near. She would be as serene as the alabaster Madonna in a

Genoese church where she had worshipped—a statue whose contours she had traced with sensitive, knowing fingers when the chapel was empty, trying to grasp the secret of the saint's peace.

All her emotional preparation was in vain, for she had had no chance to display her newfound calm. Reyner was not at the banquet. Zeus's behavior while he lay at her feet as she waited to play for the assembled nobles dining in the hall told her that fact. Just before she began to strum her lute, she reached down to pat the dog's head. He was alert and his ears had pricked forward when the English king had taken his place on the dais, but his master was evidently not among the trio of knights who had accompanied Richard on his visit ashore. Had Reyner of Winslade been there, she knew Zeus would have bounded up to meet him, barking joyously.

As she sang each verse praising chivalry, courtly love, and the beauty of the cross, she lost a little of the joy that had animated her features. Why had he not come? she wondered. Perhaps in the intervening weeks he had learned to see her for what she was—a woman bound to a vow of chaste service to God—and realized that she was not for him. That had been what she had prayed for—hadn't it?

It had required every drop of self-control she could summon not to ask the English king about Reyner, especially when he made it a point to compliment her on her singing and to greet Zeus. But her pride had won the struggle—a bittersweet victory.

"I should have expected a more . . . ah, *martial* tune as we left port," an unfamiliar voice in front of her said.

Alouette was startled, not having heard anyone approach. "Who's there?"

"I crave your pardon, Lady Alouette. I am Fulk, *Sieur* de Langres. I did not intend to intrude, but I could not help but notice your wan face. Such a contrast to the fine day! Or can it be that no one has told you that the sun shines and the wind is fair set to blow us all the way to Sicily?"

Saints! The condescension of the sighted to the blind. Normally she did not mind explaining the various sensory clues that told her everything she needed to know; but in her present mood, the stranger's presence was an imposition. She could feel the warmth of the morning sun on her face, and the freshening breeze from behind that teased the hair curled about the nape of her neck; her nose caught the salt tang in the air; her ears heard the raucous cries of the gulls and the crisp snap of the sail in counterpoint to the rowers' drumbeat.

"Ah, but I fear I trespass," said the knight kindly. "However, I must be frank, for I grieve for the *tristesse* I see in your face, knowing that one of my blood has caused it."

"What do you mean?"

"I fear I am cousin to the author of your melancholy, Reyner de Winslade."

She was truly astonished now, and dismayed. Was her every emotion written on her face? How else could this stranger know her secrets? Her hands trembled as she set the lute down. "I have met the English knight you name," she said, striving for a casual tone. "But what has that to do with me?"

"Lady Alouette, forgive me, but I watched at the banquet last night as you awaited the arrival of the English king. You reminded me of a living flame—your face was so glowing and vital. The flame flickered and dimmed as the evening went on. I was puzzled as to why this was so, until I remembered hearing the boasts of Sir Reyner de Winslade. He bragged in the streets of Vézélay and Lyon of his conquests—the latest one being closely connected to royalty, he hinted. At the time I dismissed his claims as the effects of too much good burgundy—Reyner had always been a drunkard and a strutting cock around the ladies— but as I sat there, I realized with dismay that he referred to you."

For a moment, she could not get her breath. Seeing her face turn pale, Fulk pressed his advantage. "It was my cousin you waited for, wasn't it? Ah, Lady, I am truly sorry for your pain. Reyner did come ashore last night, but I fear his destination was different from his king's. He went straight to the stews of the dockside, where he was heard to use your name in a toast—'to the whitest thighs of

France—those of the Lark.' Begging your pardon, Lady Alouette, but I thought you should know."

She was so enraged that it did not occur to her to question how Fulk knew of Reyner's visit to a brothel if he had been at the banquet. "He lies," she said through clenched teeth, pain at the betrayal ripping through her like a ragged blade. "He has no right . . . we did not . . . I am not . . ." she sputtered angrily, then the tears came in a wrenching flood and she buried her face in her hands. How dare Reyner bandy her name about as if she were a camp follower? How dare he utter such lies? The memory of her wild, abandoned embrace with him on the bank of the Rhône rose up to haunt her.

"Of course, I know there is no basis in fact for his lies, dear lady. Your piety is an inspiration to all of us who wear the red cross on our surcoats. And I promise you I will kill the blustering fool when next we meet. I only regret he will live until we reach Sicily."

New alarm flashed across her distressed features, and she forgot her earlier dislike of the intruder. "Oh, no, Sieur Fulk, you must not do such a thing, promise me!" she cried, reaching a slender hand out entreatingly. He allowed it to fall on his forearm. "Such murderous thoughts are contrary to the holy cause of the crusade! I beg you to forget any such evil intent! Pray for him, rather, as Our Lord bids us do for our enemies!"

He gazed at her earnest, entreating face, well-satisfied at the success of his campaign of slander. "I should have known you would react in such a saintly fashion," he said, patting her hand soothingly. "Very well, Lady, since you ask it of me, the blackguard may live to face a Saracen blade." *No, I will not endanger myself in open combat with the English knight, reputed an excellent swordsman*, he thought. *A dagger in the back will serve just as well*.

Alouette withdrew her hand into her lap. It always startled her to be touched unexpectedly. She hoped she did not seem discourteous to Sir Fulk, after his kindness.

"I fear I am not saintly at all," she said, thinking of how she had allowed herself to be distracted from her holy goal by that . . . that *salaud*! She remembered Reyner's words by the Rhône, just before Ermengarde had interrupted. "I want you to be my—" *He must have meant mistress,* she thought grimly. *Since I am a bastard, I am not worthy to be a wife.*

Her voice was thick with unshed tears, but she would not give way until she could do so in the limited privacy of her cabin. "I must thank you for your courage in telling me the truth. After all, such a one as Reyner brings no honor to your house. I believe you said you were . . . cousins?" Against her will, the subject held her interest.

Genoa harbor had disappeared on the horizon as they had talked, and the crowd in the aft castle had dispersed. Soon they would be interrupted, he knew. He would have to content himself with a few more well-chosen words, calculated to win her sympathy. "Reyner's father and mine were twin brothers. My father was the elder, and therefore, earl with considerable holdings under King Stephen in England. When the Angevin upstart took the crown, however, Simon of Winslade plotted and stole the title and demesne lands with Henry II's connivance. My father became just another banished outlaw, forced to seek his fortune at Louis's court. Fortunately, the saintly departed Louis saw my father's true worth and gave him the seigneury of Langres." *Just the right mixture of bitterness of old wrongs, righteous indignation at the blackening of her fair name, and oblique flattery of her not-so-secret sire,* he congratulated himself.

"We both have suffered at the hands of these unjust relatives of yours, then. It seems the lies spread by Sir Reyner about me are minor indeed, compared to the injustice done to your father," she said. "Thank you for your thoughtfulness on my behalf, my lord," she added, dismissing him as she heard Ermengarde's heavy tread approaching.

"It is my joy to serve one as devout as she is fair," he said humbly, bowing more for the servant's benefit than for the blind girl's. He walked down to the main deck, his mind full of ways to ingratiate himself to Phillip Capet now that he had won over his half sister. With a connection to the royal house, who knew what glories the future Count of Langres could achieve? Phillip might well retake the English continental possessions one day, and then, why not England? As the king's brother by marriage, he might regain his domains in England in the blink of an eye.

Alouette's professed desire for the religious life troubled him not at all. Like Fulk, Phillip's main goal in life was to please himself, and if he desired that his bastard sister wed the Sieur de Langres, then she would do so.

The written message Fulk had sent on board the English flagship *Pumbone* had been a stroke of genius, even if it had not fully achieved the goal of having Reyner murdered.

The messenger had informed Reyner that a letter awaited him at the Sign of the Three Angels, a dockside tavern frequented by sailors. "A letter from England, from Hawkingham," the swarthy, one-eyed sailor had announced, pronouncing the foreign name with difficulty.

"Why didn't you just bring it?" Reyner had asked suspiciously. "I would have paid you well."

The Genoese was all cheerful apology. "I would ha' been weeling," he said, shrugging his shoulders and smiling his regret at the tall English knight, "but Fat Maria, she don' trust me to bring de money to her. She wants the money hersel'."

Reyner sighed. Fat Maria was probably right. He wouldn't trust the fellow either. That solitary eye was entirely too shifty, and Reyner had learned that a foreigner's ingratiating smile was meaningless as a guide to his intentions.

Reyner had not checked at the harborside establishment, where mail was often delivered. He had not really expected any messages. A letter from home was probably from Aimery, and he wouldn't have gone to the trouble to send it unless something was amiss. His father? His mother? Was one of them ill, or dead? Was Prince John up to some mischief with Lord Simon's lands?

There was no help for it—he had to go first to obtain the letter, though he had been invited to accompany Richard ashore to visit the ailing King Phillip, and then attend the feast that would be held in Richard's honor. Reyner had been eagerly anticipating seeing Alouette again, but decided sensibly that a detour to the Sign of the Three Angels would only delay him an hour or so. There would be plenty of time to go to the tavern and fetch the message, read it, and find his way to Phillip's quarters—with luck, even before the meal had begun.

The one-eyed sailor had promised to show him the way for an extra few coins. This he did, chattering volubly in broken French as he led Reyner past progressively meaner brothels and taverns, into narrowing, meandering side streets going away from the harbor.

Reyner felt a prickling of apprehension along his spine, and cursed his lack of horse and armor. He would have been a lot less vulnerable on Hercules' back, but it was not practical to bring the destrier ashore for a single night. Perhaps it was foolish to have come without his hauberk, but he had been dressed for the banquet and had not wanted to take the time to locate his squire to help him arm. At least he had thought to throw a thick, serviceable cloak over his good tunic to hide its quality.

"I thought you said the tavern was on the docks—" Reyner began, and then his world exploded into darkness.

He had awakened at dawn, his head aching, the purse full of coins gone, but his sword still miraculously in its sheath—probably because it was trapped under his right thigh.

Stumbling painfully to his feet, he managed to find his way to a small chapel, where a fat old priest told him there was no such place as the Sign of the Three Angels.

There was no tavern and, therefore, no letter. It had all been a ruse. Why? Did someone want him to die, or merely to miss the banquet? Could Phillip of France feel so threatened by his obvious admiration for Alouette that he would have arranged for this ambush? He doubted it, but it certainly wasn't impossible.

Reyner found his way back to the quay and was rowed back out to the *Pumbone*. Any hope he had of lingering in Genoa and finding another chance to seek out Alouette was dashed when he saw the irritable English king pacing the deck.

"*There* you are, Reyner! I was about to weigh anchor without you! Where in the name of heaven have you been? You never made it to the banquet!"

Coeur de Lion's roar did nothing to aid his aching head. Briefly, he told the king what had happened. Richard was sympathetic, but firm.

"I'll not stay in Genoa another hour. The longer I'm here, the more the king of France wants. He was all appreciative amiability for my sick call yesterday, and then, at dawn, he sent me a message begging that I lend him five galleys! I offered him three, but he refused them, the haughty bastard! No, my boy, we sail immediately. I know you didn't get to see your sweetheart, but there'll be plenty of time once we get to Sicily. I have family business there —my sister Joanna's dowry to recover—and if that isn't taken care of quickly, we'll end up wintering there," he finished sourly, chafing at the delay in reaching his destination. "You would do well to remember that our objective is to conquer Saladin, not female hearts, Reyner."

"Yes, Sire." He could understand the frustrations causing the uncharacteristic curtness in his sovereign's tone, and remembered that before that day in Vézélay, he also had had no other goal than winning back the Holy Sepulchre and the True Cross. Once he had looked into Alouette de Chenevy's lovely face, this journey to the uttermost parts of the world seemed instead to be merely the means to a very delightful, satisfying end. He still believed in the goals of the crusade—of freeing the holy places of Palestine from the grip of the infidel, but the victory would seem a hollow achievement if he could not also have the French girl's love.

SEVEN

"Describe it to me, Ermengarde—what do you see?" Alouette demanded eagerly as they stood on deck on a morning in mid-September. The island of Sicily lay less than a league across the narrow Strait of Messina from the toe of the Italian boot.

"The harbor is sickle-shaped, my lady, and well-protected by the high jagged black rock formations along the cliffs."

"I have heard it is a land of volcanoes. I should not want to be present if one of them erupts," Alouette said with a shudder of her slender shoulders. She reached to pluck an errant strand of raven hair that had escaped her barbette and curled against her lips.

"God forfend," Ermengarde replied, crossing herself devoutly. "There are small groves of trees—olive and lemon, I think," the old woman continued as the carrack drew closer to the harbor.

"Can you see the palace? The widowed Queen Joanna, sister to Richard Plantagenet, lives there."

"Yes, there it is—a gray stone building, high on a rise above the town. I have heard that Tancred, a cousin of the king, controls the island now, though a Plantagenet female is the legitimate heir. I've heard he is a dwarf," added Ermengarde, relishing the chance to gossip.

"Then he'll be lucky if Richard doesn't make him a court fool," Alouette returned. "Are there English ships in the harbor? Is the flagship there?"

"The harbor is lined with English and French ships, but I don't see the *Pumbone*," the serving woman said, giving her mistress's face a searching look.

Alouette had been very quiet ever since they had left Genoa. A brooding bitterness, totally foreign to her usually even-tempered demeanor, lay like a heavy weight upon her slender shoulders. She spent much time at the tiny make-shift *prie-dieu* in their cramped cabin, but her prayers brought her little comfort. Nor did the near-constant attentions of a knight in Phillip's meinie, Sieur Fulk de Langres. He was always hovering with some tidbit of news to impart, some sweetmeat, or a cool goblet of wine.

Alouette did nothing to encourage the knight, but her lack of response did not visibly discourage him, either. Ermengarde suspected Alouette's actions were less *politesse* than simple lack of awareness that he was wooing her. Lately, Alouette seemed to float above mundane conversation on some private cloud of pain, though she courteously inclined her ear or accepted a proffered treat.

Ermengarde was relieved to see that her mistress seemed to care little for Fulk, whose swarthy, sullen features reminded the old woman of one of Satan's fallen angels. There was something about him that Ermengarde just didn't like—a malady of spirit that ate at him, though he was careful not to reveal it to Alouette in his cheerful remarks. But Ermengarde could see, as Alouette could not, the shadow cross the knight's face as he looked at Alouette, and the flash of resentment when Ermengarde caught him at it.

The old woman had seen King Phillip and Fulk de Langres head-to-head one day in the forecastle of the carrack. Both men had turned to gaze at Alouette, who sat in the waist of the ship, her face turned toward the warm Mediterranean sun. Their conversation was obviously about her—why?

Ermengarde remembered feeling more concerned when Reyner de Winslade was around—apprehensive as she saw Alouette turn to the Englishman, as a flower to the sun. The vow made to the girl's dead mother had seemed endangered then.

However, the servant realized that though Alouette had been torn between her vocation for the religious life and the life that had beckoned as the Englishman's lady, she had seemed genuinely happy for the first time since she had lost her sight.

Perhaps it would not be such a bad thing for Alouette to be a wife to a good man and mother to his babes, Ermengarde had thought, arguing with the shade of Lisette. *Surely you would not mind if your daughter were happy outside convent walls. Perhaps heartbreak and tragedy are not inevitable in the world.* She thought of the radiance on her charge's face as she had ridden with her rescuer from the banks of the Rhône.

Ermengarde had not uttered a word of reproach for the passionate embrace she had witnessed on the river bank, though she sensed the blind girl expected her to. But the old woman had decided it would be better just to wait and see what would happen when Alouette and Reyner met again.

Ermengarde had seen an embryonic hope die a-borning in Genoa, when Alouette had expected to encounter Reyner at King Richard's side and he had been inexplicably absent. The next day Ermengarde had seen de Langres talking to Alouette, and it was obvious that his words distressed her further.

She wished the girl would confide in her, but there was a reserve in Alouette that had not been there before. She guessed from the radical change in Alouette's spirits that Fulk had said something about Reyner, possibly given an explanation of his absence. Difficult as it was, she would have to wait until her charge chose to confide in her.

The carrack, hired from the Genoese, was anchoring, flanked by the other hired vessels carrying the rest of the French, and the sound of cheers was carried on the gentle Sicilian breeze.

"There are many waiting by the docks and on the sands to greet us," the tirewoman told her. "Crusaders, of course, but many others with dark complexions who are strangely dressed."

Sicily, Alouette had learned, had only been in European

hands for a little over a century, and it still contained many of Greek and Arabic descent.

Upon disembarking, Phillip and the royal party went directly to the palace, disappointing the crowds who had waited long for a better show. There the king and his entourage were welcomed by Tancred, the acting ruler, who gave them a suite of apartments and informed them that the English fleet (which had missed its rendezvous in Marseilles with Richard) had arrived two days earlier, on Holy Cross Day. Of the widowed Queen Joanna, Tancred volunteered nothing, and Alouette wondered where she was.

Henri, Alouette's stepbrother, would be billeted with the rest of the French in their camp outside of town. Already, Tancred complained in his whining falsetto, the French and English who had come ahead of their kings were making life miserable for the natives—stealing their goods or paying less than their purported worth, and molesting the Sicilian women.

Phillip seemed disinclined to do more than shrug his shoulders, so Tancred continued to grumble. There were yet more crusaders coming with Richard Plantagenet. Where was he supposed to put them? Would they leave as soon as Richard had arrived, or would he be forced to play host to the horde of would-be Saracen killers all winter?

"Your tone is scarcely welcoming to those on a holy mission," Phillip had retorted with lazy irony. "If you consider us a problem, however, you would be better to take it up with Richard. He's due any day now, you know. I understand he has a few questions to take up with you, as well."

Phillip's point hit home. There was the disputed matter of Joanna's inheritance, plus the aid the late King William had promised the crusade. Yes, Tancred could see the wisdom of saving his strength for dealing with the English king. Perhaps he could even make an ally of Phillip in the intervening time, and play divide and conquer.

More than a week later the rest of the English fleet filled the strait, with Richard's flagship at its head. The galleys, flying colorful pennons and banners, were crowded with armored warriors, cheering as lustily as the waiting crowd. The onlookers would not be disappointed in their desire for pageantry this time.

Henri stood next to Alouette and served as her eyes. "The English king shines like a lion with a golden mane," he said, spying Richard waving from the forecastle of the *Pumbone*. "He isn't waiting for a longboat—he's jumping into the shallows and wading ashore, greeting King Phillip with a kiss to both cheeks."

"What an impetuous man," Alouette remarked lightly. "I cannot imagine Phillip doing such a thing, can you?" She really did not care what the kings were doing, but it kept her from asking if Henri had spotted Reyner de Winslade yet.

"Ah, there's Reyner, standing in the aft castle. It will be marvelous to catch up with the news! Perhaps we shall find out what happened to him in Genoa, Alouette."

Henri was the kindest of brothers, but sometimes he could be totally oblivious to subtleties, thought Alouette. He seemed totally unaware that she changed the subject every time Reyner's name was mentioned. Of course, she dared not tell him what Reyner had done, for Henri would be honor-bound to fight Reyner. Alouette had no desire to lose her brother to that blackguard's sword.

She was dismayed by the prospect of being near Reyner again. It was too soon. She was not ready, although she had had large amounts of free time to spend in the palace chapel on her knees in prayer, arming herself for the unavoidable encounter.

Why had she come to the docks today? It was foolish madness brought about by her boredom, for there had been little to do but pray while Phillip conferred with Tancred. She could have given Reyner his dog at the palace, where she would be shielded by Phillip's presence and her role as the king's troubador.

"I'm afraid the noontide heat has given me a headache," Alouette said, touching slender fingers to her forehead in an exaggerated gesture of pain. "I believe I will return to the palace. I am to play for the banqueters, so I will see you tonight, Henri. Go ahead. I am sure you want to greet your friend. Zeus will take me back, won't you, boy?"

But just then the half-wolf caught sight of his beloved master, who had disdained riding to shore in the longboat, just as Richard had, and was splashing through the shallows to the pebbly shore. Zeus gave a series of frenzied, joyous barks and began straining at the leather leash that bound him to the blind girl. Though he was careful not to lunge so hard that he pulled her off her feet, he began inexorably pulling in the direction of the ships.

He must have seen Reyner, thought Alouette. He must not spot her here, waiting on the beach like a lovesick scullery wench! He would think she had forgiven his absence in Genoa—that she would tolerate his drunken slanders in brothels.

"*Please*, Zeus," she cried in a hushed undertone, hauling back on the leash. "Take me back to the palace. *Take me back to the palace!*" He had never disobeyed her before. The leash, which had never really been needed, now was not enough to hold him back. It was as if the dog had suddenly gone deaf.

"All right then, go! Go to your master! I'll get back to the palace without you!" Alouette cried as she dropped the leash. "Henri? Are you still there? I need you to escort me back to the palace after all!"

Henri was out of earshot, having taken her at her word. He was down at the water's edge, greeting his friend.

Zeus, however, had no intention of deserting the possession his master had set him to guard. He seized a portion of her scarlet sarcenet skirts in his teeth, resuming his gentle but relentless tugging. His job was not complete until he had reunited his master and his master's chosen mate.

"No, Zeus! Let go!" Alouette dug in her heels on the pebbly beach, but at best she could only prevent any forward progress. She knew Reyner was bound to see her, thanks to Zeus's noisy actions. All around her people walked, scuffling the pebbles and talking excitedly as they went to greet the English crusaders, but none offered to interfere with the huge canine.

"Ho, there! Zeus! Lady Alouette!" Reyner's glad cry

sent shivers of apprehension down her spine at the coming confrontation—and incredibly, regret that it must be so. Perhaps Reyner was apparently one who became drunk easily, but to besmirch her name as he had done was unforgivable. She stiffened and turned to face the sound of his rapidly approaching progress over the rocky beach. She could hear Henri at his side, still chattering volubly.

"Lady Alouette, well met! I rejoice to see you. I—"

"*Sieur* de Winslade, here is your dog. I thank you for his company in the intervening time. Henri, I am unwell. Please escort me back." Her clipped tone brooked no refusal.

She was startled to feel Reyner's warm hand upon hers, and then he lifted it to his mouth to kiss.

"I'm sorry to hear you are indisposed. I look forward to this evening, then, for we have much to talk about, Lady Alouette."

She had to be careful in her words, for repeating Fulk's accusations in front of her stepbrother would only cause disaster. Henri would be compelled to defend the Chenevy honor in a duel, and however Reyner had slandered her, she did not want his blood on her hands—or a worse reason to hate him if he bested Henri.

"We have nothing to say to each other, my lord. I trust you will remember that I am to be a nun. I will be retiring to my prayers immediately following my singing tonight. Come, Henri."

Alouette heard the sharp, surprised intake of his breath, felt him abruptly let go of her hand. "Your servant, my lady," he said coolly in that Norman-accented voice she had heard in her dreams.

EIGHT

Still stinging from the effect of Alouette's unfriendly tone, Reyner trudged up the beach in the wake of his king. *So Alouette would play the haughty "dame sans merci," would she, and not even give me the chance to explain why I did not come to her in Genoa? She kisses me as if she loves me, then retreats into her "chaste nun" guise whenever I get too close! Perhaps she's just a coquette,* he thought in a wrathful vein. "She'll talk to me tonight, or else," he promised grimly, unaware that he had spoken aloud. But only Zeus, trotting at his heels, heard the muttered words.

Richard and his retinue went first to the royal palace, which stood at the summit of a hill overlooking Messina. It was built of gray stone, but its appearance was totally foreign to those accustomed to Romanesque architecture, for its rounded domes and mosaicked arches revealed the influence of the Arabs and Byzantines who had occupied Sicily before the Normans. The Plantagenet king was intent on conferring with Phillip, but he also hoped to see his newly widowed sister, Joanna. And of course there was Tancred, with whom he had much to settle.

They were led down mosaic-tiled hallways, through a marble arch into the throne room, where Phillip, lazily quaffing a goblet of the strong local wine, awaited his royal vassal. He seemed very much at home.

"Where's Tancred? Where's my sister?" the tall Plantagenet king demanded without ceremony.

"Greetings again, Richard. Don't be in such a rush—you've only just arrived. Tancred bade me tell you he will see you at the banquet tonight. Joanna has already been sent for, and she'll be here on the morrow."

"Sent for? Where is she?"

"Palermo, I am told. She's to arrive by ship tomorrow."

"You seem very comfortable, Your Majesty," Richard said sarcastically, raising a reddish-gold brow at the robe of spotless Byzantine linen Phillip affected, "yet on the beach I see hundreds of English tents. The Englishmen who came ahead tell me the gates of Messina are closed against them. Where am I and my retinue to stay—on the beach with them?"

"Come, Richard, there's only so much room here," replied Phillip imperturbably. "We did arrive first, and after all, I am your overlord. There are lodgings prepared for you, never fear. Come, let one of my knights escort you there. Refresh yourself, wash the sea salt from your body, and we'll see you at the banquet."

Reyner was startled to see that the *chevalier* selected to guide them was none other than Fulk de Langres. Did he imagine it, or did his cousin seem just as surprised to see him? Could he have been behind the incident in Genoa? The more he thought of it, the surer he became, and stared coldly back at Fulk. Fulk made no move to address him, though, and made his face into an impassive, courteous mask.

"*He* lodges in the palace on his fat French arse while we are given the house of one of the king's officers outside the city walls!" fumed Richard, pacing through the large but hardly luxurious house set among the vineyards in the suburbs of Messina. "And Tancred doesn't even bother to come greet me. Damn their impudence!"

Reports had already reached him while he was en route to the vineyard house that the crusaders had been persecuted by the natives of the mountainous island. In addition to the indignity of being forced to camp on the beach, the crusaders had been refused the right to buy food in town, and some had even been slain when they were found wandering alone and unarmed.

The island of Sicily was populated by two groups—the Italian-speaking Lombards, and those of Greek origin, whom the Normans contemptuously called "Griffons." Both groups were united in their hatred of the "Ultramontanes," as they named anyone from beyond the Alps. More specifically, they referred to Richard and his men as "tailed Englishmen."

Tancred, it seemed, had set himself up as the champion of national rights, reminding the people that they had been unfairly conquered by the Normans in the eleventh century, and urging them to throw off the yoke of foreign oppression now that King William of Sicily had died.

Phillip had reportedly done absolutely nothing to counter the persecution or to discipline his own men, and the Messinans continued to raise their town walls as if defying the hungry crusaders.

"That will cease now, by God's toenails," Richard grimly swore, "or we will not move from this island until we are given due respect."

Reyner, thinking of the sullen, defiant looks he had been given by the swarthy Messinans, doubted that Richard's goal would be easily accomplished.

Torches flickered in the hall as the English retinue filed in, found their places at the trestle tables, and stood while the trumpet fanfare announced the entrance of King Richard, King Phillip, and the dwarf Tancred, unofficial heir to the throne of Sicily.

Reyner, seated at a point near the high table, was in an excellent position to observe that for this evening at least, the trio of rulers seemed resolved to put their differences aside. But he wasted little time watching the bland, carefully impassive faces of the kings. He had eyes only for Alouette de Chenevy, who had been assisted to her place at the far end of the dais by her brother, Henri.

Her attire gave no hint of her desired future as a nun. She was resplendent in a crimson sarcenet gown, embroidered at the neck, with long, trailing sleeves of gold fleur-de-lis. Riding low over her slender hips was a belt of gilded links interspersed with enameled beads. Her hair was uncovered, braided in a coil at her nape, and banded by an elegantly simple gold circlet.

The hue of the gown lent color to her alabaster features. Her face was innocent of cosmetics, but she needed none to accentuate her comeliness, thought Reyner. *My French lily—or rather, rose with thorns,* he corrected himself, still resentful of her biting words of the morning. *I'm going to strip her of those thorns at the earliest opportunity.*

William des Barres, seated across from him, noticed his friend's brown eyes kindle with a secret fire, but misunderstood its source.

"Phillip's mistress is ravishing tonight, *hein*?" he inquired, with a nod in the direction of the flaxen-haired wench seated at one of the tables below the dais, but near enough to exchange remarks with Phillip. In contrast to Alouette, Peronel made full use of artificial aids to enhance her blowsy charms. Her eyelids were painted azure and outlined in kohl, her lips carmined, her sallow complexion whitened with cochineal paste. Her gown of turquoise velvet seemed a poor choice for the warm evening, and too tightly molded to her lush body. All this Reyner assessed in a quick, disinterested glance.

"Not your sort, eh, *mon ami*? It's just as well. Phillip doesn't share easily. Perhaps Tancred's daughters would be more to your taste? They obviously find *you* fascinating."

Reyner had not even noticed the dusky pair of beauties who sat at their father's left, but he looked up to find them staring at him. Both had olive complexions, dark, flashing eyes, and aquiline noses, and appeared tall next to their father's diminutive proportions. When they saw Reyner looking back at them, they giggled and whispered to each other behind cupped hands, their gold dangling earrings bobbing animatedly.

One of them made so bold as to wink a dark eye at him, and he grinned in spite of himself. He did not, however, wink back, as once he would have done without hesitation. His mind was too full of a paler beauty.

"A shameless pair of hussies, are they not?" William

commented, but not as though he found them displeasing. Quite the contrary.

"Tancred probably has his hands full preserving their virtue," Reyner replied, pretending not to notice as they strove to catch his eye again.

"*If* they have any left to be preserved," retorted his friend skeptically. "See their saucy eyes! I wouldn't be surprised if he procures for them!"

Reyner glanced at the swarthy, controversial dwarf who sat in animated conversation between Phillip Capet and Richard Plantagenet, gems flashing on his plump, beringed fingers as he gesticulated and smiled genially at his royal guests.

"I wouldn't be the least surprised. Better steer clear of them, my friend. He probably has plans for them that don't include selling them to mere knights such as ourselves."

William did not look convinced, but Reyner lost interest as pages began to bring in the first course.

The meal was magnificent—a melding of Mediterranean dishes with those the "Ultramontanes" were used to tasting. The Sicilian cuisine was a reflection of their greater access to the spices of the East. In the first course, the banqueters sampled such cold delicacies as marzipan balls, Neapolitan spice cakes, grapes, olives, and pork tongues cooked in wine. In the second, roasted viands were brought in steaming on great silver platters. There were skylarks in lemon sauce, quails with sliced eggplant, pigeons with sprinkled sugar, rabbits with pine nuts, and leg of goat in a sauce made from its own juices. The third course featured boiled meats and stews: stuffed goose covered with sliced almonds, stuffed veal garnished with flowers, whole shelled almonds in garlic sauce, pigeons stuffed with sausage and onions, poultry pies, and boiled calves' feet. By the time the last course was brought in, Reyner was too sated to do more than sample a couple of the rich desserts that were offered: quince pastries, almonds on wine leaves, roasted chestnuts sprinkled with sugar, salt, and pepper, and assorted cheeses.

Reyner had studied Alouette through the meal, noticing her appetite was as light as the bird for which she was named. He marveled at how gracefully she ate, her blindness never obvious in her delicate movements. In stark contrast, Peronel and the other women were heedless of the sauces coating their fingers and dripping onto their colorful gowns.

Now, as the feasters munched on the last sweet wafers and quaffed Sicilian wine, Alouette was assisted to the gallery above the dais, and soon above the buzzing conversation the clear dulcet tones of her lute floated on the air. The word was passed up and down the trestle tables—"Quiet! The Lark is about to sing!" The chatter faded away just as Alouette launched into a sprightly tune.

> When the spring returns again
>   E-y-a
> Sadness can no more remain
>   E-y-a
> Queen of May has come to stay
>   E-y-a
> Come let us our homage pay
> For she is Queen
> Long may she reign
> Far away must care now flee
> Let sorrow come another day
> So leave your work and merry be
> A-dancing 'round the Queen of May...

Reyner sat entranced as she went from gay *pastourelles* to wry *sirventes* to pious hymns extolling the Virgin and stirring martial songs exhorting Christians to free the Holy Sepulchre. Her pure soprano caressed each note, coaxing words forth as liquid gold. It was an exalting experience listening to her. He could shut his eyes and believe he was listening to the chief angel in Heaven's choir.

The audience was hushed as she sang, but called out requests for favorite tunes in between; he noticed she avoided the *cansos*, whose theme was always love.

Perhaps the potent local wine had gone to his head, though he didn't feel dizzy, for suddenly he found himself on his feet, calling out, "Sing us a love song, Lady

Alouette! A *canso*, if you please, for a lovesick Englishman far from home."

He could not see her well behind the latticework grille, but there was a long pause before she sang again. The crowd murmured and stared at Reyner, but he was past caring. Had he glanced at the dais, he would have seen Phillip Capet grown livid, grasping his goblet as if it were Reyner's neck.

There was a discordant false start, and then the lute began a plaintive air:

> Long time I lived in wretched wise,
> By love distracted and oppressed,
> But today I recognize
> I have behaved like one possessed . . .

Just that single verse, and the lute and its player were silent. She had recognized his voice, and there was her answer; there was her feeling about that glorious, sensual kiss on the banks of the Rhône. She was throwing his love back in his face and pronouncing it worthless.

At the entrance to the gallery stairs Blondel de Nesle, Richard's minstrel, waited with his cithara, for he was to perform next. Reyner strode forward, smiling recklessly at the startled Blondel and leaning over to whisper in the surprised minstrel's ear.

"A boon of a moment only, Blondel. Do you remember that song you taught me—*'Tis Worse Than Death?* Play it for me whilst I sing, and then I promise I will steal your audience no more."

Blondel was not loath to comply. He sensed a developing drama here, and his troubador's heart was quickened. Perhaps this story could be made into a *ballade* of its own later on. He strummed a chord on the lyrelike instrument, and in a resonant baritone Reyner sang,

> 'Tis worse than death to lead a life of pain,
> Joyless, and filled with suffering and grief,
> When she who might turn all this loss to gain
> Denies her suppliant succor and relief.

Her gasp was audible even over the fading notes of the cithara. Through the lattice screen Reyner thought he saw a swirl of scarlet fabric, and then all was still as the on-lookers began to comment at what seemed to be a lovers' quarrel enacted before their eyes. Some even thought it had been carefully staged for their entertainment, and ap-plauded Reyner and Alouette on their cleverness.

Reyner ignored their questions and opinions as he scanned the apparently empty gallery. "Thank you, my friend. I owe you a favor," he murmured to Blondel, then strolled out of the hall without so much as a bow in the direction of his king.

Where had she gone? He must find her and have it out with her. Something had radically changed her between Lyon and Messina. Was it just his failure to come to her in Genoa? He would be accorded the courtesy of being heard! His jaw tightened as he stalked through the empty corri-dors, searching for a glimpse of crimson sarcenet.

In the weeks since her arrival, Alouette had learned the layout of Tancred's palace, with Zeus to assist her. Now, without the dog, she put her knowledge to good use, de-clining a page's offer to escort her to her chamber.

Ermengarde would be waiting there to help her disrobe, and she couldn't face her faithful tirewoman just yet. She wanted to be alone with her anger, alone with her flaming face. In the small pleasance in the back of the castle she could wait in solitude as her pulse slowed and her breath-ing returned to its normal rate.

She felt her way along the cool stone of the corridor, counting the doorways until the evening breeze from the strait told her she had reached the flower-scented private garden.

NINE

How dare he challenge her in public like that, as if they were a frivolous man and woman playing at the artificial game of courtly love? She was no haughty noble-woman wanting a smitten knight to satisfy her every selfish whim! She was King Louis's bastard daughter, who wished only to atone for the sin of her birth by an austere life of self-denial! The fact that she had lost her heart to a man who had such careless lack of regard for her feelings, as evidenced by his actions tonight and in Genoa, had only proven how unsuited she was to remain in the world.

She wished she had never learned to play the lute, for surely without that talent she would not have been coerced into coming along with Phillip. By now she would have been safely sheltered in some nunnery, at peace, sur-rounded by prayer and plainsong. Of all the worldly pos-sessions she would give away when she entered the religious life, the first would be the lute that had brought her to such grief. She would insist upon relinquishing it, even if she found herself in one of the more liberal orders, where the sisters kept cats and hawks and other such plea-sures.

And they would cut off her hair. Involuntarily, her slender hand flew to the coiled masses of soft, shining ebony at her nape. Her hair was her one vanity. She admit-ted to herself that she loved the silky feeling of it when Ermengarde had it all brushed out and hanging in the heavy mass that reached to her waist. Someday in its place would be a starched, stiff wimple, a sign of her belonging to a heavenly Lord.

She sighed deeply, breathing in the scent of lemons mixed with the sea breeze from the Strait of Messina. She knew from previous explorations that there were lemon trees all around the edges of the pleasance. In the middle of the lawn was a fountain whose splashing waters sounded a soothing counterpoint to her disquieted thoughts. She walked on the path made of crushed shells, feeling the cool air fan her flushed cheeks.

Alouette was so caught up in her musing that at first she did not hear a second pair of feet upon the walkway, but suddenly there was the sound of a shell cracking under a heavier foot.

She whirled, her skirt flaring scarlet about her legs in the moonlight. "Who's there?"

"Your suppliant," came his answer.

"You are my nothing," she snapped, wishing to end his pursuit of her once and for all. "I have nothing to say to you. Begone, and leave me in peace."

She looked so defiant there in the silver light, Reyner thought, as if she faced a dozen Saracen scimitars at once. Yet she was unspeakably lovely, with her chin raised proudly and her lips parted slightly as she finished her curt dismissal. But he refused to be dismissed.

"Nay, I cannot, for that is not what you really want." His answer rang confidently.

If he wanted to provoke her again, he had succeeded admirably. "How dare you presume to know what I want!" she cried out. "You conceited knave! You blackened my name in Genoa, and you've made a fair start at dishonoring it here as well!"

She heard his footsteps draw nearer on the path, and she began to back up, feeling not shell fragments beneath her slippers now, but smooth lawn.

"How good of you, Lady Alouette, to bring up precisely the grievance which is on my mind also. 'Tis about Genoa we must speak. God-a-mercy, what are you talking about, blackening your name? Do you think that I would defame the woman I long to call mine?"

As he walked toward her, she retreated with a hand stretched behind her to touch the tree trunks and hedges at the edge of the garden. She had been so startled that she was now disoriented and could not tell whether she was closer to the hedge or the stone wall.

"Surely it does not matter whether your mistress has a good name," she threw back at him, "though if I wanted that position I would still plead with you that you do not joke about Alouette when you visit the Italian brothels!"

She heard his sharp intake of breath.

"'Sdeath!" he swore. "I grow more mystified as you prattle on! Certainly I am a man, sweeting, with a man's passions, but I frequented no brothels in Genoa—or anywhere else since we began this journey to Outremer. I have taken no woman since I first beheld you in Vézelay, God help me!"

God help me, too, Alouette thought, suddenly afraid of the anger in his tone. He was near enough now that her nostrils caught the scent of the orrisroot essence that he always wore, mixed with the faint scent of wine. She felt a stone bench against the back of her legs and began to feel her way around it, but suddenly, strong hands firmly pushed her shoulders down.

"You may as well sit," he suggested in a tone that brooked no disobedience. "You're going to hear me out, *damoiselle.*"

All at once she was glad to comply, for her legs were trembling.

"I sailed into Genoa full of anticipation of seeing you again—full of the love I bear for you. I was to come with Richard when he visited Phillip on his sickbed, but I received a message that there was a letter for me waiting in some dockside tavern—a letter from England. I feared ill tidings of my family, so I followed the messenger, intending to join my liege at Phillip's lodgings as soon as I had picked up the letter. It was a trap. I was knocked unconscious, and when I awoke it was dawn. I scarcely had time to return to the flagship before it sailed."

A part of her wanted to believe him, but what of Fulk's

words? *He* stood to gain nothing from his warning, for he had said he respected her vocation.

"Lies!" she responded. "One who would make a concubine of a woman dedicated to God would not stop at sullying her name!"

"You stubborn wench! I don't know who's been feeding you this calumny, but one thing I'm sure of—it's time to rid you of the notion that you're suitable to be a nun!"

He had been standing over her; suddenly she felt herself pulled to her feet and molded against his lean, powerfully muscled body. His implacable hand tangled in the hair at her nape, holding her still as his lips descended on hers.

It was a wild, hungry kiss, full of anger in the rough way his lips massaged hers, taunting her. It was a kiss full of passion and need, a kiss that demanded an answer. With a whimper, she gave in and opened her mouth to him, and his tongue entered the cavern of her mouth, moving seductively against her tongue. She found herself leaning into him, feeling the hardness of his body and the evidence of his desire for her. As if in a dream, she felt him caress her neck, then follow its curve down her shoulder until his hand cupped the fullness of her breast. His mouth left hers to follow his hand's path down her neck and she moaned softly because of the loss. There was a fire beginning to smolder in the core of her being, a fire that had only been a spark before when he kissed her by the Rhône. She had to believe what he said, she *would* believe him.

"I love you, Alouette," he groaned, raising his head for a moment. "Please . . . let me just hold you. I won't hurt you, sweet love, I promise . . ."

She had only shreds of sanity left. She wanted much more than to be held, but she didn't want to be seen, as they had been following the bridge accident. "Reyner . . . I love you too. What if someone should come?"

"They're all at the banquet. No one will come," he said huskily, and led her back to the bench, pulling her down onto his lap.

Fulk had watched Reyner leave the hall after his musical challenge. *Good! He has offended her by his blatant innu-*

endoes. If she did not fully despise him before, she will now, he thought, guessing mistakenly that Alouette would seek her chamber in tears. *I will give her a few moments to compose herself, and then go commiserate with her. I will offer yet again to avenge her honor with my sword. Of course she will refuse, and I will acquiesce ... at least openly.*

Blondel de Nesle still held the banqueters spellbound with his cithara half an hour later as Fulk rose discreetly to his feet and went to Alouette's chamber.

A light knock brought her sleepy, befuddled old tire-woman to the door. "Lady Alouette? Why, no, my lord, she's not returned. Does she not still perform for the three kings?"

"Nay, she has finished. Perhaps she has taken a wrong turn in the palace and is lost," he suggested, counting on the alarm which he knew would flare in the cloudy old eyes. In his own heart he felt a smoldering rage, knowing now that his cousin had most likely found Alouette and was now with her.

Worry pursed the old woman's mouth. "She will be so frightened! And there are dozens of Englishmen here to-night who wouldn't scruple to molest my poor blind mistress."

Just the response he'd hoped for. Hard-pressed to hide the smirk of triumph that creased his face, he murmured, "Stay calm, my good woman. I will find her; on that you can depend."

He did not guess that his offer doubled Ermengarde's worry, rather than relieving it. She didn't trust Fulk de Langres, with his cold, reptilian stare. She quickly woke a page drowsing in a nearby alcove and sent him in the opposite direction with orders to find Lady Alouette and escort her directly to her chamber.

Reyner had just begun again to kiss Alouette's lush, swollen lips when flaring torchlight and a heavy tread announced that they were no longer alone in the garden. He knew that she had heard the sounds a heartbeat before he did, for she stiffened in his arms with a whimper of alarm.

In one fluid motion he placed her beside him on the bench and jumped to his feet, standing protectively in front of her as she hastily pulled the bodice of her dress back in place. His hand went instinctively to his sword hilt as the torch came into view, raised high and near-blinding him, preventing Reyner from seeing the intruder who held it. He felt a white-hot fury at being interrupted.

"State your errand, fool, or better yet, begone. This is a private conversation," Reyner rasped.

With an evil chuckle, the intruder lowered his torch so that Reyner could identify him.

"Is that what Richard's men call *conversation*?" Fulk's voice was laced with sarcasm. "In France we call it seducing a chaste woman."

"Lady Alouette's done nothing wrong!" Reyner raged, past caring that he was letting Fulk inflame him. "That is, unless the French call true love unnatural!"

"Enough lies, cousin," Fulk said with a sneer. "Her very name is soiled by your lips. 'Tis time you paid for despoiling her honor. Draw your blade."

Alouette was on her feet as Reyner's sword came hissing from its scabbard. "Stop it! Both of you, cease this wicked strife! How can you free Outremer if you kill each other?" She flung herself in the direction of Reyner's voice. "Stop, Reyner! I beg of you!" she sobbed, clutching his free arm.

The bloodlust had risen too high, fanned by Fulk's insinuations. He pushed her roughly from him, intent only on putting her out of harm's way, and winced as he heard her stumble and fall. He dared not take his eyes off Fulk, however, who had set the torch in a post designed for it, and was now drawing his blade.

"En garde."

Unnoticed, Alouette found her way out of the garden, fleeing the sounds of clashing steel, the scraping of broken shells, and the panting of the fighting men. It was wrong —horribly, dreadfully wrong—and it was all her fault. Two men were at this moment trying to murder each other because of her—because she had allowed herself to be tempted. It was as the Church fathers said, she thought miserably. All sin comes through womankind. But there would be time for penance later. Right now she must find a way to put a stop to their murderous combat before either was killed. But how—?

Feeling her way, she hastened along the corridor, and ran full tilt against her half brother Phillip as he came around the corner, accompanied by King Richard, Henri, and the page who had been sent to find her.

"Alouette! There you are! Your woman said you were lost! What's the matter? You are upset!" He pulled her against his broad, well-padded chest, patting her shoulder, and for a moment she leaned gratefully into him, thanking her saints she had found him in time.

"They're fighting, Your Majesty! You must stop them!"

"Who is fighting? Where?" Phillip demanded, searching his half sister's face, seeing the flushed cheeks, the swollen lips, the disarranged hair.

"The English *chevalier*, and the *Sieur* de Langres," she managed to say. "You must stop them, *mon roi*, or they'll kill each other!"

"Where?" demanded Richard angrily, for he had forbidden fighting among the crusaders and had threatened dire consequences.

"In the pleasance!" Holy Mary! Had she doomed Reyner to drastic punishment in her desire to save both men's lives? "King Richard, please don't harm them—they meant well . . ."

"Henri!" Phillip called over his shoulder. "Escort your sister to her chamber. She has had more than enough to bear tonight," he added firmly, ignoring Alouette's hysterical pleas.

A few moments later, Reyner and Fulk found their duel abruptly terminated by the arrival of the two monarchs.

Evenly matched, neither man had seriously wounded the other, though torn, bloodied tunics attested to minor touches with the deadly blades.

"What does this mean?" roared Richard, stepping between the panting combatants, heedless of his own safety, while Phillip kept a safe distance.

The red mist receded rapidly from Reyner's brain as he recognized his furious sovereign and realized in what jeopardy his foolishness and temper had placed him. Richard could be cold and unforgiving when crossed, and had made severe regulations regarding the conduct of his men.

"I . . . I beg pardon, Your Grace. The *Sieur* de Langres and I did quarrel." The words were said simply, and without excuses or groveling, looking the Plantagenet king squarely in the eye.

"And the cause?" inquired Richard coldly.

How could he say, with Phillip waiting, spiderlike, a few feet away? Would Fulk use this chance to vilify him to the French king? His eyes left Richard to stare into the icy regard of Fulk de Langres. The black eyes, glittering in the torchlight, were triumphant. He knew his power. Would he use it?

Fulk looked from Reyner to Phillip and back again.

"We are waiting."

Fulk cleared his throat. "It is a private matter, Your Grace. May it not remain so?" He looked down at his feet in a parody of submission.

There was an endless moment in which Richard was silent. In the distance, below the hillside palace, Reyner could hear the gently lapping waves and the sounds of revelry in the English camp.

Richard finally threw up his hands. "It is well you are a knight, Reyner of Winslade! A common man-at-arms knows he can expect to lose a hand for such an offense. Go to bed and no more quarrels with your fellow crusaders. Save your spleen for the Saracens."

"Yes, Your Grace." Reyner knew he had his favored position with Richard to thank for the English king's mercy. Had Richard desired, his knightly rank would have made no difference.

He could not resist glancing at his cousin one last time before he quit the pleasance. As their eyes met, it was clear that their quarrel had only been postponed. Someday there would be a reckoning.

"Well, my lord," drawled Richard, as Phillip remained silent, "have you no rebuke for *your* vassal?" He nodded at Fulk, who stood defiantly smirking back at him. Had the

French king not been standing there, he'd wipe that defiance from his face, by God!

"My men will be disciplined in my own time and way. Do not concern yourself with it. I daresay if the truth were known, my knight's cause is just. But he is too chivalrous to speak evil of a fellow knight; is it not so, Fulk?" His knowing smile told Fulk that he knew very well that the quarrel concerned Alouette. *Be cautious, and bide your time,* his eyes told the French knight, *and you shall have your desire.*

"Just so, Your Majesty," Fulk said with an appropriate display of humility.

Richard gave a snort of disgust. "Very well, my lord. I bid you good night."

Phillip was not completely surprised when he found Alouette awaiting him outside his chamber door, pacing restlessly until she heard his step.

"Your Majesty, you must tell me how Reyner . . . that is, how *Chevalier* Reyner and the *Sieur* de Langres are? Please, I must know!" she cried, flinging herself at Phillip's feet.

"Henri, I thought I commanded you to escort Alouette to her chamber?" Phillip said sternly, ignoring Alouette, and addressing her stepbrother, who stood sheepishly at the door.

"A thousand pardons, *mon roi*, but you know she can be stubborn. She would not go." Henri could not conceal a certain amount of pride in his stubborn sister.

"Yes, I know. *Eh bien*, Alouette, you will be relieved to know that the two foolish knights still breathe, and neither of them is much the worse for the event."

"God be praised!" she said, limp with relief.

"Indeed," Phillip echoed coldly.

"*Mon frère le roi*, I made a vow as I waited here for the news . . . a vow I beg you will let me carry out. My presence here will only cause strife between these two men, I fear. I would perish of remorse if Reyner . . . if one of them came to harm because of me. And I have found I am weaker than I thought," Alouette continued, her large blue eyes troubled as she remembered the way her traitorous body had responded to Reyner's touch, just moments after she had declared she wanted nothing to do with him. "I am subject to temptation after all, you see. I wish to go into seclusion in a convent until we leave Sicily."

TEN

Reyner was still asleep, blissfully dreaming of holding Alouette in his arms, when her party left Messina at dawn. They were bound for Palermo, many leagues up the coast, their destination the Benedictine convent attached to the Church of San Giovanni degli Eremiti.

Reyner had intended to find a way to see Alouette sometime that day, so that they could plan a way to be together. He knew he would first have to soothe her about the altercation with Fulk last night and its discovery by the kings, and then convince her that it had indeed been necessary to answer Fulk's challenge with his sword. He assumed his task would not be too difficult, since she had finally been willing to listen to his side of the story last night. It was obvious that Fulk had been behind the lies she had heard, and probably the attack in Genoa as well. He wanted to make sure Alouette would not listen to any more of his lies.

He was tired of fencing with King Phillip when trying to see Alouette. He wanted to marry her during this time of respite before the coming holy war, so that they could share their love. She *did* love him. She had sighed the words in the midst of rapturous passion last night, and he had echoed them back to her. If necessary, he would abduct her; he did not intend to wait for the sulky French king's permission. He rather thought Alouette would not argue if elopement became necessary. He would watch for an opportunity, and . . .

Suddenly, a firm hand on his shoulder interrupted his drowsy planning. Thomas, his squire, was shaking him awake with word that King Richard demanded he come immediately in full armor to the town gate.

At the gate Reyner found his sovereign stripped to the waist, joined with a score of his knights in the erection of a platform which could be seen over the high city walls. They were constructing a gibbet for the punishment of any who transgressed his edicts, whether they be English or French, Lombard or Griffon. Richard reported gleefully that he had heard that the townspeople already called him "the Lion," while they referred to Phillip contemptuously as "the Lamb."

Over the next few days Reyner found himself with no free time to seek out Alouette, for Richard kept him constantly busy, no doubt to remind him that he was still paying penance for his rash duel. If he were not patrolling the crusaders' camp, he was attending his sovereign as Richard met with Phillip and Tancred in an effort to resolve their many conflicts.

Reyner was present when Richard's widowed sister Joanna arrived by ship from Palermo on Michaelmas Eve. She was a female image of Richard, though her hair was a fiery auburn, far more vivid than her brother's reddish blond. Tall for a woman, she carried herself as imperiously as Richard, but all her arrogance disappeared as she embraced her brother on the shore.

"Ah, Richard, it has been too long," she cried, flinging herself at the blond giant as no one else would have dared. They had always been close. "I would have died of grief last fall, when William finally died, had I not known you would be coming!"

"God rest him," Richard said. The late Norman ruler of Sicily had been ill a long time. "William knew his end was near, I believe, when he promised all that wealth for my crusade. Where *are* the galleys he promised, Joanna? Did you bring anything else of the legacy?"

The young widow smiled wryly. "If I did not know you better, royal brother, I would say you were more concerned about the legacy than what your sister has had to endure at the hands of that ugly little bastard! Tancred has been just awful to me, Richard, shuttling me off to Palermo, rather than letting me stay·on in the palace as is my right as dowager queen! Nay, the hold of the ship bears nothing more than my bedroom furniture!" she finished with a petulant stamp of her gold-slippered foot.

"He didn't send your chair of gold, or the twelve-foot golden table, or the gold tripods and plate, or the silk tent that holds two hundred people?" Richard asked, his blue eyes narrowing dangerously as he detailed the gifts William had pledged.

"No, none of it," she sighed. "Brother, what took you so long to come to my aid?"

"One can't raise up a crusade without funds, Joanna," Richard said a trifle sharply, disappointed that he would have to fight for wealth he had expected to be handed to him. "It took many months of selling titles and benefices and assessing new taxes upon those who wouldn't come with me to get this far—not to mention the time I've wasted wrangling with Phillip and our dear little brother John."

"I heard you would have sold London itself if you could have found a buyer," Joanna commented. Her premature widowhood and recent months of struggle with William's upstart cousin had left her with a cynical attitude.

"That's God's own truth," Richard admitted with a grin. "That damn collection of merchants! I never liked England much anyway. What is that foggy, damp island, compared with sunny Aquitaine? But never fear, Joanna. I'll get you your golden throne back—*and* the war galleys to sail to Outremer."

Reyner winced to hear his land being dismissed so callously. Though he was of Norman French stock rather than Saxon, he had been born on "that foggy, damp island." Would Richard ever realize its true worth, other than as a "milch cow" for the crusade?

"I would rather you found me a new husband than a gold throne," Joanna said frankly, though she lowered her voice as she eyed the tawny-haired knight in Richard's escort, who stood at a respectful distance. "Who is *that*, for example? He's nearly as tall as you, Richard, and very handsome."

"For shame, Joanna! You are a recent widow!"

"William died last fall. It's been nearly a year, and my lord was ill of the wasting sickness for two years before that. I am still a young woman, Richard, and William gave me no babes." Her blue eyes filled with tears at the sharpness of her brother's rebuke.

Richard's expression immediately softened. "I'm sorry, Joanna. I had not considered how it must have been for you. But I'm afraid you cannot claim this handsome rascal." He beckoned Reyner forward to be presented.

Reyner knelt as Joanna regally extended her hand to be kissed. She smiled gaily. "Ah, don't tell me this handsome one is wed already!"

"Queen Joanna of Sicily, may I present Sir Reyner of Winslade? No, he's a bachelor knight, but his heart has been stolen by a winsome French lady of Phillip's court. The lady wants to be a nun, however."

"How romantic!" Joanna clapped her hands, enchanted by the prospect of a love story straight out of the tales of chivalry. Her open smile down at Reyner's upturned, flushed face indicated she took her loss in good part. "I'm sorry for our shockingly bad manners, Sir Reyner. Do we embarrass you, discussing your *affaire de coeur* as if you were not even here, my lord?"

"A little," Reyner admitted as he grinned back. He liked the widowed queen, who had been but a slender girl when he had last seen her at court. "But perhaps you could intercede for me, Your Grace?" he asked boldly. "I think I have persuaded Lady Alouette that the convent life is not for her, but King Phillip does not fancy me as a brother-in-law."

Her laughter tinkled like little silver bells. "Ah, you are indeed a rascal, Sir Reyner. I see why Richard likes and trusts you. I will see what I can do! Next to being a bride, I like the role of matchmaker best!"

Richard and Joanna were still deep in conversation as they rode into Messina. "When does Berengaria join you, brother? You must be eager for your Navarrese bride, now that you've finally left Alais behind!"

"Now, if I could just convince Phillip of that," Richard said with a snort. "No matter how many times I discuss it with that stubborn Capet, he refuses to believe I'm adamant about not wedding Father's leavings!"

"Poor Alais," Joanna sighed. "Reared to be your queen, and now she has nothing. How awful it must be for her, being shut away in disgrace like that, repudiated by Europe's most eligible bachelor!"

"She could have stayed out of Father's bed if she wanted to be my queen! I will *not* bed his castoff mistress! It's rumored she even had a child by him."

"No, I suppose no one could expect you to," Joanna said reasonably. "But what of Berengaria? I had a letter from our mother saying you'd sent her to fetch Berengaria in Navarre, at her age!"

"Mother's fine, Joanna. You should see her since Father died. Being freed from prison has given her new life. She ought to be traversing the Alps with my bride any day now!"

"Mother is a law unto herself," Joanna said, shaking her head in amazement. "At sixty-seven, she's earned the privilege. And you, brother, do you look forward to being a bridegroom?"

Richard sighed. "I suppose all men must marry eventually," he said with an indifferent shrug. "At least, Berengaria's brother can protect my southern borders."

Joanna's laugh rang out again and she laid a slender gloved hand on Richard's wrist. "Oh, Richard, you never change! You are marrying a *woman*, not an alliance to protect your lands! By all reports, Berengaria is comely, and she adores you!"

"She adores the memory of a tournament hero in Pamplona," Richard retorted. "We scarcely spoke. I spent all my time with Sancho, her brother."

"Happy marriages have been made with less," Joanna persisted. "And England needs an heir—someone better than John Lackland."

"Arthur of Brittany is my heir, and all Europe knows it—not John."

"Richard, when I left England, John was already showing what he was capable of—beating his servants, seducing the barons' wives—and if you think he'll leave England to a Breton child, you're a fool."

They argued on freely in this vein, forgetting Reyner's presence, and he marveled at the lack of true happiness and trust in the family that ruled England, and through marriage, much of Europe.

Reyner thought of the contrast of his own parents' love. After the death of his first wife, Aimery's mother, Earl Simon had taken a Poitevin wife and loved her with a passionate intensity that had not diminished with the years. Those around them were still aware of its radiant glow. And Reyner would be satisfied with nothing less in his love for Alouette de Chenevy.

Alouette had hoped the move to the Benedictine convent would restore her lost sense of vocation by removing her from the temptation posed by Reyner. His hands and lips had so easily diverted her from her holy purpose and made her long for the treacherous pleasures of earthly passion they promised. Now Reyner did not know where she was, and she was confident her royal brother would never reveal her whereabouts.

Phillip had reluctantly acceded to her request to be allowed to go into this spiritual retreat while the French remained in Sicily.

"I shall miss you, and your sweet singing, *chère soeur*," he had said, embracing her that evening in his chamber. "But I think you have made a wise decision. Perhaps I have been selfish in forbidding you the pursuit of your vocation. Would you be happier if I sent you back to France, Alouette, to enter a convent there?"

Was it the pain in his voice she heeded, or was it that ache in her heart that cried, *No, not yet, don't leave the world yet!* She was not sure which motivation caused her to reply, "Please, Phillip, it's not necessary to blame yourself. It was my weakness. I have promised to go to Outremer

with you, and that I shall do. Just give me this time away
to regain my spiritual strength, and I shall emerge stronger
than before."

"No doubt your English . . . ah, admirer . . . will turn his
lusty attentions to some wench more fitting," Phillip said.

"No doubt." She dared not show how the thought of
Reyner in the arms of another woman sent pain knifing
through her heart. She knew Phillip would have spoken
with Fulk before returning to his apartments. She wondered what the French knight had told Phillip, for she was
not sure how much he had seen before she had heard him
approach. Would he somehow stand to gain by distorting
the facts?

But those thoughts were all part of what she had come to
the convent to escape, she told herself fiercely, forcing her
attention back to the droning, Italian-accented Latin being
read from the *Life of St. Benedict* during the evening meal.

Alouette had not allowed Ermengarde to come with her,
though the old servant had protested mightily. "Who will
look after you, my lamb? Who will make sure you are
dressed properly, that your foods are prepared correctly,
that you do not fall?" she had clucked.

"Ermengarde, I am making a *retreat* from such worldly
concerns," she had told her firmly. "My clothing will be
what the good sisters wear—even a blind girl can clothe
herself in a simple habit. I shall eat the humble pottages the
Benedictines eat—there will be no need to cut up meats
for me. I must set my mind on spiritual things and maintain
holy silence when the nuns do, and I cannot do that with
you there," she had gently insisted, not wishing to hurt her
old servant's feelings, but aware that she must forgo Ermengarde's gossipy chatter, which would be a constant re-
minder of the world that waited beyond the convent walls.

A Lombardian novice, *Suora* Innocentia, had been assigned to care for her. Now, their supper finished, the two
walked through the Arabian arches of the cloisters to the
recreation area.

The days had assumed a regular, monotonous rhythm
that only partially deadened the ache in Alouette's heart.
She followed the same routine, as much as possible, as the

Benedictines. She arose at prime and went to the chilly, dark chapel for the chanting of the office. She then returned to the austere cell, furnished only with a straw pallet and a crucifix, and bathed with the cold water that had been fetched for her by *Suora* Innocentia. There followed a simple breakfast of coarse, crusty bread and sour wine before the community heard mass at tierce. Then the nuns split up to perform their assigned tasks of cooking, scrubbing, mending, working in the garden or the orchard, or feeding the livestock in the barn. Alouette was assigned very little work because of her blindness, and the fact that the nuns maintained absolute silence during the day. Alouette usually spent the work periods in her cell, composing new songs on her lute; she had rationalized that since this was but a temporary retreat, she should not give up her musical instrument yet. Sometimes she strolled the sun-drenched cloisters, sniffing the roses that still bloomed in the early Mediterranean autumn. She had become adept at finding her way from the dormer to the chapel, the refectory, the laundry, or the stable.

During these times, when she was left to her own devices, it was difficult not to think of Reyner and wonder what he was doing, whether he missed her, especially when the breeze brought traces of men's voices from the abbey situated on the other side of the church, raised in plainsong or shouting and laughing. The monks were not nearly so strict in their silence as the nuns.

The office of nones was in midafternoon, and then came the evening meal, during which a nun read to the assembled community from the lives of the saints. The Benedictines enjoyed recreation in the garth after supper. During this time the black-robed women chattered volubly as if to make up for their day-long silence. Innocentia was eagerly teaching Alouette Italian, but most of these rapid-fire conversations remained unintelligible to her. The nuns also played with balls or the pair of fat convent cats, and encouraged Alouette to play for them on her lute.

She was delighted to comply, though she was careful to restrict her songs to religious themes or innocent lyrics about the joys of nature, even though the young novices clamored for songs of love, just as the courtiers had.

The community chanted vespers as the sun sank behind the craggy Sicilian mountains and then retired to their cells. The nuns were exhausted from their strenuous labors, and it was never long before the sound of snoring drifted through the curtained-off cells.

Alouette was not so fortunate. Tormented by her memories of the warmth of Reyner's lips on hers, of his hands caressing her, of the feeling of his hard body against hers, she rarely fell asleep before midnight, when the sleepy nuns rose to say matins.

Then the cycle of the day began again, each one like the one before it—serene and monotonous.

ELEVEN

After several vain attempts to encounter his beloved while on errands to the palace, Reyner at last sent his squire with a verbal message to Alouette, imploring her to let him know where they could meet. He had sensed that King Phillip had viewed him with suspicion even before the banquet and subsequent duel, and he could assume that afterward Fulk had slandered him to the French king so thoroughly that Alouette would be forbidden his company.

Thomas had been unable to locate Alouette in the palace, or anyone who would shed any light on where she could be found.

"Her tirewoman, old . . . Ermengarde, that's her name. Did you talk to her?" Reyner quizzed the tow-headed Saxon squire.

"Yes, my lord. She would only say that the lady had gone away. She said that she could not tell me where."

"God's blood!" exploded Reyner, pounding his fist against his open palm in frustration. "Where could she go that she would not take her servant?"

Could Phillip have been spiteful enough to send her back to France? He doubted it, somehow, especially since she had not taken Ermengarde. But where was she? Why had she not sent him some message? She had said she loved him!

Reyner rode into the hills around Messina in what little free time he had, despite the stories of atrocities being visited upon solitary Englishmen by the bloodthirsty Griffons and Lombards who already chafed in the shadow of Richard's gibbet. He found nothing but the huts of those who tended the olive groves and vineyards, and his bared broadsword kept at bay those who would waylay yet another of the hated Ultramontanes.

At last, in desperation, he borrowed a surcoat with a red cross from William des Barres and stole into Messina. The town was still closed to the English forces, though the French enjoyed free passage and apparently peaceful relations with the citizens. Accompanied by Zeus, he scoured the streets, much as he had in Vézélay, asking in his limited Italian if anyone had seen a beautiful, blind, dark-haired woman of the French court—one who sang like a lark. The swarthy, thin-faced Sicilians smiled at his description, and readily took his coins, but denied seeing such a woman.

"You should not be here, Reyner de Winslade," came a voice from behind him as he spoke to the black-robed padre in the piazza in front of the Cathedral of Santa Maria.

He whirled, hand at his sword hilt, but it was Henri de Chenevy, not Fulk de Langres. Reyner dismissed the priest, who had had no information, and then said, "Why? Because I am a *tailed Englishman*?" He made a wry face at the Sicilians' hated term. "I wear a red cross. They think I'm French."

"You're hardly in disguise with that beast along," said Henri grimly, indicating Zeus. "Too many Griffons know that Richard's right-hand knight has such a pet. And Fulk de Langres still wants your blood."

"And you? Do *you* believe I dishonored your sister?" Reyner asked, pinning him with his earnest brown eyes.

The big, florid-faced Frenchman looked away uncomfortably. "I don't know."

"Listen, Henri—I love Alouette. *I love her*. Where is she?"

It was hard for Henri to ignore the steely grasp of the mail-clad hand on his shoulder; harder still to ignore the pleading in the anguished dark eyes. Henri wanted to tell him where he could find Alouette, but Phillip's threat, uttered after they had escorted Alouette back to her chamber that night, rose up to mock him: "You breathe a word of her location, and I'll wed her to Fulk de Langres."

The Sicilian sunlight was blinding in the piazza in front of the great Norman cathedral. He opened his mouth, and the lie Phillip demanded came out: "She's gone home to France, Reyner. She's going to enter a convent as soon as she arrives."

Henri would have given years from his eternity not to have seen the dawning hell in the Englishman's face.

"But she loves me!"

"My sister is . . . inexperienced. She may have been momentarily confused by passion, but her purpose is clear. She wants to give her devotion to a heavenly Bridegroom, and renounce the world. She is not for you. You must forget her, Reyner."

"Never," said the English knight bleakly.

As September turned to October, relations between the island's Greek and Italian population and the English deteriorated still further.

Recognizing the growing danger, Richard escorted his sister Joanna across the strait to the castle of La Bagnara. Then, as he recrossed the narrow sea passage, he stopped at a Byzantine monastery on a tiny island off Messina, turned out the monks who lived there, and converted it to an armory. The Griffons were furious at this desecration.

Richard's gibbet frequently bore grisly human fruit— sometimes crusaders caught brawling, but more often wealthy Sicilians who had defied Richard in his attempts to extort money from them. Still balked in his efforts to obtain Joanna's dowry, he was like a bear with an embedded arrow, turning on any who said him nay. He was determined to demonstrate mastery of this rocky little island, and Tancred's obvious preference for Phillip enraged him further. His nobles' urgings that they move on to the Holy Land fell on deaf ears.

Reyner, caught up in the private hell of his grief, cared

little whether he was in Sicily or Palestine. He moved through the autumn days in a fog, carrying out Richard's orders with quiet, sometimes deadly efficiency, and drank himself to sleep with the potent island wine. He took no woman to his bed.

The English men-at-arms, urged to avoid trouble, could not seem to resist flirting with the local women as they came daily to sell food in the crusader camp. This further aggravated the enmity between them and the Sicilians. They responded by raising the price of their foodstuffs exorbitantly, until one morning matters came to a head, when a Sicilian woman tried to sell an English soldier a loaf of bread for an unprecedented four pence.

Reyner, seated in front of his tent while he was being shaved by Thomas, saw the whole incident. "Surely the Mediterranean sun has baked yer brain," the rough, stocky Saxon said to the woman, laughing uproariously.

It was doubtful that the dusky little woman clothed in black understood his English, but the insult implicit in his guffaws was clear. Flushing, she muttered a curse and spat at his feet as she turned to leave. At that, the Englishman snatched the loaf from her hand and cast it into the mud at his feet, rendering it worthless to anyone. With a screech the woman flew at his head, fingers curved into claws, intent on scratching his eyes out, or at the very least, snatching great handfuls of hair.

The Englishman was tired of the game. He easily flattened her with a blow from a ham-handed fist and stalked off in search of more reasonably priced bread. The woman ran out of camp, still screeching vilifications and promising revenge.

Within an hour the storm broke. Word came that the citizens of Messina had barred the gates and were manning the walks, armed to the hilt. Other messengers spoke of bands of Griffons massing in the hills outside of town, preparing to lead a charge on Richard's camp.

Reyner hastily donned his armor and joined Richard on horseback as the Plantagenet king rode about the town walls, trying in vain to persuade his men to fall back and let him arbitrate the situation.

Richard failed to see that he had not served as a shining example in his petulant, capricious dealings with the Sicilians, thought Reyner as he watched the great blond warrior lay about him with a stick in the midst of mobs of Englishmen, trading jeers with the Griffons and Lombards above. Was this the same man he had idolized as a youth, followed on campaigns through Aquitaine and Normandy as he sought to wrest control from old Henry? Reyner had admired the idealism which had led him to sacrifice a luxurious life in Europe for the glories of a crusade, but since they had left Vézélay, he had seen his hero as a man with all the faults of rulers written large.

Reyner suspected the Englishmen subsided only until their king was out of sight, for reports of sporadic fighting continued as they rode to the palace to confer with Tancred and Phillip. With their help an uneasy calm was restored as the sun set behind the black, craggy mountains. A further meeting was set for the morrow to iron out differences between the crusaders and representatives of the town.

The meeting was to take place in Richard's tent, a silken pavilion at one end of the crusader camp where Richard conducted business with his leaders.

Tancred certainly seemed sincere about desiring peace, thought Reyner as he stood in attendance behind his king and studied the assembled multitude of clerics, bishops, and important townspeople, such as Reginald de Moyac, whose house had been surrendered for Richard's use. Tancred came on foot and unarmed, in contrast to Richard's retinue, all of whom wore mail and swords under their red-crossed surcoats.

King Phillip sat on a magnificent carved chair next to Richard, saying little except to encourage Richard to listen as Tancred humbly promised to satisfy all of the English king's demands, even those over and above the original legacy of William II.

Once, Reyner found the French king's eyes on him. Did he imagine it, or was there a secret gloating in the small black eyes set in that fleshy face? He dared not think of Alouette now, he knew; he needed to be alert for any sign of danger toward his sovereign. But her beautiful face, last seen flushed with passion and love, rose up to haunt him, the tendrils of her luxuriant sable tresses wrapping themselves once again about his heart.

When it seemed that agreement would be reached, for Tancred had given in on every point, suddenly outside several voices could be heard shouting, "To arms! To arms!"

An English soldier burst wide-eyed into the tent, forgetting protocol as he shouted, "King Richard! They are attacking the home of Hugh de la Marche!"

Count Hugh was the nephew of Guy de Lusignan, the king of Jerusalem and a valuable ally.

Richard arose with a roar of displeasure like the lion for which he was nicknamed. "Is *this* how you betray my faith and trust?" he shouted, glaring at Tancred and Phillip alike, his ruddy face purpled with rage. There were audible groans from the French and Messinans.

"Brother, calm yourself! Most likely 'tis another minor skirmish," soothed Phillip, laying a plump, beringed hand on Richard's shoulder. "I'm sure all will settle itself if we keep working toward a peaceful settlement."

Richard had barely been coaxed back into his portable throne, however, when another sergeant came running into the tent, panting, "My lord! Englishmen are being slain everywhere in the city!" A third followed close on his heels, saying, "Your Grace, a low party of scurrilous Griffons lies in wait to ambush you as you return to your lodgings!" With that last news there was no holding back the Lionheart.

"O my soldiers!" he cried dramatically, nearly choking with anger and turning his back on the Sicilians and Frenchmen. "My kingdom's strength and crown, who have endured with me a thousand perils, do you now see how a cowardly rabble insults us? Shall we vanquish Turks and Arabs? Shall our right hand make us a way even to the ends of the world for the cross of Christ? Shall we restore the kingdom of Israel when we have turned our backs before vile and effeminate Griffons?"

* * *

Five hours later, Messina was a conquered city, and the ships of the Sicilian navy were blackened hulks smoking in the harbor.

The citizens of Messina had fled "like sheep before wolves," as Richard had said in gleeful satisfaction afterward, as the entire English host had swept over them, destroying the barred gates, burning houses, and slaughtering indiscriminately.

Blondel de Nesle was already composing a *chanson de geste* about it:

> It took less time to conquer the Messinans
> Than a priest takes to say matins.

Reyner's sword was stained crimson with the blood of those who had threatened his life or that of his sovereign as they raced through Messina, crushing the resistance. For one afternoon he had submerged his sorrow in a murderous wrath and become a mere killing machine, as heedless of danger as his liege lord as he sought to protect Richard's right flank. Perhaps it was because he didn't care anymore what happened, for if Alouette de Chenevy wanted no part of him and preferred the austere, narrow life of a nun to his love, then it mattered little if he died in Sicily or Outremer.

Richard spent the next days consolidating his victory. He had taken hostages of the Messinan nobles, whom he vowed to sell into slavery unless his every demand was met. He had seized all gold and silver within the city. His golden lion banners flew on the ramparts of the city walls, a sight that made Phillip Capet furious.

Faced with the inevitable, Tancred capitulated, hoping to minimize further ruin until the English could be coaxed to depart. He paid Richard twenty thousand ounces of gold and another twenty thousand in earnest of the agreement to marry Richard's heir, young Arthur of Brittany, to one of Tancred's daughters.

Richard was pleased by their submission, but he, nevertheless, built a high wooden tower on a hill overlooking the city. Its name was hardly a reflection of a conciliatory spirit: *Mategriffon*, or *Kill-Greek*. It was equal to an announcement that he would subdue all of Sicily, as he had Messina.

Reyner grew weary as he helped supervise the building of the fortress and sat in on the meetings between the three kings to devise a code of conduct for the armies and their Sicilian hosts. The scope of the meetings was exhaustive. They dealt with matters as small as fixing the price of a loaf at a penny, and conflicts as large as the one brewing between the two "allies," Phillip and Richard. Phillip had been discovered plotting with Tancred and the Lombards, but the wily Sicilian had merely been playing one side against the other until he found out which was the stronger. When it became clear that Richard would emerge the victor, Tancred threw in with the English king and revealed Phillip's duplicity.

Richard eventually saw the need to reconcile with Phillip, however, if he was to go to the Holy Land with him, and so he gritted his teeth and gave in, repledging his faith with Phillip and even agreeing to see the fleur-de-lis flag flying next to his on Messina's walls.

Reyner thought surely all chance of peace would be lost when Phillip daringly demanded his "share" of the gold given Richard by Tancred, for no Frenchman had lifted a finger to help the English during the battle. However, Richard's devotion to his cause was so fervent that, amazingly, he offered Phillip half the gold.

At this point the English began to grumble, particularly those who had arrived on the island well ahead of Richard and who had been put to considerable trouble and expense. Now they were being told that they must return their share of the booty, and worse yet, that due to the long conflict with the Sicilians, it was too late in the year to cross the Mediterranean safely. They would have to winter on this miserable island!

Richard showed himself equal to the challenge of placating his men. He made a distribution of costly gifts to all the host, from his barons down to the lowliest man-at-arms, and the complaining ceased as if by magic.

Reyner himself received a gilt cup set with a large garnet. He stroked its gleaming sides, wishing he could give it to Alouette, imagining her sipping wine from it, seeing in his mind's eye the glistening red drop that would remain gleaming on her lips. With a sigh, he made arrangements to send the cup instead to his mother.

TWELVE

Chill winter winds had at last come even to sunny Sicily and had driven the nuns indoors during their recreation time.

Alouette shivered in her scratchy serge habit, drawing the rough fabric more closely about her. She suffered from the cold here as she never had at home, though France was farther north. It was as if the summer spent under the warm Mediterranean sun had thinned her blood.

The Benedictines, whose credo was to deny personal comfort, kept few fires going—certainly none in the cold dormer at night. At that time of the year there was always a mysterious increase in the number of nuns bewailing their sins and wearing hair shirts in penance. They suffered a torment of itching wearing the scratchy garments, but at least they were warm.

There was a brazier in the refectory during their recreation hour, but the seats closest to it were always taken by the oldest nuns of the community. From her bench far from the circle of warmth, Alouette could hear the old women's chatter as they tried to compensate in a single hour for the constraints imposed on them by the rule of holy silence all day.

"Like a flock of rooks, they are," *Suora* Innocentia whispered, settling beside Alouette on the bench with a rustle of skirts. Her aroma, one of garlic mingled with that of a young, unwashed body, caused Alouette to wrinkle her nose involuntarily. The order did not bathe often, counting cleanliness a pleasure of the flesh, but Innocentia bathed even less often than she was permitted. Alouette suspected it was less a matter of holiness than the way in which the Lombard girl had been raised.

She had been one of a dozen children of a poor vineyard worker and his slovenly wife. They had felt obligated to give at least one of their daughters to God—and a son as well; one of Innocentia's elder brothers served as a parish priest in Taormina. Innocentia had had no particular vocation, but as she was not expected to make a good marriage because of her unattractive scrawniness, life in the convent had at least held out the promise of sufficient food forever. Her only other choice would have been to become a prostitute in one of Palermo's harborside brothels. All this she had confided guilelessly to Alouette while respecting the French girl's reluctance to speak of her own reasons for being there. Alouette's reticence provided the Sicilian girl with a sympathetic listener who did not demand equal time to share her own woes.

But, as always, when Alouette tuned her lute, Innocentia asked wistfully for a love song.

"Please, just this once, my lady," the novice whispered. "I have been thinking of the time that Giovanni, the vineyard owner's son, made love to me in an olive grove after the harvest festival."

"Innocentia! You are to take your final vows soon!" Alouette whispered back, shocked but amused at her companion's frankness.

"Not until after Candlemas," Innocentia retorted.

It was uncanny how the Sicilian girl had unconsciously tapped Alouette's own mood, for she had been thinking all day of a song that mirrored how she had felt around Reyner de Winslade. Giving in to her companion's pleading, she began to sing:

> When I'm with him, my feelings flow
> Into my eyes and face, my hue
> Betrays the stress I'm subject to
> I'm like a leaf when tempests blow
> So deep in love am I that tho'

A lady, I'm witless as a child;
To one so hopelessly beguiled
Her love should great mercy show...

Alouette sang the words quietly, so that only Innocentia
could hear. The older, professed nuns chattered on, the
ones from noble Norman-Sicilian families in French, the
others in Italian or Greek, unaware that their French guest
had broken her own rule and was singing words of love
and longing. Soon she had even forgotten her audience of
one and was singing to Reyner in her heart.

"Lady Alouette, *cara*, you're crying." The words were
soft and sympathetic as the novice brushed away the tear
that trembled on the French girl's cheek.

"Why, so I am. How silly of me! Did anyone see?"
Alouette pretended great concentration in retuning a lute
string, ducking her head. She was startled at how completely she had forgotten her surroundings. These day-
dreams of Reyner had become more, not less, frequent as
the weeks went on.

"No, don't worry. They're all listening to Reverend
Mother's retelling of her glorious Norman ancestry, and
how she could have been Duchesa d'Apulia, or some such.
As if she didn't recite this claim once a fortnight at least!
Now, *cara*, I think it's time you told me why you are here,
since there is a man you love so much that you cry when
you sing of him."

The words of protest died aborning on Alouette's lips.
Suddenly she wanted to speak of Reyner de Winslade,
needed to tell another soul about the love she felt for the
Englishman—a love that had refused to let her go even
after she had fled from it, a love that had grown even
behind convent walls. So she told the Sicilian novice
everything, hesitatingly at first. Then, emboldened by her
friend's nonjudgmental attitude, her words rushed out,
tumbling over one other.

"You wished to see me, Alouette?" Mother Superior's
voice was as dry and flat as the parchments that rustled as
she set them aside. Alouette's pulse quickened. Always

before, the abbess had been friendly to the point of obsequiousness, obviously gratified to have a relative of the king of France in her convent. It was as if she knew what was on Alouette's mind.

"Yes, Mother." The abbess had not invited her to sit, so she remained standing, conscious of the flickers of unease rising from her viscera. "I wish to rejoin my brother and the king. Would you send him a message, please, asking him to send escort?"

Silence hung in the air. Alouette could feel the woman's eyes upon her, boring through her.

"But, my dear, I thought you were happy here? The plan was that you were to remain here until His Majesty departs for the Holy Land, was it not?"

"Yes, Mother."

"Well, with winter upon us it is obvious that King Phillip must remain in Sicily until spring. What is this wish to leave the convent all about, my child?" The abbess's voice was chill and decidedly *un*-maternal.

She couldn't tell her the real reason. "I find myself longing to be back at court, Mother. I find I miss my brother . . . and court life . . ." *Sainte Vierge, was it worse to lie to a holy woman than any other mortal?*

"Alouette, when you came to us you were very distressed in spirit. You needed the peace we offer here." A note of injured feelings crept into Mother Maria Benedicta's raspy voice.

"Yes, Mother, and I thank you for the serenity I have felt here. But I find myself longing to be back in the world again. I have resolved the conflict that was plaguing me upon my arrival."

"Indeed." The single word was drawn out, inviting her to say more.

Oh, Reverend Mother, how can I tell you that I love a man—that I would be his on whatever terms, whether I am to be his lady in all honor, or merely the mistress of his heart? She was quiet, wondering if she should further assure the abbess of her gratitude at being here.

Before she could speak, however, the older woman added, "But I thought your desire was to become a nun? I had in fact cherished hopes . . . that His Majesty would allow you to join *our* community—permanently." There was the sound of nails drumming on the writing table in front of her.

Obviously the abbess was piqued if she had expected to receive the dowry that went with a well-connected young woman of the nobility. Alouette wished there were some way she could soothe the woman's ruffled feathers without lying further.

"Once, Mother Superior, that would have been *my* dearest wish as well—to go into a convent, *any* convent, as soon as possible. If that were still my desire, I am sure I could be happy at San Giovanni degli Eremeti. But I find I no longer wish the religious life. Please, will you write the letter, Mother? I would like to be with my . . . brother . . . by the Feast of the Nativity, if possible."

She could not have known how her face was transfigured with joy at the thought of sharing Christmastide with her beloved.

"Alouette." The blind girl had not realized she had smiled until she felt it leaving her face at the staccato pronunciation of her name. "You will fast and pray for three days. I do not think we should trouble His Majesty on a whim."

Alouette had heard the abbess address the nuns this way. It always brought a meek, "Yes, Mother. Thank you, Mother," from them, from the oldest nun to the youngest postulant. Suddenly she did not feel at all meek. This upstart Lombard woman with pretensions to aristocratic Norman ancestors was seeking to browbeat her. *Eh bien!* She, Lady Alouette de Chenevy, half sister of Phillip Capet, king of France, would not allow it!

"Mother Maria Benedicta, I would not have wasted your time on a matter about which I had not already sought counsel in prayer. My conscience assures me I am on the right path. I have taken no vows, and while I am appreciative of your care, *I wish to leave*. I know His Majesty would want to know of my desire. Write the letter, please."

Alouette would have been amused if she could have seen the way the abbess's jaw dropped in astonishment at the decisive, commanding air that she had just assumed. It was evident that the woman responded to assertiveness, however, in her terse words: "Very well, *Lady* Alouette. I will write King Phillip of your request."

A week passed with maddening slowness, then two, as Alouette waited to be summoned back to the abbess's office, going about the never-changing routine that now annoyed her by its immutable dullness.

It would be Christmas next week! In a fever of impatience, she knocked on the abbess's door.

"Ah . . . Alouette! I was just about to send one of the sisters for you!" The old peremptory tone was back, and it did not bode well.

"You have heard from the king?"

"Exactly. Just today, in fact." The woman's breezy assurance was not to be trusted. Alouette suspected she had received the message days ago, and wanted to see how long Alouette would wait to ask about it.

"When will the escort be here?" She wished she felt the confidence her voice projected.

"They won't—at least, at no time soon, my child. His Majesty writes that he is very busy at present and wishes you to remain here in my care until he summons you." The old nun could not conceal the smug glee in her voice.

Alouette felt hot tendrils of rage licking about her stomach. "How do I even know you wrote him?" she demanded, surprised at her own boldness.

"I assure you that I did. Here is the vellum containing his answer." The sheet of paper scraped across the desk at her. "Feel his seal, there?" she placed Alouette's searching fingers on the embossed wax blob with its dangling ribbons.

It was indeed the seal of the King of France, though she had no way of proving the contents of the letter were as the abbess had described.

"*Maintenant*, I suggest you try those three days of fasting in penance, Alouette. Perhaps it will renew the spirit of humility that has been sorely lacking in you in the last fortnight," the abbess said triumphantly.

"I will leave, Reverend Mother. I have taken no holy vows. You have no right to hold me against my will." Alouette's heart hammered within her. Suddenly she felt like a caged beast. Was it possible the French had already left Sicily—without her?

"A blind girl? How would you find your way back to Messina—alone?" The woman's laughter was cruel now that she had dropped the mask of the kind, maternal Mother Superior. "'Tis far down the coast. In any case, it will not be allowed. His Majesty has commanded that you stay here. If necessary, you will be guarded, *my dear.*"

The abbess was as good as her word. Alouette was never alone. She discovered her new restriction that same night when she decided to try and steal out of the dormer during the longest period of sleep, that between lauds and prime, when the Benedictines' slumber was deepest.

When she had first come to the convent, she had not taken advantage of the private quarters offered her as a noble guest. She had not wanted any special treatment. Now she wished she had not been so idealistic as she parted the thin curtains that separated her pallet from a dozen others within the dormer. Rumbling, sighing snores came from up and down the rows—but how could she be certain that no eyes were open, tracking her movements? Or that all the cells were even filled?

No one challenged her as she noiselessly left the sleeping quarters, and she began to contemplate the next barrier, that of the gate, guarded at all times by Sister Portress. If that venerable nun were sleeping soundly, as Innocentia claimed she always did ("The Last Trump could not wake her, I vow!" she had said while they plotted at recreation), perhaps she could find and work the latch mechanism with her sensitive fingers. Once through the gates, she would rely on feeling the sunshine on her face to try to maintain an eastward course, using her cane as her only aid until she could find someone to help her—

"Where are you going, Lady Alouette?" the stern voice of *Suora* Penetentia, the Novice Mistress, stopped her in her tracks.

"Oh! You startled me! I? To the garderobe! Something has given me a griping of the bowels . . ."

"Lady Alouette, there is a chamber pot beneath your bed, did you forget? And you're all dressed! Surely it is a mild griping if you could take the time to don your habit first!"

Alouette was trapped. "It . . . it was cold . . ." she mumbled lamely.

"*Sí*—you would have found out just how cold it could be if you had gotten through the gate," retorted the Novice Mistress sharply, "if you hadn't fallen off the side of a cliff first. Back to bed with you now—and in chapter meeting you'll confess your sin to Mother Superior."

She received three lashes from the abbess's knotted scourge for her attempted escape, and as the first one landed on her bared back, she cursed herself for her foolishness. How could she, a blind woman, have believed she could escape with such an impulsive lack of planning? *No*, she thought, gasping as the lash descended again, feeling the taste of blood on her lips as she bit them to keep from crying out, she'd not give the abbess the satisfaction. From time to time visitors came to the convent. Perhaps she could persuade them she was being held against her will and was bound by no vows.

After she was taken to the infirmary and laid on clean sheets, her back was anointed with healing unguents in a surprisingly gentle fashion by Sister Infirmaress. The nun was evasive, however, when Alouette asked that Innocentia the novice be sent to her.

"She . . . she cannot come. She is in seclusion, I believe."

Alouette groaned aloud, causing the infirmaress to stroke the ointment more gently into the lacerated skin, but her mental anguish was the greater pain. The friendly Sicilian girl was being made to suffer because they suspected her of helping, or at least sympathizing with, Alouette.

If only they knew she had tried to discourage me, she thought regretfully, picturing Innocentia in the small, windowless building at the far end of the convent enclosure, to which the novice had taken her when she first toured the convent grounds. Nuns went there when they felt the need of a retreat while wrestling over some spiritual decision—or more often, when they were being punished for some serious infraction. There was only straw on the floor—and no heat, Alouette reminded herself guiltily, feeling the warmth radiating from a nearby brazier.

Innocentia had urged her to wait for some better opportunity, citing the dangers of the rocky terrain and the barbaric Griffons who inhabited the volcanic hills.

But to Alouette, the thought of delaying her freedom had been torture. She had to leave the convent, to find Reyner, to tell him that she loved him! She did not doubt that her royal brother had spread some false tale as to her whereabouts. What if Reyner went off, following a false trail, or worse yet, believed that she was gone forever and learned to live without her?

Her protests of the young novice's innocence were ignored. It was not until Christmas morning that a much subdued Innocentia rejoined her, just in time to march in procession into the cathedral for a joint Christmas service with the monks.

The king of England celebrated the birth of Christ in his wooden fortress of Mategriffon with his guests the king of France, the king of Sicily, and with the retinues of all three rulers.

So splendid was the great hall that Christmas day that it was hard to believe that the fortress was made of prefabricated wooden pieces, unless one felt the walls behind the colorful tapestries. Greenery was wound around upright posts and festooned the whitewashed ceiling. The trestle tables groaned under the weight of gold and silver plate, goblets, and a magnificent array of food. Richard was clearly in a generous frame of mind, for he had made presents of the silver-gilt goblets to the nobles and knights within the hall.

All were dressed in the utmost splendor, being glad to put aside, at least for Christ's nativity, the quarrels that had kept them in coats of mail most of their days since landing in Sicily. For today, at least, there was to be peace.

Reyner, though he was clothed as handsomely as the rest, could not bring himself to join in the raucous yuletide merriment around him. He looked up irritably as his trenchermate, William des Barres, who had arisen tipsily to toast the yule log being brought in by some sturdy Saxon men-at-arms, spilled his wine instead on Reyner's shoulder. There was general laughter at the log's appearance, because instead of being the stout oak the English were used to, the soldiers had brought in the smaller, gnarled trunk of an olive tree.

"'Tis the best we could do, sire—after all, this is Sicily!" roared one beefy-faced fellow, implying that the island was just steps from Hell.

Flushed with wine and goodwill, even Tancred laughed at the rude jest. "If you spend next Christmas in the desert, fellow, you may account this olive tree a tree of paradise!" he retorted good-naturedly.

Richard laughed and threw an arm around the dwarf's shoulders, lifting him from his feet in an excess of *bonhomie*. "Nay, Tancred—I trust we'll all be back home by then, with Saladin beaten and the Holy Sepulchre in Christian hands!"

"'Sdeath, Reyner, your face is as black as your tunic!" William said, indicating the sable velvet garment that was a dramatic contrast to Reyner's tawny handsomeness. "You're gloomy as a Templar tonight—not that you haven't been ever since Lady Alouette left. Come on, *mon ami*, it's Christmas!"

"Look at him," Reyner retorted dourly, indicating Richard on the dais, talking animatedly to Phillip Capet. "Repentance sits well on him."

Reyner referred to the ceremony recently held in the chapel of Reginald de Moyac's great house, in which Richard had called together his bishops and come before them stripped naked except for a loincloth and bearing several scourges.

Reyner had been the sole layperson he had trusted to accompany him to the chapel because of his selfless loyalty, the only nonclerical man present to hear Richard confess the sin of perversity that had apparently begun to lie heavily on his soul as the holy season drew near. The whole crusading army knew of Richard's repentance, though not exactly *what* he was repenting.

"Ah, well, perhaps you should do something to be penitent about, too!" William suggested gaily, downing the rest of the ruby liquid in his goblet in one hearty gulp. "Look, there's the Princess Chiara, trying to get your attention—over by the door, in the scarlet and gold-rayed dress. "I think she wants you to follow her! Go on, man—Tancred's not looking! Go prove to yourself that womanflesh is still sweet!"

Indeed, the dwarf ruler's attention was riveted on the jiggling breasts of a dancing girl who had begun to gyrate in the space between the dais and the other tables as the feast degenerated into debauchery.

Reyner's eyes darkened as he stared at the swarthy Sicilian princess standing in an inviting pose near the doorway. She was indeed beckoning to him.

"Why not?" he said out loud. Her flight back to France and convent walls had proven Alouette didn't love him. He had avoided the attractive, voluptuous daughters of Tancred before, pretending not to notice the flirting looks they cast his way, but there seemed little point in continuing to refuse what this one offered.

That she had obviously extended such an invitation to others before, he judged by her skill at evading detection by her father. As Reyner continued to gaze at her, she parted her lips and licked them, and a scarlet-nailed hand "accidentally" brushed her breast, only partially concealed by the thin, gold-shot silk of her bodice. The wine he had drunk made a wild, angry chant in his head as he arose to his feet: *Why not?* Only a certain heavy deliberation in his tread betrayed the vast quantities of Chios wine he'd consumed tonight while trying to forget Alouette.

There was indeed no doubt about what the Sicilian beauty wanted. He was scarcely in the corridor before she had pulled him into a lusty embrace, and kissed him with earthy fervency. Her musky sandalwood scent surrounded him in a cloud as she ground her hips expertly against his. Even as his head swam and his pulse accelerated, he had a fleeting remembrance of the essence of lilies that Alouette had worn.

"Princess," he laughed, when he could free his mouth for a moment, "will you come away where we can be private—alone? I would fear for your reputation, if we are seen." He continued to stroke her nipples, however, as he waited for her answer, for those soft mounds seemed to pout for the touch of his hand.

She laughed merrily, showing pearly teeth against her smooth olive complexion. "If you do, you are the only one who does. You English are so charming! My father will sell me to the highest bidder—whether it is a son of Phillip of France or Richard's small nephew, Arthur of Brittany—but meanwhile, I will do as I choose! Yes, my big, strong, English warrior—find us a chamber where we can be alone..." She giggled, her dark eyes gazing avidly into his.

His arm around her shoulder, he headed off down the corridor, intent on reaching the chamber he shared with two other knights on the floor above. Pray God they hadn't already returned to it—he could already imagine the joy of plunging into Chiara's sweet, hot flesh. It was a pleasure he'd denied himself too long while chasing after a will-o'-the-wisp.

As they reached the door to his bedchamber, however, he heard the sound of feet pounding up the wooden stairs after them and a growing din from the hall below.

It was Thomas, who had been serving at the feast. Red-faced and panting, he announced, "You're needed, Sir Reyner! The Genoese have started a battle with the Pisans and they're tearing up Messina! The king wants all his men to quell the disturbance!"

Smothering the curse that rose to his lips, Reyner gave terse orders for his destrier to be made ready, and the squire ran to do his bidding.

"It looks as though we must postpone our pleasures for another time, my lady," Reyner apologized.

Princess Chiara pouted prettily. "Perhaps. Do you suppose the French are ... occupied with this riot?"

"I doubt it—they haven't helped in any other crisis. I

can't imagine why they would start on Christmas," Reyner observed with a bitter smile.

"Then this evening need not be wasted after all," Chiara said, as she smoothed her rumpled garments and sauntered down the corridor to where the sounds of merriment still echoed.

THIRTEEN

The rival Italian factions were subdued within two hours, and Reyner went immediately to his chamber, intending to strip off his hauberk and get his squire to bring up hot water for a bath.

Zeus, who had accompanied his master as he rode at Richard's side, saw her first. He padded forward into the dimly lit chamber, wagging his tail.

As Reyner's eyes adjusted to the light, he recognized the hunched figure of Ermengarde sitting on the room's only chair.

"Is it you at last, my lord? I have been waiting forever!" The old woman sighed as she got to her feet.

"There was trouble in the town," Reyner explained. "What is it? Have you had word from Lady Alouette? Is she ill?" A thought that Ermengarde might have had a letter, perhaps even a message—any small word for him—was quickly replaced with a rapid succession of dread images: Alouette ill, pale and wan; Alouette's ship sinking; Alouette drowning beneath tossing, icy waves; Alouette dead, floating lifelessly on the waters . . .

"Nay, my lord, nothing like that," Ermengarde hastened to assure him, seeing the panic flash across those lean, angular features. So he still loves her, she thought happily, knowing she had been right to come.

"This being the season of Our Lord's birth, I naturally confessed my sins to one of the priests at the Cathedral of

Santa Maria. Oh, I wouldn't go to Père Ambrose, the king's chaplain, that toady of Phillip's—"

"I'm sorry, Ermengarde," Reyner broke in, "but what has this to do with me?" He was tired and irritable. Surely the old woman hadn't come to tell him of her religious experiences!

"I'm getting to that, my lord," Ermengarde answered imperturbably. "I had been troubled in my soul about Alouette ever since she left, and about the fact that I did not tell you what I know. But I was afraid of King Phillip."

"What do you know?" He crossed the room in two long strides, his hands closing on her wrists in his eagerness. A wild light of hope flamed in his honey-brown eyes.

The old servant was seized with a coughing fit, and Reyner had to contain his impatience as she hacked and clutched her chest, finally bringing up some phlegm into a rag she pulled from her sleeve. She waved away the tawny-haired knight's gesture of assistance.

"Thank you, my lord, but I am well enough for an old woman. It's just this damp Sicilian winter. No doubt I'll be longing for rain once we reach the deserts of Outremer..." She went on hastily, however, as she sensed Reyner's impatience.

"Alouette is still in Sicily, my lord. She never left."

"Where?"

"In a convent, Sir Reyner, somewhere beyond Messina. Oh, not to take the veil, my lord, but as a retreat," she added hastily, seeing the alarm flash in his eyes. "I'm sorry, I don't know where, exactly. Alouette would not let me go along, though I begged to, and now no one will tell me exactly where she is."

"But you have had word of her?"

"Only once, just a se'enight after she went, to assure me she was well. Since then, nothing."

"Did she go of her own free will, Ermengarde?"

The tirewoman's lined brow furrowed as she answered him, her voice troubled. "She felt guilty, my lord. She felt she had sinned, by allowing herself to... love you. She thought the sword fight between you and the *Sieur* de Langres was her fault, and that she had endangered your life. She . . . wanted to go into seclusion, Sir Reyner, for the remainder of her stay in Sicily—to regain her vocation."

Her vocation. Her damned, mistaken vocation.

"Then why are you telling me this, woman?" He was truly mystified. His heart had heard the important message, however. Alouette loved him.

"I have become convinced through my prayers, Sir Reyner, that I did wrong to cooperate in this conspiracy of silence as to her location. King Phillip's motives are not always . . . the purest."

"How well you observe," Reyner retorted wryly. He doubted the scheming French monarch ever did anything without an element of self-interest.

"And I have become uneasy in my mind, as the weeks go on and I hear nothing further from my lamb. I love her too, Sir Reyner, and something in here"— she tapped her chest—"tells me all is not well. I tried to obtain permission and an escort to visit her. Instead, His Majesty set me to being tirewoman to that Peronel, his mistress. Her own woman was abed with a fainting illness that began after Peronel struck her." She wrinkled her nose in distaste. "Find her, my lord, and go to her."

"But *how*? You can't even tell me where she is!" Reyner paced the floor, his mind whirling at the impact of Ermengarde's words. Alouette was still in Sicily. She loved him!

He thanked God that the riot had interrupted his tryst with Chiara. Now she seemed like a cheap, shiny bauble compared to the glowing pearl he longed for.

Alouette was in a convent, perhaps a prisoner there. Would they, *could* they compel her to take vows? Did Phillip's power extend to that?

"Does Henri de Chenevy know where she is?"

"Yes, my lord. He escorted her there. But King Phillip sent him to Salerno yesterday, to the medical school there to ask for a remedy for the ague that still plagues the king frequently. I don't know when Lord Henri will be back." Ermengarde's hand anxiously twisted the skirts of her thick woolen robe.

"Damn that fat French malingerer," Reyner growled.

Henri would have told him, he thought, if he had gone to him and repeated the old servant's concerns. He didn't understand why Alouette's stepbrother had lied to him, but doubtless he'd had his reasons. Reyner felt he couldn't wait and find out what they were.

"How long was he gone, when he took her to the convent?"

"Six days, my lord." She searched his face, seeing his anxiety, love and determination. A sudden thought came to her. "I remember something, Sir Reyner. I don't know if it will help—"

"Tell me," he commanded, his voice steely.

"Lord Henri mentioned the pink domes of the church there. He said it looked very odd, for a church—more like a Saracen design."

Pink domes. Perhaps it would not help him find her. Moorish architecture was everywhere on this damned rocky island, a remnant of the Islamic occupation which had ended when the Normans had driven the Arabs out over a century ago. But it was a clue, at least.

"I'll find her, old woman. But once I do I'll never let her go again," he warned her.

To his surprise, she smiled. "I used to think she was not for any earthly man, Sir Reyner. I believe now I was wrong," Ermengarde said simply. "You are the man for my lamb—the only man she could ever love. I know if you find her, she will be safe in your love forever." Her rheumy old eyes shone with happy tears as she seized his hand and kissed it.

"Thank you, Ermengarde." Impulsively he kissed the leathery old cheek and then let her out the door. He must prepare for a search he would not abandon until he found Alouette.

Leave from Richard was quickly obtained—partially because Richard saw the opportunity to annoy Phillip through his vassal's actions, Reyner suspected. It was just as well he had permission to be absent, but he would have gone without it.

"Have you any clue as to where to find your little Lark?"

Richard asked, rising from his chair when Reyner came to bid him farewell.

"The knight he rode east; the knight he rode west—" the ever-present Blondel sang with a grin, strumming a chord on the harp in his lap. "I can see it now—'twill make a fine *chanson* of chivalry and love."

"No, my lord," Reyner said, ignoring the troubador. "Do you have any suggestions?"

Richard appeared to be of two minds. Reyner assumed he was torn by the chivalric image of a knight questing for his true love and the more practical desire to have a valuable man back quickly to serve him.

At last he spoke. "A church with pink domes, eh? As you say, that could be anywhere. Tancred's own palace looks like Saladin should be living there, not a supposedly Christian king." He shrugged his shoulders. "I'm sorry, Reyner, I—but hold! I have a thought. You know how close that dwarf and Phillip are. If Phillip wanted a place to hide Alouette away, whom would he consult? Tancred! He'd have to! He hasn't bestirred himself to explore this island himself! And where is that slippery dwarf's principal seat? Palermo! I would try in that direction first, at least. What say you, Reyner?"

"My thanks, my lord. I shall take your suggestion." In truth, Reyner had no one else to guide his search. He certainly couldn't ask His Majesty King Phillip. Palermo seemed as good a place as any to look first.

Reyner, his squire, and Zeus left Mategriffon on the far southwestern edge of the city and decided to cut through Messina. The city was once again open to all crusaders; he could obtain bread, cheese, and wine for the journey and more easily reach the coastal road eastward from there.

The streets were busy with Griffons and Lombards hawking their wares to strolling crusaders of all nationalities. To see their deferential smiles and bows as they traded fat crusty loaves for pennies handed them by men wearing the white cross on their surcoats, no one would have guessed they had been at war with the English so recently, Reyner thought cynically, on his way through the narrow winding streets—not until one looked at the sullen cast in their eyes as their greedy hands seized the coins.

He stopped in the plaza opposite the Cathedral of Santa Maria, where a number of vendors were selling anything from wine to splinters purported to be parts of the True Cross. As he was purchasing goat cheese wrapped in moist cloth, a familiar, husky voice said, "Why, if it's not my fine, handsome knight!"

He looked up to see Princess Chiara, dressed in an exotic, gold-shot purple gown which complimented her dark beauty. She was accompanied by Peronel, Phillip's mistress, who was gaudily robed in cloth-of-gold. They had obviously been shopping; a servant stood by, loaded down with their purchases.

"Princess Chiara, Lady Peronel," Reyner murmured, bowing politely. He hoped the Sicilian princess would not detain him long with her chatter. It was already midmorning; he had wasted hours waiting until Richard had arisen and broken his fast to give him an audience, and was eager to be on his way.

"You are up early for one who banqueted all day and then went out to fight," Chiara said, smiling coquettishly and batting her long, thick eyelashes up at him as she seized his arm. "Ah, but you are going somewhere!" she exclaimed, eyeing their saddlebags. "I am so disappointed! I was hoping to encounter you, in fact, and see if we could perhaps reschedule our little . . . *rendezvous*—perhaps even today?" She looked appealingly at him through archly slanted eyes.

Reyner darted a look at Phillip's mistress, who looked amused. She was no more fooled than he. Chiara had had no such plans, but now that she had encountered Reyner, she wanted to see if her feminine charms were strong enough to dissuade him from his purpose.

"My lady, I am devastated that I must refuse such loveliness—at least for a while," Reyner answered, trying to inject regret into his voice. "But I confess I am surprised. I had thought you would have no time for such as myself, after last night. Had you no joy in the hunt, then?"

He had meant just to tease her, and did so to counteract

the feeling of distaste he got from the cloying scent of her perfume and the possessive way she touched him, which made him feel that she viewed him as much a thing to be owned as the packages in her lackey's arms. He saw from the narrowing of her eyes and the tightening of her lips, though, that he had gone too far. She thought he was mocking her.

Her laughter was brittle as she whirled back to Peronel, her purple skirts flaring. "Do not suppose you are the only man who has caught my eye, milord Reyner," she retorted over her shoulder. "A handsome Frenchman consoled me in your absence last night. In fact, he tells me he is a cousin of yours—Fulk de Langres."

Perhaps unwisely, Reyner could not resist getting the last word. "Ah, I would never *presume* to think I was the only man in your life, Princess."

He bowed, then turned and mounted his destrier, but he felt her glaring at him until he turned a corner out of sight. He would not have been surprised to feel a dagger in his back.

"The lady looked angry," observed Thomas, his squire.

"Yes, that was stupid of me." What doubly foul luck that the woman who had enticed him had later succeeded with his deadly enemy, and that he had met her in the company of Phillip's concubine, who was probably privy to her lord's feelings about him. By noon, Phillip Capet and Fulk doubtless would know that he had left town.

Once through the gates, however, he decided there was nothing he could do but forget the confrontation and concentrate on finding Alouette. He felt none of the sluggishness that should have followed a night with little or no sleep. He was energized and happy—a feeling he saw reflected in Zeus, who was trotting alongside his destrier.

The huge canine grinned up at him, tongue lolling out and gray, plumed tail waving merrily.

"We're going to find Alouette, old friend, but I need your help, all right?"

Zeus barked his joyous assent. It was not the first time Reyner and his pet had seemed so perfectly in tune, but it added to the warm glow of confidence Reyner felt, none-theless.

As Messina receded in the distance, the little talk he and Thomas exchanged about the chill weather and the wind-ing, steep track that followed the northern coast left Reyner plenty of time for the solitude of his own thoughts. The more he contemplated Richard's idea that Phillip would have asked Tancred where to place Alouette, the more convinced he was that the theory was correct. He spurred Hercules into a canter, and the war-horse's rolling gait seemed to echo the refrain in his heart: *Palermo, Palermo, Palermo.*

Princess Chiara was unsuccessful in finding Fulk, to tell him of her encounter with Reyner that morning. With typi-cal Mediterranean indolence, she shoved the information to the back of her mind. It was not until the following night, during their midnight tryst in a borrowed chamber of the palace, that she broached the subject of his hated cousin.

Replete with satisfaction after an impassioned coupling, she yawned sleepily and told the sprawled Frenchman be-side her of seeing Reyner de Winslade and his squire in the streets of Messina when she and Peronel had been shop-ping. Both the English knight and his squire were mounted, she went on, and the squire was leading a sumpter mule.

The pleasant, relaxed afterglow evaporated as soon as Fulk had digested her words. Immediately he sat up and began pulling on the shirt and chausses he had discarded so hastily only an hour before.

"Packed as if for a journey, you say?" he repeated, gaz-ing at her over his shoulder as he dressed. She was sprawled in naked splendor on the borrowed bed, disdain-ing to cover her voluptuous breasts or the dark triangle between her legs. What he felt now, however, was irrita-tion, not lust. *The stupid bitch!* She should have found a way to come to him as soon as she had seen Reyner, so he could have followed him—not waited to tell him a day and a half later when the trail was cold! Had she been a peas-ant, he would have struck her in his anger.

"Yes, but he didn't say where he was going," Chiara said, eyes smoldering and mouth tightening as she remembered the thinly veiled insult Reyner had dealt her. "Where are you going, my love?" she purred. "I had hoped you could stay until dawn! I have many more delights to show you, *cara*," but Fulk was already pulling on his tunic.

"It will have to await another time, *ma douce*," Fulk said, covering his anger and kissing her pouting mouth. "This information must go to the king immediately."

Still she reached out to him, kneeling on the bed, breasts thrust out invitingly. "In the middle of the night? Surely it can wait until morning, and you can stay with me until then! You Frenchmen are all mad!" She collapsed in a petulant heap as he closed the door without looking back.

Phillip Capet was not pleased at being awakened in the middle of the night, for he had drunk heavily before retiring and was enjoying a very erotic dream as he lay nestled against Peronel's well-padded hips. He knew Fulk would not dare disturb him unless it was important, however. Pulling the velvet bedcover about him, he drew the curtains around Peronel and confronted Fulk.

"My apologies for disturbing you, sire, but I have just learned some vital information . . ." Quickly, he told the king about Reyner being seen in Messina, obviously embarking on a journey, although he didn't mention who had told him.

"So? Why should I care where Richard's knights go? No one knows where Alouette is—I made sure of that!" Phillip retorted coldly.

By now Peronel's tousled head was peeking through the bed hangings. "My lord," she began hesitantly, "perhaps you had better listen to the *Sieur* de Langres. Something that seemed unimportant to me at the time is beginning to fit into place."

Phillip stopped pacing and waited impatiently as his mistress wrapped herself in a furred robe and joined the two men. "What is it?"

She pushed a brassy blond ringlet away from her face and told him. "You recall that King Richard and his knights left the banquet yesterday because of the squabbling Italians and returned at dusk—" Out of the corner of her eye, she noticed that Phillip was becoming infuriated. "I saw Ermengarde leaving from the upper floor that evening," she added quickly.

"What has that to do with this, you silly baggage?" Phillip exploded, his shout making her cower against the bed curtains. "Why should I care where one old woman was?"

"Because only Richard's favored nobles—and *knights*—have chambers in the upper floors of Mategriffon," Peronel replied. "And because only Ermengarde—and Henri de Chenevy, who is away—know that Alouette has not truly gone back to France. Ermengarde had no reason for being there, unless she was telling Reyner what little she knew, my lord. In fact, I slapped her when I saw her, for I had ordered her to mend a certain cloak of mine, and she admitted she hadn't done it—"

"Stupid bitch!" Phillip shrieked. "This happened two nights ago, and you didn't think to tell me about it?" In a motion too swift for the eye to follow, he backhanded the cringing woman, his ruby ring cutting her cheek. "Get out of my sight!"

Peronel managed to dodge the kick the enraged king aimed as she hastily quit the chamber.

Phillip turned back to Fulk. "Empty-headed slut," he growled. "None of them is worth the time it takes to copulate."

"*Vraiment,*" Fulk agreed. "They either talk too much or not enough. But you agree with me, Your Majesty, that the English knight's destination is Lady Alouette's convent?"

"It seems likely, but for one thing—even the old woman doesn't know *where* in Sicily the convent is."

"Henri—"

"—Wouldn't dare to have told her, before he left for Salerno. I made him swear," Phillip said, black eyes gleaming as he added, "and when I informed him of the dreadful fate that would be Alouette's if he told, he turned a rather interesting shade of green."

"But all the same, Your Majesty, don't you think it prudent to send a contingent to guard the convent?"

Phillip laughed mockingly at his vassal and, stepping over to the brazier, poured himself a goblet of wine from the flagon that sat beside it. He did not offer any to Fulk. "It is well that I am king and not you, fool. After just concluding a peaceful season with my vassal, Richard of England, would I now send an armed force out to murder one English knight? Richard would know their purpose before they left Messina's gates, I assure you. And as this simple knight is rather a favorite of his, for some unknown reason—he doesn't seem to be one of his catamites, so I'm at a loss to explain it—that might annoy Coeur de Lion just a trifle, don't you think?"

Fulk was forced to nod, though he saw where this was leading. Sicilians might call Phillip a lamb, but he was actually a snake. "What is it you want me to do, sire?"

"I want *you* to go to Palermo, which is where the convent is, and guard it. Perhaps the English knight will figure out where she is, perhaps not. But you are to intercept him, if he comes there—and eliminate him. Quietly, of course. He is just to disappear. Do you understand, my lord?" Phillip asked quietly, his dark eyes opaque and his voice cool.

"Of course, Your Majesty. My cousin Reyner will never reach the Lady Alouette. And if he comes to Palermo, he will never be seen alive again."

"*Bien.* Do not fail me, Fulk. I have a long memory of past sins—yours in particular. If you expect to wed Alouette—and finally atone for the most heinous of your crimes—do not blunder."

As Fulk was taking his leave, Phillip stepped into the hall, yelling, "Guards! Bring Ermengarde the tirewoman to me for questioning!"

FOURTEEN

It was an unusually fine day for the first of January, and Mother Superior had decreed that recreation could again take place in the cloister garden before supper. The Benedictines put on their cloaks and happily munched upon the oranges and almonds the abbess had given them because of *Hanguevelle*, or the giving of New Year's gifts. The citrus fruit was only a little the worse for wear after being shipped from Jaffa by way of Cyprus.

"Just think, dear Alouette, 'tis the year of Our Lord 1191," mused Innocentia, who had finally begun to be herself again after being let out of seclusion. "Do you wonder what great things will happen this year? I will take my vows . . . and doubtless the Christians will free the Holy Sepulchre."

"*I* wonder if I shall ever be free," Alouette said sadly to the novice. "It seems as if my time here will never end."

"Certainly it will, my lady! You have told me that King Phillip was not willing to go on crusade without you," her friend—her *only* friend in this collection of austere women—said, scoffing at her fears.

"Perhaps that was my pride speaking," Alouette suggested. "He has certainly managed to do without me these long weeks. Perhaps he has decided I am just too much trouble," she continued, thinking of the duel she had caused between Reyner and Fulk. But she could not be sorry now. Indeed, all she had to comfort her in this haven that had become a prison were those moments in the garden, when Reyner had held her, and kissed her, and touched her. She remembered even now the orrisroot scent of him, mingled with the taste of wine on his lips, the feel of his hand on her breast, burning her through the silken gown . . .

Beyond the convent walls, a pair of horsemen, leading a sumpter mule, paused and studied the pink-domed cathedral which stood between the monastery and the convent.

"Alouette, please sing the song he sang to you that night at the banquet," pleaded Innocentia, breaking into her daydream. Alouette had always refused such requests before, but now, caught up in a whirlwind of remembered love and passion, she could not stop herself. She felt rebellious, her blood racing frustratedly through her veins on this sunny day. *Why not?* she thought, and strummed a loud opening chord.

'Tis worse than death to lead a life of pain
Joyless, and filled with suffering and grief—

Her voice rose on the gentle wind, truer and stronger than ever before, and suddenly it was joined by a male voice beyond the gates:

When she who might turn all this loss to gain
Denies her suppliant succor and relief.

Alouette's hand froze on the lute and she stopped singing, staring sightlessly into the vacant air as the resonant bass voice continued:

But 'tis Paradise when at last
She turns to me, my lady true
'Tis gain indeed, all sorrow past
And adores me with eyes of celestial blue . . .

"Who is that?"

"Some monk from the monastery—his prior will soon silence him!" sniffed the novice mistress, who nevertheless turned her suspicious gaze on Alouette.

Alouette's face was transfigured. She gripped the lute as the tears poured down her pale cheeks, but they were tears of joy.

"Reyner," she breathed. Then, as she heard the pounding on the gate, and the portress refusing him entrance, she lifted her voice: "Reyner!"

The knocking grew louder, accompanied by a frenzied barking, as the intruder ignored Sister Portress's screeching imprecations. His voice rang out: "Open! In the name of King Richard of England, open the convent gate!"

Alouette could hear the rustle of Mother Superior's serge skirts as the woman arose to deal with the problem, her muttering like the buzzing of an angered wasp. Alouette stood up also, trembling, and took Innocentia's proffered arm.

She reached the solid wooden gate soon after the abbess. There she was seized by the Novice Mistress, who held her in a grip of iron, a hand over her mouth.

"What is the meaning of this disturbance, Sir Knight? We are all holy women here!" Mother Maria Benedicta cried indignantly as she unshuttered the grille in the gate.

What she saw through the small square aperture was a startling view of a knight in full mail, wearing a white cross on his surcoat and bearing a naked sword. It was the hilt of that sword he had been using to hammer so loudly on the gate.

"I am Sir Reyner of Winslade. You hold one among you, I believe, who is no nun—a Frenchwoman, Lady Alouette de Chenevy. She has taken no vows and is being held against her will."

"We do indeed give Lady Alouette *sanctuary*," corrected the abbess icily. "She is here at her own request. Only on order of His Majesty King Phillip of France can we release her, and I believe you said you are a subject of the English king?" She affected to ignore the sounds of a struggle going on to the side of her. A very determined Alouette was attempting to free herself from the Novice Mistress's fierce hold.

"I have an axe across my saddlebow, my lady abbess," warned Reyner. "Reluctant as I am to desecrate the property of nuns, I shall reduce this wooden door to kindling in a trice if I am not permitted to see Lady Alouette free and unhindered. If she tells me she wishes to be here, I will go my way and leave her in peace."

There was silence from the abbess. Alouette went still in *Suora* Penetentia's grip. Behind her she could hear the curious, scandalized whispers of the Benedictines.

Then, in haughty tones, the Reverend Mother said, "You leave me little choice, Sir Knight. I am responsible for the property, as well as the souls in my care. But be yourself warned that you may well face excommunication for your actions."

At a signal from the abbess, Alouette found herself loosed from the other nun's hold. With a jingling of her massive key ring, Sister Portress opened the gate.

Surely saints entering Paradise were greeted by no less glorious beings, Reyner thought, catching sight of Alouette standing a little apart from the black-robed nuns, waiting for him. She was clothed exactly as the Benedictines were, in a white, unbleached linen undergown with a coarse serge veil and cloak of black. A white wimple stretched taut over her forehead hid any sight of her midnight-hued hair, but even in these anonymous robes she was Alouette, the Lark—his Lark. Her eyes were luminous with joy and tears, and bluer than the vaults of Heaven. Her full lips quivered as she stretched out wind-chapped hands in his direction. "Reyner—?"

He didn't remember crossing the lawn to her, but in the next heartbeat she was in his arms, laughing and crying at the same time as he kissed the tears from her cheeks and held her close.

It was several minutes before he could bear to stop kissing her. In the background, Alouette was vaguely aware of the abbess dispersing her nuns to the kitchens for the preparation of the evening meal. Naturally, she must be loath to have her community view this successful challenge to her authority.

Finally, only the abbess remained, her face a tightly controlled mask when Reyner looked at her over Alouette's head. His brown eyes danced with mischief as he stared the woman down while addressing Alouette: "My love, do you wish to come with me, or remain with these *good* women?" His ironic emphasis left no doubt of what he thought of Mother Mary Benedicta's particular sanctity.

But the abbess did not give up easily. "Stay with us and preserve your soul, dear Alouette," she pleaded, glaring at the English knight as she faced the end of her dream of a fat dowry from King Phillip. "The lusts of the flesh are the lures of Hell, my dear. You will notice he promises you nothing, Alouette—not even the protection of his name."

Alouette frowned. "I want nothing promised but his love, Reverend Mother," she said proudly, facing the abbess from the safe circle of Reyner's arms.

The abbess shrugged, knowing she had lost. "I will send *Suora* Innocentia to help you pack, then. Please be ready to leave as soon as possible. I will not have my community still in turmoil at vespers," she said crisply, and stalked off across the cloister, her shoes rustling the winter-dried grass.

Wistfully, Innocentia assisted Alouette as she stripped off the Benedictine habit and donned the dark blue woolen dress she had worn on her journey to Palermo.

"Your knight looks like someone from a troubador's song," Innocentia told her. "Such tawny-gold hair! Such eyes—like warm honey, when he gazes at you!"

Alouette, remembering Ermengarde's remarks about Reyner's plain features, assumed the young novice was easily impressed by the rare sight of a knight in the full regalia of a crusader.

"I will miss you, Lady Alouette. You have been kinder to me than the abbess—or my own *madre*, for that matter."

Alouette could hear the tears Innocentia was struggling to hold back. She was touched, and gathered the novice into an embrace. She was surprised to realize how much she would miss the Lombard girl's companionship. She was like the sister Alouette had never had. Without Innocentia's loving prodding, she wondered whether she would have had the courage to look within herself and discover the love she bore for the English knight who waited outside her cell.

"I will never forget you, Innocentia. You will make a lovely bride of Christ. Will you promise to pray for me?"

"Of course, my lady, always. . . ." Innocentia's words became muffled in sobs.

Alouette wanted to stay and comfort her friend, but Reyner was waiting. "I suppose I had better be going, before Mother Superior changes her mind," she said with an attempt at a laugh, gently disengaging the clinging arms that held her.

"Lady Alouette, please—take me with you!" Innocentia cried suddenly, dropping to her knees and grasping the astonished Alouette's skirts pleadingly.

"But Innocentia, you wanted to be a nun—you told me so!"

"Nay, not anymore!" sobbed the Lombard girl. "I was here because my parents told me it was my duty. *I* wanted to have a husband and be a mother to his babies. But once they knew Giovanni had taken my maidenhead, they knew no good Sicilian boy would take me as anything but a *puïana*, a whore. Let me be with you! I'll be your servant! I'll do anything for you, I swear! And perhaps someday I could meet some man-at-arms who would want a good wife. *Please*, Lady Alouette! If I don't leave with you I will have to take my vows next month. I don't want to be a dried-up old woman behind these walls!"

Alouette could not help but sympathize with Innocentia's desperation. Wasn't it similar to how she had come to feel? "Very well, I suppose my lord would not mind. Ermengarde is growing old, and I think she could use some help. But I have one condition, Innocentia—"

"Anything, my lady!" sighed the novice, kissing the blind girl's hand rapturously. "I will sleep on the floor, and I don't eat much. I will bring you hot bath water whenever you wish . . ."

"The condition is that *you* bathe regularly, also, Innocentia," said Alouette gently. "Now that you are not to be a Benedictine, there is no special holiness about odor."

* * *

Alouette found Reyner waiting in the chapter room where important visitors such as the bishop were entertained, or the nuns visited on rare occasions with family members. He was perfectly agreeable to having Innocentia come along as Alouette's tirewoman.

"However, sweetheart," Reyner murmured, pulling her against his chest and stroking her cheek gently, "I hope you will dismiss Innocentia now and then and allow me to play lady's maid for you."

His words brought to mind images of his assisting her to bathe, scrubbing her back, his strong hands massaging the soap through her hair, sensitive fingers roaming down her neck and shoulders—pictures so intimate that her breath caught in her throat. She felt herself flushing, the heat spreading above the neck of the gown and into her cheeks. There was much they had not spoken about, after all. She had no idea of his plans once they left the convent walls, but it was clear that he was eager to make her his. And she was eager to be his, she discovered with a pleased little quiver in the pit of her stomach.

"You know, I did not want to give the old dragon the satisfaction of hearing it, but I do love you, darling Alouette, and I—"

As if mentioning her had the power to make her materialize, the "dragon" swept into the room just then with a chastened-appearing Innocentia in her wake.

"It is not enough that you are stealing a lady against King Phillip's express orders! You want to rob me of one of my novices as well?" she huffed, shoving Innocentia toward Reyner and Alouette. It was obvious that she was already resigned to the loss, however, for the Lombard girl was dressed in the shabby, threadbare gown and cloak she had worn when she had been brought to the convent half a year ago. That it no longer fit the growing young woman, and was inadequate even for a sunny winter day, did not seem to trouble Mother Mary Benedicta.

Reyner was suddenly tired of the abbess's venal nature. He suspected the tyrannical old woman had made life hellish for Alouette while she was there.

"What's the trouble, Reverend Mother?" he inquired in a

silky drawl. "Are you afraid I will free all your flock, and you will have no one left to dominate?"

The abbess's face went first livid, then purpled with anger, but she caught the purse Reyner tossed contemptuously at her to compensate the convent for the loss of the novice.

It was dark by the time Reyner, Alouette, Innocentia, and the squire rode from the convent gates, so Reyner inquired of Innocentia whether there was an inn in Palermo where they might shelter for the night.

"There is, my lord," responded Innocentia in a worshipful tone. It was clear she was totally in awe of the tall, handsome knight who had rescued the French girl and changed her own life in the course of a single winter afternoon. "But it is very shabby, and not worthy of you or my lady. Besides, it is much frequented by Griffons and other low, thieving types."

Reyner had to smile at the Sicilian girl's earnestness. She seemed to feel that he and Alouette deserved little less than royal accommodations. Though he appreciated the warning, there seemed to be little choice, for the nearest town to the east, Bagheria, was several leagues away. Though he was loath to spend this special night sleeping with one eye open against thieves, riding through the winter darkness did not appeal to him either. Damn the abbess! Had she a spark of true Christian charity, she would have offered them quarters for the night, he thought, weighing the unappetizing alternatives.

"My lord," Innocentia said, "if I might make a suggestion. The abbot of the Benedictine monastery over there—" she gestured toward the terra cotta-tiled buildings on the other side of the pink-domed cathedral "—never speaks to the Reverend Mother, and his guest hostel is famous for its hospitality. Why not apply there for lodgings?"

Within half an hour Sir Reyner and Alouette, with Zeus curled up at their feet, were comfortably seated in front of a crackling fire in the guests' dining room and were being served capon cooked in wine, a selection of fruits from the Holy Land, and Sicilian cheeses. They were still chuckling at the audacity of simply riding their mounts around the cathedral to the monastery just a few hundred yards away from the convent.

The genial abbot was the abbess's opposite in his kindness, as well as the bounty of his table. It must be true that he and the abbess did not communicate, Reyner mused, or else he would have certainly realized that the beautiful blind lady in his guesthouse was in fact the famous minstrel of the French court, lately a guest at the neighboring convent.

Since there were not many travelers abroad on this winter night, the little party had the common room to themselves. Reyner and Alouette sat separately, however, for Innocentia and Thomas had by tacit consent moved across the room.

"I'm not so sure if they are trying to give *us* privacy or themselves," Reyner remarked with a chuckle, serving his beloved another morsel from the delicious capon. "Your new little Sicilian servant will not be hard to look at once she obtains some better clothes and has a bath. It's apparent that the Benedictine robes hid a buxom figure, and Tom is already ensorcelled by those big, sloe eyes of hers."

"And you, my lord?" she could not resist asking.

"—have no eyes for anyone but you, of course."

She felt foolish for her moment of insecurity. Reyner was no Phillip, to go lusting after her servant. "I'm sorry, Reyner. That was silly of me. It's just that . . . now that I have abandoned the secure life of a nun, I realize how vulnerable I am."

His big hands closed over hers, and squeezed reassuringly. "There was a time I despaired of hearing you say you care, let alone that you could feel jealous."

She relaxed further in the caressing warmth of his voice.

"Did you know I was told you had gone back to France?"

She did not, of course.

"If Ermengarde had not become troubled about the lack of any word from you—for Phillip would not even tell her where you were—I would have gone on believing that you hated what had happened between us and despised me, at least until he brought you to the Holy Land."

"If he ever truly meant to let me out of the convent at all," she responded bitterly. "I can't go back to his court, Reyner. He's a selfish, venal man—I won't be his puppet anymore!" Her slender hand clenched into a fist on the wooden plank table, and her pink lip quivered as a glistening tear rolled past.

"You will never have to be," Reyner assured her, trying to communicate all his sincerity through his touch, for she couldn't see it in his eyes. "I will never, ever let you go again. You are *mine*, lovely Alouette, and I will love and protect you all the days of my life."

"But the king—"

"Will not dare to stand against my king," he told her. "Richard will aid us, I know. If the Lionheart supports our cause, even Phillip will bluster in vain. Besides, your brother Henri can be persuaded, I believe, to give his consent when he arrives back in Sicily. You are not a slave, nor even Phillip's ward. If your brother agrees to our marriage, what can . . ."

He broke off his musing as he saw her pale and begin to tremble.

"Alouette, what is it? You're as white as your wimple! Don't be afraid of Phillip, love, it will be all right!"

She had thought never to hear him speak of their marriage—thought he only meant to make her his mistress. She had hidden from a fundamental truth deep within her —one she didn't fully understand, but that made it nonetheless true. If she loved him, *truly loved him*, she couldn't tie him to her, knowing that she was somehow unworthy.

"Oh, Reyner," she managed at last, through her sobs. "I can't marry you!"

FIFTEEN

Now it was Reyner's turn to lose his color. He stared at her, thunderstruck. "Alouette, what are you saying? Of course we'll be married!" He couldn't believe his ears, but another glance at his beloved, who had now buried her face in her hands, confirmed what he had heard.

He darted a look across the room at Innocentia, who had noticed her mistress's disquiet and was obviously wondering if she should do something. He liked the gawky Sicilian girl, but the very last thing he needed at the moment was interference.

He crossed the room quickly. "Lady Alouette is overtired," he informed Innocentia and Thomas curtly, "and needs to retire for the night. We will need nothing further."

He had bespoken two rooms, but there had been no discussion as to the sleeping arrangements. Now he was grimly determined to escort Alouette to her chamber, and at least get to the bottom of her ridiculous statement. Not marry him? What female foolishness was this? He had just threatened his way into a convent, risking excommunication and the wrath of a vengeful king, and she didn't think she could marry him?

He returned to their table and commanded quietly: "Come upstairs, Alouette. We have much to discuss." Something deep festered in the girl's soul, and by God, he'd know what it was.

* * *

At the thud of the bolt when he locked the door behind them, Alouette jumped like a startled doe. She had sensed his anger in the rigidity of the forearm she had held as they walked back to the chamber.

The room was not large, but was comfortably appointed with a backless chair, a bed on a rope mattress with clean but patched blankets, a crucifix on the whitewashed wall, and a glowing brazier near the bed. It was scarcely the luxurious sort of chamber one would wish for a first night together, but it would have to do.

"Now, Lady Alouette," he began with icy formality, "suppose you tell me why you refuse to marry me. Is there someone else?"

"Nay, my lord, there is none other in my heart but you," she whispered, her eyes downcast.

He breathed deeply in relief, but there was another painful possibility to explore. After all, she was a royal bastard. Perhaps, having decided the celibate life was not for her, she had evaluated her prospects and decided she could look considerably higher than the second son of an English earl. However, she was known to be sensitive about her illegitimacy, and she did not know he knew the truth of her birth.

"Perhaps, then, you have decided I am not good enough to claim your hand," he accused, not really trying to keep the hurt from his voice. "Good enough to brave the wrath of the church and the king of France, perhaps, but after that, just a gallant *chevalier* to be rewarded by the privilege of kissing milady's hand—and then to be dismissed."

She was standing across the room, facing his accusations, but at his last words she whirled from him as if he'd slapped her. "Nay, you mistake me, Sir Reyner," she said quietly, sadly. "It is I who am not worthy of you."

His hands clenched at his sides, while his heart twisted in pity for her. She was referring to her bastardy. He had hoped they could avoid speaking of it, at least until she felt more secure, but he'd be damned if he'd lose her again, just to preserve a secret that was no secret.

Before he could open his mouth to confront her, however, she said, "I never meant to deny you my *love*,

Reyner. You have that, always. I would be your mistress willingly." She turned then, lifting her head proudly, a trifle defiantly, eyes dilated as she waited for his reply.

He was speechless for the space of a hundred heartbeats as he stared at her, unable to believe his ears. Then he burst out laughing.

At the rich sound of his merriment she drew herself up stiffly. "You are amused, my lord. Would you mind telling me what you found funny? I was not jesting, Sir Reyner." Her voice was full of hurt pride.

"I don't want a mistress, I want a *wife!*" he exclaimed, and crossed the room with quick, catlike grace, pulling her gently, reassuringly into his arms. "I'm only laughing because all the *damoiselles* I ever attempted to seduce as a youth wanted exactly the opposite of what you want!"

He saw immediately that his attempt at humor had only made things worse. "No doubt there have been many," she said coldly, going rigid in his embrace. "I'm certain I would not compare to the least of them. Perhaps I have made a mistake in offering my poor self to you." She struggled to break free, but when he would not let her go, she contented herself with again averting her face, trying hard to ignore the seductive scent of orrisroot that was always about him and the tingle in her shoulders where his hands held her captive.

"God-a-mercy, Alouette! I'm not comparing you to anyone! Nor would you expect me to have been a monk before we met, would you? I merely cannot understand why you claim to prefer being my mistress, rather than my wife. Where did you get the idea you were not worthy to be the Lady of Winslade?" He wanted to give her the chance to reveal her secret "shame" in her own way.

"I'm blind," she answered, much too quickly. "How could I run a household?"

"God's death!" Reyner exploded in frustration fueled by fatigue. "I'm sick of hearing you hide behind that excuse! Being blind didn't stop you from becoming an accomplished troubador, nor did it keep you from considering the convent, though there was very little you could have done there without your sight but pray, chant, and eat! What's the real reason, Alouette? Say it. I want to hear you say it."

He took her chin in his hand, forcing her head upward so that he could gaze down on her pale, unhappy face. The blue eyes blazed through unshed tears so that they looked like dewy aquamarines. "I am a bastard, Sir Reyner. Count Édouard de Chenevy was not my father. Are you content? Now you know why I cannot be your wife," she said, her whole body shuddering with sobs.

He clutched her to him, stroking her hair while she wailed like a child. It was the first time she had said the word with which she labeled herself: *bastard*. It was not until her sobs quieted to whimpers that he spoke again.

"And since when does bastardy make one ineligible to be a knight's lady, my poor sweetheart?" he said into the midnight tresses he ran his fingers through. Her hair felt like silk, and smelled of lilies, for she had used the essence in the bottle that had been put away with her clothes. "The very first of the Norman kings was a bastard, and won such respect that his status became his sobriquet! The issue of royal liaisons are sought-after marriage parties all over Europe. Why shouldn't I offer you honorable marriage, Alouette, my love?"

"You know who was my sire, then," she said through her tears. "When did you find out? Who told you?"

She was so like a wounded fawn who would bolt for cover if loosed that he continued to hold her and stroke her, feeling the trembling beneath his long, tapering fingers through the wool of her bliaut.

"I have always known," he assured her, "since the first day I saw you in Vézélay. It is an open secret, my proud love, that you are the natural daughter of Louis of France. But none thinks any the less of you for it!"

"Your mother would," she said stubbornly, lower lip slightly outthrust. "She would think you could do better than a blind, illegitimate girl—even the daughter of a king."

"Lady Ysabeau?" He chuckled at the thought of his mother's reaction to that statement. "Not likely. She came from the notorious courts of love of Aquitaine, where affairs of the heart are a way of life! She was wed to a mad Catharist knight who tried to murder her and my father because they loved each other. Nay, love," he said, kissing her cheek as he imagined their homecoming reception at Hawkingham Castle, "she would love you as I do, simply because you loved me."

"There is another reason I cannot marry you," she repeated adamantly, "some stain within me...something wrong...something I cannot really explain, Reyner, my love, but is *there*—I feel it."

He could see he would not be able to move her further —at least, not tonight. He knew, also, that even if being her lover were all that he wanted, he could not expect Richard's support against Phillip unless they had an honorable relationship. Though a homosexual, Richard was curiously moral when it came to heterosexual relationships. That was why he had so piously refused to wed Alais of France; he could not accept the fact that she'd been his father's concubine. Reyner thought it likely he could change Alouette's mind—particularly if he could discover the nature of the fear she kept hidden even from herself. But first he would have to bind her to him with the invisible silver cords of physical love.

"Very well," he said at last, voice husky with suppressed feeling. "You have said you are willing to be my mistress. I will accept (at least for now, he added to himself) what you are willing to give."

The words hung between them in the air.

"What did you say?" she asked in a small voice, having heard exactly what he said. She had longed for this moment; indeed, had he taken her in the garden in Messina, she would have given herself willingly, swept away by the passion he had aroused in her that night. But to have him accept her offer so baldly confused her. Now that the moment had come, she was not ready. Her heart hammered in her throat and her mouth had gone dry.

"Come here, Alouette," she heard Reyner say, and as if she had no will of her own, she followed his voice until she stood close enough to touch him.

"What are you going to do?" she whispered as he put his

arms around her again and held her, his lips so close to hers
that she could feel his warm breath.

"Sweet Alouette, I am going to kiss you until your knees
grow weak," he said, "and caress your breasts until the
nipples are hard between my fingertips. Then I will strip
off your bliaut and undergown and chemise, and touch and
stroke your womanhood until you are moist and moaning
and hot with the need of me. You will be ready for me
then, and I will lay you down on that bed as naked as God
made you, and take you while your cries of pleasure echo
in my ears."

His words had a life of their own, caressing her with
promises, exciting her with the expectation of delights to
come. Her fears and doubts vanished, and she surrendered
completely, waiting for him to fill her with his love.

Framing her face in his hands, he claimed her with his
mouth, kissing her slowly and thoughtfully at first, his
tongue tracing the soft fullness of her lips before it parted
them and stole inside. The kiss sent a rush of heat to the pit
of her stomach, and her hands, which had been clenched at
her side, stole around his neck and twined into the long
hair that curled at the nape of his neck. She arched against
him as his hands left her face, one of them cupping her
breast, burning her through the soft woolen stuff of her
gown. Just as he had prophesied, she felt both nipples—
even the one he was not touching!—become erect. His
other hand splayed out against her lower back and one
round buttock, holding her tightly against him, where she
could feel the increasing evidence of his desire. A moan
stole from her parted, moistened lips as his mouth left hers
to trace the line of her jaw down her slender neck.

When he began unlacing her bliaut at the back, murmuring love words and stopping to rain kisses on her forehead
and cheeks, her legs were already so weak from the waves
of desire washing over her that she doubted they would be
able to hold her up until the task was done. She felt the
swish of the soft woolen fabric around her ankles as the
bliaut slid to the floor, then the warmth of the brazier-
heated air against her flaming skin as the linen undergown
joined the bliaut.

"By all the saints, Alouette, you're beautiful," he breathed as she stood before him clad only in a thin, lace-trimmed chemise, so sheer that it did little to hide the dark triangle between her legs. Then he pulled the chemise over her head, and slid one arm beneath her trembling knees to place her gently on the bed, where he covered her tenderly with the blankets. She heard the rustle as he removed his velvet tunic and the linen shirt beneath and untied the chausses from the belt around his waist.

As Reyner pulled the covers back and joined her, she sighed, "I wish I could see you." Her voice was thick with longing as she reached for him, determined that her finger-tips should tell her all that her eyes could not.

"I am but an ugly fellow, as you know," he said lightly. "But I will leave the candle lit, for you are all things beautiful in its light, my sweet Lark."

Lark, he called her. She thrilled to the husky caress as his voice shaped her name in English. He allowed her precious minutes to explore the contours of his body, holding himself firmly in cheek as her warm fingertips traced his sensitive features—his powerfully muscled warrior's shoulders, the trim, flat belly, and the muscles of his thighs that quivered at her touch.

"Nay, but you *are* beautiful," she murmured.

He took her hand then, gently guiding it to the tumescent shaft, watching her face as she gingerly felt its warm, trembling length, gasping in surprise as she reached its swollen head and it pulsed in her hand.

"Feel how much I want you, beloved," Reyner said as he pulled her against him. He parted her legs with his knee and allowed his hand to slip between her legs, gently stroking, delighted at the moisture he found already there as evidence of her desire. She did not seem afraid, only increasingly aroused as his finger penetrated her damp entrance, and so he lowered himself onto her, teasing her with his manhood, thrusting, not enough to pierce her maidenhead, but enough to spread the moisture and set her writhing beneath him.

She gasped with delight as his long, naked body met hers without any barrier of clothing between, glorying as his expert touch sent her even higher in a dizzying spiral of passion. She knew no fear, only a desire to satisfy the wonderful ache within her. Her body felt as if it were on fire, as if it would explode if he did not soon quench the flame raging within her.

"Please, Reyner," she breathed into his ear, barely able to find the air to speak.

"Ah, you are so ready, my love," he said into her neck. "Hold onto me now . . . it will hurt but once . . ." He set his jaw and thrust forward.

She thought it a miracle of love, and evidence of the tender care with which he had initiated her into the joys of coupling, that there was no ripping, tearing pain, such as she had heard servants gossiping about—just a lessening of resistance as he buried his length within her.

He stopped for a moment, studying her upturned face, seeing only loving expectancy there, but no guilt. Could it be—? But no, his mind dismissed any possibilities as his passion took control, setting the tempo for her to follow, watching in satisfaction as she experienced the sweet agony of her approaching climax, slowing his thrusts until she dug her nails into the small of his back, then moving harder and faster within her as her world dissolved into a shower of fiery sparks. Then, before her body could relax completely, he spent himself within her, groaning her name aloud.

They slept, still joined, until he woke and moved to blow the candle out and lie beside her. His movement awoke her and she nestled closer to him in the dark.

"I love you, Alouette."

"And I, you." How inadequate the words were to describe the depth of emotion she felt for Reyner de Winslade! She was already beginning to regret the time wasted until this night. She almost wept for what she had come so close to missing. Celibate nuns never knew such joy! She would never be parted from this man, never!

She giggled suddenly as a thought struck her. "Reyner—the sheets. What will Innocentia think—or the abbot?" She had been told there was blood at a virgin's deflowering; indeed, on the morning after a wedding, the sheets were proudly displayed as proof of a bride's prior chastity. Surely the abbot would be surprised when the monks gossiped after cleaning the room, for he had assumed them already a wedded couple.

Reyner swallowed uncomfortably in the dark, wondering what he should say. There had been enough lies, enough evasions. He was satisfied from her innocent response that she was concealing nothing from him.

"She will assume we have slept together since I . . . did not come back downstairs right after escorting you up here. But you need not worry about the sheets. There was no blood."

He waited in the darkness for long moments, almost holding his breath.

"But . . . I was a maiden! I came to you virgin! There was no real pain, but . . ."

"Alouette, sweetheart, it means nothing. Girls sometimes tear their maidenheads accidentally while riding or playing. Possibly you do not remember such a time . . ." His words sounded false, even as he said them. A blind girl would not have been riding at anything more than a decorous pace, nor would she have played strenuously enough to tear that internal membrane. Whatever had happened, it didn't matter.

She was not reassured, however, and he groaned inwardly as he heard her begin to cry softly next to him.

"I told you there was something wrong with me. I am accursed! Perhaps an incubus . . ."

"That's utter nonsense," he said firmly. "I don't care what Holy Church teaches. There are no demons that lie with innocent females as they sleep, stealing their virginity. I believe you, Alouette. It was obvious to me that such pleasures of the flesh were new to you. And," he added, caressing her shoulders and pulling her closer against him, "I am honored to have been your teacher in the ways of love." He would have liked to make love to her again, but she lay still when he kissed her cheek a few moments later and he thought she slept.

SIXTEEN

She was a child, walking through a torchlit room of an ancient castle, clutching her blanket to her and looking for Ermengarde. Through the mists loomed a door —a door with a shadowy, sinister aura outlining it. Going through the door, she found not her nurse, but her half brother. Phillip was ill . . . or so he seemed, with red-rimmed, dull eyes, unsteady gait, and slurred words. There were others in the room who stared at her, all hot-blooded youths of the court and blowsy female companions. Some of these she recognized. Coming to greet her, Phillip collapsed on the floor. Then she was seized by a man near her. She couldn't see his face, but his words mocked her illegitimacy and labeled her fair prey . . .

And then there was roughness, and terror, and pain— tearing, searing pain. And blood—so much blood. She screamed. Then there was nothing.

Reyner awoke to Alouette's screams, bolting upright in bed. In the faint light from the smoldering brazier, he could see her, curled tightly away from him, eyes clenched tightly shut, mouth frozen open in a rictus of terror as the screams became moans of fear.

"Don't! Please, sir knight, don't!" she cried over and over.

"Wake up, Alouette! You're dreaming! Please love, it's just a dream! *Wake up!*" he insisted, holding her close and smoothing her hair.

161

She was drenched in sweat as she turned to him and sought refuge against his warm, furred chest. "Oh, Reyner!" she sobbed, still trembling like a leaf. "My dream was so awful!"

"Can you remember—"

His question was interrupted by a pounding at the door. "Is aught amiss, my lord?" came a voice, obviously one of the monks.

"Nay, my lady has merely had a nightmare," he called out, and turned back to Alouette as the sound of padding feet died away.

He asked again if she remembered the dream, wondering if it had aught to do with her stubborn insistence that she was somehow stained.

"I'm sorry, Reyner. As you were talking to the monk, most of what little I recall of the dream crumbled into dust and faded away. But I do remember there was someone evil, and of being held captive . . . and in my dream, I could see, so it must have been before my illness . . ."

Suddenly she started. "Reyner! A moment ago something extraordinary happened. I just realized it! For just one moment, as I woke up, *I could see!* I remember now . . . *seeing* your shoulder as you were holding me. Then the monk knocked, and the room went black again. Oh, God, I could *see*! I wish I had seen your face! Will it ever happen again?" Her tears flowed against his chest, and he let her weep them, continuing to hold her until the paroxysm of terror was past and she dozed, exhausted.

There was no more sleep for him, and he pondered many things as he let her sleep through the early dawn. Had the dream revealed the source of her lack of self-esteem? Was the harm symbolic, or had someone actually hurt her? If literal, who was the evil one who haunted her soul? And that momentary, miraculous flash of vision—was it possible that her sight was recoverable? Was there some mysterious connection between her blindness and the dream?

They departed the monastery's precincts at dawn, for the day promised to be sunny and mild. Reyner was determined to cover many leagues so that they could arrive back in Messina as soon as possible.

Alouette had awakened to the sounds of Reyner's squire arming his master for the journey. She had slid further under the covers, blushing and wondering what Thomas must think of her. Nay, but she must grow a thicker skin than that, for she had chosen to become Reyner's mistress, she told herself.

Before summoning Innocentia to help her dress, she had waited until the squire had gone and Reyner was breaking his fast with some watered wine and bread. As she waited for the Lombard girl, she felt suddenly shy with Reyner. *What did one say the next morning to the man who had made you a woman?*

"Did you . . . sleep well, my lord?" she essayed at last.

"So formal, after last night?" he teased, coming over to touch her cheek. "Say rather, 'my love.' Yes, very well," he lied, "for you were beside me." There would be time enough later to speak of the nightmare. "You are beautiful in the morning, Alouette," he added, dropping a gentle kiss on her brow as Innocentia entered. Reyner left then, intent on seeing the horses readied for the journey.

"You are well, my lady?" the former novice asked, surveying the rumpled sheets and her new mistress's blushing radiance.

"Very well. Oh, Innocentia, I love him so! He is so good to me," she sighed, thinking of how Reyner had soothed her following her nightmare.

"He is a good man. His squire, Thomas, is quite charming, too. He paid a monk to bring me a tub and hot water for washing."

Alouette smiled, thinking that the squire probably had done it as much for his own sake as Innocentia's. The Lombard girl was definitely more pleasant to be around now.

Alouette wished she had something beautiful to wear for Reyner, but the few garments she had brought on her journey to Palermo had been serviceable ones in sober hues. Her mood last fall had been one of guilty self-denial, and she had thought to have no need of beautiful raiment among the nuns. It was just as well. They had a journey of several days until they reached Messina, she told herself, and perhaps it was best to be warm. She did trouble to scrub her teeth with fine twigs, however, and put on her sheerest linen wimple after dabbing some of the lily essence behind her ears and at her throat.

On a grassy hill overlooking Palermo, Innocentia, riding the sumpter mule, reined in and asked them to pause that she could look one last time at the pink-domed Cathedral of San Giovanni degli Eremeti and the adjoining convent which had been her home.

"No second thoughts?" asked Alouette, who was riding pillion with Reyner. "I'm sure the Reverend Mother would take you back if . . ."

"Nay, I have no wish to go back!" the girl replied so hastily that Reyner and Alouette had to laugh. Reyner did not miss the flirtatious wink Innocentia had given his squire. Alouette's maid was going to be a handful.

It was here that Fulk de Langres finally caught up with them. He was in a foul humor, having ridden all night, for when he had pounded on her gate last night, the abbess had informed him that Alouette had left a few hours earlier. He had checked the rude, shabby inn in the town, then assumed they had pushed on to Bagheria. It was surprising that he had not encountered them on the road, but he rode to Bagheria nonetheless and had found no trace of them. They must still be in Palermo, he had decided, spurring his weary mount eastward again. Perhaps the ill-tempered old abbess was even concealing them, though she had seemed truthful enough when she had told Fulk they were gone, adding spitefully, "May you get more joy of the stubborn wench than I did." If she was lying to him, Fulk swore, he'd tear the convent—and its abbess—apart.

Alouette heard the pounding of hoofbeats, the creak of leather, and the jingle of harness that announced the newcomer, but was merely curious until she heard Reyner mutter, "It's Fulk. Tom, help Lady Alouette down and protect her."

"Good morrow, cousin," Reyner greeted him, pleasantly enough.

"Prepare to die, Reyner de Winslade," growled Fulk, drawing his sword.

"Whatever for?" drawled Reyner innocently, though he drew his sword anyway.

"For abducting the Lady Alouette de Chenevy from sanctuary and staining her honor," retorted Fulk, his dark eyes glittering.

"I fear you are mistaken," replied Reyner in a deceptively mild voice, though his face had taken on a hardened cast. "Lady Alouette was being held against her will in that convent, for she had changed her mind and wished to depart. As for the rest of your accusation, 'tis groundless as well. I would wed the Lady Alouette in full honor. 'Tis her wish and my fondest desire."

"You lie, foul dog!"

"Nay, Fulk! Listen to me!" Alouette called from several yards away where Thomas had withdrawn her and Innocentia at his master's orders. "It is as Sir Reyner has said! I love him, and wished to leave the convent!" She would argue with Reyner over the issue of marriage again later; for now, she had to prevent this combat.

"I suggest we postpone this fight, cousin, until your mount is rested, at least," Reyner suggested with maddening sensibility. "He is obviously winded. I would be glad to meet you whenever you choose. Why not in the lists at Messina where King Richard and King Phillip could judge the right?"

Fulk dared not allow his quarry to return to court, of course. His life would not be worth a sou if Phillip lost face as a result of his half sister's accusation of imprisonment and open liaison with Richard's knight. And he himself wanted Alouette so badly. *She has lain with him*, he thought viciously, as he noted the still-swollen lips and the violet shadows beneath her eyes. *Damn the bitch!* She'd suffer for coming to him soiled by another man. But he *would* have her . . .

"Nay, I will kill you here and now, de Winslade. Let us dismount and fight on foot." He suited action to his words, dismounting his lathered charger.

"Very well, but you seem weary as well. Would you like to rest a while? I would not have it said the odds were uneven, Cousin Fulk." Reyner dismounted as he spoke, giving Hercules into Thomas's care.

Reyner's exaggerated reasonableness goaded the Frenchman, as he had known it would.

"*En garde*, de Winslade!"

Alouette was in agony as she waited with her maid and the squire, listening to the clanging of broadswords and the heavy breathing and grunting of the men. She had never been so frustrated at her blindness, for though Tom tried to keep her informed of the combat's progress, the movements were so quick that his eyes could scarcely follow it.

"Fulk is attacking . . . my lord is parrying his thrusts easily. He feints . . ."

"*Who* faints, Tom?" cried Alouette, thinking one of the men was down, but the clanging of swords went on, so Alouette realized that Tom meant a distracting movement.

"My Lord Reyner, Lady Alouette. He draws Fulk off, pretending to go one way, then thrusting in another."

She was terrified, standing there helplessly. There was no doubt that Fulk meant this to be a duel to the death. What would happen to her if her beloved were killed by this man? She would not want to live if Reyner were not alive! She heard a bellow of rage.

"He is hit, my lady!"

"Who is hit?" She felt dizzy with fear.

"Fulk is hit! My lord cut his left arm! He still fights, though, being right-handed . . ."

But the pain, coupled with overwhelming fatigue, slowed Fulk, making him clumsy. He suddenly wished he had taken Reyner at his word, and rested. Reyner would have allowed him an hour . . . But it was too late. He would have to see this through to the finish now, even if it meant his death.

"Sir Reyner is on the attack! He presses Fulk sorely! He

is hit again! He is down! Fulk is down!" cried Thomas exultantly, going to assist his master.

Fulk had received a wound to his right flank. It was not a fatal one, though it bled steadily. He lay on the ground, having pulled off his helm, and stared up with hate-filled eyes. Reyner now had the right to dispatch his opponent; and in his place, Fulk would have killed him before he had time to utter a Paternoster, Reyner realized, staring down at his cousin.

"Kill me and be done with it, cousin," grated Fulk, grimacing in pain.

"Nay, I cannot. We are of the same blood. We could have been friends."

"We want the same woman. We can never be friends."

His words confirmed what Reyner had suspected. For a moment, the bloodlust rose again, but he suppressed it firmly and called over his shoulder to Thomas: "Go down to the monastery and summon the good brothers to carry this scoundrel to their infirmary. Then rejoin us on the road." He turned on his heel after adding to Fulk, "If infection and meanness don't put an end to you, cousin, I hope to see you use your blade against the Saracens yet."

Fulk watched through pain-glazed eyes as Reyner embraced Alouette and remounted, riding off with her and her servant. I have failed, he thought desolately. He'd never dare show his face to Phillip of France again. But he'd have Alouette de Chenevy someday. Oh yes, even if he had to make a pact with Saladin himself, Alouette would be his.

The rest of the journey passed without incident, and they arrived at the outskirts of Messina at noon on the fourth day.

"I am taking you directly to Mategriffon," Reyner informed Alouette as he directed their path around, rather than through the city. "I want you safe in Richard's keeping before Phillip ever learns you're back."

"Reyner, what of Ermengarde?" Alouette asked a trifle guiltily. If it hadn't been for her faithful old tirewoman, she might still be languishing as a prisoner in the convent. She had hardly spared her a thought, preoccupied as she had been with the threat that Fulk had posed, and then caught up in the new delights of love. She worried that Ermengarde would be jealous, perhaps, of Innocentia, who was proving invaluable as a lady's maid. She was younger, and her fingers were nimbler, her eyes better, her reactions quicker. Alouette would not hurt the old woman's feelings for the world, however. Reyner had told her as they traveled of Ermengarde's change of heart regarding himself, which made Alouette even surer of her own decision to give herself to the English knight. She would have to caution Innocentia to be extremely diplomatic in her first dealings with the old retainer.

"I will send for Ermengarde," Reyner promised her. "Right now, our first concern must be to talk to King Richard about you."

They found Richard in a genial mood, lounging on a couch, listening to Blondel at his feet playing the lute. Reyner thought he had seen Richard hastily withdraw his hand from where it had been caressing the minstrel's neck, but he could not be sure.

Briefly, he reported what had taken place in Palermo, including the duel with Fulk de Langres and the reasons for Alouette's reluctance to return to the French court.

"I see," said Richard pensively, stroking his beard. "I think you did as well as possible under the circumstances. Perhaps 'twould have been safer to kill the whoreson— saving your presence, Lady Alouette," he added hastily, "but I understand why you did not. I don't blame your lady for not wanting to return to...Phillip," Richard said, catching himself just in time. "We had best conduct the betrothal ceremony as soon as possible, to forestall any hypocritical hysteria from Phillip regarding milady's honor."

"*Betrothal?* But I can't..." Alouette began in protest, but stopped in confusion, hectic color staining her cheeks. How could she explain her reluctance to Richard when she didn't fully understand it herself?

"Cannot what?" Richard looked to Reyner for illumination.

"My lady has certain . . . ah, maidenly reservations about the wedded state," Reyner temporized, not wanting to embarrass Alouette further. He did, however, give the monarch a meaningful wink.

Richard studied his handsome vassal and the lovely, blushing blind woman, and was not fooled for a moment. He'd wager his soul Reyner had already made her his, and that Alouette had enjoyed every bit of it.

"Do you love him, Lady Alouette?" he asked with sudden bluntness.

"I? Ah . . . yes," she stammered, the flush becoming more pronounced.

"And you're not precontracted? Nor have you taken the veil?"

"Nay, Your Grace."

"Will your brother Henri consent, do you think?"

Alouette felt as if she were being swept along by a whirlwind. "I believe so, Your Grace, unless he feels too threatened by King Phillip, his liege lord."

"Ah! Then it's Phillip I shall have to persuade," Richard chuckled, already enjoying the thought of forcing the fat French king to do something disagreeable.

"But Your Grace—" began Alouette, not knowing what she should say, but feeling obliged to voice her objections somehow. However, a sharp elbow from Reyner just then (his motion hidden by the folds of her cloak) warned her not to speak.

"Yes?"

"Oh . . . 'twas nothing, Your Grace. I . . . will await your direction . . . and thank you." She curtseyed gracefully, and allowed Reyner to lead her away.

He found her a tiny chamber, no mean feat in the crowded wooden fortress, and would have left to summon her maid, but Alouette placed a slender, detaining hand on his wrist.

"Reyner, you must explain to the king somehow—you know we cannot be betrothed!" she said, worry coloring her voice.

"I know no such thing, Alouette," her lover answered firmly. "Foolish love, how long do you think Phillip would let you remain in my company without at least a betrothal to preserve your good name? You would have no choice but to rejoin the French court." Once again he was frustrated by her apparent willingness to be labeled his mistress rather than marry him, simply because of some mistaken notion of her worth.

"*Never* will I go back under Phillip's roof," she vowed, shuddering.

"Then agree to the betrothal. A betrothal is not a wedding, Alouette. You could say we were waiting until we could be wed in Jerusalem—or whenever you choose. But meanwhile we could be together. You *do* want to be with me, don't you, sweetheart?" His voice was caressing and persuasive as he took her into his arms, his warm breath on her neck causing little thrills of excitement to race down her spine. It was hard to think when he did that . . . except of the delightful nights they had had on the journey back to Messina as he instructed her further in the arts of love . . .

"Yes," she sighed, and was rewarded with an encouraging hug.

"Excellent. I'll have Innocentia come to you now, and send for Ermengarde. I probably won't see you until we sup, you know. Richard doubtless feels he's allowed me to play the lover long enough, and will have a dozen things for me to do."

For his part, Reyner considered her agreement to the betrothal a victory, even if she accepted it as a means of staying out of Phillip's hands. Though easier to dissolve than a marriage, betrothal was still a legally binding tie. Perhaps he would have to accustom Alouette to the idea of marrying him in gradual steps, but marry him she would.

Richard waited no longer than the next morning to confront Phillip. Bored with lounging around, waiting for the winter to pass, he approached the palace as eager as if he were going to attempt a passage-at-arms with Saladin himself. He had considered briefly taking Reyner with him; he would have spent another year in Hell to see Phillip blanch at the sight of the knight he'd ordered assassinated. Richard hoped he'd get the chance to do unto Fulk de Langres as Phillip would have done unto Reyner. Richard had temporarily forgotten his Christmastide repentance.

When he was shown into the throne room where Phillip Capet lounged comfortably against plump cushions, sharing a game of chess with Tancred, he stood in the entrance a moment, watching them, before he allowed himself to be announced. Phillip had grown fatter than ever during this inactive winter, Richard thought with distaste. He was aware that he himself presented a startling contrast: well over six feet tall, flesh kept lean by constant exercise, even in pleasurable Sicily.

Phillip and Tancred affected to be pleased to see him. Richard smiled tolerantly, sure that they had been plotting or gossiping about him before he interrupted their play.

"My lord, I have some news," he said suddenly, cutting through the pleasantries. Rapidly he told Phillip of how his vassal, Reyner de Winslade, had "happened" upon Lady Alouette de Chenevy in a Palermo convent, found that she was being kept there an unwilling prisoner, and had returned with her to Messina.

"Now Phillip," Richard went on reasonably, "I am sure you were unaware that your little troubador had changed her mind about staying in the convent. Perhaps the abbess had become overzealous, hoping for a rich dowry. But, in any case, my knight loves the lady and wishes to wed her."

Richard enjoyed watching the rapid progression of emotions over Phillip's fleshy face: surprise, irritation, rage.

"Never! Never will my . . . my minstrel marry an Englishman!" Phillip sputtered.

"He's Norman, actually—speaks French just as you do," countered Richard with maddening logic. "Very few English are anything but serfs or clerks."

"I do not care to be educated about that damned foggy island," gritted Phillip, neck veins bulging dangerously above his furred collar. "He can't have her."

"Surely that is up to her *brother*," Richard suggested, baiting him further. "She is but your troubador."

"The Comte de Chenevy is my vassal."

"And will do as you say. *Certainement*. I would expect no less of my own. But I draw the line at sending a man of mine out to *murder*, my lord."

"Murder? What do you mean?" stammered the French king, his face suddenly as white as the ermine of his collar.

"You know very well I mean the *Sieur* de Langres, Phillip." Richard stepped closer to the seated monarch until he towered over him like an avenging angel. He was enjoying himself immensely. "I thought you'd appreciate knowing that he failed miserably. If he recovers from his wounds, I should see that he doesn't show his treacherous face around me, if I were you."

"My knight's quarrel with yours is a personal matter between them," Phillip said stubbornly. "I am a Christian king soon to be fighting the infidel. I do not deal in murder."

Richard's blazing blue eyes revealed what he thought of that particular bit of self-righteous hypocrisy.

"As you say, Your Majesty. Therefore, I am sure you will agree to this betrothal."

"You can't blackmail me, Richard," Phillip said, his voice becoming strident.

Richard darted a glance at Tancred. The dwarf king was watching this verbal duel with intense interest, alert to any advantage to himself. Richard knew he could be counted on to throw in his lot with whichever side was stronger.

"Nay, that was hardly blackmail, Phillip. *This* is blackmail: Remember those six vessels of which I made you a present only yesterday, *Your Majesty*? The two roundships and four galleys? I'd hate to have to withdraw them, but I will, unless you allow the betrothal."

Phillip's black eyes cursed him, but he said only, "Very well, Richard, but surely you would allow me an audience with my si—with my troubador, before the ceremony."

Richard's grin told Phillip he had noticed the slip. "But, of course. The ceremony will take place in Reginald de Moyac's chapel tomorrow. Come a little early. I know you want to give Lady Alouette your best wishes—and your temporary farewells."

"Temporary farewells?"

Richard savored Phillip's blank look before loosing his final shaft. "Yes, I've decided Alouette would serve best as Berengaria's lady-in-waiting. I've had word my intended bride has reached Naples with my mother. She'll be in need of ladies, and Alouette would fill the post admirably. It's quite an honor, you know."

Phillip looked a likely candidate for apoplexy. "Richard, you're not free to be betrothed! You're still affianced to Alais!"

Richard, who had been heading for the door, turned around for a moment. "My lord, I've told you time and again I will not marry your sister. She was my father's mistress. Berengaria is to be my bride."

"Then return Alais and her dowry."

"You can have Alais. The Vexin remains with me. Calm yourself, Phillip, or you'll never survive to fight Saladin." With that parting bolt, he left Phillip.

SEVENTEEN

Alouette waited alone in a small anteroom off the chapel of the Sicilian nobleman Reginald de Moyac for her audience with her royal half brother. Her heart quailed within her at the thought of putting herself within striking range of that adder again, despite Reyner's assurances that Phillip could do nothing to harm her.

"Don't let him make you feel guilty," Reyner had encouraged her. "I'll be waiting for you in the chapel, my beautiful love."

She concentrated on his words, remembering also the admiring remarks of Innocentia, as she had dressed her in the sky-blue velvet gown with its golden girdle and matching fur-lined cloak. Innocentia had let Alouette's hair hang loose and cascade about her slender shoulders in a midnight cloud, confined only by a gold circlet encrusted with pearls.

"Ah, my lady!" the Lombard girl had cried. "You are as beautiful as the statue of the Virgin in the Cathedral of San Giovanni!"

Alouette had hushed her maid, cautioning her against blasphemy, but the compliments pleased her, and assured her that she would indeed be beautiful in Reyner's eyes. Innocentia had informed her that her soon-to-be-betrothed was as handsome as any prince, clothed in a creamy velvet tunic with matching hose and scarlet shoes, all provided by his generous liege lord, Richard.

She smiled at her servant's extravagant praise. Innocentia always saw Reyner through a haze of hero worship, Alouette thought.

The door to the anteroom creaked on its hinges. A draft of cold air eddied about Alouette's ankles. She knew before he said anything that Phillip had arrived.

"Well! You look very comely for one who once aspired to wear only the humble robes of a nun." Phillip's voice was laced with contempt, which stung in spite of her resolve not to let him hurt her.

"Thank you, Your Majesty."

"'Thank you, Your Majesty,'" he mimicked cruelly. "You conniving traitor! You had me convinced you were so chaste and holy, and then you pant like a bitch in heat for my enemy's vassal! An Englishman! Tell me, Alouette, do the English fornicate as well as Frenchmen?"

"I wouldn't know," she said, fighting desperately to maintain her dignity. "Please, Phillip, I did not do this to hurt you, I swear. I feel no disloyalty to you or France. Reyner is a good man, and I love him. It just happens he is Richard's vassal!"

Phillip fought down the pangs of conscience that urged him to let her find her happiness. Certainly, she had suffered a great injury because of him. But he'd repented long ago, hadn't he? Alouette was of his blood, which made her his. What was Phillip's stayed Phillip's.

"Very well—the betrothal may take place," he said, ignoring the hurt in her eyes as he prepared to inflict greater pain. "Your brother—ah, *step*brother—waits to sign the agreement. Do you love Henri, Alouette?"

"Love Henri? Of course." *Why was Phillip asking that?* "He has always been good to me, as if he were in truth my brother."

"Then you wouldn't want anything to happen to him, *would you, Alouette?*"

"What do you mean?" she whispered, fear forming like a cold icy ball in her belly.

"Merely that I believe your protestations of loyalty to France, and I am France, *ma chère*. I know you would still wish to serve us, even though you are to marry an enemy."

"I thought our enemy was the infidel, Phillip, not fellow Christians," she pointed out stoutly.

"Don't expect me to believe you are such a fool, Alouette!" Phillip snapped. "Richard intends France no good, nor ever shall. But you will be my eyes—or at least, my ears—in Richard's household."

"You want me to spy for you?" she gasped at his effrontery. "Nay, I won't do it!"

"You will, if you want Henri de Chenevy to remain alive," he said, as casually as if he were discussing the January weather. "Refuse me, and there are a dozen ways he can meet his end in Outremer—and any of them could be blamed upon the Saracens."

"You . . . you demon!" she exclaimed, backing away from him in horror.

"Softly, *ma soeur*, softly. Your betrothed and the witnesses are just outside the door. I'd hate to have to renege on my agreement. Just furnish me with regular reports about Richard's doings and his plans concerning the Navarrese wench—congratulations on your appointment as her lady, by the by—and your brother remains hale and hearty. Of course, Henri is to know nothing of our little chat, Alouette."

"Of course." She did not have a choice. Spy for Phillip, or her stepbrother would be killed. She knew she would be privy through Reyner to all sorts of information that Phillip could use. And if Reyner ever found out he loved a spy, his love would turn to hate. Phillip had planned this trap very neatly. Her mind scurried through a maze of thoughts like a frightened mouse, but she could find no answer.

"Very well, Phillip," she said stiffly. "You leave me no choice."

"You are wise, sister," Phillip said silkily, and would have left her, but she called him back as he reached the door.

"Your Majesty, where is Ermengarde, my tirewoman? We have sent for her, but all the squire receives are polite evasions."

"Ermengarde . . ." he said, as if trying to place the name. "Ah, the old woman! I am sorry. She was not well after you left. And after she came to talk to me . . . well, she just faded away. She died in her sleep."

Ermengarde . . . dead! The thought hit with the force of a falling ceiling beam. She couldn't even cry. Alouette realized then that the old tirewoman had stood as a mother to her, indeed, had loved her with a mother's love. Alouette stood there for a moment, swaying like a sapling in a strong wind, as the rest of Phillip's words penetrated her shocked brain.

"Came to talk to you?" she asked. "What did Ermengarde have to talk to you about, Your Majesty?"

He wished she wouldn't train those limpid blue eyes on him like that, even though she couldn't see. The momentary pang of guilt her gaze caused within him was enough to make his voice falter just enough. "Talk to me?" he repeated stupidly. "Why . . . ah . . . many things. She longed to know if I had heard from you, for example. She was old, Alouette, and not strong . . ."

Suddenly she knew what had happened. His tone was too hearty, too forced. "You had her arrested and questioned, didn't you? You found out somehow that Reyner was looking for me, and you wanted to find out how he knew I was still here. Murderer!" she accused, retreating from him again.

"Nay, *ma soeur*! I never touched her, nor did any of my men, I swear it! I merely asked her if she had told Reyner. How was I to know her heart was so weak?" he protested, but the knowledge that the old woman's heart had failed her when he had threatened various unpleasant means of extracting the truth stole conviction from his voice.

"And *you* are the leader of a Christian cause," Alouette mocked. Yet what she knew was not enough to save her from Phillip's demands, she realized. Phillip was the king of France, armed in his divine right, and no one would bring about his fall merely because of the circumstances surrounding the death of a frail old woman. Henri was still in jeopardy unless she complied and became a spy in Richard's household. Reyner must never find out, or she would surely lose him.

* * *

Reyner and Alouette, accompanied by Thomas, Innocentia, four men-at-arms, and of course Zeus, departed Sicily the next morning, crossing the narrow Strait of Messina just as the late winter sun was beginning to dance off the sparkling azure water. They would travel up the province of Calabria, the toe of the Italian boot, and into Campania, stopping at Salerno before going on to Naples.

"Why Salerno?" questioned Alouette, standing out on the deck of the galley below the forecastle. The way Reyner had said "Salerno" indicated it was significant.

"It is the best medical school in the Christian world," Reyner answered her, excitement tingeing his voice. "Perhaps they can cure your blindness, Alouette."

The deck seemed to sway alarmingly beneath her feet. "Cure?" she reiterated, not believing she had heard him aright. "Oh, my love, I don't know . . . I've been blind for years. What makes you think—"

"I think it possible because of that flash of vision you had that night with me. Surely, if your affliction were permanent and absolute, that could not have happened?" The anticipation in his voice was painful; she must not let him hope and be disappointed.

"My father took me to all the best physicians of the time, Reyner. King Phillip even called in a Jew. They tried everything from poultices made of mares' milk to infusions of powdered unicorn's horn. Nothing cured me."

"Salerno is famed throughout Europe, sweetheart. Perhaps the doctors there can do more than the court physicians. There may have been some new treatment devised. It would be a shame to pass through without consulting them—without trying." His arm about her shoulder gave her a little encouraging squeeze, as if to say he knew how afraid she was to hope, after resigning herself to a world of darkness for so many years.

"But what about Queen Eleanor and Princess Berengaria? Surely we must not leave them waiting in Naples . . ."

"Naples is a pleasant enough port," Reyner said. "You must learn to think of yourself first on occasion, my Alouette. If you must stay in Salerno any great length of time, I will go on to their graces and come for you on the way back."

It seemed he had thought of everything. How could she object? She could not begin to verbalize the anxiety that ran through her at the thought of seeing again. Since childhood her blindness had been a shield against the world. Would she be able to live the life of a normal woman of her station, or would the demands be more than she could fulfill? Would Reyner think less of her then?

Worse yet—and more likely—what if this were one more source of disappointment? When she had first become blind, she had let herself believe, with each new physician who examined her, that *this* would be the one who would make her see again. After a while she dreaded the coming of each new man of medicine, for it became harder to overcome the crushing disappointment as each man tried his potions, unguents, charms, and treatments, and she was left in darkness.

It was too much to bear, on top of the weight of the grief she felt for Ermengarde—a grief mingled with rage at Phillip and a feeling that she was in some way responsible for the old woman's death. If she hadn't refused to let her accompany her to the convent, Ermengarde would still be alive. Phillip would pay someday, somehow, for his sin against her dear old nurse, she swore.

Demetrius, a spare, lean-limbed Greek physician, lifted his hands from Alouette's face and smiled deprecatingly.

"I am afraid there is nothing we can do that has not already been done by my learned colleagues in Paris." He sighed. "I suppose you have already prayed to the patron saints of the eye, my lady—Brigit, Triduana, Lucia?"

Alouette nodded.

Reyner turned anguished eyes on the man clad in black flowing robes which bore, embroidered at intervals around his neck, the insignia of a snake curled about a staff. "But sir," Reyner protested. "She has had a flash of vision. Surely that would indicate that her blindness is not incurable!"

"From my examination, I can tell you there is nothing

functionally wrong with the eye. I can detect no apparent reason for the blindness. But blind she is."

"I was told Salerno is the best medical school in the world!" Frustration colored Reyner's voice.

"In the *Christian* world," the Greek corrected gently. "Though our school is open to persons of any faith—indeed, we were founded by a Jew, a Latin, an Arab, and a Greek—yet, we have not the skill of the great physicians in the Muslim world. Ah, the things I have heard of the great hospitals of Cairo and Baghdad! Here we have made many great discoveries, too—we take the pulse, we examine the urine, we teach the importance of diet, we have discovered the formula of a draught for pain so effective that we can open a man and he sleeps on undisturbed—" He saw that the English knight was becoming impatient. "But you did not come to hear of the glories of Salerno. My advice to you, since you are going to the lands where the faith of Mohammed holds sway, is to seek the counsel of a physician of Islam."

"How can I allow the hands of an infidel to touch her? They are the enemies of Christ," Reyner protested.

"A physician is no man's enemy," reproved the old Greek. "You must open your hearts and minds as you journey to Outremer. You may find that those you count as allies are enemies, and those you thought inimical seek only peace." His words were hard for the young knight to accept, he knew. "The Arabs, I have heard, have become skilled in treating disorders of the eye . . . and the mind."

Reyner, who had been studying the sparsely furnished examining room, whirled on the Greek, hand on his sword hilt, eyes lit with a dangerous glint.

"Are you implying that Lady Alouette's mind is not sound?"

"Not at all, my lord," Demetrius said in calm tones. "I merely admit that there is much we physicians do not know about the connection of the mind with the physical organs; in this case, the eyes. But be open, I beg you, to those who could help your lady."

Demetrius could see the beautiful, ebony-haired noblewoman was as shocked by the idea of consulting a Mohammedan physician as her handsome knight was. He bid them farewell with a smile, not at all discouraged. They loved one another; and where there was love, there was always hope. He had learned a certain acceptance of fate—*kismet*, as his Arab colleagues called it. If the blind Frenchwoman was meant to find her sight again, she would. If not, well, she nevertheless had the obvious devotion of her stalwart knight. He watched admiringly as Alouette picked up the strap affixed to the back of the huge wolf-mastiff, and walked as gracefully out the portals of the medical school as any sighted person.

EIGHTEEN

Reyner had feared that Alouette would be depressed after their disappointing visit to the school of medicine, but he found that she was determined to look forward instead to their coming encounter with the legendary Eleanor of Aquitaine, dowager queen of England, and Richard's prospective bride, Berengaria of Navarre.

"Just imagine," Alouette said of Eleanor as they strolled the streets of old Salerno. "She must be in her sixties, and yet she just crossed the Alps to bring her son his bride!"

"She is a formidable woman," agreed Reyner, remembering the amazingly vital woman Richard had sent him to meet the year before, after she had left her castle prison.

"And Berengaria—I wonder what she is like," Alouette continued. "I cannot picture myself journeying across half the world to wed a man I met only once, years ago."

"Such is the lot of princesses. Let us pray she is patient," Reyner said cryptically, thinking of Richard's proclivities and hoping fervently that the Navarrese princess would be the key to change. England needed an heir. If Richard died without issue, life under King John would be awful indeed.

They walked on in a companionable silence, Alouette on Reyner's arm, which left Zeus free to investigate interesting sights and smells.

"Reyner," Alouette said suddenly, breaking into his reverie. "When I am Berengaria's lady-in-waiting, I suppose I shall be at her call, perhaps even have to sleep near her?"

"I suppose so. My mother did, as Queen Eleanor's attendant. But 'twas not every night, love. Doubtless she will have other ladies as well, and the duty will be rotated."

"God send that you are right," she said with relief. "I am pleased to be chosen as Berengaria's lady, but I couldn't bear it if we were always to be apart at night!" She lifted her lovely face toward him invitingly as they paused in a dark archway.

He obliged her, kissing her with growing hunger, molding her body to his hard one, feeling the ache within him matched by the ardor of her embrace. He had been astonished and pleased by the enthusiasm with which she had learned to welcome his lovemaking and initiate it on her own. It was hard to believe that only weeks ago she had been determined to be a nun and forgo the love between a man and a woman.

His caresses grew bolder, encouraged by the growing dusk that hid them. It was not until Zeus barked at some passers-by that they were brought back to reality.

"Are we far from the inn?" Alouette sighed, breaking the contact with reluctance, her face flushed.

"Nay, love. Are you tired?" Reyner asked, thinking the disappointments of the day might have wearied his Lark.

"It's not that. I confess I want you, beloved—I need to be alone with you, tonight, now, for after we reach Naples I shall be at Berengaria's beck and call. Does that make me a shameless wanton?"

He loved the way her eyes shone, the way her lips, luminous with his kisses, smiled mischievously.

"Yes, shameless," he said with a husky laugh. "But, tell me, what will you do when you're alone with me?" he teased.

She pulled him close so that he could hear her husky whisper. "When we get to our chamber, I will kiss you until your knees grow weak," she began in conscious parody of his seductive speech the night she had first given herself to him, "and I will strip off your tunic, then your shirt and chausses . . . and lay you down on our bed, as naked as God made you, and kiss you all over, until you are trembling and hot with the need of me . . . but I will not let you take me yet. Oh no," she said, smiling as he groaned in a torment that was only partially pretended, "no, first I will—" She found she could not even say the words aloud, but stood on tiptoe to whisper in his ear of the delights she would inflict on him—delights he had taught her for their mutual pleasure. She had been a most willing pupil.

They reached Naples by late afternoon on the following day and went to the monastery where the two queens were staying. After taking time to bathe and change their travel-stained garments, Reyner and Alouette were shown to the apartments occupied by Eleanor and Berengaria.

The rooms were luxurious, in spite of the fact that they were in a monastery. Obviously the good monks were used to receiving important visitors. Tapestries lined the walls, depicting religious scenes in somber colors. Tiles arranged in a colorful mosaic lay beneath their feet, while in front of the fire two woman waited, a thick Oriental rug cushioning their slipper-clad feet against the chill.

Reyner led Alouette a little way into the room, then bowed, his gesture warning Alouette to drop into a deep, graceful curtsey.

"Rise, Reyner of Winslade, and let me look at you," a husky voice called warmly. "It has been too long. And bring the Demoiselle de Chenevy close to these old eyes as well."

How animated and beautiful this legendary woman still was, old though she might be. It was the eyes, Reyner decided. Even though the brow beneath the snow-white wimple was furrowed with wrinkles, the glowing jade-green eyes lit Eleanor's face, imparting a vibrant glow to her entire countenance.

"Greetings, Reyner, you young rascal. You took the devil of a time arriving here to escort us!" she scolded affectionately, sighing as he bent to kiss her hand. "I do believe you're more handsome than your father, with your dear mother's Poitevin eyes! And betrothed to this lovely thing, I hear," she said, turning to Alouette. "Come closer, my dear—I won't bite. Ah, no wonder no English girls were good enough! She's enchanting, Reyner."

As her betrothed murmured polite thanks, Alouette felt her hand being clasped by a thin, cool, gnarled one—a hand that was at once strong and soft as silk. Eleanor smelled of roses. Alouette wondered if Berengaria was in the room, for thus far only Eleanor had spoken.

"You have lately come from Phillip's court," Eleanor went on, still holding her hand, as if to substitute for the link that could not be made by their eyes. "Tell me, how does the young king-who-might-have-been-my-son, had I stayed married to that monk Louis?" she asked dryly.

"He . . . was well when I left him, *ma dame*, though he chafes to go to Outremer," Alouette said, unsure of how Eleanor felt about him. She was reluctant to discuss King Phillip, even though she assumed Eleanor did not know of their secret kinship. She would have been astonished to know that the aging queen did know she was Louis's daughter; little escaped Eleanor's information-gathering network.

"'Well' when you left him—ha! That means he's fat and lecherous as ever, I suppose! I'll warrant he's as anxious to go on crusade as a courtesan to wear a hair shirt! But enough of that, *mes enfants*. I have the honor of presenting Berengaria of Navarre, my son's affianced bride."

There was a rustle of clothing as the princess, who had been content to watch the byplay between her future mother-in-law, Reyner, and Alouette, extended a hand diffidently for Reyner to kiss.

Reyner's first thought, as she turned to greet Alouette, was *Saints, Richard will eat her for breakfast and swallow her without chewing*. She was pretty, or could be if she were not dressed so severely. One hoped the dove-gray robes she wore now were a concession to traveling, and would go to the bottom of her coffer when she had met her royal bridegroom. Richard, with his preference for the arts of war over the ways of heterosexual love, needed to be dazzled by a handsome woman who dressed in bright colors—a strong woman. She'd have to be, to compete with the firm hold Eleanor already had on Richard's heart.

He saw the goodness shining in Berengaria's limpid gray eyes, and his heart sank within him. His king would make her miserable unless she changed, he thought.

Reyner was relieved to see nothing in the dowager queen's demeanor to indicate other than approval of her son's choice of bride. If Berengaria had Eleanor's backing, that would count for much with the Lionheart.

"Tell me, Sir Reyner, may we depart on the morrow for Messina?" Berengaria asked eagerly. "How fares my lord? Did he send any messages for me?"

Reyner was forced to make polite excuses for his liege, pleading the press of preparations for departure to Palestine, but he damned Richard for the necessary lie. The Lionheart had not thought to send so much as a brief note or some token gift, yet he had written Eleanor a long and affectionate letter. He'd have to see if he could present the missive to Eleanor privately. Berengaria would experience hurt soon enough.

She brightened when he said that they could indeed leave at dawn the next day. "Oh, it is so *good* of you to be willing to depart again so soon after your long journey! I am eager to make my lord's acquaintance again!" A happy flush animated an olive complexion grown pale after months away from sunny Navarre.

Eleanor's eyes met Reyner's. Hers were troubled in their green depths, reflecting the dismay he felt.

Berengaria's maidenly eagerness was to be frustrated. Before they reached the tip of the peninsula, the traveling party was met by a peremptory message from Tancred, forbidding them entrance into Sicily. They were to stay, it directed, in Tancred's comfortable castle in Brindisi until summoned.

"We'll see about that!" snapped Eleanor. "I've not journeyed halfway around the world to be kept from my son and daughter by a dwarf. Send a message to Richard—*he'll* overrule that bastard usurper."

But Richard's reply, when it came, directed Eleanor and Berengaria to remain at Brindisi. No explanation was offered, no softening of the harsh order, no information as to when their separation would end. Again there was no private love note from the bridegroom-to-be. Richard did, however, inform them he was sending Joanna to them.

The old queen was cheered at the mention of her favorite daughter. "That will be nice. It's so long since I've seen Joanna. And you'll see, my dear," she comforted the crestfallen Berengaria, "Richard will come visit us here. Apparently he has to placate Tancred—and likely, Phillip—but he won't be able to resist coming to see his affianced bride."

There was an order included in the packet for Reyner, which commanded him to return to Messina immediately, and hinted of trouble with Tancred and Phillip.

Alouette had been trying to steel herself for this moment. She knew she could not expect the English king to leave one of his most trusted warriors dancing attendance on a woman's household, even a royal one. Parting from her lover for an indefinite time was hard, particularly since she was being left alone (except for Innocentia) among people who were still relative strangers to her. She resolved to put on a brave face, however, for she reasoned that the crusading armies would inevitably be leaving for the Holy Land soon.

Reyner arrived back in Messina in time to be among the king's escort to Catania, midway down the eastern coast, where Richard had scheduled a meeting with Tancred. Apparently the dwarf king had decided that Richard was the monarch to favor, for he offered him lavish gifts of gold, silver, expensive cloth, and fabulous horses during a three-day celebration.

Richard, not to be outdone in chivalrous generosity, refused all gifts but that of a small ring "in token of friendship," and presented the diminutive monarch a sword which he asserted was the famous Excalibur of King Arthur.

Reyner heard a disgusted clucking nearby and turned to see the earl of Leicester shaking his head cynically at the grandiose gestures being made on the dais.

"Richard has no great reverence for English things; but

even if he had Arthur's actual weapon, he'd not dare give away a relic so sacred to the English people—especially to that upstart." The earl appeared just to be venting his feelings to a convenient ear, but then he said, "Reyner, did you hear about the Lionheart's confrontation with your friend des Barres? It's quite the subject of gossip in Messina."

Reyner had not, of course, having had only enough time to rest his destrier and gather his gear before departing with his liege's retinue.

"While you were gone," the earl began, clearly delighted to have a chance to recite the scandalous tale to a new pair of ears, "a few of us rode out on Candlemas Day, including three Frenchmen, to do some hawking. We found little game on this rocky island worth our loosing the birds, but on the road we met a Lombard carrying a cartload of bulrushes. Richard was bored, and bought a handful, decreeing that a mock joust take place on the spot, French against English."

It sounded like a typical whim of the Lionheart, and not one without covert malice, for Richard was always eager to prove his superiority over the French.

"He commanded that des Barres ride against him, for he declared the Frenchman in his debt for breaking his parole when held by Richard in some previous battle. However, the mood of all was so merry that William was agreeable and charged, splintering Richard's lance easily. Well, you *know* the unpredictable Angevin temper," the earl went on, rolling his eyes as he referred to Richard's most terror-inspiring fault. "He charged des Barres before the young knight even had the chance to recover, but failed to unseat him, and his own saddle slipped. By this time he was in fury, and would listen to none of us. I expected him to start pounding on the ground and chewing the grass, as old Henry did before him! I tried to calm him, but he pushed me from my mount and charged William again! He never did unseat des Barres, and ended by screaming at him, 'Get you hence, and take heed that we see you no more, for you and I are henceforth enemies forever.' He's demanding that des Barres leave Sicily and go home, Reyner."

"Poor William," murmured Reyner, thoroughly in sympathy with his friend, apparently the latest victim of a Plantagenet temper tantrum. "I wonder if it would help if I interceded for him?"

"Nay, I doubt it—the best of France's chivalry have gone down on their knees before our sovereign, but Richard is adamant. He wouldn't even listen to Phillip."

Reyner glanced back at the dais, where the high-flown speeches were still going on. "Where is William now?"

"I know not—only that he had to leave Messina. King Phillip would not support his vassal in the face of the Lionheart's wrath."

Reyner gave a cynical laugh. "I wonder when Richard will stop fighting fellow Christians and depart to fight the Infidel..." Such comments were a common refrain on everyone's lips.

A general buzzing, signifying that something important had taken place, caused him to ask Hubert Walter, the king's military aide, what he had missed.

"Tancred finally offered something Henry wanted," the stout Englishman chuckled. "Richard's just been given four roundships and fifteen galleys. The man must be desperate to get us off his island!"

From Catania they traveled back up the coastal road toward Taormina, where Richard was to meet Phillip. On the way there, however, Tancred produced a letter sent to him by Phillip.

Reyner watched his sovereign's face purple as he read the parchment. "How dare he, the whoreson?" Richard grated, when he could speak at last. The entire horseback procession stopped in its tracks on the dusty road. For a moment Richard looked as if he would crush the vellum to powder, then evidently thought better of it, for he carefully put the letter into the saddlebag.

"What is it, sire?" Hubert Walter asked carefully, and all held their breaths.

"My 'fellow crusader' King Phillip names me a 'traitor who would not keep faith with anyone,' and offers France's assistance to Tancred if he should desire to attack me by night! I can hardly believe it!" The blond giant was shaken as he turned his azure gaze on Tancred, who rode beside him. "My thanks, King Tancred. I am in your debt for this revelation."

"It was my duty to my friend Richard of England," Tancred said piously, eyes downcast, but Reyner did not miss the sly gleam of triumph in them at his successful mischief-making.

Suddenly Richard raised his hand, pointing to a fork in the road that ran slightly westward. "Can we reach Messina by that road?" he asked the dwarf king.

"Eventually . . . but it's not the most direct route. The quickest way is the coastal road, through Taormina."

"I'll not meet that scoundrel Phillip," sputtered Richard. "If I saw him now I would run him through. I have to think what to do. We return to Messina!"

Richard snubbed Phillip the next day when the French king rode up to Richard's headquarters. All innocence, Phillip pressed the issue, until Richard finally produced the incriminating document and waved it in his face, his own florid features flushed a dull red with righteous anger.

Reyner had to admire the French king's nerve as he blustered that the letter was a forgery, even though his sudden pallor proclaimed the lie.

"You created this yourself, Richard," accused Phillip.

Richard's mouth dropped open at the other's audacity.

"I? What need have *I* of forging letters full of perfidy, Your Majesty?" he inquired, his lip curling at the ridiculousness of the charge.

"It's just another excuse not to do the honorable thing and marry my sister Alais."

"I'd not marry my father's whore, even if my overlord were the Pope himself!" thundered Richard, his wrath kindling at this familiar refrain.

And so it went. Reyner, wearied of the intrigue and conflict that had punctuated the boring months of waiting for the spring sailing, daydreamed as the French and English kings continued to hurl charge and countercharge at one another. He thought of Alouette, and wondered what his beloved was doing, and if she longed for the day they could be together again. Did she dream of the nights she had spent in his arms, sighing rapturously as he brought her again and again to the peak of fulfillment? He thought of each one of her perfect features, dwelling in his mind's eye on the perfection of her lush, inviting lips, the ebony wealth of her hair, the rose-tipped breasts that were so exquisitely responsive to his touch, the womanly curve of her hips, and her long, sweetly curved legs.

He felt himself growing hot and hard with the aching need of her and was grateful that he stood behind Richard's high, carved chair, where none could glimpse his embarrassment. He found that he had not missed much while he fantasized. Richard was still producing witnesses to his late father's relationship to Alais of France, and Phillip was still indignant, but willing to be persuaded to drop the matter if Richard would go with him next month when the "March passage" opened up.

Incredibly, Richard declared that not only would he not go in March when Phillip departed, but that he was even considering going back to England for a short time and could not depart until August! Reyner knew that his king had received word of trouble in England, of disputes between Prince John and Longchamp, Richard's chancellor; but it was impossible to believe that Richard would even consider delaying his participation in the crusade longer than he had already. Reyner heartily damned all princes in his heart, thinking that he and Alouette could have seen more of each other had they been serfs in the field at Winslade.

NINETEEN

Though Eleanor had two attendants from England, older women who had been with her throughout her imprisonment, and Berengaria had brought one, Ramona, from Navarre, Alouette quickly became the favorite of the royal household at Brindisi.

There were many small tasks that usually fell to a lady-in-waiting, of course, that Alouette as a blind woman could not do, such as reading from the illuminated manuscripts and books from Tancred's library or assisting Berengaria to dress, but Ramona usually handled these things. Occasionally even Innocentia was pressed into service, though the Sicilian girl was openly awed at serving royal personages when she had not even aspired to being a lady's maid short weeks ago.

The royal women treasured Alouette for her unique musical talent. She spent endless hours playing her lute and the small harp Eleanor had brought with her, singing to them in her clear, pure voice. First she went through her repertoire of French songs, then learned the songs of Aquitaine and Navarre that Eleanor and Berengaria remembered, improvising accompaniment with the great skill that was her gift. Shyly at first, she even included the songs in English that Reyner had taught her, finding the tunes attractive, even though she occasionally stumbled over the strange, guttural sounds of the Saxon tongue. She felt the Navarrese princess should be exposed to the culture of her future subjects.

It was as Berengaria's confidante and sounding board that Alouette proved her greatest value. Once the vivacious Joanna arrived to join their exile, Berengaria had someone of her own age and rank to relate to, but she frequently felt shut out by the Plantagenet mother and daughter. It was not that Eleanor and Joanna meant to make the princess feel that she didn't belong, but they often became caught up in Plantagenet family anecdotes and spoke of things unfamiliar to Berengaria. As a Frenchwoman, Alouette was similarly new to Joanna's childhood memories, but she had met Berengaria's future husband.

She would quiz Alouette for hours about each facet of the Lionheart. Though Alouette could not describe Richard's appearance, Berengaria had little need of that, thanks to the *chansons de geste* which already praised his physical beauty and handsomeness. Berengaria wanted to hear about the subtler things: his voice, the words he chose, the scent he wore, his personality. Berengaria seemed sure that, being sightless, Alouette had some special insights into Richard's soul.

Alouette naturally kept Reyner's misgivings about the English king's character flaws to herself. No sense in piercing the princess's happy bubble of belief that her bridegroom was the epitome of all chivalrous virtues. Perhaps Richard would be so enchanted with his bride that he would rise to the occasion and be all that Berengaria expected, leaving his selfishness, his temper, and his perverse lack of interest in the female sex behind.

Joanna's presence considerably enlivened the little household. She had a quick wit, but unlike her giant of a brother, was never cruel. It was clear that her marriage to the late King William had been happy, and having spent nearly a year in mourning, she was ready again to take on life with customary Plantagenet enthusiasm.

She frankly admitted to Alouette that she had found Reyner of Winslade attractive, but had seen immediately that it would be useless to flirt with him "because he is quite ensorcelled by you, Lady Alouette!"

The blind woman responded modestly to the compliment, thinking it was probably Reyner's winning charm that had caught the Plantagenet widow's interest, and warming to Joanna for her good-naturedness. Many high-born ladies would not have been so sanguine about their failure to win any fellow who appealed to them. Berengaria had described her future sister-by-marriage as auburn-haired, blue-eyed, and breathtakingly lovely, and Alouette did not doubt that Joanna Plantagenet's widowhood would be short.

As the days of March wore on with no royal visitor, Berengaria grew wan and anxious, and Joanna openly peevish in her irritation at their enforced boredom. Eleanor joined in Alouette's efforts to keep them amused, but it was largely in vain.

Then, at the end of the month, as rumors flew around the castle and feminine tempers frayed, the letter bearing the royal seal came.

They were at last bade to join Richard. Phillip would be setting sail on the thirtieth of March, his destination Acre, the besieged city on the coast of Palestine. Richard would escort him out of the harbor, then turn aside to Brindisi to pick up the royal women and their household and take them to Sicily until he, too, was ready to leave for Outremer.

"High time it is, too," grumbled Joanna.

"And high time I went home," Eleanor added tartly. "He has kept me dangling in Sicily long enough. There's no telling what mischief John may get into if I don't hasten back."

Alouette was amused to hear Richard's younger brother being talked about as if he were merely a recalcitrant boy, rather than the dangerous troublemaker he was.

Of the three royal women, only Berengaria's joy was unalloyed. "By the Virgin, I am so happy he is coming at last! Is it possible that the marriage may take place before we depart?" It was a question that none of them could answer. No one could compel Richard Plantagenet to do anything before he was ready.

Alouette had been relieved to hear of Phillip's imminent departure. *Good*, she thought as she sat among the excited women. *Until we also depart and reach Acre, I am free of Phillip.*

She had reckoned without Phillip's cunning. Two evenings before the departure date, Alouette was enjoying a peaceful time alone in the chapel, glad to escape for a short time the frenzied preparations for Richard's coming.

Suddenly she heard stealthy footsteps approaching where she knelt. Perhaps Berengaria had come to join her, for the young woman was more devout than the pleasure-loving Joanna. But no, the footsteps were heavier, more like those of a man. And then she smelled the musky scent that Phillip habitually wore, and knew he knelt next to her.

"Greetings, *ma soeur*. Surprised to see me . . . ahem, I should say, that I am here? Never underestimate me, Alouette—and do not call out. I should not like to meet your new mistresses. They do not know I am here, nor do we want them to, *hein*? Are you enjoying your new post?"

"Yes, Your Majesty," she said through lips gone stiff with fear and resentment. "Their Graces are very kind . . ."

"And the woman who is usurping your half sister Alais's place? Is she kind, too? Are you like a bitch dog that fawns on any new master?" he hissed. His hand shot out and stroked her under the chin as one would stroke a faithful hound, but when she would have wrenched out of his reach, the cold fingers held her firmly.

"When does she expect to wed Coeur de Lion?"

"There has been no date set, Your Majesty," she said, glad it was the truth.

"Nay," Phillip sneered. "Nor has the royal bridegroom been exactly eager to meet his bride, has he? When does he plan to sail?"

"Again, *mon frère le roi*, no date has been mentioned in the letter to Eleanor, Joanna, or Berengaria, at least in any passage that was read aloud."

"*Merde!* You're useless!" he fumed, and smacked the altar railing in frustration.

Alouette waited warily, not knowing if he would strike her or depart. The king of France had another thought.

"But you must have heard from your precious Englishman! When does he say Richard will sail?"

Alouette had indeed heard from Reyner, the letters being read to her in secret by Joanna, to spare Berengaria's feelings.

"If he knows, he has not said."

Sometimes Reyner had mentioned his frustrations at the crusading army's inaction, but his missives were mostly full of love and longing, so poignantly written that Alouette frequently felt tears in her eyes. Joanna had freely admitted her envy, for William had been too ill to be a true husband in the last years of their marriage. It was clear she was glad for Alouette, though.

"Bah!" Phillip grunted in disgust as he arose. "See that you have more to tell me when next we meet. And never assume I won't know if you lie, Alouette. Henri's life depends on you."

The next morning the women stood watching from the crenellated tower as the bay filled with red-crossed sails.

"There—there's Richard's flagship, the *Trenche-Mer*," Joanna said as she pointed to a large dromond whose sail bore a snarling scarlet leopard, the Plantagenet emblem. As they continued watching, trumpeters on the dromond gave a final salute to the French fleet, then the ship came about, heading for Brindisi.

"To think I will actually meet my husband-to-be this morning!" sighed Berengaria, next to Alouette.

The castle held a commanding position above the bay, so the women continued to watch as the majestic, long-prowed ship drew nearer and nearer, until at last Joanna pointed triumphantly. "There! There's my brother Richard, Berengaria!"

"Ah . . . what magnificence!" Berengaria breathed. "Such a warrior's physique, such golden hair."

While Berengaria was rhapsodizing about Richard, Joanna told Alouette that she had also spotted Reyner of Winslade, an easy task because of the massive canine who walked beside him.

Alouette's heartbeat quickened. She felt the reflected glow of Berengaria's excitement, but her own happiness would not be complete until she heard his voice and felt his arms around her. She wondered if there would be a way for them to be together.

She had been astonished at how her body, as well as her heart, had longed for Reyner of Winslade. Once he had made her his, he was like some magic potion that she had to have—her senses clamored and begged. She flushed at the thought, grateful that the others, from their cries and remarks, were apparently still intent on watching the long-boat bearing the king and his retinue to the shore.

Only when the boat had been beached did the ladies go below to the hall, for Eleanor insisted they receive her son "with some semblance of royal dignity, and not as wanton tavern wenches blowing kisses at a soldier's procession."

No wedding took place while the English crusaders remained in Sicily, however, for while Richard had professed himself well-pleased with Berengaria, he pleaded the excuse that it was Lent. "Perhaps it would be most fitting for a leader of the crusade to be wed in Jerusalem," he proposed grandly.

Though Lent was not an absolute barrier, Berengaria said she was pleased her future spouse was such a devout, principled Christian. She passed the days in supreme contentment, enraptured at every small saying of her betrothed, agreeable that they should wed when Richard decreed. Surely, with Richard leading the host, they would be entering the gates of Jerusalem within the month.

Eleanor, however, was not so sanguine. "See that he espouses her speedily," she had commanded Joanna tartly as she left Sicily, only four days after their arrival.

Joanna had promised, but confided in Alouette that the more one pushed Richard, the more he balked, so Berengaria would be better off if no pleading were done.

Only Reyner and Alouette were mutually happy, using whatever hours were free of duties to be together. They spent hours strolling the cobbled, narrow streets of Messina, or riding out into the hilly countryside, enjoying the early Sicilian spring. Whenever Alouette was not attending

Berengaria at night, it was possible for them to have discreet, passionate *rendezvous* in her chamber.

To Alouette, this time was like the calm before the storm. Surely, once the English army reached Outremer, Reyner would be caught up in battling the infidel and she would have to wait as he devoted himself to the holy cause. In these halcyon days the lovers seemed to have tacitly agreed to defer the conflict-ridden subject of marriage until later. Alouette had no idea when Reyner planned to bring it up again—perhaps during the sea voyage, perhaps not until they reached Palestine, or even until the crusaders had conquered the Saracens—but she was certain he had not changed his mind. He expected to marry her. Something in the way he told stories of his family back in England, and of the gray stone keep of Winslade, where he was castellan, told her that he had not abandoned his plan that she would join the family as his lady.

It was inconceivable to Alouette that Reyner would be willing to install her at Winslade as his mistress. Eventually, he would want a legitimate heir. Perhaps he would be agreeable to finding her a small manor house nearby. But she was more and more sure, as he spoke fondly of Earl Simon and Countess Ysabeau, his parents, of his elder brother Aimery and his sisters, Rohese, Nicola, and Blanche, that he must not marry her—a bastard, a woman of tainted blood.

She knew he worried about the possibility of their conceiving a child, and once had even attempted to practice that age-old form of contraception, withdrawing from her just as he was about to spill his seed. Alouette had been on the brink of her own climax, and when she sensed what he would have done, gave a small cry and dug her nails into his back, moaning, "Please, Reyner, please! Don't stop, my love, not now..."

And of course he did not stop, reaching his own peak at that moment and thrusting wildly into her.

It was Innocentia who solved the problem, shyly volunteering to Alouette that she knew of an herbal infusion which, taken regularly by the woman, prevented conception safely. So Alouette dutifully swallowed the bitter brew, gagging at its taste, always with a pang in her heart, for she wanted above all things to have Reyner's child. But it was not fair to make an innocent babe a bastard. She above all should want to avoid bestowing the stain of illegitimacy on another being, she told herself sternly.

TWENTY

"*Mes dames*, I regret to tell you that we have lost sight of the king's ship and the rest of the fleet," Stephen Turnham, captain of the *Mermaid*, said, maintaining an upright stance with difficulty on the pitching, tossing dromond. He brought in with him the scent of rain and sea salt—a welcome change from the stench of vomit and fear that permeated the cramped cabin.

On the bunk beside her, Berengaria moaned. Alouette put a comforting arm around her quaking shoulders, though her own heart was pounding with terror. She could remember only too well her near-drowning in the Rhône. Zeus lay at her feet now, growling uneasily occasionally, but even the huge dog would not be able to save her from a storm at sea. She could think of nothing to do but pray, as she could hear Innocentia doing, and hope that the skull of the sailors on the dromond—and the intervention of the saints—would bring them to safe harbor.

Joanna spoke up with Plantagenet directness. "Where are we, captain?" If she was afraid, it did not show in her voice.

"A few leagues off the southern coast of Cyprus, I believe, my lady. I am hoping to make the harbor of Limassol."

"Pray God that we do, and that my lord is safe also," Berengaria murmured, and Alouette guessed from the motion of her shoulders that she crossed herself.

* * *

They had started out so bravely, three days before. The crusaders' fleet was two hundred ships strong, with Richard's ship, *Trenche-Mer*, at the head of the procession, a lantern burning day and night in its masthead to keep the fleet together. A storm had blown up, however, and now the *Mermaid* was alone at sea.

Alouette had had misgivings about sailing on a different ship from Reyner and his king, but she had kept them to herself, fearing to add to Berengaria's discomfiture at being parted from Richard. She could see the logic of distributing the important passengers—as well as the treasure—on more than one ship; sea travel was feared by all for its hazards. Why risk losing all if one ship was lost? She could only pray that this great ship was as seaworthy as Richard's.

At dawn the *Mermaid* lay at anchor outside Limassol, the ships rocking gently with each swell. As Joanna, Berengaria, and Alouette came on deck, the bright sunshine revealed a scene of stark horror on the shore.

Two other English ships, their red-crossed sails tangled around splintered masts, had run aground ahead of them during the night. Their hulls lay broken on the sharp, jutting rocks of the shore. On the sandy beach lay mounds of sodden cloth, which Joanna realized, after she borrowed a spyglass from the captain, were the drowned bodies of many sailors and passengers. There were more of them floating in the bay, Berengaria noted, gasping. Several figures bent about the still bodies appeared to be concerned with the tragedy at first, but then it became obvious that they were only looting. As they stripped the corpses, ripping off jewelry and pawing the pockets for coins in callous disregard for the dead, Joanna ground her teeth in rage.

"The scoundrels! They shall repay every last penny!"

"Look there!" Berengaria pointed to where the path led from the shore. Several men were being herded at swordpoint toward the port city.

"Survivors! We must rescue them!"

"I'm afraid we will have to wait for reinforcements,

Your Grace," apologized the captain. "We'd be outnumbered, and our men have nothing but short swords suitable for sea battles, and a few clumsy crossbows."

"Then let us sail back out and find Richard!" suggested Joanna confidently.

"Again, I must apologize, but that is not possible. Our mainmast was cracked and the sail torn during the storm. We are not seaworthy. And judging by what we have just seen, we dare not trust the Cypriots to help us."

"Then what—" sputtered Joanna, with the impatience natural to a Plantagenet.

"King Richard will catch up soon," Alouette spoke up, her calm voice surprising the other two women. "We must wait until the *Trenche-Mer* arrives."

In a few hours, however, a ship put out from Limassol harbor, making straight for them.

"Oh, Virgin Mary, protect us!" cried Berengaria. "They're going to board us!"

"Not without a fight!" growled Stephen of Turnham, calling out orders to his sailors to ready their defenses. The women watched from the shelter of the aft castle as wiry, tanned figures climbed into the rigging, armed with crossbows. Still others, wearing boiled-leather jerkins for protection, waited on deck with spears and cutlasses. Zeus also paced the deck, fangs bared, growling.

As the purple- and gold-striped sails neared the *Mermaid*, Berengaria described a rotund figure lolling on a couch on deck, being fanned by two brown youths.

"Probably Isaac Comnenus, the so-called emperor," Joanna said. "They say he is in league with Saladin himself. And his island is populated with treacherous Griffons like those in Sicily."

"*Deus juvat mea,*" Berengaria prayed devoutly.

As the ship sailed within range, the crossbowmen tensed, awaiting the order to loose their bolts, but the other ship's captain called across the water in passable French that the emperor's ship meant them no harm. He wished only to have speech with them.

"Let them draw closer, then, but see that they don't get close enough for grappling hooks," Stephen of Turnham warned his sailors. Alouette could feel the hackles rising on Zeus's shoulders.

The plump figure stood erect as they watched, and made his way ponderously to the side of the boat nearest them.

"Queen Joanna! Princess Berengaria!" he shouted across the water. "I, Isaac Comnenus, Emperor of Cyprus, bid you welcome to my island! I would like to welcome you in the manner your rank deserves. Please follow my ship into the harbor, where we will take you ashore and escort you to the palace for a royal welcome!"

"Dare we trust him?" Berengaria inquired anxiously.

"Of course not! Once there we'd be prisoners, as our countrymen no doubt are," Joanna replied with an un-queenly snort. "No!" she called across the water. "We have seen our sailors marched away as captives. Free them, and we may then trust your hospitality!"

"I regret that that is not possible. The Englishmen offered hostility to our peaceful people, who sought only to give them succor," Isaac called back, shrugging his shoulders. "I am sure that once you come ashore, however, this misunderstanding can be cleared up."

But Joanna stood firm, even though Berengaria worried that their ship would be attacked, or that they would starve if they did not give in.

By the end of a week, the ship's stores were indeed running out, but by this time, Isaac Comnenus had begun to ferry supplies out to them: a minimal amount of fresh fruit, cheese, drinking water, and wine, always with the promise of much more if the royal ladies would trust him. He professed himself much wounded that they remained so suspicious. Each time the boat came out from the harbor, Zeus stiffened, the growls rumbling from his bared teeth.

Berengaria was inclined to give in, once the food deliveries began, always willing to take people at face value. "Surely he would not dare harm us with the king of England due to arrive at any moment," she reasoned.

"But where *is* my brother? His ship may also have come to grief," Joanna answered, then softened her tone as Berengaria began to cry. "I'm sorry, *chère*, but we must act on our own until Richard is here."

Each day the emperor's messages became less placating and gracious and more threatening.

By the end of another fortnight, he stopped delivering food, and as the last of the drinking water ran out, anxiety ran high.

In the afternoon, a flotilla sailed out in the harbor, expertly surrounding the ships, their decks bristling with men, some armed with crossbows. At a signal from one of the captains, the pitch-soaked bottles were set alight.

"Ladies of England! Come ashore, or we will set the *Mermaid* afire!"

"Master Stephen, I believe we have no choice," was Joanna's terse comment. The captain gave the signal, and the dromond, flanked by Cypriot ships, sailed into Limassol harbor.

"Ladies, I bid you a proper welcome to Cyprus at last," Isaac said, smirking as Berengaria and Alouette prepared to descend into the longboat. Joanna would board last, having gone back to the cabin for her mantle.

"Nay, I don't think we'll be joining you after all, Your Magnificence," announced Joanna, her arm shooting out to restrain the other two.

"But you have no other option!" sputtered the fat ruler.

"I think we do, as of now." Joanna allowed a smile of triumph to light her features. "Look there, Berengaria, on the horizon!"

"The *Trenche-Mer*!"

There was a brief, pitched battle on the sands of Limassol, in which the Cypriots put up an ill-trained resistance behind piled-up furniture and doors, but soon the crusaders had the Griffons fleeing toward the mountains that flanked the city. They pursued them, gaining much booty, for the emperor and his attendants discarded silver plate, bolts of silk and purple cloth, livestock ready for slaughter, laden horses and mules. But the crusaders were unsuccessful in capturing the slippery emperor, who moved with astonishing speed for a man of his bulk.

Six days after his timely arrival in Cyprus, Richard wed Berengaria in the chapel of Limassol Castle.

"I wish you could see King Richard," Reyner whispered during the ceremony. "He quite outshines the bride. On his head is a scarlet cap, while his tunic is of rose-colored samite, and over that he has a cloak with solid silver moons and golden suns encrusted on it in rows."

Alouette had been present in Berengaria's chamber that morning as Queen Joanna, Ramona, and Innocentia had helped the nervous girl into the soft lavender silk gown, and had braided pearls into the thick ebony coronet of her hair. Berengaria was a quietly lovely woman, Alouette surmised from their descriptions of her, but certainly one who would not steal Coeur de Lion's thunder.

It had been Alouette's task, since she could not help her dress, to talk soothingly to her mistress, for Berengaria was quite paralyzed with excitement, hardly able to believe that the anticipated wedding was at last taking place.

"Does he look happy?" Alouette whispered to Reyner as the choir's singing filled the air. "Queen Joanna confided in me that she had to take her brother aside last even and keep him from postponing the ceremony again. He was so distracted, with the coming of Guy de Lusignan from Acre, begging him to come and help the crusaders who have already landed in Outremer, that Joanna feared he would balk at taking time for the sacrament of marriage."

"That doesn't surprise me. Yes, Richard appears happy enough. I only hope he maintains his pretense, so that the poor little princess never knows it's only the alliance with Navarre that makes him choose her over any other candidate." Then, as if to soften his cynical tone, he leaned down and said, "I am glad that what we have, my lady, is not based on territorial agreements but upon love. After you have put the bride to bed tonight . . ." He whispered a suggestion as to how they should spend their time that had her blushing and trembling as she stood next to him in the chapel.

But that was the last time they found to make love while the English remained in Cyprus. The bloodied sheets of the marriage bed had scarcely been shown—a traditional morning-after sequel of the bedding ceremony—before Richard tore away from Limassol in hot pursuit of Isaac Comnenus. It seemed likely, too, that he wanted to avoid the envoys of Phillip of France who had arrived that morning, robed in importance, bringing a royal summons to Richard to join the French outside the walls of Acre. Richard's response had hardly been polite, let alone the obedient answer of a vassal to his liege.

As the next two weeks went by, Isaac was hunted down and captured and his Griffons forced into submission. The Lionheart had succeeded in turning Cyprus, just one day's sail from the Holy Land, into a strategically important power base.

Berengaria had been radiantly happy the morning after her marriage, when it seemed all her hopes had been fulfilled. She was the crowned Queen of England, and more important, wife of the most chivalrous, most handsome king in Christendom.

As the honeymoon sped by and Richard made no further move to share her bed, even when he spent the night in Limassol, her newborn contentment died. Alouette and Joanna spent endless hours trying to reassure her, telling her that all would be well as soon as they departed for Acre—surely by the time they entered Jerusalem! But Alouette could not be confident of her words even as she spoke them. What kind of man was Richard that he did not desire to share his wife's bed? That minstrel, Blondel, was always with him, even when he rode out on campaign.

Joanna had described Blondel de Nesle's mincing gait and soft, effeminate hands, much to Alouette's amusement, but now she resented him—and his master—for the tears he had put on the face of the Navarrese princess for whom she had come to care deeply. Berengaria seemed like a wilted flower these days.

Alouette was hardly surprised when one of the French envoys managed to confront her in the corridors of the castle. She had been expecting it.

No, she did not know when Richard planned to sail. *Yes*, Richard had made Berengaria his wife in fact; hadn't they heard of the bloodied sheets being displayed, as was customary? *No*, Berengaria showed no signs of breeding. It had only been a fortnight since the wedding! *Yes*, Richard had agreed to support Guy of Lusignan, king of Jerusalem, against the attempts to take his crown and give it to Conrad of Montferrat, Phillip's candidate, in return for his assistance in conquering Cyrus.

She trembled as she answered the last question. It was the first *real* information of substance that she had passed on in her forced role of spy. Not even the knowledge that she was helping to preserve her stepbrother's life sufficed to console her. Alouette felt unclean—so much so that she wanted to plead a headache when a page came to the ladies' bower, saying that Reyner had come to see her.

Surely he would detect the guilt on her face if he saw her! But she had no logical excuse that would not make the queens suspicious—not when she had always been so eager for her lover's visits before—so she laid aside the lute she had been strumming and left the bower.

Reyner was accompanied by Zeus, who greeted Alouette with his customary enthusiasm, licking her outstretched hand and putting his head under her hand to be petted.

"Isaac Comnenus is captured, my love—in fact, Zeus sniffed him out from the pile of old clothes in the hovel where he was hiding! He surrendered on condition that Richard would not put him in 'irons,' and Richard agreed—but then he found himself in chains of silver!" He laughed richly at the joke, and even Alouette had to smile. "Richard is mightily pleased to have Isaac's great courser, Fauvel. A swifter horse I have never seen! As for Isaac, he lies in captivity in Margat, a 'guest' of the Templars. His young daughter, Chloe, will be brought here as hostage and will go on to Acre in Berengaria's charge."

"Poor child," murmured Alouette, thinking of the unfortunate girl caught up in the intrigues of her elders. However, she thought, it might be a very good thing for Berengaria to have a little girl to fuss over. Perhaps it would distract her from the feeling of being a rejected wife. Her thoughts were interrupted, however, as Reyner took her hand.

"Richard plans for the queens and their households to sail tomorrow. We will leave also, but not for a few days."

"We are to leave . . . without you? Why?" The thought of sailing separately again filled her with unease, after the disastrous storm that had struck before.

"I'm not sure, but I believe Richard has agreements to be completed concerning the government of the island. However, I've thought of a way you can stay with me . . ." His voice had become husky, caressing, and his warm breath near her ear turned her knees to jelly. Forgotten was her fear that Reyner would sense her guilty conscience as she waited to hear his scheme.

"How is that?" she responded in her most seductive tones.

His words were like cold water to her. "Marry me, of course!"

TWENTY-ONE

He saw her flinch as if from a blow, saw the slender body, which had been inexplicably tense, grow rigid once more.

"Marry you?" she repeated, as if he had never asked her before.

"Yes, of course! How else would Richard permit you to leave the queen and stay with me, even temporarily? I know we had pledged to wait until we could marry in Jerusalem, but surely you see how foolish it is to wait when we love each other so—"

"You are pleased to call me foolish," she said icily, pulling away from him. "I'm sorry, but I must stay with Berengaria. She'll be frantic when she hears she's to travel without Richard—again."

"Berengaria has Joanna, and her Lady Ramona," he snapped.

"But she depends upon me," she returned stubbornly, turning away so that he would not see her lower lip quivering, or the tears forming. How badly she wanted to say yes, to know that tonight she could lie with him as his wife, in all honor!

"Well, then, go with her. Mayhap you deserve each other," he growled. He didn't believe she was refusing him for the sake of staying with the queen. He had been confident that she had changed her mind, thanks to the tenderness of his love and the passion they had shared during those secret rendezvous. Suddenly he didn't believe the other excuse anymore—that babble of some mysterious "stain" within her. She must be playing a deeper game. erhaps a mere knight was not enough for her. Perhaps she hoped to snare some earl or count in either king's court— some poor fool who didn't know he had taken her maidenhood!

"Perhaps I'll see you in Outremer, then." He bent to kiss her hand, his lips and fingers as cold as his voice.

At the very moment that the *Mermaid* set sail for Acre, a meeting was taking place outside the walls of that city.

The forces of Islam were bottled up inside the besieged city. The crusaders waited outside, daily hurling large stone missiles over the high walls with their mangonels, but largely relying on starvation to achieve the desired goal.

In turn, Saladin hovered in the hills beyond, harassing the fringes of the Christian host, but mostly impotent to help Acre due to inferior numbers.

Phillip fanned himself languidly inside the spacious tent. He had just broken his fast, yet it was already oppressively hot.

"You took a gamble, coming to us like this," he said, addressing the figure who stood before him, dressed in the flowing white garments of a Moslem. Only the cold blue eyes in the tanned face identified the man as a Frank. "How did you know we would not have you executed on sight?"

"Because I know you to be a fair man, a just king . . ." Fulk began, then saw that he would have to change his tune. Insincere flattery had never worked with Phillip Capet. One had to appeal to his selfishness. "Very well, Your Majesty. I acknowledge that I failed you grievously in the matter of Reyner de Winslade's assassination."

"I would tend to agree," Phillip said dryly, "since the damned fellow is not only hale and hearty, but betrothed to Alouette."

He was pleased to see that Fulk paled beneath his dark tan. "Betrothed—to that man? You must forgive me for asking, sire, but why did you permit it?"

Now it was Phillip's turn to grow livid. "Because thanks to you, we had no choice," he growled, his jaws clenched with the effort not to attack Fulk de Langres where he stood. He did not relish being reminded that he had been virtually forced by Richard to allow the betrothal.

"I'm sorry, Your Majesty..." stammered Fulk. "The news about Alouette caused me to speak overhastily. I only thought you disliked the idea of such a union, too." Fulk's tone was smooth, but inwardly he seethed with disappointment and rage. Reyner would die even more slowly and painfully for claiming what was his.

"Of course I hate such an idea," Phillip said, impatiently abandoning the royal pronoun, "but what else could I do when Richard was in a position to expose my hand in the plot? Besides, a betrothal is not a marriage, though you may be sure my lovely half sister would no longer be a virgin bride. I was hoping... ah, events would conspire to remove the handsome English knight from this world." He quirked an inquiring brow at Fulk, who was quick to see his cue.

"You may count on me, Your Majesty."

"So I thought before," retorted the French king, swatting at an irritating fly. "What do you have to recommend you now?"

"The ear of Saladin." Now he had Phillip Capet's full attention. He settled himself on one of the many cushions without waiting for a royal nod. "I have not wasted time since you banished me from court in Messina," continued Fulk. "Upon arriving in Palestine, I managed to meet the great Salah-al-din himself, and impressed upon him my close relationship with you—which I believed would again be the truth, sire, once your royal anger had cooled," he added hastily, watching Phillip as one would a coiled adder. "I offered to be your liaison. Surely you can see the advantages of making an alliance with Saladin before Coeur de Lion ever lands. Then you can present Richard with a *fait accompli*—which will surely diminish his fame in Christendom—or you can keep the treaty secret, using it when it is most advantageous."

"Yes, hmmm..." Phillip drummed his fingers on the

table next to his couch. "And your reward for these 'diplomatic' services?"

"For that and the annihilation of de Winslade, I still ask nothing more than the hand of Lady Alouette," Fulk said modestly, "and, of course, restoration of my lands in England, when you conquer it."

"My dear *Sieur de Langres*," purred Phillip. "Such a humble request." *You must think me a babe in arms, and Saladin, as well. Do you think I believe you promised him nothing in return for your services? You will bear watching—close watching, indeed.* "Naturally, you cannot return to our ranks until Richard has been humbled," continued Phillip. "To him I must continue to be an ally—for now— and as his ally, I will deny having seen you." When Fulk appeared perfectly content with his terms, Philip inquired, "Do you have a place to stay while you engineer de Winslade's downfall?"

"Yes, sire. Saladin has found me lodgings, from which I can move freely from the Christian to the Moslem world and back again."

I'll wager he has, indeed, thought Phillip, wondering for what price Fulk would have betrayed him to the Saracen leader, or if indeed he had not done so already.

Reyner decided that enduring the heat of this land was like standing in front of the ovens in the kitchen at Winslade when old Griselda took out the freshly baked loaves, except that one could not get away from the heat by walking back outdoors. This heat was everywhere, accompanied by a blinding sunlight, and the combination of the two made his hauberk unbearable by midmorn.

The mood of the fleet was jubilant as it sailed into the horseshoe-shaped harbor of Acre, with its high seawalls and Mt. Carmel visible in the distance. Sailing down the coast between Beirut and Sidon, they had sighted a huge, three-masted ship which, when hailed, claimed to be Genoese. One of Richard's sailors had been suspicious, however; and when one of the galleys gave pursuit, the "Genoese" ship opened fire, proving it was Turkish. Richard had succeeded in taking the ship, which had been loaded with Turks bound for the relief of Acre, Greek fire, foodstuffs, and two hundred poisonous snakes, which were to have been loosed in the Christian camp. After choosing a few emirs to be ransomed for handsome sums, he sank the ship, leaving the rest of the Turks to drown.

His victory did much to assuage the sting of Tyre's refusal to open its gates to him. Controlled by Conrad, the Austrian marquis of Montferrat, who was already Phillip's ally, the city had been as unwilling to be turned into another English supply base as Cyprus had been. Conrad's lack of welcome had enraged Richard, but thoughts of revenge seemed far from the golden Plantagenet giant's mind now as he viewed the tumultuous welcome that awaited him on the beaches in front of Acre.

Crusaders of every nation—French, Flemings, Germans, Pisans, Genoese, Swabians—stood cheering on the sand, blowing trumpets and waving brightly colored banners. The noise was deafening.

As Reyner watched, Phillip Capet waded into the surf to greet Richard, his arms open in an apparently fervent embrace. Then the embracing became general as crusaders— some of whom had been there as long as two years already—rushed to meet the English newcomers, babbling joyously in a dozen tongues, tears of joy in their eyes. One could almost ignore the gibbet above the camp, whose swinging fruit was mute evidence of the discord and low morale rampant in the ranks, and the stench arising from the deep ditch in front of Acre's walls.

"Faugh! What *is* that?" gasped Thomas, Reyner's squire, holding his nose against the overpowering smell.

A Burgundian man-at-arms standing nearby was amused to enlighten him. "Oh, that? That's just what's filling the ditch, *mon vieux*! We've been packing it with whatever was most noisome and awful, to stink the scoundrels out, so to speak. Mostly, we've used the carcasses of dead animals —but it's considered quite the chivalrous deed to direct that your own corpse be placed there if you are dying. And since plenty *are* dying from the heat, the poisonous arrows and Greek fire, and *leonardie*, we have lots o' fill for the moat."

" 'Leonardie?' " questioned Reyner.

The Burgundian was flattered to have the attention of such an obviously important *chevalier* in Richard's retinue. "Leonardie, my lord, is the wasting sickness one gets here —if the infidels don't get you first. The hair, toenails, and fingernails fall out, and the skin becomes all scaly. . ."

At that moment, Reyner heartily damned his king for sending his bride, his sister—and, most important to him, Alouette—ahead to this hideous land while he dallied in Cyprus. They'd probably be there still if Richard had not heard a rumor that Acre's fall was imminent, and come hotfoot, unwilling that a victory should take place without him.

"The queens of England and Sicily, fellow, where are they?" Reyner queried, anxious to make sure Alouette was all right. He would learn to live with the fact that she hated him, if only she were well!

The Burgundian soldier pointed to a dromond anchored near the French camp. "They've stayed aboard the ship, my lord, except for brief visits with Phillip. It was felt to be too dangerous for them to leave it, with Saladin making such frequent raids on the camp from those hills. I saw them once, though—beautiful ladies they are. Even their attendants are like angels from heaven—especially the blind one they call *Alouette*, the Lark . . ."

"Indeed," murmured Reyner, breathing a silent prayer of thanks for common sense on someone's part. Evidently Alouette was safe and well, then. He wondered how soon he'd see her. If she was still angry with him, her face would still be haughty, her tone cold as ice. He could still feel the hurt of her refusal to wed him on Cyprus. Would she have realized her error in the ensuing fortnight? Would she perhaps seek him out, with a sweet apology on those luscious lips? Should he welcome her at once into his arms, kissing away any repentant tears she would shed, or hold aloof a while himself, so that she would not be tempted to think she could lead him around by the nose once they were wed? But he would keep his lessoning brief, and afterwards, reconciliation would be sweet, indeed.

However, duty intervened. When Reyner would have preferred to be going out on the barge which summoned Berengaria and Joanna to the feast of celebration that night, he was in fact riding at Hubert Walter's side, suffering the noonday heat in full mail as they checked the walls of Acre to find the best position against which to place the English siege engines in relation to the French ones already there. After that, he listened as scouts reported on Saladin's strength in the hills behind them, and spies in Acre described the worsening conditions in the besieged city. Reyner wondered why those who seemed to be Saracen themselves betrayed their people, but he understood when he saw them paid in loaves of bread and wheels of cheese.

It was late afternoon before he finished his duties. By the time he had located his tent, had had Thomas assist him from his hauberk and sweat-stained gambeson, washed himself, and changed into a blue linen tunic, he was already late for the feast.

He would have been distressed indeed to learn that Alouette was actively trying to avoid meeting him. She couldn't face him just yet, with the memory of his scorn still ringing in her ears, all the way from Cyprus to Palestine. Now that Richard's fleet had arrived, they would inevitably be thrown together as she attended Berengaria, but cowardlike, she wanted to postpone the moment as long as possible.

She even volunteered to watch Chloe, Isaac's hostage daughter, while Berengaria and Joanna went ashore, only to be told that Berengaria intended for the volatile thirteen-year-old to come along! Berengaria had made a pet of the Cypriot princess, lavishing upon her all the care and attention she would have tried to give to Richard, had they not been separated these two weeks. Nothing was too good for "sweet Chloe," Berengaria declared, determined that the "poor child" should not suffer for the sins of her father.

Joanna and Alouette were of the same mind regarding Isaac's daughter. Chloe had never been so happy, having been freed from a tyrannical, cruel father and given a naive, indulgent guardian all at once. They felt, however, that Richard's bride might care for her better by providing fewer sweetmeats and baubles and paying more attention to preserving the girl's questionable virtue.

Berengaria had accepted, with alacrity, Alouette's offer to take care of the girl, never guessing that Alouette had meant to avoid the feast. "How good of you," she enthused, dropping an affectionate kiss upon Alouette's brow. "You must have guessed how eager I am to see my lord. Since you will be with Chloe, I can spend my time with Richard!"

Behind Alouette in the ship's cabin, Joanna commented that there was little likelihood that Richard would even notice Berengaria's efforts, as his bride stopped to explain in stammering Greek to Chloe that Lady Alouette would be her chaperone at the event. Then she had flown on wings of giddy joy to have her trunks brought up from the hold.

"I doubt if her efforts at the Griffons' tongue are necessary anymore," Joanna observed as she, Alouette, and Chloe remained in the cabin together. "You're understanding every word now, aren't you, Chloe?"

Chloe returned her look sullenly. "I understand *some* French, my lady," was all she would say.

Playing nursemaid to the mischievous Chloe—especially in the tumult and confusion of the crusaders' celebration—should certainly be worth some time off her stay in Purgatory, Alouette thought grimly as she attempted to keep up with the exuberant girl. Of course, she had planned on having Innocentia's assistance in the task, but as they came ashore, her stepbrother Henri had greeted them, and Alouette knew she could no longer count upon her maid's help. Indeed, after a few minutes of polite conversation as they strolled through the crusader camp, Henri and Innocentia had lagged farther and farther behind, until Alouette could no longer hear their voices over Chloe's lilting chatter.

Henri had first noticed Innocentia when she and Alouette had returned from the convent, and had been paying the Lombard girl marked attention ever since they had come to Outremer.

Alouette knew from Joanna's remarks that Innocentia was becoming a winsomely pretty girl, with curves blossoming under her bliaut and a sparkle dancing in her attractively slanted sloe eyes. Not until Henri de Chenevy started teasing her, when he came to visit Alouette, did the roses begin to bloom in Innocentia's cheeks, however.

Alouette hoped her serving woman was not cherishing unattainable dreams. True, she was not of the nobility, and not a virgin by her own admission, but she had been chaste ever since entering the convent, and Alouette did not want to see Henri become the instrument of Innocentia's heartbreak. Even though her stepbrother was the soul of chivalry, Alouette was determined to be realistic. The nobility looked on servants, complaisant or not, as fair game for their attentions.

Her warnings to Innocentia had thus far fallen on deaf ears. "My lord Henri is just being kind," Innocentia had protested in her Sicilian-accented French. "He knows I am a long way from home, as is he. There are very few white women here. He flirts, that is all."

Alouette very much doubted that Henri meant to leave his attention at kindness. Innocentia was too ripe a morsel not to be tempting to a virile young Frenchman, despite the easy availability of prostitutes, both Christian and Saracen.

"We're here, Lady Alouette! And there is Uncle Phillip, waiting to greet us!" shrieked Chloe as they drew near to the giant silken pavilion which would hold a thousand crusaders, the location of Phillip's feast of welcome.

Uncle Phillip, indeed. She would have to speak to Chloe later about the unseemliness of calling the king of France uncle, no matter what he had told the girl. "All rulers are in some fashion brothers," Phillip had said, leering at the nubile Cypriot princess when they were introduced, "and since your father and I are brothers, therefore I must be a sort of uncle to you, *hein*?"

Berengaria had been pleased by his friendliness to the young hostage, but Alouette had heard a distinctly ununclelike tone to Phillip's oily courtesy. She would have to warn Berengaria, for she certainly didn't trust Chloe's common sense. Perhaps Phillip was tiring of Peronel and casting about for an even younger concubine. He certainly wouldn't scruple to use the pretty hostage, since it was Richard's honor that would inevitably suffer more.

"You're looking well, *chère* Alouette." Phillip turned his attention to her after greeting Chloe effusively with a very Gallic kiss on both cheeks. "You seem to have adapted well to the heat."

The climate, and its debilitating effect on Europeans, seemed a safe enough topic. "I . . . I thank you, Your Majesty. Yes, I . . . seem to have recovered my appetite, finally."

"*Bien!* I think you will find much to appeal to your palate tonight. And I hope you will favor us with a few songs later? Doubtless Blondel will lend you his lute."

Richard summoned Chloe to a seat upon the dais with Berengaria, in recognition of her rank. While Berengaria might be dismayed at having to compete for her lord's attentions, even with a younger female, Alouette was glad to be relieved of her charge during the feast and found a place with Innocentia and Henri.

She was tense as the other banqueters found their places, expecting at any moment to hear the Norman-accented voice of Reyner de Winslade. Would he speak to her because it was a social occasion, his courtesy masking the fact that he thought her a silly fool? As the feast began and she heard no such familiar voice, Alouette relaxed a trifle and allowed herself to savor the enticing smells as Phillip's servants commenced to serve the vast array of foods.

Phillip was true to his promise. The banquet consisted of endless courses, some foods still exotic to Western palates, but found abundantly in Outremer. In addition to the usual meats and poultry, there were crane, ibex, and roebuck, spiced liberally with pepper, mustard, and garlic, accompanied by dishes made with artichokes, asparagus, and cucumbers. Carved wooden or silver platters of fruit sat on the trestle tables, laden with bananas (called "apples of paradise" by the crusaders), oranges, figs, peaches, plums, quinces, and almonds. The fruits were liberally sprinkled with sugar, which delighted tongues used only to honey as a sweetener.

Alouette relished the strange fare, listening with only

half an ear to the grandiose speeches of welcome being given by Phillip, Giles Amaury, Master of the Templars, Conrad of Montferrat, and Leopold, Duke of Austria. Tonight was all peace and amity, but by tomorrow, her royal half brother would be back to his *metier*: looking out for Phillip Capet's interests while undermining Richard's cause.

Alouette was not precisely sure when she became aware that Chloe was gone.

TWENTY-TWO

Even as the crusaders began their feast, Fulk was summoned into the Presence.

The tent that housed Salah al-Din Yusuf ibn Ayub, known to the crusaders as Saladin, was larger than those that sheltered his men, but hardly more luxurious. Fulk had heard stories of the fabled splendor of the sultan's palaces in Cairo and Damascus, but this tent boasted only a few cushions, a bed, a bedside table, a few dishes, cups of brass and carved wood, and a chest, the meager personal belongings Saladin carried on campaign. His one concession to his position as ruler over Islam was the beautifully bound copy of the Koran which lay open on his bedside stand, its cover of finely tooled leather, its pages full of flowing Arabic calligraphy. Saladin, when fighting for his homeland, had no need of silken clothes, or the ministrations of his wives or slaves. He would return to these things only when the Christians were defeated and the Cross no longer threatened his land.

The person of Saladin himself, rather than luxurious trappings, supplied the regal aura in this tent. Fulk was struck again by the contrast between the English and French kings and the sultan. Though tall for a Saracen, Saladin was a foot shorter than Coeur de Lion, and swarthy in contrast to Richard's golden fairness. He was closer in height to Phillip Capet, but solid of build, where Phillip was stocky and tended to obesity. Yet Saladin was easily more regal than either of these royal invaders of his land;

his mien had neither Richard's swaggering nor Phillip's blustering cruelty.

Fulk was not conscious that he was staring until Saladin's brown eyes became hard as marble. Remembering where he was and what was required, he hurriedly lowered himself to the floor, touching his forehead to the packed earth in a gesture of respect and submission. His murmured "O Sultan, live forever," was muffled in the folds of his *kafiyeh*, or turban, but the ritual had been completed.

"Rise, Infidel."

Fulk suppressed the feeling of resentment at the term. To either side, he reminded himself, the other was "the infidel." Someday he would be in a position to receive rather than to give obeisance.

The voice commanding him in Arabic had been that of the Kurdish soldier who had escorted him; Saladin himself waited calmly on his cushions. Next to him were seated two elderly men, a Moor and a hawk-nosed Jew, but Fulk saw them only in the periphery of his gaze. His attention was seized by the compelling, lambent eyes of Saladin.

"*Salaam alicum*—peace be with you," said Saladin politely, for he knew Fulk was not free to address him until he was spoken to.

"Your Majesty . . . my lord . . ." he began in his halting Arabic. He was never sure how to address the sultan, and Saladin let him wonder. "I come to bring you a report. Richard arrived at Acre this morning, in a fleet of thirteen fishing boats, one hundred transport ships, and fifty trireme galleys." He waited expectantly, but no praise was forthcoming for his important news.

"You tell me nothing I did not know in the same hour as they arrived," Saladin retorted in flawless French.

Fulk lapsed back gratefully into his own language, and tried again. "On the way to Acre, Richard became suspicious of a ship that appeared to be French and challenged her. She was Turkish, my lord, and the English king sank her, sending most of eight hundred troops and its cargo of arms and serpents to the bottom. They kept the stores of cloth, foodstuffs, and several of your emirs."

"A grievous loss, and one of which I am already well

aware. The ransom demands from *Melech-Ric*, as we call the English king, have already reached me, in addition to his demands for the return of the True Cross and the prisoners I hold. In return, he will free the garrison of Acre—a garrison he has not even conquered yet!"

Obviously Saladin had no need of Fulk's reports; his network of Saracen observers was already well-established. The Sultan's tone told Fulk he had better prove his value, and quickly.

"I had audience with the king of France, for whom I am a trusted confidante," he began, unconsciously puffing out his chest a little. "I told him of my ability to act as a liaison with you, O mighty Saladin." He touched his hand to his breast in the Moslem gesture of respect.

"And what was Phillip Capet's response?" Saladin's opaque glance and passionless tone betrayed nothing of his thoughts now.

"He was most pleased. He begs me to tell you, O ruler of Islam, of his utmost respect, and puts himself at your disposal, should you desire to make a separate peace."

Saladin laughed mirthlessly. "If he respected me in truth, he would not be here, is that not so? However, it is good to know I have a way to communicate with King Phillip of France through you, Sir Fulk. I shall call you when I need you."

Though nothing in Saladin's polite demeanor said so, Fulk knew he was being mocked, and that he was the subject of the rapid Arabic being spoken as he made his retreat. It was a mistake to have come—foolish to have supposed that Saladin would not have been informed already of the strength of Richard's fleet or the sinking of the Turkish ship. Ah, well, he was content as long as they stuck to the original terms of the agreement for his services: a position as an emir, and the promise that one Alouette de Chenevy, half sister of the king of France, would be spared for him alone.

"Do you trust him?" asked the Jew, after Fulk had bowed out of the tent.

"No farther than I could throw him," admitted the Sara-

cen sultan. "I grow old in my struggles against the Franks,
and therefore, I do not boast much. Of course I would not
trust one who would play Judas against his own people,
especially for the sake of a woman." His lip curled in disgust. "What kind of woman could respect such a man? But
let the infidel dog and his master Phillip think he has my
trust, and that he passes valuable information. I will find
out much more from his artless chatter than he ever does
from me. I will use him—and then toss him back on the
dung heap where he belongs, Maimonides."

The man who had been so addressed was Saladin's personal physician, a Hebrew who had fled the persecution of
Cordova and found peace in the younger Saladin's court,
just as Saladin had become heir to the throne of Nuredin.

"Some sherbet, my friends?" Saladin inquired, gesturing
toward an ornately jeweled pitcher. "It is cooled with snow
brought to me from the mountains daily by runners." At
the old men's pleased nods of assent, he poured cups of the
sweet, cool beverage and handed them to his companions,
a gesture full of respect for their learning.

"Now, my old friend El Khammas, you were on the
point of speaking when the Frank intruded upon our pleasant conversation," Saladin prompted, turning to the venerable Moor. "I believe you were about to tell me exactly
what you thought of me for luring you from Acre with this
ruse of my being ill."

"Indeed," the black-skinned Moor said with a gentle air
of reproof. "I could not imagine an illness my good col-
league Maimonides could not cure without my assistance,"
he said, with a deferential nod to the famous Jew. "But I
was willing to come, since your message was urgently
worded. How was I to know it was only a trick to spirit me
out of Acre against my will? Saladin, my lord, the besieged people of Acre are starving. Disease will soon be
rampant, if the Christians do not batter down the walls
first. As a physician, I am needed there!" His voice had
become more impassioned as he spoke.

"It is precisely *because* of Acre's danger that I lured you
hence," Saladin responded firmly. "Good El Khammas, I
know your art is life and breath to you. But could I stand

idly by and watch you endangered with the rest of Acre's faithful, when without your skill my brother Safadin would have died?"

"Any physician could have saved Safadin," retorted the Moor with a self-deprecating gesture. "I am but a humble man, the son of a tenant farmer—" (Indeed, his name, El Khammas, meant exactly that.) "—who is fortunate to have found favor in your sight. But I feel guilty knowing that I am here, out of harm's way, while down there, the garrison suffers without my aid as a physician."

"You are seriously worried about the fate of Acre, then?" Maimonides asked, with the familiarity of an old retainer.

Saladin's mahogany-brown eyes grew troubled. "I wasn't, until word came of the sinking of the Turkish ship —and the size of Melech-Ric's fleet," he added. "But now I have grave misgivings, my old friends. Richard will demand the return of the Christian prisoners from Hattin and the True Cross if he conquers Acre. How am I to satisfy these demands? Many of the prisoners have been dispersed across Islam as slaves, and others have died. I don't possess their holy relic—no one does. I suspect it is a chimera—a phantom that will cause the deaths of many of the faithful and infidels alike. I could not lose the opportunity to save at least *you*, good friend!"

Alouette, in her seat near the dais, suddenly became aware of the absence of Chloe's constant babble and the tinkling of her silver bracelets as she ate and gesticulated.

"Princess Chloe?" she called. "Lady Ramona, is Chloe still at her place?" she asked Berengaria's Navarrese lady-in-waiting, who was seated across the table from her.

"No. That's strange . . . I did not see her leave . . ." the older woman replied vaguely.

Alouette did not find it strange at all. Lady Ramona had been flirting with a Gascon knight, laughing much too loudly as she consumed more Tokay wine, and the Gascon's tipsy compliments grew bolder. Alouette cursed her blindness and her offer to take care of Chloe.

Hastily she called to Innocentia and Henri, and they hurried out to search for Chloe. Berengaria had been radiant at the high table, basking in Richard's reflected glory, but eventually she would remember her pet and wish to show Chloe off. Soon the sweet wafers would be served and Phillip would call on Alouette to sing. Blondel was already taking his turn with the entertainment, though his pleasant tenor was difficult to hear above the noise of the drunken merrymakers.

"You don't suppose she's been lured off by some lecherous knight, do you?" Henri asked as he guided Alouette down the narrow alleyways between the sea of crusader tents.

"Anything could have happened to her," Alouette replied grimly, though she could imagine the scandal throughout Christendom if Isaac's daughter were ravished while she was hostage to her father's good behavior. "What if she's found her way to the waterfront and has bribed someone to sail her back to Cyprus?"

"Be calm, *ma soeur*, she has scarcely had time enough to do that—nor does she have the funds!" Henri reassured her.

"She could pay them with those cursed bangles that make such a clanging racket—or herself," retorted Alouette darkly.

Suddenly, her pessimistic musings were interrupted by an excited barking, and before she had time to think, a warm, wet tongue was licking her hand. "Zeus!" she cried. Zeus's presence meant . . .

"Reyner!" Henri called out gladly, as the knight and his half-wolf, half-mastiff dog stopped in front of Alouette. "I had wondered where you were. You could not have shown up at a better hour! Can that animal of yours track a human?"

Reyner had just now left his tent and had been heading for the banquet, intent on finding the very woman who stood before him, an anxious expression furrowing her brow. In the silence that followed, he realized that, in his surprise at seeing Alouette before him, he hadn't heard Henri's words.

A trifle embarrassed, he greeted Alouette's stepbrother and asked him to repeat himself.

The genial Henri de Chenevy was not the least put out. "There will be time for *amour* later on," he teased, not knowing of Alouette and Reyner's quarrel in Cyprus. "For now, could you and Zeus help us find Chloe, the little Cypriot princess? She seems to have eluded my sister, here . . ."

Reyner grasped the importance of the situation without another word. "I had a feeling that wench would be more trouble than she was worth. Of a certainty, Zeus can track a person. He once followed an outlaw's scent clear through Hawkingham Wood and across the River Meon! But do you have a garment, some article of clothing that Zeus can sniff to get the scent?"

Now Alouette was glad of Chloe's offhand way of treating her like a servant. As they had been seated for the banquet, Chloe had deposited her light cloak in Alouette's hands, to keep until they left. She hadn't seen the need for bringing it at all, she added petulantly, though Alouette reminded her of the abruptly cool nights in Outremer. In her haste to find Chloe, she had absentmindedly brought the cloak along. Now she offered it in Reyner's direction. "Will this work, my lord?"

"Probably." He held it in front of Zeus, who sniffed it intently. Clearly the canine knew what was expected of him. "Now, it is best that we return to where she was last seen . . ."

Back at the pavilion, Blondel could still be heard singing inside as a drunken couple stole out the side entrance, intent on celebrating in another fashion. Alouette could hear Reyner's dog running this way and that around the perimeter of the tent, casting about for the scent. Her heart pounded, not only from her anxiety about the wretched Chloe, but also from Reyner's presence. His voice had given her no clue as to the state of his feelings for her. Was he still affronted by her refusal to marry him? Didn't he know he possessed her heart and soul anyway? If only she could convince him that love had prompted her decision, that she desired only the best for him.

Suddenly the wolf-mastiff's noisy snuffling changed to a triumphant baying, and he set off at a rapid trot, nose to the ground, toward the shore. A few moments later he led them onto the beach, where Chloe was in animated conversation with a sailor.

Dizzy with relief, Alouette still found the energy to scold her charge. "You wicked girl! Don't you know what could happen to you here? You could have been kidnapped by the Saracens!"

Alouette could not see the sullen sloe eyes turned on her or the pouting mouth, but her anger was plain. "And would that be so bad, Lady Alouette? My father was a trusted friend of Saladin's! Besides, I was only trying to get Jacques, here, to row me out to the ship so I could go to bed. I'm tired! Your Frankish music gives me a headache!" She stamped a tiny, slippered foot for emphasis. "And how dare you address me like a babe escaping from the nursery! I would remind you I am a princess in my land!"

"Be careful, Princess, or you will find yourself turned over my knee and spanked like a peasant," growled Reyner, cutting her tantrum short. "Henri, *mon vieux*, would you and Innocentia be so kind as to escort *Princess* Chloe back to the ship so that she may seek her rest? Perhaps it will sweeten her temper," he said with a wink, ignoring the look of raw fury the Cypriot girl shot at him. "I will see that Alouette returns safely later."

Within moments Alouette found herself alone on the rock-strewn beach with Reyner. Several yards away, a group of French crusaders sat around a campfire, their laughing talk humming in the background, but between Alouette and Reyner stretched a long, uncomfortable silence.

A cool breeze ruffled the tawny hair that curled about Reyner's neck and playfully ruffled the edge of Alouette's veil. The sun setting behind the hills that sheltered Saladin's troops cast a fading golden glow as it sank, leaving behind a sky streaked with amethyst, crimson, and orange. It was more beautiful than any cathedral window, but it seemed drab indeed when Reyner compared it to the beauty standing before him. He watched the pulse beat in her throat, for today she had left behind her wimple and wore only a sheer veil over her ebony tresses. He knew he should still be angry with her, but suddenly all he wanted was to kiss those trembling, lush lips and soothe the troubled brow. He pulled her into his arms with a hungry urgency.

It had been in her mind to ask if he was still angry, but his lips communicated their own message: *Forget about matters affecting our future, love—lay it aside for now. For there is only this moment, and it is more needful that I hold you and kiss you and touch your soft skin . . .*

She clung to him, marveling as always how their bodies joined as if carved from the same block of wood. But there was nothing wooden in his kisses, which sent shivers of desire racing through her, or the way his warm hand cupped her breast, thumb and forefinger lazily encircling the nipple, which grew rigid under his ministrations. If she had been made of wood, she surely would have been consumed by the flames of passion lit when he whispered hoarsely against her ear, "Come to my tent, love. 'Tis the only place we can be alone, and I want you."

Berengaria would not need her, or even remember her existence tonight—why not? She wanted him, too. Every inch of her skin tingled. Only he could quench the flame that he had sparked within her.

They had scarcely taken three steps in that direction, however, when out of the darkness Thomas called, "Sir Reyner, King Richard commands your presence in his pavilion."

Reyner's muttered curse echoed her own fiery disappointment. There was nothing she could do but acquiesce gracefully as he procured a longboat to take her out to the queens' ship. They were in the Holy Land, and until the crusaders rescued Jerusalem, their desires must give way to the cause that had brought them here from hundreds of leagues away.

TWENTY-THREE

Richard set to work with a will, appointing crews of sappers to tunnel under the wall into Acre. The ends of the tunnels would be lined with brush and other combustible material, then lit. When the tunnel caved in, the wall would collapse, thus providing a breach in the wall for the waiting invaders. The work was tedious, because the undermining must be started far enough from the wall that it was beyond bowshot. Timbers were needed for shoring up at intervals lest the tunnel collapse prematurely, and there was always the threat of a counter-mine dug by the defenders. Each sapper listened as he dug for the *chink* of another pick, operated by an enemy, coming *toward* him. The fate of the town might rest on hand-to-hand struggle underground.

Reyner was willing to do anything his liege lord required of him, for he had come to the Holy Land to serve, but he was relieved that Richard did not direct him to be in charge of the sappers. If he died on this crusade, he did not want it to be in a dusty tunnel underground, suffocating amidst collapsed earth.

Richard promised him a prominent position among the first invaders into Acre, once the walls were breached, but in the meantime, Reyner was put in command of one of Richard's catapults. Phillip's catapult, the *Malvoisin* ("Bad Neighbor"), and one erected from the common crusaders' purse, called "God's Own," were already hurling great stones into Acre and against its walls.

The English catapults were better than these. Armored with layers of rawhide and rope, they carried farther than their predecessors, raining terror on the Saracen inhabitants of the walled city. Of such size were the stones that they either shattered whatever they struck or ground it into powder. Blondel made an epic song of the incident in which one of the English missiles killed twelve men.

Richard seemed equally intent on sowing dissension among the nations wearing the Cross, for on that first full day of work he had it loudly proclaimed that those knights who served him would get four gold bezants a month—knowing full well that Phillip was offering three. Men flocked to the leopard standard, particularly the Pisans and the Genoese, though Richard refused the latter because they had already pledged themselves to Phillip.

Phillip had arrived two months earlier than Richard, and had assumed the leadership of the crusade. He had pitched his camp in front of the Accursed Tower on Acre's walls—the very one, in legend, where Judas supposedly received the thirty pieces of silver. He had begun bombardment, but had achieved no great progress, partly because of Saladin's cavalry, which came pouring out of the hills to harry the rear whenever the French attacked. Now Phillip watched in helpless rage as many of those who had welcomed him so enthusiastically deserted his ranks for those of the Coeur de Lion, singing the praises of Richard's mightier catapults and military prowess.

The disassembled Mategriffon had been delivered two days after Richard's landing, and it was now erected so that Richard's archers could look down into the city of Acre from the tall wooden towers that had first been built to intimidate the Lombards of Sicily.

This time the queens and their retinues were not invited to inhabit the wooden fortress, since its position so close to the Saracen walls placed it in danger of being struck with Greek fire, the deadly Saracen liquid whose flames could only be extinguished by vinegar.

Except for occasional excursions ashore, Berengaria, Joanna, and their ladies remained on board the galley, growing more restless as June wore on. The heat was stifling, and Alouette could not imagine how the crusaders tolerated their armor. The women had packed away their woolen clothing, wearing only light silks and new gowns made up of Egyptian cotton. They spent most of their time under an awning on deck, catching the rare breezes that could not reach their tiny cabins, whiling away the hours with gossip and embroidery while Alouette played her lute.

Tempers grew short in the heat and indefinite waiting. They could see the bombardment going on against the walls; however, no kingly visitor came on board to inform them of any progress being made.

Reyner became their link to the shore. When his duties allowed, he rowed out for a brief visit. When he came, all the women greeted him, starved for diversion. He sat with them, regaling them with tales of the siege and news about Richard.

Alouette was glad her lover could relieve the tedium of their days, but she was frustrated, too. Surrounded by Joanna, Berengaria, and the other ladies, she seldom achieved a moment alone with Reyner, but guiltily labeled her feelings selfish.

She heard the weariness in his voice and sensed there was much he was not saying in front of Berengaria about the grim realities of war. She would have liked to hold him and soothe away the tension and fatigue that tinged his voice during those brief visits.

The rest of the time, Alouette found herself with the increasingly impossible task of calming the distraught Berengaria, who had been almost totally ignored by her royal husband since their arrival.

Richard had not shared a bed with her, Berengaria tearfully told her one evening when they were alone in the cabin, since the night after their wedding. He had not invited her to remain ashore with him on the night of her arrival at Acre, but had peremptorily secured a longboat for her to be rowed back to the galley, saying something about an urgent meeting with his advisors. Was this the behavior of an eager bridegroom? Berengaria questioned angrily. How dare he treat her, a princess of the House of Navarre, as if she were a stone statue, to be ignored at will? What was offensive about her that he continued to avoid his marital duties?

"I'm sure there is nothing, Your Grace," Alouette answered carefully, hearing the hurt underlying the proud princess's angry tones. She wondered how much Berengaria had already heard or guessed about Richard's proclivities. Despite the king's renunciation of sin at Messina, Reyner had remarked to Alouette that Richard always had the delicate-featured Blondel or some girlishly pretty page with him in camp.

"I wish I could believe that the blame did not lie with me," muttered Berengaria. "But how am I to conceive his heir when he makes excuses rather than spend the night with me? Alouette, he's in so much danger every day—prowling around beneath the walls of Acre, exhorting the sappers, shooting at the Saracens along with the archers, when he could command all from a distance."

"He has been a warrior all his life, my lady. 'Tis not his way to merely supervise." She had begun to comb out Berengaria's long raven tresses, which the Navarrese woman always found relaxing.

"But what if he is killed, and dies without an heir? What then?" In the anguished cry, Alouette could hear another unspoken fear. If Richard persisted without issue, what place would there be for her, his widow? Alouette privately doubted she would be any more secure—probably less so—if she had a male infant, with Prince John as regent.

"Such things are in the hands of God, my lady," Alouette murmured, then decided her words sounded grim. "Perhaps you could get Queen Joanna to speak to him?"

"Oh, no, I could never do that, never! Promise me you will not mention it! To Joanna, Richard can do no wrong —he has no faults. She would only think of me as a spoiled child if I complained about him!"

Alouette was surprised. The two queens had a very cordial relationship, especially because of the nearness of their ages. Joanna, slightly the elder, enjoyed teaching Berengaria the demeanor of a queen, and had a rapt audience when she told her stories of Richard as a youth. But as

Alouette pondered Berengaria's words, she realized the young queen was right. Joanna had loved Berengaria instantly because of their mutual worship of Richard—a love which could remain undiminished in Joanna since she had lived most of her life apart from him, and need never know his darker secrets, as a wife did. She might indeed turn from the Navarrese woman if she knew Berengaria was dissatisfied with Richard. Berengaria, a foreigner among all these Normans, was loath to lose any of her friends.

Poor little princess, she thought, married to the legendary Coeur de Lion, and lonelier than before, an unclaimed wife among virtual strangers.

Alouette had not realized how the silence had lengthened as she pondered these thoughts until Berengaria spoke again, her voice cooler now, regality regained: "Please forget my words, Alouette. It was wrong of me to criticize the most puissant king in Christendom. I am indeed an ungrateful wretch—I who am the luckiest woman in the world to be married to such a man. I will do penance for my sin, if you will excuse me."

Before Alouette could formulate a word of comfort and understanding, she heard the rustle of cloth as Berengaria knelt at her prie-dieu and began to tell her beads.

Alouette was dismissed for the evening. There was nothing to do but go above, where she strummed her lute desultorily and half-listened to Joanna's Sicilian lady-in-waiting debate with Lady Ramona on the merits of several perfumes.

Berengaria beat her breast in earnest the next day. News was brought to the ship that Richard lay ill of the *leonardie*, that mysterious affliction of Outremer. Many had died of it. In addition, Richard was suffering an attack of the intermittent fever which had gripped him briefly in Sicily and again in Cyprus. Rumor had it that his life was despaired of.

Berengaria fell into hysterics, threatening to throw herself into the bay if he died. She would give herself to Saladin, if God would but spare her lord's life! 'Twould be fitting punishment for her sinful thoughts to have to be a concubine of the infidel ruler, she vowed to Joanna and Alouette.

Joanna did not know of Berengaria's complaints, of course, but she replied sensibly, and rather dryly, that she imagined Richard would have plenty to say about such a penance for his recovered health. She suggested instead that they go ashore and see if they could minister to the ailing king.

Richard accepted their visit with ill grace, obviously displeased that his wife and his sister should see him so. Alouette could not see the lank, faded gold hair which had fallen out in clumps, or the sunken blue eyes which glared in response to Berengaria's loving looks, but she heard the querulous way in which he responded to her solicitousness. There was nothing he needed of them but to be left alone until he felt better, he growled to the two hovering queens. The only consolation he enjoyed was that Phillip was struck down with the same sickness and could make no progress while he, Richard, lay dying!

However, he would accept Berengaria's offer to let Lady Alouette stay and play her lute for him. One grew tired of the same minstrel all the time, the king added in a pettish voice. At the last, there was a sharp intake of breath and Alouette heard footsteps leaving the tent.

"I haven't given you leave, Blondel!" roared the sick lion.

"Pardon me, sire. Your dismissal was implicit in your words," said Blondel, affronted, and kept walking.

None of Richard's nobles or knights would have dared address him so coldly, yet the silence that followed Blondel's rudeness was tantamount to giving permission for it. Did Berengaria grasp its significance?

The two queens soon took their leave, and though Berengaria's kiss on her brow was affectionate, Alouette wondered if she was not piqued that Richard would allow her to stay, but not his own wife. However, it was not up to her to question the ways of the Lionheart.

She played and sang for an hour, her performance punctuated by Richard's applause and complimentary remarks.

When he knew the song he would join in, his rich baritone blending beautifully with her clear soprano.

At length, the ailing king bade her stop, saying he would sleep now. "You have given me much pleasure, little Lark. Ask anything of me, and if 'tis in my power, I, Richard Plantagenet, will grant it."

What should she ask for? In truth she wanted nothing of a material nature, and even Richard could not give her a cool spring day in the Île de France, with gentle breezes and a friendly sunshine on her face, rather than the overwhelming heat of Outremer. He especially could not give her what she most craved—freedom from that overwhelming, causeless guilt within her.

Then she thought of something she could ask for—if she dared. The words were out before she could lose her courage: "The only boon I would ask, Your Grace, is for my mistress, your wife, and Queen Joanna. They fret so, without contact with you, my lord, and life on the ship grows tedious. They would not mind the hardships of camp life —or the danger. They did not come to Outremer to be pampered queens, sire, but to be fellow crusaders with you." In the silence that followed, she wondered if she had presumed too much upon a casually kind offer.

Suddenly there was a loud clunk as Richard threw an empty goblet against his shield in a temper. Alouette flinched at the loud crash, sure the next object would be aimed at her for her audacity.

She stood, uncertain whether it was best to freeze in place or try to find her way out of the tent.

"Nay, stay a moment, milady Alouette," Richard's voice came repentantly. "I'm sorry if my sickbed crotchets frightened you—'tis ill payment for your lovely singing. Tell me—do you never ask anything for yourself? No wonder Reyner loves you! What a change from Joanna, with her ceaseless nagging for a new, rich—but lusty, mind you!—spouse, and Berengaria, with her clinging, cloyingly sweet ways! They put you up to this, didn't they? Nay, don't deny it! I'm not angry at you for asking, but you tell those baggages they'll come off that ship when I enter Acre, and not a moment before! I'll not have women cluttering up this camp, distracting good men dedicated to a holy cause with their feminine wiles. It's bad enough there are camp followers everywhere, and the king of France has his mistress by his side."

"Yes, Your Grace," she said meekly. There was no use arguing that the idea had come from her, not from the queens. Richard's mind was made up. "Perhaps I should return to the galley and let you rest, sire."

"But we have not settled upon a reward for you, little troubador." Richard's voice was once again genial. "Ah! I have it! A wedding in Acre once the city is liberated! A wedding to be held as soon as we have swept the infidel muezzins from the bell towers of the finest church and installed proper Christian bells there again, to ring out the tidings of your marriage to my best knight. What do you say, Lady Alouette! Is it not a grand idea? Page! Send for Sir Reyner—he's at the catapult, directing the bombardment."

What could she say that would dissuade Richard in his enthusiastic rush?

Just then the sound of footsteps outside the pavilion came to her ears, and the page, who had just left to carry out the king's bidding, re-entered to announce: "Your Grace, the sultan Saladin sends his own personal physician, having heard of your illness."

Richard was thunderstruck as he looked away from the blind woman to behold the figure before him—an ancient Moor swathed in dazzling white robes, his walnut-hued, wizened face framed in a *kafiyeh* of the same spotless linen.

"*Salaam alicum,*" the old man said, bowing low and touching his hand to his forehead. "O King Richard, live forever. The Sultan of all Sultans, Salah al Din Yusuf ibn Ayub, known to the Franks as Saladin, bids me, Haroun El Khammas, to see how I, a physician, may aid you. Word has reached Saladin of your grievous illness, and it gives me sorrow. But I must correct your page in that I am not Saladin's personal physician, but the humble assistant of Maimonides, who has taught me all his skills . . ."

"No matter," Richard interrupted with careless rudeness.

"I would rather have you. I have heard this Maimonides is a Jew." Apparently he saw nothing inconsistent in preferring an infidel Saracen to a Jew, though he was here to fight the Saracens. Clearly he was impressed by the chivalry of the gesture—and Richard could always be reached by great acts of chivalry.

"Who is this with you, physician?" he asked, pointing to the dark-robed figure who had been busy bringing in silk-covered bundles, which he laid before the king.

"Even a humble assistant may have an assistant of his own," El Khammas answered. "He is no one of importance, O great Lionheart—just Rashid, who carries my bag of instruments and the gifts Saladin has sent."

Rashid bowed jerkily to Richard, his face hidden among the folds of his dark *kafiyeh*, but Richard ignored him. He was distracted by the graceful gesture El Khammas made toward what the servant had unloaded in front of him: silver bowls of exotic fruits and a gilt ewer whose sherbet beverage was packed in snow from the distant mountains.

"How princely of the sultan! How very Christian of him!" Richard crowed. "Of course, you must inform the sultan that Melech-Ric is already on the mend," he added, uncertain as to whether he should admit weakness before this representative of the man he had come to best. It never occurred to him to be suspicious that his enemy had sent presents and the services of a physician. Such treachery would not be chivalrous.

"Rashid" was delighted with the success of his ruse. The old Moor had been loath to allow him to come along, and he made no secret of the fact that he despised the French spy, whose real name was Sir Fulk de Langres.

Confident that his presence was forgotten, Fulk looked up, allowing the *kafiyeh* to fall back from his face a little. Fool that Richard was! Didn't he realize he could be assassinated at will, either by himself or the Moor, were they so inclined? Fortunately for the English king, El Khammas was bound by his physician's oath and he, Fulk, forbidden by Phillip to eliminate his rival just yet.

Fulk knew the only other occupant of the room could not

know that his features, though swarthy, were decidedly European, rather than Saracen. He gazed in satisfaction at the object of his nightly dreams and lustful fantasies. Even in his wildest hopes he had not imagined that Alouette de Chenevy would be right here in Richard's tent! He was glad he had appealed directly to Saladin to let him come along in disguise.

He watched her, sitting so serenely on a backless chair in the tent, her lute cradled on her lap. Apparently the fiery heat had yet to wilt her, his little lark. He imagined her as she would be in the harem he would have someday—his first wife, dressed in gauzy pants and a short little vest that would betray the presence of those glorious, rose-tipped breasts as she rose to satisfy his needs, dismissing his other wives as she followed him to the couch, there to do his bidding. Oh, yes, there would be others. As a convert to Islam, he would be allowed five wives, if he could support them, and that would be easy in his new status as emir of Saladin. And he could have as many concubines as he wished. There would be graceful, sloe-eyed Saracen *houris*; statuesque Numidians when he had a taste for black flesh; blonde, blue-eyed Circassian slave girls. But Alouette would be his first wife, and he would only use the others to slake his lusts when she was carrying his sons or having her monthly flux.

His reverie was interrupted by the words being exchanged by the physician and his royal patient.

"I need to examine you, O Melech-Ric. What of the woman—?"

Richard had forgotten all about Alouette. "Ah, good physician, what an ill-mannered fellow you will tell Saladin I am! I have the honor to introduce Lady Alouette de Chenevy, who has pleasured my ears with her lovely singing this past hour."

"And your eyes with her beauty," added the Moor gallantly, though he had heard the rumors about Richard and doubted the woman's beauty moved Richard deeply.

"Lady Alouette is blind," explained Richard, "but doubtless we should excuse her before you begin, physician. My dear, thank you for beguiling the last hour for me—and for your unselfishness. Go outside to the palm grove, *damoiselle*. The page will bring Reyner to you there."

El Khammas watched her go, appreciating her comeliness and graceful movements, which were unhindered by her handicap. Even Saladin's chief concubine was not so lovely as this woman. "You say she is blind? She has not the look of one denied sight from the womb." He was suddenly intrigued by the woman's handicap, puzzled that she should be blind despite the limpid clarity of those sky-blue eyes.

"Nay, I'm told she became blind during childhood, due to some illness. But can you help me rise from this accursed pallet?" Richard demanded of the Moorish physician.

With difficulty, El Khammas dragged his attention back to the man before him. He would rather have run after the slender figure, and gently asked if he could examine her eyes. *Ah, well. Such things were in the hands of Allah*, he thought. If Allah willed, he would see her again.

Alouette was excessively glad to quit Richard's pavilion. She had enjoyed performing for him, for her music always gave her joy, and the English king was a knowledgeable, appreciative audience of one. Her unease was not because of the confrontation they had had over the queens, or even the arrival of the Moorish physician, surprising as that had been. She had listened to the Arabic-accented French spoken by El Khammas and not found it surprising that Richard had trusted the man instinctively. His voice was soothing, competent, and rich with goodness.

There had been a presence of evil, however, in the tent, she told Reyner moments later as he joined her in the shade of the palm grove. She was at a loss to explain it, she said, for she had a deep conviction that the man Saladin had sent to aid Richard was one who intended the king no harm.

"You said he had an attendant?" Reyner asked alertly.

"Yes. I believe he said his name was Rashid. Reyner, do you suppose—? There were men-at-arms within call, you know..."

"I don't know," Reyner said grimly, "but if Richard was

alone with two Saracens and they *did* have evil intent, he could nevertheless be in danger. Come on, Alouette!"

He pulled her along with him, toward the azure-and-gold silk tent that housed Richard. Reyner ignored the pair of men-at-arms guarding the entrance and burst into the cool, dim interior.

Inside lay Richard, king of England, on his pallet, and seated across from him on a cushion sat a wrinkled old Moor. From Richard's relaxed posture, it was evident that his Saracen visitor had offered him no harm. There was no one else in the tent.

"Reyner? Has the sun's heat addled your brain? What mean you by bursting in here without so much as a 'by your leave, sire'?"

Reyner went down on one knee, feeling foolish, but his sense of apprehension remained.

"Sire, forgive me, but I felt you might be in danger."

"From the physician Saladin himself has sent me? Nonsense, man. 'Twould not be chivalrous."

Reyner was familiar with Richard's weakness for grand gestures, so he forbore to point out that it was conceivable that Saladin could wish to harm Richard in such a devious way. In addition, he too felt the impact of the Moor's honesty shining from the liquid black eyes directed on him. The Moor's gaze contained no hostility, suspicion, or irritation at being interrupted, only friendly curiosity.

"Again, forgive me, sire, but where is the servant who came with the physician—I believe he is called Rashid?"

Reyner watched as the old physician looked around the tent in honest bewilderment. "Why . . . he was here just a moment ago . . ." El Khammas shrugged his shoulders at them both. "He said nothing about leaving, but I doubt he has gone far. He must be ready to aid me, he knows, and should be within range of my voice."

Unfortunately, Zeus had been left at Reyner's tent. A quick search of the camp was made, but no "Rashid" was found—not in the latrines, or in the tents of the camp prostitutes—because by this time Fulk had removed the billowing dark Saracen robes and wore the anonymous clothing of a French man-at-arms as he made his way to Phillip's tent to report his findings.

After the futile search, Reyner, still accompanied by Alouette, returned to apologize to Richard and the Moorish physician for his precipitate, unmannerly intrusion.

"But I pray you, sire—have a care. Keep a guard with you while you are ill. I beg you to realize that not all Saracens believe in chivalry," he could not resist adding.

"Nor do all Franks," interposed El Khammas mildly, thinking of the French spy he had been compelled to bring along with him. Saladin had pledged he meant no harm to Richard through this man, but El Khammas nevertheless loathed him. No honorable man would work against his country and his faith. What did Fulk hope to gain?

"God's toenails, de Winslade, you're turning into an old woman! I'm not so ill I can't defend myself!" Richard cried in annoyance. "Perhaps you'd better see that your Lady Alouette gets back aboard the dromond safely. 'Tis all you're suited for, if you see assassins behind every trunk!"

Reyner spoke little until they were in the longboat being rowed out to the *Mermaid*. Alouette sensed that the king's rebuke had embarrassed him, especially because it was undeserved. It was indeed foolish for a sick, unarmed man to allow two strangers into his tent, trusting in the code of chivalry to protect him.

She laid a gentle hand on Reyner's wrist and felt him stiffen, then relax at her touch.

"I'm sorry, Alouette, my love," he said, his voice flat with weariness. "I must seem like a cross old bear to you. I'm fatigued with this accursed heat. Sometimes it seems we'll never breach these walls—that the Saracens have endless pots of Greek fire to pour down on our archers and flaming arrows to burn up our siege engines." He allowed a great sigh to escape him. "But how are *you*, love? This heat must be awful for you, too." As if for the first time he studied her face, and noticed that it looked thinner. Her eyes, however, gleamed like two shining sapphires, full of love for him.

"I'm fine, *chèr* Reyner, just worried for you."

The loving concern in her voice was like a cool drink in this desert, especially after Richard's harsh words.

"Ah, Alouette . . ." he whispered, "when will I be free to hold you in my arms, and love you again and again through the night?" Passion vibrated in his tone—a passion he was relieved to feel revive in her presence. For too many nights he had fallen on his pallet, too exhausted even to yearn for her. But she was here now, and feeling her sweet response, he gathered her into his arms and kissed her, oblivious to the fascinated stares of the rowers.

Reacting either to Reyner's "excessive" concern, or to news that Phillip of France had already made his recovery, Richard had himself carried out to the walls of Acre the next day, still weak, but strong enough to exhort the sappers, archers, and men-at-arms to fight harder. And at their leader's command, the men redoubled their efforts, in spite of the fact that every time some portion of Acre's walls was assaulted, the Saracens within beat upon their drums, calling forth an attack from the rear by Saladin's forces in the hills. Fighting on two fronts at once was a challenge, but one at which the crusaders were succeeding.

The garrison within Acre was becoming weary. Their food supplies, after two years of siege, were growing short. The messages sent to Saladin by means of carrier pigeons—the only fowl that had not been eaten yet—were increasingly desperate. A collective moan of anguish went up from the walls when one of the sharp-eyed English archers succeeded in shooting down a winged messenger. They gleefully roasted the bird afterward over a campfire, just out of bowshot, but well within the view of the besieged Saracens.

On the eleventh of July the Accursed Tower fell with a tremendous crashing roar, succumbing at last to the sappers and catapult operators. Acre was not taken that day, however, for although a huge contingent of crusaders poured into the breach, hacking off Saracen heads and limbs with great ferocity amidst the swirling dust and rubble, they were finally repulsed.

While cries of "Christ and the Sepulchre!" rang out on the walls, the main force of crusaders were under orders to take their suppers as if nothing were happening. Richard was determined to hold his men back for the final assault —let the French, Pisans, and Austrians spill their blood, while he negotiated with Karakush, the commander of Acre! Richard knew the Saracen general was being urged by Saladin to drag out the negotiations until reinforcements could arrive from Egypt, but he kept up an unrelenting pressure by continuing bombardment and vivid threats of massacre, and agreement was reached the next day.

On July 12, the fall of Acre was proclaimed.

TWENTY-FOUR

Richard entered the city in triumph, mounted on a captured snow-white Arabian decked in purple silk trappings. Accompanying him were his fellow crusade leaders—Phillip of France, Conrad of Montferrat, Leopold of Austria, and Guy de Lusignan, king of Jerusalem.

Reyner rode on the right flank of the procession, alert for any attempt by the defeated Saracen inhabitants to harm the monarchs as they passed.

It seemed there would be no resistance. The Moslem inhabitants were too gaunt and dispirited, gazing with hollow, wary eyes at the crusaders who rode in among the rubble they had created. Behind gauzy curtains in silent stone buildings, Reyner glimpsed veiled women peering anxiously out at the hordes who marched in behind their rulers. Here and there on the streets, scrawny women stood with whimpering babies on their hips. Would the hundreds of crusaders, eager for booty and revenge for the slaying of their comrades, be able to obey the edict?

Heralds had proclaimed the terms of surrender in the crusader camp the evening before. The infidel captives were hostages who had fought bravely and were to be treated with honor, though they would be confined. They were to be exchanged within a month for the True Cross, fifteen hundred prisoners held by Saladin, two hundred thousand bezants to be paid to Richard and Phillip, and an additional fourteen hundred to Conrad for his negotiating services.

The two chief leaders parted and rode to the establishments they had selected for their own—Richard to the Palace of the Kings, Phillip to the Palace of the Templars, while Conrad of Montferrat rode about the city, accompanied by Duke Leopold, planting Christian banners where Moslem ones had proudly flown—on the minaret of the Great Mosque and on the Tower of Battle.

The English king was drafting a message summoning his wife and sister ashore and had not even had time to remove his armor when a wide-eyed soldier burst into the great hall. "Sire! Sire! The duke of Austria has planted his banners alongside yours and those of France!"

In the space of time it took to drop the quill, Richard changed from the genial "Golden Warrior," flushed with victory, to a livid, snarling lion.

"How *dare* he claim equality with me!" Richard crushed the sheet of vellum in his clenched fist. "He may have arrived sooner than Phillip, but he's done naught since with his piddly contingent but drink and wench!"

"Your Grace, 'tis but a small demonstration of vanity," soothed Blondel, who was once more in Richard's favor. He ducked just in time to avoid being struck by the pot of ink, and straightened as the dark liquid dripped down the tapestry at his back.

"Vanity?" the Lionheart roared. "That drunken sot's vanity is the least of my worries! If his banner is equal to France's and England's, fool, then so is his share of the booty, and I won't have that! That banner cannot be allowed to remain!" He whirled from the cringing minstrel to his retainers, flaring at them in turn as if each one had planted the offending banner.

Finally, the blazing blue fires settled on Reyner. "You— de Winslade. *You* were so eager to save my life when 'twas needless—go save my honor now. Go fetch that disgraceful Austrian rag hither!"

With a sinking heart, Reyner bowed in token of his obedience, realizing he had no choice. The Lionheart was offering him a chance to redeem himself after embarrassing Richard in front of El Khammas.

Once, in the hot flush of faith and new knighthood, he would have volunteered for the mission, joyfully laying low any who dared oppose him in its completion. Today, however, he had been about to carry the message to the queens bidding them to their new apartments in the palace. He had been looking forward to seeing Alouette and helping her settle into her chamber, and finding his own quarters among the captured stone houses. Perhaps there would have even been time for them to be alone together.

He trudged back out into the noonday sun, pulling on his helm and calling Thomas to lead Hercules out. He motioned Zeus into the shade of the building and bid him to stay, aware that the presence of his huge pet would only draw unwanted attention.

Was his love for Alouette turning him womanish, as Richard had accused? He didn't think so. He was as eager as ever to fight the Saracens, to regain the True Cross, to secure the holy places for the pilgrims of the faith. But he found this endless quarreling among "Christian" princes, this ceaseless jockeying for preeminence, wearying and disgusting. Richard wasn't interested in what he thought, only in the results, so he resolutely cleared his mind of all other hopes and dreams.

The square where the Great Mosque stood was crowded with milling crusaders, all celebrating the victory, many clutching wineskins, many others dragging half-clad Saracen women around. The conquerors were already laden with jewels, fancy cloth, ornamented dishes, and even furniture.

Reyner would have preferred not to have an audience watching while he took down the Austrian duke's banner; the fewer wine-soaked men to carry tales or offer battle, the quicker he could accomplish the task. This was not the Lionheart's way, he knew —Richard would have sounded a trumpet as he snatched down the flag.

"Men of Winslade," he ordered, quietly motioning them forward with his arm, "surround the mosque."

"Ho—Reyner! A happy day, is it not?" William des Barres staggered up as Reyner prepared to dismount. Obviously, he had had more than a sip of the potent Syrian wine.

"William," Reyner responded, although he chafed at the interruption, "it's good to see you. I wasn't sure if you'd come from Sicily, after that little confrontation with my liege."

"Yes, he finally relented, and I sailed with Phillip. I've been here since April—an old-timer!" he laughed. "Those flags are a brave sight, *hein*?"

"Only two have a right to be there," Reyner said, still striving to keep his voice down, so the drunken throng didn't divine his purpose until it was accomplished. If he were stealthy as he climbed into the minaret, perhaps they might not notice Austria's banner was gone.

"What d'ya mean, Reyner? Austria's? Oh, let Leopold have his fun—it won't mean anything!"

Reyner's whispered hints for William to be quiet were lost on the tipsy Frenchman, who continued to remonstrate with his friend in a penetrating voice that turned heads— particularly blue-eyed, bushy-mustached ones whose stocky features had a Teutonic caste—Austrian heads.

"You can't mean you're going to pull it down? Reyner, *mon vieux*! Can't Richard take a jest? That's all it is, a jest!"

Reddened, bleary eyes were beginning to stare hostilely in their direction. "Shut up, William," he said quietly. "I'm under orders from the King of England."

William complied, tardily realizing the effect his loud words had had on the crowd, but it was too late. It was useless to attempt discretion now.

"Guard me," Reyner growled at his men, and at his command swords were unsheathed, pikes made ready, maces displayed menacingly. Baring his own blade, he backed up the stairway of the tall, thin tower, watching the faces in the crowd until they were out of sight.

Removing the gaily colored Austrian banner from its place next to France's fleur-de-lis and England's snarling leopard was easy, though he heard a buzz begin in the crowd as he leaned out from the muezzin's platform and ripped it from its standard.

By the time he reached the street again, however, the angry rumbling of the Austrians had become a roar, and weapons were being drawn to match those already held by his men, who were in position around the entrance to the minaret in a semicircle.

Reyner hoped that getting himself killed in such a silly errand in the name of chivalric honor would make Richard happy. Imagine, to be willing to die under a Saracen blade, assured of instant salvation, and to be slain by fellow "Christians" instead! After taking a deep breath, he leaped off the top three steps, screaming at the top of his lungs: "Winslade! *À moi! À moi!*"

Realizing his fault in the confrontation, William des Barres's shouted battle cry—*"Dieu nous sauve! Des Barres!"*—summoned his own retainers to aid his friend, which was all that enabled Reyner to escape alive. Nevertheless, during the course of the fray the banner was snatched from Reyner by a stout Austrian eager to retrieve his duke's honor—an action for which he was rewarded by receiving the flat of Reyner's sword squarely on his shoulders. The banner fluttered to the ground, was muddied by spilled wine, and was trampled underfoot many times before Reyner succeeded in retrieving it.

By the time it reached Richard's satisfied hands, the banner of Austria was a ripped, dirty rag. The story of its "dishonoring," by the time it reached Leopold's enraged ears, no longer bore resemblance to reality.

The furious duke of Austria was at the palace within the hour with the king of France in tow, blustering threats against Richard Plantagenet.

They were kept waiting in the great hall for nearly an hour while Richard settled his faithful knight on a silk-cushioned couch in a darkened room on the roof of the palace, which was cooled by the evening breeze off the bay and the ostrich feather fans wielded by two of Richard's pages.

Alouette, who had come ashore with her mistress during the time Reyner was seizing the banner, was sent for, as well as Innocentia, the latter to stitch up a small laceration opened in his left cheek by an Austrian dagger.

Reyner's hauberk and shield had saved him from most of the damage the Austrian men-at-arms had attempted; nonetheless, he had several painful bruises and aching muscles. Richard remained for several minutes, praising Reyner's daring raid as if his knight were a new Roland, as if he cared not a whit that Leopold and Phillip waited below, and that his petulant action would cost the crusade the entire Austrian contingent. At last he arose and stretched, lion-like, before leaving them.

"It seems I am restored to favor," chuckled Reyner, grimacing intermittently as Innocentia finished closing up the last edges of his gash, plying her bone needle and horsehair thread as if she were mending a seam. The willow bark infusion Alouette had sent for to ease his pain was beginning to work—or was it the Syrian wine, iced with snow from the mountains?

"You could have been killed," grumbled Alouette. She had heard the indrawn breaths revealing his pain as she had examined him with sensitive fingers. "And all for a colorful pennant and Richard's vanity."

"Sssh, love. After all the infidel arrows I've dodged this fortnight, that was child's play. And as little as I care for currying favor, it is well the king thinks I can do no wrong for the moment," answered Reyner dryly. He was imperturbable now that the fracas was over and Alouette was with him. "He's secured me the use of a villa not a stone's throw from here—I didn't even have to fight for it!—for as long as we're in Acre. Thank you, Innocentia," he added, as the Sicilian girl deftly snipped the horsehair thread and applied a balm to prevent festering of the wound.

"'Tis nothing, Sir Reyner." Innocentia beamed at him, reacting to his kind tone, then turned to Alouette sitting on the chair near Reyner's couch. "My lady, will you be need-

ing anything else for a while? Shall I return to escort you to
your chamber later?"

"I'll see that Alouette is taken care of," said Reyner.
" 'Tis a pretty new bliaut you wear. Is it in celebration of
the victory, or for some sweetheart?"

He was rewarded with a blush and a shy smile. *"Sieur
Henri*—my lady's brother—promised me he would show
me the house he claimed today. May I go, Lady Alouette?"

Compassion warred with good sense in Alouette. She
didn't want her maid to be hurt.

"Innocentia, go, by all means . . . but be careful. I love
my brother, but young noblemen are used to taking what
they want. I would not have him play with your feelings . . ." she warned.

"Henri—that is to say, *Sieur* Henri," Innocentia protested, "would never hurt me, my lady. He loves me, and
I, him."

The simple declaration hung on the cooling night air.

"Then go, and send him my greetings."

They dismissed the pages wielding the fans at the same
time, for the night air was now pleasantly cool. When they
had gone, Reyner said, "My sweet love, you cannot protect
others from their mistakes."

She sighed. "And I'm too late, am I not? I'm certain my
stepbrother has bedded her already. I'm not worried about
her conceiving his bastard—you know of the potion she
makes—but of his breaking her heart. Oh, he may make
her his mistress while in Outremer—but what is there for
her when he goes back to France? He is a count, Reyner.
He is overdue to marry, and he was besieged by neighboring barons before he left, all offering their daughters to
him. Will he wed my tirewoman, Reyner, when he is offered dowered *damoiselles*?"

He pulled her from the nearby chair onto the couch
where he lay. "You would shield everyone from dishonor
but yourself, sweet Alouette. Would you really go back to
England as my mistress, when you could return as my lady
wife?"

She could not think when he was this near—when the

scent of him was in her nostrils, when his hands were stroking her back and stealing around the side to caress her breasts.

"Lie down with me, love..." His voice, husky with desire, floated to her ears on the sweet night air.

"Reyner, what of your injuries? We'll tear open the stitches!" she argued, already feeling him pressing her down on the couch.

"So? I'll have one more scar and be just a little uglier. What does it matter? A wonderful woman loves me and is blind to my faults," he joked, drawing her against him, loving the feel of her body through the embroidered cotton bliaut.

Already stripped to a loincloth so that Innocentia could tend his injuries, he quickly relieved Alouette of her clothes, barely able to restrain himself from ripping them, in his haste to feel her soft skin against his own. "I hope Berengaria was not expecting her attendant back tonight, sweetheart, for I intend to keep you very busy all night through."

"No, I think she was expecting the king to visit..." Alouette sighed. It was difficult to breathe when he touched her like that. And like that...

With one swift movement he unwound the loincloth, and now his manhood lay pulsing against her thigh, erect and demanding. She felt that inner core of her moisten, ready for the entrance of his shaft.

He slid teasingly above that opening, inflaming her with need, until she moaned with the intensity of it. He lowered his mouth from her parted lips and suckled her breasts, circling each sensitive aureola with his tongue, gently nipping with his teeth, until she thought she would go mad.

"Please..." she whispered. She would climax as soon as he entered her, she knew; she *must*, or surely her heart would burst.

"You want me to take you?" he murmured into her ear, his voice honeyed with passion, and paused to give her a mind-drugging kiss.

Frantically she writhed under him. He knew what she

wanted without asking! Why must he torment her so? "Yes! I want you to take me, Reyner, *please*!"

"Do you love me?"

"Yes, I love you! I love you, Reyner, my love, my own..."

Still he made no move to end her delicious agony. "And I love you, Alouette, my heart, my darling. But if you want me to take you, you have to agree to one little thing —a whim of mine, only..."

"What is it? Anything!" she gasped. Indeed, she would have given half of eternity, just to end this sweet pain in pleasure.

"Marry me—here, in Acre—as soon as it can be arranged."

She stopped her movements as if she were suddenly paralyzed. "Reyner, I can't... we mustn't... please, I've explained why—don't ask it of me."

He ground his hips against hers, tantalizing her, knowing how close she was to her peak and reveling in his power. "Marry me!" he demanded, his own breathing ragged with the effort of restraint.

She was on fire, and only he could put out the flames. "Oh, damn you, Reyner!" she cried, tossing her head back and forth on the bed linens, digging her fingers into the small of his back. "All right—I'll marry you!"

He laughed triumphantly, then sucked in a breath and drove smoothly into her, burying himself within her in one stroke.

Her orgasm came, not on his first masterful thrust but the second, and she screamed with its intensity. Reyner allowed himself his own release then, and groaning her name, thrust into her in a rhythmic frenzy as the spasms shook him.

She must have lost consciousness for a short interval, for when she came to herself he was curled up against her and his regular breathing told her he slept. The single rush light he'd left burning must have guttered out, for she smelled only the smoky traces of it. It didn't matter, she reflected with a smile, she wasn't afraid of the dark.

Alouette lay on her back, savoring the feeling of his body against hers and the hardness of the well-muscled arm possessively holding her close. The call of night birds, foreign to her ears, mingled with the far-off sounds of revelry somewhere in the captured city below.

By Our Lady, what had she agreed to do? She should never have put herself in the position where she was as butter in his hands, for both their sakes! Now she was honor-bound to marry him. Reneging on her agreement, even though it was made under the sweetest sort of duress, was out of the question.

Perhaps her misgivings had been foolish, all along. Maybe he was right. Bastardy, after all, was a common enough thing, and Reyner loved her despite her blindness. Yet how she wished that she were as perfect as the wife he deserved to have! And that other reason to refuse him, though it hovered at the edges of her memory, could not be so important. She looked within herself and the thing rumbled and shook itself, rather like a dragon slumbering and moving in its sleep—enough to remind her it was still there.

At last she, too, slept.

In her dream she heard the voice—that hated, sneering voice—laughing at the terrified child who stood screaming, pointing at the crimson stain on the sheets, a stain that matched the bloody traces of her virginity in streaks down her legs.

"There's nothing like the feel of a young virgin, Phillip —you really ought to try it. Why don't you have a go at her? After all, I've done the hard part, ha, ha . . ."

The drunken Phillip had only raised red-rimmed eyes, apparently still too intoxicated to make any sense of the fantastic image before him: of his crony, transformed into a naked satyr, looming over the screaming child, the man's blood-stained organ . . . Then his head slumped forward again, but his snores could not be heard over her broken whimpering and the mocking laughter of her violator.

She woke up, drenched in sweat, still hearing the scream

that echoed down the years, but realizing the room was quiet.

It was pitch-black, for dawn was long off and there was no moon shining in the window to illuminate the shapes within the room, but as her eyes accommodated to the dark, she found them resting on the figure lying next to her, half-covered by a sheet.

Reyner lay on his stomach, tawny hair covering most of his face, which was turned away from her. She saw the rise and fall of his massive shoulders as he breathed in sleep.

She saw him. She could see.

Alouette screamed then, clutching his shoulders. "Reyner! The light! Light the lamp! I can see, Reyner! I can see!"

He woke quickly, completely alert, as a warrior trained to battle must learn to do. Most of his face was hidden from her by the dark shadows, but she could discern a hawklike profile with a determined, slightly cleft chin.

"You can see? What miracle is this? Never mind, I'll get a torch!"

Alouette heard him run from the room as tears of joy blurred her vision. She was going to see him! She was going to *see* the face of Reyner de Winslade, the English knight who loved her and would become her husband!

Holy Mary, it didn't matter if his eyes were crossed or his mouth misshapen or his face scarred and hideously birthmarked. She could hardly contain herself in her excitement.

She turned in the direction of the door, eager for her first glimpse, as the sound of his running footsteps returned. She smelled the resinous odor of the burning pine pitch, but still her eyes could not pierce the inky blackness of the room.

"Reyner? Bring the torch inside, love. I can hardly wait to see you!"

"It . . . it is inside."

"Stop jesting with me, love! I've waited too long as it is!"

"Alouette, I make no jests. See the flame, sweetheart?"

She felt the first stirrings of panic slide like icy slivers into her belly.

He held the torch so close that she could feel its radiated heat, but no glowing flame filled her vision—only the continued hellish darkness she'd lived in since she was eight years old.

"Oh, Holy Christ, no! *Nooooo!*"

TWENTY-FIVE

"I trust this is a matter of sufficient importance for you to intrude, despite my instructions that you were to wait until summoned," Saladin said, settling himself comfortably among the cushions, while the veiled, sloe-eyed concubine he had been fondling glided noiselessly behind a screen. Her eyes were discreetly downcast; she betrayed neither by resentful look nor panting breaths that the sultan had been within a hairsbreadth of bringing her to joy, merely by the skillful use of his hands. To be interrupted at such a point—and for a despised infidel at that—was frustrating to the young woman, but to betray her feelings would bring dishonor to the sultan and cause a loss of his favor. She could tell he wasn't going to tolerate the Frank for long, in any case.

"I think you will agree that it is of *vital* importance, once you have heard what I have to say. By the by, I applaud your taste," Fulk said, nodding in the direction the lithe-limbed *houri* had gone.

A wiser man than Fulk de Langres would have known not to refer to Saladin's concubine. For an infidel especially to do so was to degrade the sultan's exclusive property. And Fulk had made a grave error in assuming he could speak to Saladin in such a man-to-man fashion. He was not Saladin's equal, any more than a snake was equal to a falcon.

"Say on," Saladin directed him, and since Fulk was cunning rather than wise, he missed the curling of the sultan's lip and the coldness of the black eyes that stared at him.

"His Majesty the King of France bids me to offer you a proposition." He waited, but Saladin did not betray by so much as the flicker of an eyelid any eagerness.

"He offers, for a certain consideration, to leave the Holy Land and return to France."

"'A certain consideration?' Is this the infidel way of referring to money?"

Fulk pretended not to notice the sultan's lashing scorn. "For the sum of two hundred thousand bezants, he will sail away from Palestine's shores within the week," Fulk said, with the air of one who drops a stone into a deep pool and stands by to watch it splash. He was astonished to hear Saladin laugh.

"Two hundred thousand bezants to bribe him to leave, eh?"

Fulk nodded.

Saladin laughed again, as if it were indeed a matter of great amusement. "The French king will leave anyway— why should I beggar myself? It is no secret that he is ill, both with the disease you Franks label leonardie and with dysentery, so that he can barely leave the close-stool, and he shakes like an old man. Also, he can scarcely wait to invade Richard's possessions while the Lionheart remains to fight me. Let him do what he is fated to do, but never let him think I will pay him to do it. And once he leaves, I can more easily sweep the remnant into the sea."

Fulk swallowed nervously. That Saladin knew of Phillip's most intimate infirmities spoke of a larger spy network than he had imagined. "I shall convey your message, O Saladin."

At that moment the tent flap opened, and the white-robed El Khammas strode in. He salaamed to Saladin, then eyed the sultan's visitor with unconcealed distaste.

"I am sorry to intrude, O Sultan of Sultans. Your guard did not tell me you were in conference."

"The Frank was just leaving," Saladin said shortly, then switched to French. "You were finished with your message, were you not?"

"Yes, my lord. That is all Phillip ordered me to say. But I need to make my own plans, O Sultan."

"Your own plans?"

Fulk had decided the best course was boldness. "I would know, O Sultan, of the emirate you will award me, that I may secure the woman you promised me—Lady Alouette de Chenevy. I worry about her safety, lord—that she may accidentally be caught in the crossfire when you crush Richard's forces." *Or that Reyner de Winslade would succeed in persuading Alouette to marry him.* Fulk had begun to doubt his ability to kill his handsome cousin, and was increasingly reluctant to risk his life in the attempt. If Alouette were already married, the legitimacy of any children he might sire on her was in doubt. That wouldn't matter if he stayed in Outremer and became a Moslem, but someday he wanted to return to England and reclaim his father's stolen estates.

"We will discuss the matter of a reward when you have merited it, de Langres. Now go, and do not come again until you are summoned—or until you have real news."

With relief Saladin turned to the old physician, knowing his guards would prevent Fulk from lingering outside to eavesdrop.

"My old friend, how are you? How goes it in Acre?"

"Peace be with you, O Sultan. We will speak of Acre in a moment. For now, I am troubled at the furrow between your brow, and the churning of your liver the Frank has caused. Why do you tolerate him?"

Saladin's shoulders twitched in genuine amusement. Only his physicians would dare upbraid him thus. "You see inside of me as if I were glass, old friend. The bile indeed is sour within me after I speak to that scoundrel. Like his French master he would sell his grandmother—or his soul —for the brightest coin. But never fear—he will get naught of value from me. When I am tired of his vainglorious antics, I will send for the Assassins. They will rid me of him—like that." He snapped his fingers.

Even El Khammas gasped at his casual mention of the murderous Assassins, whose headquarters were deep in the mountains. "Saladin, have a care! Their ears are every-where!"

"Don't worry, physician. They have already demon-strated to me that they can penetrate even my closest guard, if they wish. But there is no need. All they ask of me is respect, which I give them. Beyond that, we operate in separate spheres, unless I need their services."

"I say again, have a care, lest they demand your soul in exchange for their *services*," El Khammas retorted darkly.

"Enough of that! Tell me of Acre! How does my con-quered garrison fare?"

"Your people are well so far, housed comfortably in Phillip's and Richard's care, and treated with respect by royal decree. I have been allowed free access to them to care for the wounded. Will you be able to ransom them or rescue them, my lord?"

Saladin heaved a deep sigh. "I don't know. If only they had been able to hold out until the reinforcements came from Egypt. But 'twas not as Allah decreed. Melech-Ric will treat them with all chivalry, certainly—until it be-comes evident that I cannot meet his impossibly greedy demands. Then—who knows? He cannot stay bottled up in Acre forever, nor can he spare any of the army to stay and act as jailers. Jerusalem is his destination. What will he do with two thousand men then? He can hardly afford to leave them to nip at his rear!"

The answer was too troubling to contemplate. The old Moor saw with regret that he had only reminded the sultan of his greatest worry. He decided to distract Saladin with the matter that had made him start with surprise as the infidel knight was talking.

"If I may change the subject, dear friend—?"

Saladin made a gesture of assent. "Please. I would be grateful for any diversion. Even as I pleasure the concubine I brought from Damascus, my mind runs hither and yon, like a mouse in a labyrinth, fleeing the lion. If you can make me forget, even for a few moments . . ."

"The woman the Frankish knight covets—I have met her. You must not let that pig of an infidel have her."

"Ah! So even my ancient Moor is not proof against

love!" Saladin crowed in amusement, then stopped as El Khammas held up a hand with a wry smile.

"Nay, friend. 'Tis not lust that motivates me. What need have I for a woman, except to warm my old bones? I would waste her youth and loveliness upon the desert of *my* body!"

"Then what is it that is so important about a mere woman that you bring her to my notice? Are you suggesting that I take her for my harem?"

"No, though she is the equal of your most favorite wife. I met Lady Alouette in Melech-Ric's tent when I went to minister to him in his illness. She was singing to him, my lord—fittingly enough, her name means 'lark' in the Frankish tongue. Her loveliness surpasses the moon and the stars, Saladin, and if I am any judge, her heart is the equal of her beauty. She loves a knight in Melech-Ric's retinue, and he, her. He is stalwart and brave, a fitting spouse for this lovely lark as Fulk, that scorpion, can never be. And I believe I can help her."

"Help her? In what way?"

"She is blind, my lord, though her eyes are as unclouded as a mountain pool. I wonder if her blindness is of the soul, rather than of the body. I wonder if I could—"

"Restore her vision? Surely that would be a miracle blessed by Allah. Go to her, my friend, and offer to do so!"

The old physician chuckled, pleased at the boyish enthusiasm which betokened the success of his diversion. " 'Tis not so simple as that. The women of the Franks are well-guarded by their men, and walled in by the ignorance and superstition that clouds the Western mind. If I were to approach this beauteous lady, she might well flee from me in horror, as if from Satan himself, even if she knew I could heal her. Nay, I ask only that you prevent her from falling into Fulk's greedy grasp. I will leave the opportunity for her healing up to Allah. If He wills that I am to be the instrument of her healing, He will bring it to pass."

"I think the azure veil would complement my coloring . . . and you should purchase the dark green one with the gold threads. It would set off your fiery red hair, Joanna.

Alouette, you too must have a veil, as a present for tolerating these endless trips into the marketplace. I think . . . this burgundy-hued one for you."

"What about me, *Tante* Berengaria?" Chloe wailed, and was soon placated with a gaudy ring that had caught her eye.

The two queens, Chloe, and their attendants were in Acre's *souks*, as was their wont almost every morning, before the merciless sun climbed too high in the sky. Afternoons were for napping in their apartments in the cool interior of the palace. There was little else for them to do until evening, when Richard, sometimes accompanied by Phillip, usually came to dine with them. They were always disappointed when he held his own entertainments and they were left to their own devices.

The bulbous-nosed old merchant was delighted that the royal ladies had stopped at his booth. They rarely haggled, and seemed to have an endless supply of coins for the gold and silver jewelry, bolts of cotton and silk fabric, fresh fruits, vegetables, and meats that were sold in these open-air stalls. Furthermore, they never allowed their escort to harass the merchants, as some of the crusaders took pleasure in doing now that life in the coastal town was beginning to resume its normal rhythm.

The harassment consisted of various "tests" designed to prove the merchants were eastern Christians, as they claimed, rather than secret Saracens or Jews. For Syrian Christians, with their swarthy features and long beards, looked identical to their counterparts in the other faiths. Often, they were merely required to recite the Pater Noster and Ave Maria—at swordpoint—but sometimes the "proof" was more humiliating; as when the swords were dipped to pull up the hems of the merchants' garments to expose their manhood. Only infidel Saracens and Jews were circumcised—and the plea that one had undergone conversion to the Christian faith after infancy was generally ignored. If the merchant were found to be lying about his religion, he could count on having his booth smashed, his goods stolen or trampled—or might even lose his life.

Even bona fide eastern Christians were having difficulty

reclaiming their property in Acre these days, for the greedy crusaders refused to release the dwellings they had taken over, even if the real owners, who had been driven out two years earlier by the Saracens, returned. Descendants of the first crusaders, who had come more than one hundred years ago, found themselves as dispossessed as the Saracens, and crowded the palace with their grievances.

Alouette murmured her thanks for the veil. Perhaps she should wear it with her wedding dress, the silk cloth for which had been the object of an earlier shopping trip.

It was hard to believe that in a fortnight, she would become Reyner's bride.

It had been a week since Acre had fallen, since the night of love when she had promised to become Reyner's wife. A week since she had had that agonizingly brief flash of sight before she was submerged in darkness again. Since that night, she had known a depression so black and enveloping that even the excited chatter of Joanna and Berengaria, delighted at having a wedding to plan, could not penetrate. She smiled politely, answered questions about her preferences, and went where they bid her.

Her body did these things, but her soul remained trapped in a morass of despair.

The queens had not noticed she was merely going through the motions, as if in a dream. Reyner, though he seemed to suspect all was not well with her soul, had been kept so busy by Richard that he had little time to be with her.

Alouette would go through with the marriage because she had promised. She would not dishonor her word. And she really was in love with him and wanted to be his wife. However, now more than ever before, something was festering within her—some noisome creation that must soon cause her destruction.

It would have been better if those moments of sight had never happened, she thought. The transient phenomenon seemed designed by the Devil himself to torment her. It did no good to berate herself as an ungrateful wretch, or to remind herself how fortunate she was to be marrying the most loving man in Christendom, whose touch—whose very voice—aroused her, who promised her a secure life in England, away from her treacherous half brother. She had been blind for more years than she had been sighted; but until she had *seen* again, she had been resigned to her handicap and had almost forgotten what it was like to see. Now that she had been allowed to experience sight again, she resented the capricious way that sense was being dangled in front of her, only to be cruelly snatched away. Ah, blessed saints, surely she should go confess her base ingratitude. If God realized what an ungrateful wretch she was, he would take away the love of this good man, perhaps by letting Reyner find out about her spying for Phillip, minor as it had been.

The French king had come to her in the last week, managing as he always did to discover her when she was alone.

Phillip had asked her about Richard's plans—what he proposed to do if the ransom was not raised; if he would intervene in the increasingly bitter wrangling between the two claimants to the throne of Jerusalem, Guy de Lusignan and Conrad of Montferrat; and what news he had of Prince John's antics back in England. As usual, she could shed very little light on those military and political matters. Reyner had scarcely been allowed any time with her since that night on the roof of the palace, and Berengaria was so little in Richard's confidence that she was not a useful source either.

Oddly enough, Phillip had not seemed that disgruntled. He made none of the usual threats about Henri's safety. Alouette thought he was on the point of leaving when suddenly, as if out of the blue, he said, "But here is something I vow you *can* tell me, *chère soeur*."

"What is it?"

"Does your mistress quicken, as yet? Has Richard of England succeeded in planting a babe within Berengaria's belly?"

Alouette was honestly puzzled. "Why, Your Majesty, would you be interested in such petty gossip? What possible business could that be of yours?"

"What an innocent simpleton you are, Alouette. If Rich-

ard remains true to his perversion, then Berengaria of Navarre remains barren. If Richard creates no legitimate
issue, then the crown will one day be available and coveted
by greedy John Lackland and Richard's callow nephew,
Arthur, whose duchy of Brittany lies close to my borders.
Oh yes, little sister, it is of very great interest to me if
Richard is acting the man with his wife, or not."

Alouette could not help thinking of the time that Berengaria had come to her on the dromond, upset at Richard's
lack of desire for her bed. As far as she knew, Richard had
not bedded his wife since then, though Berengaria had not
complained of it to her lady-in-waiting. Perhaps she felt
she had confided too much to her already, or perhaps she
was becoming resigned to her strange state. Alouette had
been too absorbed in her own melancholy to wonder about
it, these last few days.

"I'm waiting, Alouette. Remember your brother's
life—"

It must have been the heat making her irritable, but suddenly she was weary of Phillip's threats.

"I know, I know. Don't bother harping on that string,
Your Majesty. No—as far as I know, Berengaria is not
enceinte—"

"Because Richard can't bring himself to touch her. She
doesn't look enough like a pretty boy," Phillip jeered, fin-
ishing her thought for her.

Deep in her thoughts, Alouette shook her head. Surely
what she had said could not have been such a traitorous
revelation.

"I do believe she hasn't even heard us," giggled Joanna,
and Alouette suddenly realized that Berengaria had been
addressing her.

"I'm sorry, my lady. I fear I was woolgathering. What
did you say?"

Berengaria was not annoyed. "'Tis a bride-to-be's privilege," she said kindly. "I said, why don't we visit the baths
before we return to the palace. I vow I am drenched with
sweat after even this little walk."

Alouette readily agreed. She enjoyed the cool stone
bathhouse, which had no counterpart in Europe. Once in-

side, they were taken into private rooms reserved for female patrons, their garments removed by solicitous female attendants, and served iced wine and sherbet while attendants scrubbed them all over with a soft cloth and shampooed their hair with sweet-smelling soap. Frequent bathing was a necessity in this hot climate, but the bathhouses made it a treat. She would have to ask Reyner if they could construct something similar back in England.

As Alouette and the queens were entering the bathhouse, Reyner had just arrived in the great hall of the Palace of the Kings.

He could see that Richard was not alone, however, so he would have to wait to make his report. Besides, judging by the importance of Richard's visitors, this would be a most interesting wait.

The duke of Burgundy and the bishop of Beauvais were pale as they stood before the English king and exchanged greetings. Clearly something was amiss.

"We come as ambassadors of His Majesty the King of France," the Bishop began in a careful fashion, staring at his red leather-shod feet. "I am asked to announce to you, King Richard of England, that King Phillip will be departing these shores for Europe as soon as it can be arranged. He begs me to tell you he is 'weary of sacrificing his health and interest on this barren coast,' and feels he has fulfilled his vow as a crusader, having left his kingdom for a full year."

Richard rose to his feet, his face purpling as he worked himself into a true Plantagenet rage.

"If your king leaves undone the work for which he came hither, he will bring shame and everlasting contempt upon himself and France. But if he feels he will die if he stays, let him go."

Reyner could imagine the anger that boiled within his sovereign—an anger that was only partly mollified when the Duke of Burgundy announced that Phillip was leaving a generous portion of his army under the duke's generalship. Richard must be smarting with humiliation as he remembered that the night before, he had entertained Phillip in this same hall, and had proposed that all the crusaders bind themselves to an oath to remain in the Holy Land for three years—unless Saladin surrendered sooner. Phillip had flushed and looked away, muttering something noncommittal. Now all knew why.

Reyner was sure that once Richard's rage had cooled, he would see the benefits of having a free hand in Outremer, for his orders would be unchallenged. Even though Phillip was leaving and Leopold had already left, Richard would still retain an impressive force.

It would take hours, though, for Richard to calm down; and in the meantime, he would be looking to vent his spleen on the next poor fool who bothered him. Reyner left word with Richard's seneschal that he could be summoned at the king's convenience, then went to see if Alouette was in the queens' apartments.

Reyner knew Alouette would be interested in the startling news of Phillip's imminent departure, and relieved as well. With her royal half brother back in France, they could begin their married life free from the ominous cloud of his presence. Perhaps Phillip's departure would even free her of the sadness that had clung to her since the all-too-brief flash of sight she had had that night on the roof. He wondered also if Henri would choose or be ordered to return to France, and if Alouette would be very distressed if he left.

He decided he would tell her about his trip into the hills as Richard's envoy to Saladin. Negotiations had gone on daily as both sides attempted to secure further concessions. The evening before, Richard had received a trio of turbaned ambassadors from the sultan and had sent Reyner and two other knights to Saladin's headquarters with his answers to the sultan's proposals.

He looked forward to telling her about the fabulous meal set before them of roasted kid, quail, and spiced gazelle; of fruits so exotic he did not even know their names; and almond cakes, all washed down with *kaffe*, the dark Arab drink with the white powder called sugar, which was so much sweeter than European honey.

He would describe Saladin to her, telling his love of the

intelligence that shone from the sultan's dark eyes, and the gentle courtesy with which he had treated the Frankish knights, even when they had to tell him of Richard's obduracy concerning certain proposals. He had been surprised to find himself liking the older man, who looked far younger than he was rumored to be. Reyner was impressed that Saladin seemed singularly free of arrogance and illtemper, and that his regal air seemed unstudied and natural. He had asked each of the knights his name, and a little about his background, nodding with genuine interest as he drew each one out. The knights found themselves talking of home and kin, unaware of the longing that tinged their voices.

Saladin came last to Reyner. When Reyner had given his name, the Sultan seemed startled.

"Sir Reyner of Winslade? I have heard of you, through my good physician, El Khammas. Are you not betrothed to a lady of Melech-Ric's court—a blind troubador named Alouette?"

Reyner was astonished that Saladin, with the cares of the entire Moslem world upon his shoulders, should know his name—and Alouette's—merely because his physician had seen them in Richard's tent.

"You guard your lord well, and are a credit to him. As the old Moor has told me, your lady loves a worthy man. Here—take this as a token of my respect and goodwill." Saladin held a small gold ring out to Reyner, chuckling at his dumfounded expression as he took it.

"I will understand if it is never on your finger," Saladin had continued as Reyner studied it, noting the crescent design engraved on the ring. "You're too intelligent a man to believe that this crescent conveys some malevolent power, but your fellow crusaders will shun you if you wear it. Keep it on your person, and show it at need, Reyner of Winslade. It will bring you freedom if you are captured by my men—and it will even win mercy from The Old Man of the Mountain."

At Reyner's blank look, he explained: "The head of the sect who feed their courage upon the drug hashish—hence their name, 'Hashasheen,' or in your tongue, 'Assassins.'"

When he arrived at the queens' apartments, Reyner found Alouette's tirewoman alone.

"Lady Alouette has not returned as yet from the *souks*, where she went with Queen Berengaria and Queen Joanna," Innocentia told him. "Frequently they stop at the baths on the way back."

Reyner would have liked nothing more than to meet Alouette there (though he would have had to wait for her outside, to avoid damaging her good name!), but he gave Innocentia a regretful smile.

"I'm afraid I must linger in idleness here until Richard sends for me. I will look for Lady Alouette later."

TWENTY-SIX

When Fulk heard the news of Phillip's imminent departure, he lost no time in seeking an audience. It was the answer to a prayer, he thought fervently, forgetting that he had not prayed in years. Saladin seemed cooler and more disdainful every time he paid him a visit, and his information never seemed to please the sultan. Fulk had grown more and more worried each time the rapid-fire Arabic died down in the tent just as he arrived, and flared up the moment he exited.

He had begun to doubt that Saladin would grant him anything if he turned coat permanently—and while the sultan affected yawning disinterest when Fulk spoke of Alouette, the dark eyes became colder and more distant. Perhaps it was only that the Saracen leader couldn't understand his obsession for one woman, since Moslem law allowed polygamy.

Fulk had to wait an annoyingly long time while Phillip saw an endless number of merchants and landowners, all pressing their claims upon the French king. They thought him more amenable to granting their demands for redress since he was leaving—and they were right.

At last, Fulk's turn came. Phillip sent even his guards from the room, smiling derisively at his henchman, who was disguised as a Syrian Christian, complete with long dark robe and beard, with a patch over one eye to further hide his identity.

"Wait, don't tell me—let me guess. You have heard that we are leaving, and the idea of returning to France appeals more to you than staying and currying Saladin's favor."

Fulk could only stare shamefacedly at him, mouth agape at the French king's perception. "Yes, sire. If you will have me, I shall serve you faithfully the rest of my life."

"Oh, I'm sure you will—if it suits your interests. Tell me, how am I to explain your sudden reappearance, when all are aware I had banished you for your sins against Richard's favorite knight?"

"Everyone knows of your clemency, Your Majesty," Fulk began smoothly, then saw that Phillip was immune to his flattery. "Or you could levy a fine to be paid—"

"You begin to speak my language."

"—which you will magnanimously forgive as my wedding present."

Now it was Phillip's turn to drop his jaw. "Your wedding?"

"But, of course. You *would* rather that Alouette wed me —incidentally, righting an old wrong—than have her marry Reyner de Winslade, wouldn't you? Their nuptial vows are set for the first day of August, as you know."

Fulk had the satisfaction of catching Phillip off guard. Phillip's cruel eyes narrowed dangerously in his pudgy face. "No, I did not know. My dear half sister has been remiss in informing me. The day after we are to sail, eh?"

"Exactly, sire. Now, here is what I propose to do . . ."

Two evenings before her wedding day, Alouette sat at the window of her chamber, enjoying the slight evening breeze.

Tomorrow Phillip—and those of the French who felt they had done their duty as crusaders—would be leaving the shores of Palestine. It would be a relief to know he was no longer near enough to cause her misery.

When he had taken his leave of her earlier today, Phillip had been in a buoyant mood, overjoyed to be returning home and leaving behind the wearying climate and cares of this crusade. Perhaps that explained his cheerful tone as he announced that her brother Henri was staying behind, with his royal permission and blessing.

Alouette was surprised. It was the last thing she had expected him to say. "Henri will stay? But—I thought . . ."

"You thought I would take him with me as a hostage for your behavior. *Chère* Alouette," he cried, swooping down on her and catching her in a too-tight embrace, "you *wound* me with your suspicions! Even if I wanted to, I would be too far away to regulate your actions, even with Henri at my side. No, I have accepted the way things must be. You will marry your English knight someday, but I've already lost you to him, haven't I? However much I would have loved seeing you married to one of my nobles—or praying for your royal brother as the abbess of a French convent—I must accept that things have changed. Be happy, sister."

"Thank you, sire . . . Phillip . . ." she breathed, hardly daring to believe her ears. It was too easy. Was he actually freeing her of the obligation to spy for him?

A scratching at the door interrupted her thoughts. "Innocentia? Is Reyner here?"

"Nay, Alouette—'tis me, Peronel. May I enter?"

Peronel—King Phillip's mistress. Since coming to Acre, the sergeant's daughter-turned-courtesan had scarcely spoken to her. What did she want now?

Without waiting for permission, Peronel came over to her with rapid steps, her kid slippers making a swishing sound against the stone floor. "Lady Alouette, I beg your pardon for the intrusion, but a note addressed to you arrived at the Palace of the Templars. I don't know why 'twas misdirected—my tirewoman had sent the Arab boy away who fetched it—but I thought it might be important, so I brought it to you without delay."

"A note to me? Surely all know I am lady-in-waiting to Queen Berengaria! Why should they send it to King Phillip's headquarters?" Suspicion rose in Alouette.

"Have I not said I don't know?" Peronel replied patiently, and stepped closer. A musky wave of perfume wafted to Alouette's nostrils. The vellum crackled as it was waved about.

"I haven't broken the wax, Lady Alouette," she said, handing the folded sheet to the blind woman so that she could feel the flat, round seal. Alouette's sensitive fingers could discern no design in the hardened blob; no lord had pressed his seal ring into the melted wax to indicate its sender.

"Do you want me to read it to you?" Peronel offered helpfully.

Alouette could imagine the girl's curiosity—any message in it would be all over the Templars' Palace in an hour. "Nay, if you would but send for my tirewoman, Innocentia, I will not keep you further. Thank you for bringing it."

But Peronel was not to be so easily dismissed. "The Sicilian girl? I saw her strolling down the street, arm in arm with your brother, Count Henri."

Alouette could not suppress a grimace of irritation. Innocentia had not even asked permission to go. Now she would have to have Peronel read the message, or wait an unknown length of time until someone else was available. She only hoped it wasn't a private message from Reyner. Her lover rarely chose to commit even the most mundane messages to her on paper because she must have someone read them to her. Still, he might have needed to inform her of something that was detailed, she thought.

"Very well, Peronel, then I suppose I must depend upon your kindness," she said, trying not to sound grudging. "Read it, if you please."

There was a cracking sound as the seal was breached, then the rustle of the vellum and the sound of Peronel clearing her throat. A moment later Alouette heard her gasp.

"'Lady Alouette,'" she read, "'your lord lies seriously wounded in a house in the Pisan quarter. A physician is in attendance, but his injuries are grave, perhaps mortal. Please come without delay.'"

Alouette felt curiously numb. "Who sent the note?" she asked, amazed at the lack of emotion in her own voice when she wanted to scream or run.

"There is no signature, Lady Alouette. What will you

do? The Pisan quarter is the farthest one from the Palace of the Kings, right on the waterfront!"

"Wherever it is, I must go to him," Alouette said, her knuckles up against her teeth in an effort to quell the rising panic.

"I will help you," Peronel announced. "The pair of men-at-arms who escorted me here can take us there. Come— the message said not to delay, and we have lost valuable time already."

As if in a dream, Alouette found herself following Phillip's mistress out of the palace and into the streets.

They met no one of importance as they left the palace. Alouette would have liked to leave word of her whereabouts with Berengaria or Joanna, but doubtless the queens were still enjoying their evening repast, and the entertainment which was to follow.

In her haste to leave her apartment, she had been unaware of the sheet of parchment Peronel had left behind in Alouette's clothes chest, where it would not be found right away. It was not the message she had read to Alouette.

Fulk watched with satisfaction from the roof as the king's mistress, with Alouette holding onto her arm and flanked by the two burly soldiers, reached the waterfront house. Peronel had done her work well. Once he had control of Alouette's dowry, he would have to buy her some bauble in payment for her services. He couldn't wait to have Alouette in his power, unable to refuse him anything. He meant to make a leisurely banquet of the lovely Alouette de Chenevy. There would be no inch of her silken flesh he would leave untouched—perhaps bruised if she fought him, as he hoped she would. At the thought, he felt himself growing hard.

"Where is Sir Reyner of Winslade? I received a message that he was hurt . . ." Alouette began as footsteps sounded in the entranceway of the house to which she had been led. Dear God, what if she were too late? Unconsciously clutching Peronel's arm in her anxiety, she waited with her heart hammering in her ears.

"Good even, Lady Alouette. I fear we've played a nasty trick on you to bring you here. I'm sure you'll be relieved to know that your English knight is quite unharmed, and no doubt anticipating his approaching wedding."

"Fulk de Langres," she said dully, acknowledging her recognition of the voice, and feeling the danger of her position simultaneously.

"Indeed, I'm flattered you remember my voice. It's been months since you heard it last in Sicily."

"'Twas your *smell* I remember," she retorted, "if a serpent can be said to have a smell."

Even Peronel twittered as the barb struck home.

"Very glib, little Alouette. I wonder if you will be so glib when you are taken on board ship tonight, knowing that you are completely in my power—and will never be with Reyner de Winslade again?"

"Phillip is helping you with this plot?" she asked, her mind moving at lightning speed. "They'll search Phillip's fleet, you know. He's not leaving until late tomorrow. I'll be missed—and that's the first place Reyner will look if I disappear," she pointed out with some satisfaction.

"I'm sure you're right, my sweet, but you and I will sail *tonight*—in an hour, in fact. No one will miss you tonight. They'll all guess you are trysting with your betrothed, you slut." He moved closer, his cold, hard fingers caressing her cheek, his breath hot on her neck. "And he will assume you've been delayed by your duties to your queen. By the time your disappearance is discovered, we will have sailed for Tyre, where we will meet with Phillip in two days. By then your servant—or your distraught English knight—will have found your note explaining your change of heart. You have decided to become a nun after all, realizing that you have sinned by your wanton behavior with him—only we won't tell him at which convent. There are a score of convents in Outremer, Alouette—many of them behind Saracen lines. He'll break his body and his heart looking for you—and then he'll forget you."

"Never."

"So confidently spoken, so full of faith in your English lover," Fulk leered. "But even if he remains faithful to your memory, he can't have you. You'll be my wife—and I'll kill him if he ever finds us."

"No! I won't go with you! Whoreson! Traitor! *Reyner!*" she screamed, launching herself at the hated voice, her fingers curled to scratch and tear.

Alouette had the satisfaction of knowing she had raked a painful, bloody furrow in Fulk's face before she was yanked backward by a hand clutching her wimple and a fistful of hair. She felt a thudding blow to her head, and was consumed by an overwhelming blackness darker than her blindness—then nothing.

Peronel had been lying when she had told Alouette that Innocentia had gone off with Henri de Chenevy. The servant had merely stepped out to take some of her mistress's linens to one of the many laundresses who did a thriving trade in Acre. Therefore, when Reyner arrived, she was in Alouette's chamber, humming a tune and thinking of how blissful it would be to dance with Henri at his sister's wedding.

"Nay, she's not here. I thought she was with you, my lord," she said in response to Reyner's question. Funny, she knew Alouette had planned to be with her betrothed tonight—she suspected they would steal away for a last night of unwedded bliss, tomorrow being given over to the farewells to the departing French, and later, confession to the priest to prepare themselves for the sacrament of matrimony. She had thought it very romantic, knowing the thrill of clandestine hours of passion herself.

Together they searched the palace, making sure that Alouette was not in the kitchens, or consulting with the steward over some detail of the wedding feast, or wandering the lemon-scented gardens. No one had seen her—not even Joanna, who had retired early, and who looked sleepy and confused at seeing Alouette's maid and Reyner at the entrance of her apartment.

"You had better check with Berengaria, just to be sure."

"She left word she was not to be disturbed, Your Grace —that she was expecting Richard tonight," Reyner put in grimly, "so I don't think she'll be there."

"You never know—perhaps Berengaria asked her to comb out her hair, or sing duets with Blondel to entertain Richard," Joanna said, but without real conviction. "You're really worried, aren't you, Sir Reyner? Tell Berengaria I take all responsibility for your intrusion. And be sure and send me word if Alouette is not there," she called after the rapidly departing pair.

They did not find her with Berengaria (nor was Richard there). Reyner kept his feelings of uneasiness from blossoming into full-blown alarm until he and Innocentia had reached his house.

She will be there, he had told himself during the short walk to the house he had claimed on the Street of the Angels. She has merely decided to disregard my instructions to wait for me to escort her there. She probably wanted to surprise me by coming early. Perhaps we missed crossing each other's path by moments. When I arrive she will be lounging comfortably on a chair on the roof, with Zeus at her feet, waiting for my return.

But only Zeus was waiting for him, barking furiously—as he did only when something was wrong—and clawing at the door until Reyner opened it. The dog sniffed frantically around Reyner and Innocentia, commencing an anxious whining that did nothing to calm their growing panic.

Reyner quickly climbed the stairs to the open area on the flat roof that had become their private haven in the cool of the evenings. It was deserted, with everything neatly in place as he had left it.

Returning to the ground floor, he gave the anxious dog a command: "Find Alouette."

Zeus picked up Alouette's scent outside the back entrance to the palace. From there he took off into the city, loping along with his nose to the ground, stopping every now and then and looking back so that the human pair following him could catch up. Going deeper into the center of the ancient seaport town, Zeus led them at last to the Pisan quarter, to a simple house made of *kurkar*, a coastal rock of rough sand and sea pebbles.

The Pisan merchant from whom Fulk had borrowed the house had been warned that the English knight might trace the woman's path to his door, though he had not expected him so soon. He was nevertheless prepared, though, having eliminated all signs of the surprising struggle that the blind woman had put up—until a blow to the back of the head collapsed her like a child's rag doll. The French knight and his henchmen had left an hour ago with the unconscious girl wrapped in a form-concealing blanket, and had headed for the docks.

The Pisan had also taken the precaution of vacating the premises himself, though he could not resist watching from the edge of the roof across the street. Catching sight of Reyner from his concealed position, he breathed a sigh of relief that he didn't have to face the tall Englishman who stood in the street, pounding on his door. Neither the naked sword he held at the ready, nor the ferocious beast dancing excitedly at his feet and barking at the door looked as if they would have accepted his denial.

". . . And so I finally kicked the door in, sire, but no trace of Alouette did I find. I know she had been there, Your Grace. I could *feel* it, and Zeus seemed to scent traces of her, too—yet when we returned to the street, he found no further trail."

Richard turned away from the brown eyes so full of blazing anger and worry, stroking his golden beard. "This is indeed a serious matter. What do you want me to do? Somehow, I doubt you awakened me just to confide in me," he added gently, when his knight seemed hesitant.

Reyner was relieved that Richard was willing to hear him out, though he would have dared anything if it would bring Alouette back safely. He might not be so patient, however, when he heard what his vassal proposed.

"I wish a boon, sire—I need your backing on the docks this morning when you go to see King Phillip off. I wish to search the French fleet."

For a long moment Richard was silent, frankly gaping at his knight's effrontery. "You want my support while you, in effect, accuse Phillip Capet of kidnapping your be-trothed?" he asked in a quiet, intense voice.

Reyner could only nod, miserably aware of the enormity of what he was asking. Such a tacit accusation could pro-voke severe reprisals—perhaps even the withdrawal of the entire French army.

Surprisingly, Richard did not explode, but stood consid-ering the situation, endlessly stroking his beard. "Yes, I suppose Phillip snatching her back is the best explanation —he never did seem too happy to have his natural sister marrying an Englishman. And it will be my last chance—until I return home, at least—to tweak Phillip's beard." The chance to annoy the king of France while granting his vassal's wish was too good to pass up.

If Phillip were annoyed, it did not show as he stood waiting to be rowed out to his flagship at midmorning, surrounded by the banners of all the represented nations of Christendom and the crusaders of these nations who had come to bid him farewell.

"You certainly have gall, boy," said Phillip to Reyner, with a smile meant for the massed crowds, but his eyes were as cold as the grave. "But so would I, I suppose, with Coeur de Lion at my back, giving me courage.

"I have no reason to hold onto my little troubador against her will—she made her choice, didn't she? Trou-badors are a half-dozen a *sou*, so why should I begrudge you one? When I have such beguiling company, I don't even need music," he said, pulling Peronel closer and ca-ressing her crimson silk-clad shoulders. The blowsy blond wench flashed a defiant glance at Reyner as she leaned against the king.

Reyner was puzzled by what he saw there—something more than the disinterest she'd always exhibited toward him. Could it be smirking triumph he saw on her face?

"Your Majesty, I swear to you that I wish no offense to France. But I must explore the ships to be sure that no one is hiding my betrothed," Reyner said evenly.

"Perhaps he has not considered the possibility that the damoiselle de Chenevy herself could have changed her mind," purred Peronel, eyes full of mocking pity as she loosed the barb.

Reyner felt the blood draining from his face as he fought the urge to slap Phillip's mistress in front of the assembled throng. That wouldn't solve anything—and there'd be no way Richard could save him after that, he told himself firmly.

"Anything is possible," he said grimly at last, avoiding Peronel's triumphant eyes. "But I'd prefer to hear it from her lips. Your Majesty, with your leave—?"

Phillip answered with a mocking bow. "Just don't delay our departure, Sir Reyner. We sail with the tide."

He did not find her. Shoulders slumping dejectedly, he entered the longboat after searching the last of the galleys and dromonds that made up Phillip's fleet, oblivious of the hostile looks and jeers of the sailors. He was unaware, too, of the cloaked figure on the dock who had been following him at a safe distance ever since he had left the Palace of the Kings with Richard. The man had watched and listened with interest as Reyner had his confrontation with the French king, and now melted back into the crowd, intent on returning to his master with his report.

TWENTY-SEVEN

Reyner spent the afternoon searching the narrow streets of Acre. Accompanied by Zeus, he poked his nose into every tavern, church, bathhouse, brothel, and private dwelling, asking courteously where he could, demanding information at swordpoint where he had to, becoming more morose and quarrelsome as the day wore on and everyone denied having seen his betrothed. He began to see sympathy as pity, then contempt, in the faces of those he interrogated. The word spread ahead of him: beware of the tawny-haired Englishman with the cold brown eyes and the wolf at his heels—he's spoiling for a fight, and he'd just as soon spit you on that wicked blade as look at you. No wonder his woman fled him!

Innocentia found him on his rooftop at dusk. He had already been drinking steadily for two hours, thinking with great self-pity that this was to have been the eve of his wedding. Peronel's mocking words had come back to haunt him: "Perhaps he has not considered the possibility that the damoiselle de Chenevy has changed her mind . . ." Damn her for reinforcing the painful doubt in his mind, and damn Alouette's tirewoman for confirming it with that cursed letter!

"My lord," she'd begun apologetically, waving the folded sheet of vellum, "I found something when I was rummaging through my lady's belongings, looking for any clue. It's . . . addressed to you, Sir Reyner . . ."

He wanted to ask the Sicilian girl if it contained some good news—some message from Alouette that would make him smile fondly at some foolish whim she'd had—but the look on Innocentia's face spared him the trouble.

"I . . . I'm afraid I read it, I was so desperate to know where she'd gone. I . . . I'm sorry, my lord."

He didn't know if she meant she was sorry she'd read it, or sorry for the letter's contents, but after he perused the few lines, it didn't matter.

To Sir Reyner, Knight of King Richard:

If I could ever love an earthly man it is you, Reyner, but I have seen a vision as I contemplated our marriage and know that I would be cheating Our Lord of one of His brides. Surely only tragedy would follow if I fail to heed His clear call. Please do not try to find me this time. I have chosen a convent in this land, far away from worldly temptations and close to His footsteps. I am at peace, and hope that you will be. I am sorry for any pain I might cause you.

Alouette de Chenevy

He crumpled the vellum in his fist, his face a mask of anger and pain. "No," he breathed. "No! She wouldn't do this again—she loves me! She was glad we were to wed tomorrow! She wanted no further part of that life—she learned that in Sicily."

But there it was, mute testimony that Alouette had decided, after all, that she was not strong enough to be part of the world—of *his* world. She preferred living in some spiritual ivory tower, communing with long-dead saints and a God who, if He cared, hadn't proven it in over eleven hundred years—if the Carpenter's crucifixion proved He ever cared.

"So she chose to run and hide in her nun's habit after all," Reyner snarled. "Very well, then, so be it. Why should I let it ruin my life? After all, I'm here to kill Saracens, not play at love games."

Innocentia backed down the stairway to the roof, frightened by the look she had seen in his eyes. Gone was the spark of warmth and friendliness that had set him apart from the bloodthirsty rogues who also bore the cross on their surcoats. There was no light in those dark brown depths—nothing.

She followed him and Zeus at a safe distance as he left the stone house and went into the city. Occasionally the big dog would look back at her and whine, as if to convey his concern, but Reyner was like a man walking in a nightmare. At last he stopped at one of the many taverns that had opened up all over the conquered city and sat down at the first available table. After setting out a handful of coins, he began drinking whatever they set in front of him.

Fulk de Langres had been delighted with his success in getting Alouette aboard the little roundship while she was still senseless, for the sight of a struggling, squirming mass in a blanket might have aroused curiosity and difficult questions as they carried her through the streets that led to the Acre docks. She had remained limp as a rag doll even after she was unrolled from the blanket and laid on the bunk within his cabin—so motionless that he had to place a hand over her breastbone to detect the shallow rise and fall of her chest. Feeling her breathe, he relaxed somewhat, planning in his mind how he would bring her to tearful submission when she awoke.

To pass the time while he waited, he went up on deck for a while, smiling broadly as he saw Acre slipping behind them with the sun setting over Mt. Carmel. Feeling generous, he offered the Genoese captain of the ship a drink from the wineskin he'd brought with him, and affected not to notice when the Genoese accepted with ill grace. What difference did the captain's surliness make to him? Perhaps the fellow was jealous! He must suspect that Fulk and his henchmen had carried a wench aboard—but let him. Fulk had paid an extra two gold bezants to have the captain's cabin all to himself for the overnight voyage, and to ensure that he was undisturbed, no matter what the other passengers heard.

Despite the soothing effects of the wine, he was not

nearly so carefree when he returned below, to find the object of his lust still deeply unconscious, still unaware, by so much as a twitching muscle, of her bonds.

With a hand lightly held over her nostrils, he reassured himself of her breathing and, just to be sure, he pushed back her lids and gazed at the unseeing eyes. Alouette's dilated pupils constricted as he shone a candle near them.

Taking out his dagger, he ripped open the already loosened bodice of her azure silk gown and the fine Egyptian cotton chemise beneath.

In the gathering darkness of the cabin he stared at the regular rise and fall of her blue-veined, rose-tipped breasts, reaching out and fondling the nipples, but still Alouette showed no sign that she was aware of his invasion.

For a time he considered taking her as she was—unknowing, but unresisting as he thrust into her woman's passage and spent his seed. Strangely, the thought left him limp as a eunuch. He needed her to be aware and resisting, fighting him with every ounce of her womanly strength— which would be no match, of course, against his. Then, by God's breath, he'd ram it to her! He sat back, pulling her bodice closed and covering her torso with a sheet. He'd wait—and she'd be worth it.

By dawn, with the city of Tyre in sight, he was truly panicked. Alouette de Chenevy was as insensate as before, and showed no signs of movement that would indicate her coma was lifting. Dear God, had he struck her too hard? What if his single blow had fractured her delicate skull?

He imagined going to Phillip and admitting that his half sister was dead, as the result of a blow only meant to keep her quiet for a few precious minutes. Hell would be nothing compared to what Phillip Capet would do to him before he died!

He debarked just long enough to determine that his luck still held. Phillip had not arrived yet, and the harbormaster did not expect him before eventide, as planned. Good, he thought. With any shred of luck, I can find one of these cursedly clever Saracen physicians—or even a Jew—and have the wench cured before Phillip arrives.

"Ho! You there!" he hailed a brown-skinned fellow loitering near the dock. "I have urgent need of a physician. Find me one, and I will pay you—and the physician—handsomely."

"For yourself, *effendi*?" the Saracen asked, staring at him insolently. Though he used the Moslem title of respect, there was none in his tone.

"Of course not!" blustered Fulk, feeling the flush of anger rise above his surcoat. "Do you see a mark on me? Nay, it's for Lady—it's for my wife," he amended hastily. The infidel dog needn't know the details.

Still, the turbaned fellow made no move from his lounging position against a post, his gaze as unblinking as a lizard's.

At last Fulk held out a gold bezant, which the fellow leisurely bit before pocketing it somewhere in the folds of his filthy robe. "Follow me," he said.

"Am I to bring my wife?" Fulk asked.

The Saracen had already walked away, but he paused and turned. "Of course," was all he said, but his scornful glance was openly contemptuous.

The Saracen balked when Fulk's nod brought two of his armed retainers to his side as escort. "We must go alone, or I will not take you."

Follow this scoundrel alone, through the streets of an unknown city? Fulk suddenly realized he was being recompensed for the murderous trick he'd tried on Reyner back in Genoa. Still, he had no choice, he considered, staring down at the limp figure he carried. If he had any hope of ever leaving this godforsaken country for the cool green forests of France and England, Alouette had to be healed. Cutting off his head would be the least painful thing Phillip would do to him if she died. He wondered briefly why Phillip was so obsessed with his bastard sister. Perhaps the king even harbored some unnatural passion for her himself.

"Very well, but do not think to cheat me," he answered in a lordly fashion. "I am armed also." He felt foolish as soon as he said it, for how could he reach the sword across his back or the dagger which hung from his sword belt, as he carried Alouette? The Saracen's eyes told him he was thinking the same, but he said nothing further, just turned and set out at a brisk pace.

Fine-boned and light, Alouette was not a heavy burden, but carrying her became difficult as they wound through the city under the hot sun. It seemed they walked for an hour past open-air marketplaces, mosques, and churches, through streets so narrow that the second- and third-story inhabitants could touch or hand laundry between the buildings. Once he and Alouette narrowly escaped being doused with the contents of a chamber pot being emptied from an upper room.

At last the Saracen stopped in front of a kurkar dwelling distinguishable only by a plaque above the arched doorway, bearing a serpent twined about a staff.

"Enter, *effendi*."

Inside was a room with a half-dozen cots, each filled with a brown-skinned patient. They were obviously beggars—two men, a woman, and three children—but the sheets they lay on were clean, their wounds covered with spotless linen, their sores medicated with pleasantly aromatic ointment. The curious black eyes they turned on the Frank were unclouded by pain.

Fulk turned to the Saracen who had brought him, only to find him gone. Quickly Fulk went to the door, but the street was empty of all but veiled women and playing children.

A man had come on noiseless feet into the quiet room. He had that quality of agelessness that men in desert climates often have; once past youth, it is impossible to tell if they are forty or sixty.

"I—I'll not have my lady wife treated with street scum!" Fulk announced.

"You are scarcely in a position to dictate terms," the man said quietly. "Yours is a rather desperate case, is this not correct?" His calm gaze took in Alouette's motionless form; her parted, slack lips; her shallow breathing. "But I have a separate examination room. Bring her in here." He motioned toward a room leading off to the left from the entranceway.

Fulk had the eerie feeling he had been expected.

At the physician's gesture, Fulk set Alouette on a raised cot in the middle of the floor. Lining the wall were shelves containing stoppered jars and glass bottles with multihued liquids. Dried herbs hung from the low-beamed ceiling. Windows along one side let in a wealth of light, as did the glazed opening in the roof above the cot.

Free now of his burden, Fulk felt it necessary once more to assert his authority. He drew his dagger and held it at the physician's chest. "This woman is the sister of the king of France," he said, "and my wife. If she dies, so will you—most painfully."

The Saracen did not flinch, but continued to examine Alouette's arms and legs. "It will not help her to make threats," he said.

"Perhaps not. But know that there are armed men who know where we are. They would crush you if any harm came to either of us."

Did the Saracen believe his empty lie? Fulk looked away as he uttered it, conscious that his retainers were no doubt caught up in a heated dice game by now, and probably had not even thought to try to follow him. He had never paid them enough to think for themselves.

The Saracen looked at him again; he seemed to have reached a decision. "Hassan!" he called, snapping his fingers. A slim youth strode into the room. The physician gave an order in Arabic, at which the boy salaamed, and after darting an assessing glance at Fulk, scampered out the door.

"What did you tell him?" asked Fulk, suspicious.

"I merely sent him to the apothecary for some herbs I do not possess," came the smooth, unruffled answer. "Now, may I inquire as to the mode of your wife's head injury?"

Incredible. He had not even told the Saracen what Alouette's problem was. "How did you know that? Do you deal in the black arts?"

The Saracen didn't bother to laugh. "It is no magic. She has a boggy, swollen area—here." He indicated the back of her head. "There is blood matted in her hair. What did you hit her with?" he asked, as calmly as if he inquired about the weather.

The effrontery of the man! Still, denials failed when Fulk tried to bring them to his lips.

"My mailed fist. You . . . you don't understand! She was . . . I had to . . ."

"It is not necessary to tell me more," the physician said.

"Can you save her—wake her up?"

"I believe I can save her life, but she may not wake at your convenience. Your blow sent her to a place where her mind is safe from you while her body heals. You cannot rush the journey back, *effendi*."

"I tell you she must awaken before Phillip arrives!" shouted Fulk, frantic at the thought that he might yet have to face Phillip's wrath, or miss his ship home. Could Phillip be made to believe Alouette's condition was an accident? Once the physician had administered whatever potion he would give her, Fulk could silence him with his dagger and hope that Alouette would not remember struggling to avoid capture.

Henri and Innocentia finally succeeded in dragging Reyner from the tavern on the evening of the second day after Alouette's disappearance. It took a full night of rest to get him sober enough to do more than rave about the unfaithfulness of women.

"We must go after her, we must!" Henri insisted, plying him with cup after cup of the bitter dark Saracen beverage, *kaffe*. The first two cups had been generously laced with some liquor, which did much to ease the throbbing of his temples, but it was nevertheless difficult to focus his eyes on Henri's earnest face.

"Why?" Reyner's voice was dull and flat. "She's made her choice. This time I will believe that is what she wants. If you want her, why don't you go look for her?"

Henri's face fell. "I lacked the courage to go alone," he admitted after a moment. "Besides, I thought if I found her, she would not return unless you asked. And something else I have thought of—how do we know she's in a convent? She could not have written the note herself, so we have no way of knowing. Perhaps she was kidnapped!"

"I thought of that, but you know I searched the French

ships. She wasn't on them. I looked into every chest in the hold, every barrel, under every blanket. She wasn't there," he finished with an air of finality.

"All that proves is that she wasn't kidnapped by the French. What about the Saracens? What if she is in Saladin's harem, being pawed by that infidel dog?"

The thought of some lustful Saracen touching Alouette, his Alouette, brought a fresh wave of pain to Reyner's face.

"Saladin wouldn't take her," Reyner answered with more certainty than he felt. Saladin had been told of her wondrous beauty and her singing. "The sultan is an honorable man—one who believes in chivalry." But he was human. *Could even an honorable man hold to his honor if he could possess the Lark?*

"I will send to Saladin. If he has her, I believe he will admit it," Reyner said, reaching for the pouch at his belt and bringing forth the crescent ring. Possibly some lesser emir had kidnapped his love. In that case, Saladin would command the man to restore her to her betrothed. But if it were the sultan who held her, and if he tasted of the delights of Alouette's body—however unwilling Alouette was—nothing would convince him to relinquish her.

"We must not wait for the reply," Reyner said briskly, standing to pull on his tunic. "It may take days to locate the sultan. Meanwhile, we can visit the convents in the desert, and assure ourselves Alouette is not in fact there."

"Travel? Beyond Frankish lines?" gulped Henri, his florid complexion paling. "But how—?"

"This is our safe conduct," said Reyner, flashing the ring. "I will use it to seal the letter to the sultan, then wear it as we ride. Saladin led me to believe it will protect us. Frankly, I would trust his word before Phillip's."

"You have a point," conceded Alouette's stepbrother.

Reyner expected, and received, a full portion of the Lionheart's verbal wrath. "I don't give a *damn* about Saladin's ring. It wouldn't matter to me if you had Saladin's privy seal as your safe conduct!" roared Richard. "Why should I risk one of my best men, and one of the nobles

Phillip was 'kind' enough to leave me—" he said, giving an ironic nod in Henri's direction "—by letting you go off on a hopeless chase across the sands? Did it occur to you I might have other duties for you here in Acre besides chasing women?"

Reyner knew he was on dangerous ground if he argued. Richard's temper had been none too even these days as July had become August and he received no answer to his ransom demands. Feeding the captive Islamic garrison was a serious drain on his finances, and it kept him anchored in Acre.

But Reyner was too anxious to play the courtier with Richard, so he plunged ahead. "Sire, there has been naught for most of us to do but stand guard over the prisoners while Your Grace negotiates. I am bound by chivalry to help my lady if she needs succor."

"She chose the convent instead of your chivalrous self, it appears," grumbled Richard. "She needs no aid from an earthly man, 'twould seem."

"I cannot trust that written missive, sire. I must hear it from her lips. If 'tis so, I will return immediately and there will be no deed you may ask of me that I will not do." His brown eyes, the color of Saracen *kaffe*, met Richard's determinedly as only he dared to do.

"You mean you won't give a damn about your hide if she rejects you," shot back Richard. "God's blood, I don't need a suicidal knight. Go and be damned to you!"

As Reyner and Henri were bowing and murmuring their thanks, Richard added a final condition. "'Tis now the second of August. Be back before the twentieth whether you find her or not. That is all the time I can give you, for the ransom is due from Saladin that day, and we will be starting down the coast to Jerusalem."

The day after Fulk had brought her to the Saracen, the knight stood staring at the bed on which Alouette still slept, though now she occasionally moved an arm or leg, or moaned.

He did not hear the two men enter the room. They were

simply there when he turned around, warned by some sixth sense of another presence.

The men were swathed in thick black robes and *kafiyehs*, draped in such a way that only their cold, red-rimmed black eyes showed.

"Who are you? What do you want?" Fulk demanded, fingering his dagger.

"We are from Rashid-ed-Din Sinan, may his name live forever—the one you know as The Old Man of the Mountain. We want you, Fulk de Langres."

The man's voice was curiously dreamy, and Fulk scented an odd, pungent odor clinging to the sleek, black-robed figures who glided imperceptibly closer as he attempted futilely to draw his sword.

TWENTY-EIGHT

Alouette was aware of little but that the voice of her caretaker had changed, and that an ominous presence which had hovered near her had been removed.

She still floated on some cloud above the mundane world, though now her eyes were open and she responded appropriately to simple commands: "Sit up," "Turn on your side so that I may examine your wound," "Here is soup; eat, please." She obeyed when she smelled the delicious aroma and felt the spoon against her lips. Gradually, strength returned to her weak limbs and her head stopped spinning when she sat up. Little by little the horrendous, lacerating pain in her temples subsided.

She could not have said who she was or how she came to be here—wherever *here* was—only that she had been kindly treated by the two soft-voiced men who insisted she down the bitter herbal drinks that left her feeling better. Her mind was a blank sheet of parchment.

Alouette had heard the voice of the newer caretaker before. She could not have said when, though the low-voiced conversations in Arabic would have explained all, had she understood them. Alouette felt curiously detached from the need to know, however; she accepted that she would be told eventually.

"I came as soon as I got your message, Omar al Karem. It is good to see you again."

"And you, my good teacher, El Khammas. Is this the woman whose blindness you felt you could heal—the woman who was unlawfully taken by the Frank, Fulk de Langres?"

"It is. 'Lady Alouette de Chenevy' is how she is known among the Franks. She is indeed blind, but I felt it to be a malaise of the soul, rather than a disorder of the eye. She was in a coma when the French knight brought her here?"

Al Karem briefly described her unresponsive state, and the hematoma his sensitive fingers had found at the base of her skull. "She is much improved now, as you see."

The old Moor glanced at the beautiful woman reclining upon the bed, her glossy ebony tresses spread fanlike over the bolster and covering her slender white shoulders. She was awake, and appeared to be enjoying the breeze as Hassan waved an ostrich-plume fan above her. "And the Frank who brought her here—where is he?"

"I did as your message requested, El Khammas. The Hashasheen were summoned. I doubt if Fulk de Langres still lives."

El Khammas breathed a sigh of satisfaction, though as a physician, he could not rejoice in the agony Fulk had undoubtedly experienced before he breathed his last. He wondered if the knight had been killed in Tyre, or if the Assassins had toyed with their victim, dragging him up to their mountain fortress of Alamut, so that The Old Man of the Mountain himself could administer the *coup de grâce*.

De Langres was evil, and deserved to die. All that mattered now was that Alouette was free of danger from him —free to let her mind heal. If Allah willed, El Khammas would be the instrument of that healing. At the proper time he would send for the young woman's lover, and if Reyner was large of heart, he would help complete the restoration of her mind.

"Will you try a different infusion, Teacher, or perhaps the Therapy of Dreams?" his former pupil asked the old Moor.

El Khammas considered before answering. "Your infusions were effective in sedating her, and preventing fever and convulsions that could come from the pressure on her brain. You have learned well. And dream therapy is all very well if the patient is fully aware, and there is much time. No, I believe I will try hypnosis, a skill I learned from a sojourn among the Greeks. Watch now."

He pulled up a stool in front of the Frenchwoman, who seemed to notice the sound of it scraping against the tile floor.

"Alouette... Alouette de Chenevy... Listen to me, Alouette. I am El Khammas, the physician. I will help you, but you must relax and do as I say. Your eyelids are getting very heavy, Alouette. Close them, and listen only to my voice..."

His pleasantly modulated, low-pitched voice was compelling. She had no will to resist, for the voice was soothing and promised only good things. Her lashes brushed against her face as her eyelids closed over cobalt eyes. She felt herself drifting, her limbs weightless, following that voice. It could have been moments, or even weeks later that she heard the voice ask her, "Do you remember that you are Lady Alouette de Chenevy, formerly of King Phillip of France's court, now lady-in-waiting to Berengaria, Queen of England?"

She realized that it was true, but it was a realization that as yet had no importance. "Yes," she said softly.

"Good. You will return to that role when it is time. For now, I wish you to revisit your childhood. Tell me, Alouette, what is your first memory?"

Obediently, she went back in her mind down the passage of time, to Chateau de Chenevy, situated over the River Yonne. She could picture herself, she said aloud, a cherry-cheeked, black-haired child of four, giggling delightedly as she played hide-and-seek along the crenellated parapet with her brother Henri, screaming in mock terror when he pounced upon her hiding in the barbican tower.

"You smile as you describe the chateau and your brother Henri. You were happy then?"

"Yes, I was. Everyone loved me—Henri, my step-brother; my father, Count Édouard; my nurse, Ermengarde..."

"What about your mother, Alouette?"

A slight frown furrowed the perfect alabaster brow of the

blind woman. "She was not there. She . . . died when I was born."

"What did your father tell you of your mother? What was her name?"

"Lisette. He said she was very lovely—that she had the same black hair as I, the same laughing blue eyes, the same pouting lips."

"What was her full name? Did she come from some noble's house? Was she, perhaps, the daughter of a baron?"

"Her name was just—Lisette. She was . . . a laundress, before she caught the king's eye."

Ah, thought El Khammas. *There is more here than I thought.* "She was the king's paramour. And am I to understand that you are the fruit of that liaison?" he continued.

"Yes," she said simply. For the first time she felt no shame, no guilt about her parentage, as she talked to the mellow voice. It was just a fact—one for which she bore no responsibility.

"And did your stepfather resent you?"

"Never. Once I was old enough to understand that my real father was King Louis, he told me the truth, though I knew it was a fact not all would find a source of pride and honor. But he told me he accepted my mother gladly in marriage, and grieved when she died. He had come to love her very quickly, you see . . . and hoped that she could forget the pain her royal lover had brought her and come to love him—more than as someone who had given her daughter honorable birth." Even now she remembered the catch in Édouard de Chenevy's voice as he remembered pretty Lisette.

"And did you ever meet King Louis, your real father? Did he acknowledge you?"

"Not by public pronouncement, lest it cause me shame. My father—that is, the count—told me King Louis settled upon me a sum of money to be used as my dowry."

"Tell me about your meeting with the king, Alouette," the voice prompted.

"I met him more than once. We went to court, my father and I, about once a year. King Louis was always kind to me . . ." Even as she said it, however, the pain in her temples recommenced, first as a low throbbing, which rapidly built into a crescendo of pain.

El Khammas was quick to note the change in his patient's demeanor—the quickened rise and fall of her chest, the dilation of her unseeing pupils, the shrinking posture, as if she wished to avoid something that lay ahead on the path of her memory. Too much haste now could destroy everything.

"We will continue another day," the voice said comfortingly. "Rest now. I will give you a draught of the poppy and you will sleep, the pain gone. When you awaken, you will remember that you are Alouette de Chenevy, and that we have spoken of your childhood, but you will not remember that we touched upon anything painful."

Together, Reyner and Henri had traveled the length and breadth of Palestine searching for Alouette. They rode the smaller, fine-boned Arabian steeds they had bought from a Saracen trader in the *souks*, knowing these native mounts to be swifter and more able to negotiate the shifting dunes of the desert than the heavier European destriers. They were also capable of enduring the heat without water for longer periods and drinking deeply when they came to the rare oases.

Reyner and Henri had made further concessions to the desert heat, leaving behind their chain mail hauberks and helms for the white robes and *kafiyehs* of the Saracens.

Reyner had even begun to look like a Saracen, Henri thought, as they rode from *wadi* to *wadi*. The desert sun had darkened Reyner's arms and face till the hue resembled the coppery bronze of a Saracen's skin, which made the dark brown eyes seem darker; in fact, Reyner could have passed as a young Saracen emir himself. Henri, cursed with a fair, ruddy complexion, had suffered sunburn and had to seek relief from the soothing aloe balm sold to them by a trader.

They traveled mostly at night to avoid the heat, so they met few patrols—only a few Bedouins and an occasional caravan. Those who challenged them, however, withdrew instantly when Reyner showed them the ring. Henri watched admiringly as his sister's betrothed conversed with the mounted soldiers in increasingly fluent Arabic, asking directions, determining distances to the next oasis, the next convent.

Besides the Catholic convents that had been founded in lonely places in the hills and the more populated towns, there were other places of retreat from the world founded by Christian sects. They visited convents of the Syrian Jacobites, the Maronites, Copts, Nubians, Armenians, and Georgians. After a fortnight, Henri could rattle off the places they had been—Mt. Tabor, Aba Ghosh, Quruntal, Rantes, Bethany, St. Brocardus, Nabi Samurl, Tayibe, Deir al-Asad. But none of them held a newly arrived European woman who was blind.

Wearily, they turned their mounts back toward Acre, trying not to feel that they had failed. They would arrive back in the Crusader-held city on the eighteenth of August, two days before deadline.

"Perhaps Saladin will have responded to your message," Henri said encouragingly as they rode over the moonlit sand.

"I hope so," muttered Reyner grimly. His eyes were bleak. If she wasn't in a convent, then there was every possibility that she was in mortal danger—perhaps even dead. No, his heart would sense it, wouldn't it, if the Lark no longer breathed?

What if he heard nothing from the sultan, despite his promise? He would not know where to look. He would have no option but to become a killer of Saracens, hoping at last to reach the harem of Saladin, where Alouette might be held.

Acre was a city on edge as the deadline for the ransom drew near, with no sign of the money demanded by the crusaders, no True Cross, no redeemed Christian prisoners. As Reyner and Henri rode into the city, the very streets buzzed with the question: what will the Lionheart do with the captive garrison?

There was indeed a message from Saladin awaiting

Reyner as he returned to the cool stone dwelling in the evening shadows.

From Salah al Din Yusuf ibn Ayub, known as Saladin, Sultan of Sultans, to Sir Reyner of Winslade, greeting:

It has come to our attention that you have undertaken to search the countryside, looking for your lady in the convents that have always been tolerated under Islam. It grieves us somewhat that you have journeyed unnecessarily—if ever a journey can be said to be totally unnecessary, for it always accomplishes some good for the soul, and is undertaken only as Allah wills.

We are pleased to tell you that the woman of your heart is safe, and if you will ride out from Acre at dawn on the twentieth, I will restore her to you. You must be willing to follow my instructions. Go with Allah, and may Alouette de Chenevy give you many sons.

Was Saladin admitting responsibility for Alouette's disappearance? He read it over until the bold black characters blurred on the page, but could not be sure. Henri had thought the Saracens had taken her; maybe Alouette's stepbrother was right. But then, why would Saladin be trying to restore her to him?

And why was Saladin so insistent that he leave at dawn on the twentieth, the day the Saracen garrison was due to be released—*if* the ransom was paid? Did the sultan know that that was when Richard had specifically ordered Reyner to attend him? Was he testing Reyner's loyalty, trying to make him choose between his allegiance to his sovereign and the safety of his beloved? Was he threatening Alouette's safety or her freedom? The more Reyner read the letter, the less he was sure of anything but that he had to go to Alouette. With a muttered oath, he scooped up the much-read message and set off for Richard's palace.

* * *

The king looked up from the missive and scowled. "I suppose you think I should give you permission to go lay your head on Saladin's block. It's just a trick, you know, to lure one of my best men into danger. I'm surprised at your gullibility, Reyner."

Reyner had expected Richard to be furious when he proposed leaving yet again, but accusing Saladin of treachery left him momentarily speechless.

"I believe this to be a true message, sire. He has her, or he knows where she is. Saladin is a man of honor." He stared unblinkingly into the storm cloud that brewed in Richard's eyes.

"A man of honor, is he?" Richard shouted, slamming his fist into the table beside him. He seemed even more annoyed that Reyner did not flinch. "The same 'man of honor' is going to renege on the ransom terms, fool! No, you can't go chasing after a phantom *woman* anymore. I've lost over a month—when I could have been advancing on Jerusalem—waiting for that Saracen snake to come through. I'm not going to lose you to him, too!"

Richard had been pacing up and down in a fury before Reyner, but now he whirled away from his knight as if he had said too much. He stood by the open window that looked out over the city, his back rigid.

If Reyner had been speechless before, he was astonished now. Had he imagined the jealousy that had colored Richard's voice when he had accused him of chasing after a phantom *woman*? Or the passion that underlay the cry, "I'm not going to lose *you* to him, too?" There had been more there than just a king's reluctance to risk one of his best knights.

Richard turned to face him from across the room, his flushed face ravaged by the agony of his emotions.

"I'm sorry, Reyner. I don't mean to . . . well, make you uncomfortable. I know you . . . don't feel that way. I'm not asking you for anything, don't worry. I'll stay with my . . . men like Blondel, and the pretty pages that seem to find their way into my service." He took a deep breath, as if the air in the room were diminishing, and his blue eyes were chill and wintry again. "I'm sorry, Sir Reyner, but I must refuse your request. Be ready to move out of Acre with the rest of the army tonight. We will camp on the plains in front of the city, between Al Ayadijeh and Keisan, to deal with Saladin if he surprises me and brings the ransom—or deal with the garrison if he does not. You are dismissed."

Reyner had to try. He knelt before Richard, and striving to keep his voice calm, began: "Sire, I beg of you—"

"No more, Reyner! Don't think to take advantage of what I've said! It won't make me weak where you're concerned, I warn you! You will be under house arrest until you return to me in your armor, do you understand?"

"Perfectly, sire."

Richard meant what he said. A trio of men-at-arms escorted Reyner to his house. Two of them stationed themselves at the front entrance and rear exit, while a third accompanied him from room to room as Thomas armed him and they readied their belongings. Richard had not said when, or if, the crusaders would be returning to Acre.

What did the English king intend to do with the two thousand men, with their women and children, if Saladin failed to meet his terms? He could not afford to remain in Acre guarding them, either financially, or from the standpoint of his mission to rescue the holy places of Christendom from the infidel. There had been a cold ruthlessness to those brilliant blue eyes when he'd discussed dealing with Saladin—or with the garrison. Reyner's heart was troubled when he thought of the Moslems he'd seen in the prison compound. Many of them had veiled, sloe-eyed wives with them, and beautiful dark-haired, brown-skinned children whose laughter was stilled when the Frankish soldiers looked their way. *What would the Plantagenet king do with these innocent families, caught in the crossfires of religious war?*

Noon of the following day found Reyner in full armor on his destrier, with Zeus sitting beside them, on the plains outside Acre. The chained-together Moslem garrison stood in a mass, together with their families, surrounded on all four sides by the Christian army.

It was a hot, airless day. No clouds diffused the burning rays of the fiery ball in the sky. The crusaders sat their horses or stood, according to their rank, roasting in their chain mail and helms despite the white surcoats and turbans they wore over the metal.

Richard rode the perimeter of the captives and his army, mounted on Fauvel, the swift charger he had taken from Isaac Comnenus. From time to time he stopped, looked at the sun, then at the hills where he knew Saladin's forces lay hidden, then back at the chained captives. Messengers rode out from Acre at intervals. Though Reyner was not near enough to catch their words, it was obvious that they bore no encouraging news of Saladin's response.

Noon came and went, and still the frozen tableau was maintained in the broiling heat, until Richard suddenly pointed to a dozen men within the crowd of Moslems, and a pair of men-at-arms moved in to break their chains. The men fell at the prancing feet of Richard's steed, salaaming and murmuring their thanks. Reyner watched as one pressed a fabulous golden necklace which sparkled with fiery rubies and green gleaming emeralds into the king's hands before walking way. These, then, were the wealthy among the captives, and Richard, ever in need of wealth, was allowing them to ransom themselves. The remainder of the Moslem garrison shifted uneasily and stared at the golden giant who held the power of life and death over them.

As if sensing the adults' anxiety, babies in their mothers' arms who had been quiet before began to whimper, then wail their fear, and women to moan as they tried unsuccessfully to still their children.

Reyner watched the barely suppressed panic rippling through the Moslem ranks, but his mind was filled with a whirling mass of anxiety for Alouette, mixed with rage at Richard, who held him here to accomplish God knew what when he should be riding to her side—wherever she was, no matter if it cost him his life.

He and Zeus were situated in the portion of the guard nearest the hills. Would it be possible for him to quietly back his horse toward the rear guard, until he was far enough from the main force to spur Hercules into a gallop? He'd race straight for the Moslem lines, waving his unfolded turban as a white flag of peace, and demand that they take him to Saladin! Did he dare? Richard would never forgive him, of course. Love for his woman warred with his vows of loyalty as Richard's vassal.

Reyner looked up and saw Richard's eyes on him, cold and assessing. It was as if the king could see within and know the debate that raged within his soul. As blue eyes remained locked with brown ones, Richard gave a small, almost imperceptible shake of his head. *Don't do it.*

Another hour passed. Richard called his chief nobles to him—Leicester, the Duke of Champagne, Guy de Lusignan—and conferred with them. All looked grave as they spurred their horses to opposite corners of the quadrangle around the prisoners. A decision had been reached.

Reyner looked down from his horse and stared as Zeus set up a low-pitched whining. What did the dog sense was going to happen?

Richard's voice rang out over the plain. "Saladin has failed to meet his obligation to pay the ransom. We have received neither the money, nor the Christian captives, nor —most importantly—the True Cross, which the infidels hold in their filthy hands. Therefore, the lives of these captives are forfeit!"

Those few Moslems who understood French began to sob and moan, communicating their terror, without words, to those who did not. Excited chattering began in the Christian ranks as knights straightened in their saddles and readied their swords. Then there was silence as every eye was trained on Richard's upraised arm.

The arm was waved forward as Richard cried, "Let them now pay for Saladin's treachery! Kill them, Christians! Send their souls to Mohammed! Every Saracen you dispatch to Hell sends your soul closer to Heaven!"

All around Reyner knights spurred their horses forward, some jumping off with bared swords, leaping into the chained masses of cowering Saracens. Screams rent the hot afternoon as blades fell and came up crimson, the screams often dying in midnote as throats were slashed. The air became thick with the stench of blood and fear and the lust of murder.

A destrier behind him brushed Hercules as he thundered past, causing the stallion to rear and trumpet resentfully. He returned to the ground, uncertain as to why he felt no spurs ordering him forward. His nostrils flared at the scent of carnage, for the stallion was no stranger to battle. Zeus stood poised to protect his master and carry out any orders Reyner should issue.

Reyner felt sick within, knowing he was expected to fall on the helpless captives and kill them, until all of the two thousand lay dead in their blood on the plains.

He had come to Outremer knowing he would have to slaughter Saracens in the course of freeing the holy places, yes—but soldiers, armed for combat, understanding the risk, believing in a cause as he did! Not helpless chained men, who had surrendered in honor, with their wives and families! How could it be *Christian* to be spearing babies on pikes, as he saw men-at-arms doing—or gutting a pretty, terrified Saracen maiden as she begged on her knees for her life?

He wouldn't do it! Calling to Zeus, he hauled hard on the reins, and the obedient war-horse reared and whirled, responding to the golden spurs Reyner set into his flanks as he galloped for the hills.

As he reached the outskirts of the Christian ranks, however, he found a desperate battle going on. The rear guard was busy fending off scores of white-cloaked, scimitar-waving members of the *ramieh*, Saladin's mounted cavalry, who had raced down from their concealment in the hills, howling their rage at the murder of the helpless prisoners.

The Saracens wouldn't be able to break through and stop the slaughter—there were too few of them, too lightly armed against the Frankish forces in their chain mail hauberks and helms. But their presence made it impossible for Reyner to spur off into the hills, for when he tried to make use of the confusion, he nearly got a scimitar in the back for his pains. A quick thrust of Reyner's sword in the abdomen of his attacker, and the Moslem was sent screaming to Allah.

Reyner whipped off the white cloth he wore to shield his helm from the sun and waved it about, hoping the charging *ramieh* would see it as a peace symbol, since they did not seem to understand the French he screamed from a hoarse, raw throat. He had to abandon it, however, when he saw a Moslem on a gray horse spurring straight for Zeus, who was looking back toward his master as if urging him on. That enemy, too, was dispatched to Paradise, then Reyner and his wolf-dog looked around them for a way out of the battle.

There—a hole on the right flank! Reyner set his mount toward it and drummed on his flanks, though the stallion needed no encouragement, and then plunged toward the open space where no one was fighting.

A blur on his right side was the only warning Reyner received before a blow to the head caused all the dazzling lights of Heaven to flash inside his mind as he flew through the air. Then darkness descended.

TWENTY-NINE

The headache to which he awoke was a familiar one. Was he back in Genoa, where he had awakened to find he had been robbed and left for dead? A cautious opening of one eye told him he wasn't in his field tent, or better yet, back in Acre.

The tent was crimson silk. On a low bedside table sat a golden bowl filled with pomegranates and the long, yellow fruit called bananas.

The veiled *houri* who had been bathing his forehead sat back on lithe haunches barely concealed by the gauzy loose trousers she wore. Her dark eyes looked as if for approval to the robed figure sitting in the shadows.

"You have done well, Fayeh. You may retire now," the figure said. Reyner's head throbbed as he endeavored to bring the dimly lit shape into focus, but the image crossed and doubled in his blurred vision. The woman salaamed and glided gracefully out, leaving Reyner alone with the owner of a voice he had heard before.

Reyner's eyes widened as Saladin strode into the circle of light shed by the oil lamp beside his pallet. The sultan sat down, waving an arm to prevent him as Reyner tried to arise.

"No, stay as you were. I'm sure getting up would cause your head to ache most miserably."

Reyner would have liked to tell Saladin that his head already ached as miserably as possible, but he forbore to do so as the sultan settled himself closer to the knight.

"I see you wear the ring I gave you. It is well. 'Tis all that saved your life, did you know that? My *ramieh* were frantic to kill any Frank they could, while the slaughter took place just out of their reach."

Saladin's black opaque gaze bore into Reyner's brown eyes. "Ah, yes, the slaughter. Approximately two thousand six hundred men, together with their families. It went on for hours, and then the *Christians*—how your Jesus must laugh at the term—slit open many of the dead, looking for the jewels they were sure the captives had swallowed. Already the ravens feast on the carrion before Acre's walls, while the stench of the dead should waft clear to Rome—if not Heaven itself."

Reyner lay back on the cushions, shame on behalf of his people overwhelming every other emotion that dwelled within him. What could he say in the face of such a deed? He assumed that, despite the woman's ministrations, he was going to die most painfully. Perhaps Saladin meant to send him back to Richard a piece at a time. He could accept his death, however horrible, if he knew Alouette was safe. He opened his mouth to plead for her life, but Saladin raised a regal hand.

"Previously, I have dealt chivalrously with Christian captives whenever possible, ransoming those I could, freeing more who could not have afforded to free themselves. Courtesies have flowed between Melech-Ric and myself. All that is at an end, because of what your king has done. I will show no more mercy than did he."

Now he was going to say the words—now he would tell Reyner how he would die.

Saladin smiled gently, as if he discerned Reyner's thoughts. "You do me an injustice, Reyner of Winslade. Whatever anger I hold toward Melech-Ric, I have already promised you my aid. Your life was preserved today because of the ring you wore, and because I saw that you were disgusted by the massacre. I know this does not mean you would scruple to kill in a fair combat with a Saracen soldier, but you are intelligent enough to realize there is a difference.

"Rest now. In the morning I will have you taken to Lady Alouette."

Reyner studied the Saracen man dressed in a robe of wide, somber-hued stripes standing before him. He had introduced himself as the physician Omar al Karem.

"You're telling me that Lady Alouette de Chenevy is in that room?" he said quietly, his heart beginning to race with joy. He had been escorted all the way to Tyre, and now he was about to see his love! Impulsively he started toward the door, only to be halted by a gently restraining hand.

"You must not burst into the room. Lady Alouette is in the middle of a therapy session, deep in a trance. To interrupt now might cause irreparable harm."

Reyner stared, dumfounded at the calm statement. "You have *ensorcelled* her?" he demanded, his hand going instinctively to the hilt of his sword. If these Saracens were practicing the black arts on his beloved, he'd slay everyone in the building.

"Nay, sir knight, my master, El Khammas, merely uses the Greek art of *hypnosis* on your lady. While in a trance, the mind surrenders troubling secrets that it jealously guards from consciousness."

Reyner shook his head. It was too much to comprehend. "Lady Alouette's mind is sick? Not her body?"

On the journey he had already been told how Alouette had come to be here; how the word had gone out to watch for the Frankish knight who had foully kidnapped her; how the knight had been lured to bring her here when she needed medical attention. He remembered the ancient Moorish physician who had been sent to help Richard when he suffered from *leonardie*, and he relaxed somewhat, knowing Alouette to be in good hands.

"She was unconscious from a blow to the head given her by the French knight, Fulk de Langres. We saved her from the ill effects of her injury, through the skillful use of medicines known to my people," al Karem told him proudly. "But, then—"

"Wait a moment. Fulk de Langres was the one who kidnapped her?" Reyner interrupted, wondering if he had heard aright. "He isn't even supposed to be in Outremer! He has been banished to France!"

The physician shrugged. "He has been in this land for months, spying for Phillip and Saladin. You will want to know, doubtless, that he was turned over to the Assassins for his treachery to this woman."

"And what will the Assassins do to him?" Reyner asked. He had heard of the fanatical sect of killers who used the drug hashish to lend courage to their murders. Even Saladin was known to respect them.

"They have taken him away for execution," al Karem said. "He was an evil man."

Reyner agreed, but he felt a tinge of sadness, knowing his cousin was dead, even after so much treachery.

"You say Alouette's head injury is healed," Reyner said, coming back to the subject of his love. "Then, why—"

"She is healed from the effects of her concussion," the Saracen physician explained patiently, "but the wise El Khammas felt her deeper need was to be healed of the sickness which causes her blindness. Her eyes are sound, sir knight; therefore, her blindness is of the mind."

Reyner's heartbeat quickened. "He can heal her blindness through this . . . *hypnosis*?" Was this the kind of treatment the doctors at Salerno had in mind when they urged him to seek out the Saracen physicians?

The Saracen raised slender brown arms deprecatingly. "There are no guarantees, Infidel. It will be as Allah wills. Come, there is a side chamber where you can listen and watch without disturbing the session, if you are absolutely quiet."

The room into which Reyner was shown had no windows. For a moment he stood still, allowing his eyes to adjust to the darkness, then he was shown to one of a pair of chairs in front of an ornately carved grille which formed a door between the two chambers. Through the many whorls of wrought iron, Reyner could see into a sunlit room on the other side.

Had al Karem not warned him specifically, he would have gasped aloud as he gazed into the other room. As it was, he sat down so heavily that the chair scraped protest-ingly against the tile floor.

There, on a white-sheeted bed, sat Alouette, her eyes staring, unfocused, straight at the grille. It was obvious that she had heard nothing, however, but the pleasantly modulated voice of the ancient Moor who sat by her side.

El Khammas looked once at the grille and raised a finger slightly to indicate he knew of their presence, then went back to the monotonous message he was giving her.

"He is just inducing her trance. It was fortunate you could arrive at this point. My teacher has been hypnotizing her every day, and he felt he was on the verge of a break-through."

"If he can help Alouette to see . . ." began Reyner. Tears pricked his eyes at the thought. As he watched her eyelids fell, long, sooty lashes brushing her cheeks.

"Sssshh. Listen. She is in trance now."

"Alouette, when I ring the little bell that ends our talks, you will waken refreshed and remember only that which I have told you you should," El Khammas was saying. As always when they talked, her limbs felt light, as if they weighed nothing, but her eyes were so heavy that she could not keep them open. She felt utterly at peace.

"Alouette, as we have talked, you have remembered much. You have told me of your love for music, which only developed fully after your blindness began. We have discussed your fervent desire to be a nun, though you did not understand this compulsion. We have talked about your coming on this crusade only to please King Phillip, your half brother. You have told me about meeting the chival-rous English knight with whom you fell in love, who con-vinced you to become his wife, rather than be a celibate nun."

Even Reyner could see the heightened color which stained her cheeks and the half-smile that curved those sweet lips.

"But we are not going to talk of these things today, Alouette. We are going to go back to a time we visited when you first came here. Let us go back to the time when you became blind."

Alouette's face immediately lost its serenity. She shrank back, one hand clenched in her lap while the other went to her mouth. "Nay, I don't want to," she said softly and clearly.

"But we must, Alouette," the old Moor said gently. "We have avoided it long enough. It is what troubles you—perhaps what *made* you blind. Somewhere, deep inside you, you *know* what robbed you of your sight, but your innermost soul keeps this secret from your mind, and that is not good. We must unlock that door, Alouette."

She sat quietly, but her expression was still fearful.

"How old were you when you lost your sight?" El Khammas queried in that seductive voice.

"Eight years old."

"Return to that time in your mind—the time right before you became blind."

As Reyner watched, Alouette's face relaxed and underwent a subtle transformation. Somehow, she seemed suddenly younger, more girlish.

"Where are you now?"

"At the Cité Palace in Paris. We come every year to visit King Louis." Alouette's voice was higher, more breathy, excited—the voice of the child she had been.

"Ah yes, King Louis, your secret father," continued El Khammas. "Do you like him?"

"Yes, he is kind to me when none of his nobles are in the room—when it is just Papa and me. He smiles and pats my head, and tells me how pretty I am getting, though he looks sad when he says this, and whispers, 'Just like Lisette,' to himself. He thinks I don't hear, but I do. And he tells Papa he will always provide for me."

"Alouette, did your real father, King Louis Capet, harm you in any way?"

"Never."

"Who else is at this palace? Does Louis have any daughters for you to play with? Are there any royal princesses?"

"The only one close to me in age is Alais, and she has been sent across the channel to the royal household of England. She is to be reared with the Plantagenet children, and one day is to be Richard's bride."

"And what of the princes? Does King Louis have any sons?" continued the gentle questioning.

"Only one, Phillip. He is six years older than I."

"And do you like him?"

"I used to." Alouette's voice became hesitant, her manner wary.

"But not now? Tell me, what is he like?"

"He dresses in silks and velvets and furs. He has a pointed beard now. He has many friends, and ladies who come to drink and play."

"Alouette, you have said you *did* like Prince Phillip, but now you do not. Tell me, please, why that is."

A dew of perspiration broke out on the blind woman's forehead, but she was silent.

"Alouette?" prompted El Khammas.

"I . . . He didn't protect me . . . He let me be hurt."

"Be hurt? What do you mean?" the old Moor probed.

"Nay . . . I can't . . . 'tis too painful."

"Alouette, you must. I promise you, once you have said the words aloud, the pain will be gone—forever. Did this event in which you were hurt cause you to be blind?"

"*Yes.*"

Reyner felt beads of perspiration breaking out on his own forehead, and he leaned forward to catch every word drawn so unwillingly from her lips.

"*Alouette, what is your last memory before you became blind?*"

She was again silent for an endless moment, but just as the physician was about to prompt her, she began to speak, slowly and hesitantly.

"I am in my chamber in the Cité Palace. I awaken in the night, and Ermengarde is not there. I am lonely, so I get up to look for her. I wander down the corridors, wrapping a blanket around my nightgown. At last I come to a room. I am scared . . . but I think, perhaps Ermengarde is there, and I push open the door . . ." Alouette's voice died away as her breathing quickened.

"Alouette, *what is behind that door?*"

"It is dark in the room, except for a few guttering torches. I smell wine . . . and women's perfume . . . Several young nobles are lying about . . . with women . . ."

"Is Phillip one of them?"

"Yes."

"Did Phillip hurt you?"

"Nay. He . . . is very drunk."

"Go on."

"I am walking toward him, thinking perhaps he knows where Ermengarde is. He gets up to come to me, but he wobbles and falls down. Then, another man stops me. He . . . says I am a good girl, then he laughs at me . . . touches me. Says things . . ."

"'Says things?'"

She whimpered like a little child. "Mean things . . . about how I am a bastard and nobody cares about me. Things like I am ripe for the plucking; that a young girl's maidenhead is the sweetest of all . . ."

"Does Phillip do nothing?" El Khammas asked, a note of incredulity creeping into his voice.

"He tries, but he falls down. His eyes are closed."

"Alouette . . . do you know the man?"

"No . . . I can't see his face. There's a shadow in the way. Now I see! He's Fulk de Langres . . . Once I saw him beat the little boy who helps in the kitchen. He is cruel. Make him go away! I'm afraid of him!"

Reyner sat bolt upright in his chair, clutching the arms. A sour taste of bile rose in his throat as he watched the terror rise on his beloved's face. "Stop," he cried softly, clutching al Karem's sleeve. "Stop it now! Can't you see it's hurting her too much!"

El Khammas heard his cry and flashed alarmed, forbidding eyes at him through the grille.

"Silence!" al Karem begged. "If you disturb her now, in the midst of the agony she is reliving, I cannot promise you her sanity! It may well break her! Hush now, and trust that Khammas will bring her through safely!"

Fortunately, Reyner's outburst did not appear to have broken Alouette's trance. Since he apparently had no choice, Reyner sat down again, watching fearfully as she began to speak again, her voice full of childish horror.

"He's holding me tight, too tight, and pushing me back onto the couch. Help me, please, you ladies, stop giggling . . . Why are all those men cheering him on? Tell him to stop. He's ripping my clothes and touching me . . . where no one is allowed to touch me. His hands are hurting and hard. He's pinching me. He's pulling apart his own clothes . . . what is that thing?"

"Thing? The male organ?"

Alouette shuddered and nodded. "It looks so swollen and red . . . and disgusting. He's on top of me, grunting and panting, like an animal. No, no, stop . . . it's tearing me apart . . . No! No!"

Reyner watched helplessly as the tears poured down Alouette's face. So much was clear now—her nightmare on the night he had first made love to her . . . her lack of virginal bleeding . . . her insistence that she knew deep down she was not worthy to be his wife, that she was somehow stained, and not merely by her illegitimacy. He rubbed a hand across his eyes, and was surprised to find it came away wet with tears.

The old Moor let Alouette cry for a few minutes, then began to speak again, his voice tender with compassion.

"What is happening now, Alouette?"

"I . . . I don't know. Everything is black, but Ermengarde is here. I can hear her voice. She's crying. Oh, Ermengarde, I hurt so! I hurt everywhere, but especially between my legs. I feel sticky, on my legs. I'm dirty. I will never be whole again, never clean again. Bring me a candle, Ermengarde . . . I can't see! I can't see!"

THIRTY

"Alouette, rest for a few moments. Sleep. When I speak to you again, I will tell you what will happen when you awaken."

Reyner watched through tear-blurred eyes as Alouette's body visibly relaxed. He had not known how rigidly she had been holding herself until then. Her shoulders rose and fell with the regular respirations of deep, restorative sleep.

El Khammas arose then and padded on soundless feet to the grille and opened it, joining Reyner and his fellow physician in the shadowy room. His shoulders sagged with exhaustion. His face looked, if it were possible, a score of years more ancient than it had before. Suddenly Reyner had some inkling of how draining it must have been for El Khammas to have gone on this journey into the past with Alouette, knowing he bore the responsibility for the healing of a wounded spirit. With one careless word, he could have sent that fragile soul plummeting into the morass of insanity. He became aware that his own body was drenched with cold sweat. While she had been talking he had felt her terror, had imagined the pain of the child's body being cruelly torn by that monster. Ah, God, that such a fiend had been related by blood to him! He hoped the Assassins had not let Fulk die too quickly, but had made his torture a foretaste of the Hell he was now surely experiencing.

"Sir Reyner, did you hear me? I said, you have a decision to make." The physician broke into Reyner's anguished reverie. "It is only natural that you find this ... how shall I say it?—shocking. I must confess, I had no idea such a psychic trauma underlay her blindness. I thought perhaps she had only seen some horrifying sight ..."

She did, thought Reyner. The sight of her own brother failing to protect her from that demon. He realized then that Phillip must have known what had happened as he lay there in a drunken stupor, too sodden to do more than listen to his half sister's screams as she was violated. He knew that his crony Fulk de Langres was responsible; and instead of reporting the heinous crime to his father, and seeing that justice was done, he had kept shamefully silent. He had continued to tolerate Fulk's existence, knowing that within the man still burned an unclean lust for Alouette.

But El Khammas was waiting patiently for an answer to a question. "I'm sorry, sir. As you say, it is much to take in. I have a decision to make? What can that be?"

"My son," began El Khammas, "I believe you love this woman very deeply. I see it in the tears that have run down your cheeks. But men are merely human creatures, unlike women, who have a spark of Allah's divine perfection— however much we males like to think of them as 'mere females,'" he added wryly. "I must ask you to tell me honestly how you feel about Alouette de Chenevy, now that you know the nature of the suffering she has undergone— now that you know you were not the only man to possess her? Nay, do not be tempted to speak too quickly, to say it will not matter, out of pity, for pity corrodes over the years, sometimes turning to contempt. Look deeply into your soul, Reyner of Winslade."

Reyner did as he was bidden, fighting the urge to answer immediately. After a long moment, he said, "I swear by all that I hold holy, revered physician, that it makes no difference to the love I feel for Alouette de Chenevy. I want her as my lady, in honorable marriage, to be by my side, to bear my children, to love me and be loved by me always."

El Khammas smiled as Reyner looked into his eyes. "I knew you were worthy of her!" he said with quiet exultation. "But it was necessary that I ask. This is a harsh land of harsh men. Here, a Bedouin chieftain whose Arabian mare gets loose and is mated by an inferior stallion will not breed her again, considering her forever soiled. He will kill one of his wives if she takes a lover, or divorce her if she is stolen or raped. Your European ways are not so different, for you put women away in nunneries to die a slow, abandoned death for their sins. But I sensed you were different, Reyner of Winslade.

"Perhaps, if life were perfect, Alouette could have come to you, an untouched maiden on your wedding day, knowing you were the man who would shed her virgin's blood, the same man who would teach her of passion.

"But life is not perfect. Nevertheless, you will be her lord and love her, for Allah—or God—has chosen you to be together."

"There could be no other decision, sir."

"Indeed. Knowing that, I can now awaken Alouette . . ."

"Sir," interrupted Reyner, "do not let her remember . . . what happened to her as a child."

El Khammas shook his head. "Perhaps you do not understand, in your desire to protect your beloved from harm. It is the struggle to repress this dreadful memory that has perpetuated her blindness and the nightmares she has told me about. I can cause her to remember in such a way that it is no longer painful to her, because I will tell her it will no longer be a source of shame. And she will know that you, also, know the truth and love her just as before. When she awakens, she will have no more need to be blind, Reyner."

Reyner nodded in amazed acceptance. "Truly, you are blessed by Our Lord and all the saints," he said. "Christians believe that Moslems are damned by their own beliefs, and yet you have a gift of healing far beyond the pitiful efforts of European medicine. Surely, such a one as you deserves Heaven far more than I. Thank you, my lord."

He would have kissed the old Moor's hands, but El Khammas arose. "You are welcome, Reyner of Winslade. Perhaps you had best save your kisses for your beloved," he said with a twinkle in those bright black eyes. "After all, she has another shock to go through. From what she has told me while in a trance, she has been informed that you are a rather ugly fellow. Oh, it makes no difference in her love for you, and wouldn't if she could see you, she assures me." He chuckled. "What a surprise she has in store!"

Alouette rose from the deep, comfortable depths of the trance as she heard the gentle voice of the physician summon her.

"Alouette, when I sound the bell, you will awaken with full knowledge of what you have learned while in the trance. You will remember the events of your childhood, even the horrible crime that resulted in your blindness. But you will know henceforth that you were in no way to blame for the heinous act of a selfish, cruel man—no more than you were when you fell and scraped your knee when first learning to run. All sense of shame regarding that event will be gone, Alouette. You will feel free to wed Reyner of Winslade, who is here waiting for you to awaken. When I ring the bell, Alouette, you will see. And this ability will never be lost to you as long as you live. You will see the face of your beloved, and later, the babes that you will give him."

Alouette tensed, feeling like a diver about to surface after a long submersion in the inky depths of some subterranean pool.

The little brass bell tinkled.

El Khammas had drawn the shades in the sunlit room, knowing that at first any light would be blinding. Even so, she had to shut her eyes for a few moments as the dim light penetrated her brain in a searing flash of white. Tears stung her eyes, and she let them flow, taking a deep breath and letting the lids gradually admit more and more light. At first all was gray and indistinct, with blurry shapes.

The physician had said Reyner was here. She could not comprehend that miracle, either. There would be time to find out how, later. For now, all she wanted was that he be the first thing her eyes focused on.

A form loomed in the doorway—a form that gradually assumed the outline of a man. He was swathed in shadow, but as he moved forward into the lighted room, Alouette could see that he was tall, with broad, muscular shoulders that tapered to a lean torso and slim hips. He was clothed in a linen tunic and chausses that molded themselves to powerful thighs. As he drew closer she could see a thatch of unruly, tawny gold hair that curled at the back of his neck, and a pair of extraordinary eyes, whose brown velvet depths glowed with an inner fire. His nose was patrician, his lips finely chiseled, yet sensual. Despite a fresh scar on one cheek, it was a face of rugged masculine beauty.

Had Reyner brought some companion with him? She looked beside the tall, handsome man, then behind him, for the man who had held her in his arms and made her irrevocably his. Perhaps Reyner was afraid that she would see his ugliness and turn from him in disgust. She was eager to prove that was not so.

"Who are you, sir? I beg you to pardon me, but I want to see Reyner de Winslade," she said, finding her voice at last.

She felt a flash of irritation as the stranger began to smile, the dancing amusement in his eyes matched by the quirking of those sensual lips.

Alouette tried again. "My lord—"

"Alouette—don't you know me?"

That voice! It couldn't be coming from that mouth in that handsome face! The man was like the image in her mind of every hero of chivalric legend wrapped together. How could it be Reyner? Ermengarde, the beloved caretaker from her childhood, had assured her he was not comely—in fact, far from it.

"Alouette, I will introduce myself. I am Reyner of Winslade, knight in King Richard's service, and your betrothed, I assure you . . ."

"But . . . Ermengarde said . . ." She began to laugh and cry at the same time as she stared at him, incredulous.

Suddenly, she was in his arms, being kissed with fervent expertise. "Ermengarde thought to shield you from a lecherous English knight, sweetheart, by telling you I numbered ugliness among my faults. She meant well, love. She truly thought her charge could only be happy behind convent walls."

Alouette realized the truth of his compassionate words about her old servant, and knew with a flash of insight that the life of a nun had never been her own dream, but that of the old woman . . . and of Lisette, her mother, who saw a retreat from the world as the only safety. But life is to be lived, she told their hovering spirits, and forgave them.

There was yet one cloud upon her horizon—one secret sin to be exposed before she felt worthy to accept Reyner's love. Perhaps, when he heard what she had done, he would turn away from her, but she had to know that now.

"Reyner, there is something you must know about me . . ." she began, trembling.

"What is that?" he asked fondly. "Do you turn into a unicorn by the light of the full moon? I have not seen it happen, but I assure you, I look forward to it—"

"Reyner, please! 'Tis important!"

He saw then how distraught and anxious she was, and was silent.

"I think you should know that Phillip made me spy for him."

Her words made no sense. "'Made you spy?' What do you mean?" She had seemed totally free of the French king's influence ever since she had left the French court.

"I mean that he threatened to kill Henri if I refused to pass along information—"

"But what information could you know—a blind woman?"

"There was much I couldn't tell him that he wanted to know—when Richard would sail from Sicily, for example —and much that was pure curiosity on his part, as whether Richard was bedding his wife or not, and if Berengaria was with child. But Reyner, 'twas I who told the French that Richard would support Guy de Lusignan as king of Jerusalem." She dared not look at him as she made this last admission.

He came to her, tilting up her head and pulling her close. "Sweetheart, it's obvious that you told him nothing of real value, and that this was merely Phillip's last attempt to dominate and intimidate you as he felt you slipping from his control. You have nothing to apologize for—nothing."

"But what about Henri? I fear for him, Reyner! He will have to go back to France eventually, and if Phillip still lives—"

"With the power that Richard and Saladin wield between them, I'm sure that we can arrange something so that Henri lives to a ripe old age, unmolested by that scoundrel of a king. Now, my dear, unselfish Lark, stop thinking of others for a moment and think only of us . . ."

Upon reaching Acre, the Saracen escort that had seen Reyner and Alouette safely from Tyre bade them farewell and turned their swift Arab mounts back toward the desert.

The pair went straight to the palace, where, after savoring Berengaria's and Joanna's amazed joy at Alouette's safety and the miracle of her regained sight, Reyner asked for the king's whereabouts. He was informed that Richard had moved out two days after the massacre and was heading down the coastal road toward Jerusalem.

Reyner knew he had to find Richard and tell him what had happened. He had no idea whether he would be forgiven for disobeying his liege's orders, or if he were not, how severe the penalty would be. Richard was a man of whims. Despite the deep affection he had professed for his vassal, it was possible that he would call Reyner's disappearance desertion and treason.

Even in the best case, it might be months before he could send for Alouette, assuming he survived the advance toward Jerusalem. Saladin would not be able to make full use of his cavalry as the crusaders marched along, vulnerable to attack as the line became strung out. Keeping the shoreline at their right would help to protect the army, but the terrain became forested and hilly after Acre, giving the Saracens numerous opportunities to ambush the invaders.

With a heavy heart, Reyner left Acre with Thomas and Zeus. The image of Alouette's stricken face as he kissed her goodbye filled his thoughts. She had fought tears, not wanting him to see her cry, but she could not quite hide the fear that Richard would exact some severe vengeance on her lover.

He wished for the tenth—nay, hundredth time that

morning that he had made love with Alouette before leaving. She had left no doubt in his mind that she was more than willing. When he thought of how long they could be parted, his noble resolution not to bed her again before the wedding night seemed mere vainglorious posturing. Somehow he felt compelled to make some gesture to show God how thankful he was for restoring Alouette to him, but now the ache in his groin matched the ache in his heart. He supposed that it was one more sacrifice a crusader should accept cheerfully.

It had been easier during the journey to deny himself the well-remembered delights of her body. They had slept out by the campfire, surrounded by the half-dozen friendly Saracens Saladin had provided for their escort. It had been enough to hold her in his arms, look deeply into her eyes, and delight in the fact that she could see the love in his own.

He caught up with Richard in Caesarea, where the Plantagenet king was resting with his forces before they tackled the next leg of the journey between there and Jaffa.

As Reyner waited in the anteroom outside the king's chamber, he was joined by two familiar figures—Henri de Chenevy and William des Barres. When he told Henri that his sister was not only safe back in Acre, but had miraculously regained her sight, Henri had cried for joy, vowing to found a monastery in gratitude to God when he returned to France.

"God is good," Reyner agreed, "but this miracle could not have happened without the intervention of the Moslem physician, El Khammas. The Saracens' knowledge of healing is centuries ahead of our Western learning. Why not spare a Saracen's life, if it lies in your power, in tribute to what they have done for Alouette?"

Henri looked thoughtful as talk progressed to the campaign. Both men told him how Saladin's forces had paralleled their line of march, sending skirmishing parties to attack the rear. Stragglers were picked off without mercy, and their severed heads sent to Richard. It was evident that Saladin meant to avenge the massacre of the Acre garrison.

"Our infantry marching at the rear is taking the brunt of the attacks," William told him, "for it is difficult to turn and face the attackers and march backward. Our first day out, the Duke of Burgundy's troop lagged behind, and Richard himself had to spur back and lead the counter-charge. Since then, we have been under orders to march in tight formation. You couldn't throw an apple into the ranks without striking a man or a horse. And a good thing came of that day—I managed to convince Richard to forgive his old grudge against me by a bit of conspicuous bravery," William finished with a grin.

"I am glad for you, old friend." He hoped William could hold onto Richard's favor longer than he had. "And what of you, Henri? You're looking very smug. Did you play the hero as well?"

"Only in the marriage bed," replied Henri, with a smile. "Undoubtedly you didn't remain in Acre long enough to hear the news. I have married Innocentia! She carries my child, but I would have wed her anyway. I have grown to realize, here in Outremer, that many of the ways we judge a prospective wife back home—the size of her dowry lands, her noble birth—are silly and meaningless. This Sicilian girl loves me, and I, her. I want to spend my life with her, to have her son be my heir and not just a love child. I expect Alouette will be furious with me for stealing her excellent tirewoman, but relieved that I have made an honest woman of her. I could tell she feared I would treat Innocentia as Louis had her mother."

"I think you have made an excellent choice," Reyner said, embracing him.

Joining the crusade had changed the course of their lives; none of them would return to Europe the same person. They had seen other cultures, encountered other philoso-phies, and learned from them.

Now Richard's seneschal entered the room to announce that His Grace would see Sir Reyner now. Buoyed by his friends' good wishes, Reyner went through the door, feel-ing much like Daniel entering the lion's den. He would face only one lion, but one with formidable teeth.

* * *

Richard listened without interruption as Reyner recounted the events that had taken place, from the moment he had spurred his horse away from the massacre and was knocked unconscious, waking to find himself in Saladin's tent, to the point where Alouette had been healed by El Khammas. He made sure to include King Phillip's part in the scheme.

"I stand ready to accept what punishment you may seem suitable, sire, or rejoin your ranks to serve the crusade, whichever you decree." He bowed deeply, unable to meet that unblinking blue gaze any longer.

"Sir Reyner, I have already received a communication from Saladin, interceding on your behalf. He tells me of the dreadful fate suffered by your scoundrel of a cousin at the hands of The Old Man of the Mountain—and I suppose I am to incur a like fate should I punish you now for deserting my side in battle." Richard seemed amused, rather than discomfited, by the implied threat.

"In any case, his request does not counter my own inclinations. I fear that after the wondrous miracle the Saracen physician wrought for you, you might feel ambivalent about slaying any more of them—and that indecision could cost you your life.

"You are aware of my affection for you, Reyner," Richard continued, abandoning his regal air and speaking openly to his vassal, "as I am aware that you cannot fully return it, except as the love and duty you bear your king. I want you to be happy, Reyner, even though you have chosen a different path. Your way lies with Alouette. Wed her, and be happy—though you will perhaps understand why I cannot bear to witness your choice.

"I think it best that you return to England with your bride. I do not want you to feel you are being sent away. You are not in disgrace. A man can serve me other than on crusade, you know. The letters I have been receiving from Queen Eleanor suggest I need another pair of eyes to observe my dear brother, Prince John.

"Go back to England, Reyner. I'm giving you an excuse —a grant of land in Kent on which you may erect a keep. Why not call it 'New Acre?' You'll be a baron, holding directly of me. That won't cause friction with your father, the earl, will it?" Richard asked, enjoying himself now as he watched the dumfounded expression on Reyner's face.

"Nay, sire! You know I am his vassal for Winslade, but I cannot picture Earl Simon's course counter to the royal house's interests. I . . . thank you, Your Grace. Words are inadequate to express how I feel."

"They are, aren't they?" Richard agreed, husky-voiced. "I suppose that's why there are troubadors. You have your Lark; I, my Blondel. Go with God, Reyner. Remember, I shall expect regular reports!"

Reyner journeyed to Acre, his heart so light it might have had wings. To be allowed to return to the green hills and forests of England with his bride was better fortune than any man deserved. And to return a newly created baron! Lord Reyner, Baron of New Acre, he said to himself, liking the sound of it. And his lady, Countess Alouette. He knew his brother, Aimery, would be as glad for him as their father would. Jealousy had never had any part in their relationship, and in any case, Aimery would inherit the earldom someday. His mother would be worried only that she wouldn't get to see him and her new daughter-in-law often enough to suit her!

Berengaria and Joanna, bored in Acre without the presence of Richard and the major part of the crusading army, were delighted to arrange a wedding with very little prior notice—a good thing, since Alouette was so completely astounded by Reyner's unexpected return that she laughed and cried for joy. She had been prepared to wait months to see her lover again; yet here he was, back in a few days, with the incredible news that they could wed immediately, that Richard had given Reyner a barony, and that they were to return home! Home would be England; her love's land would be hers.

Reyner and Alouette were married at sunset, when the day's fierce heat surrendered to the cool breezes sweeping in from the desert. Their wedding took place in the chapel of the palace, which was packed with well-wishers who had remained behind to guard the Christian-held city.

The two queens stood as witnesses, both with tears of joy sparkling in their eyes. If Berengaria harbored a trace of envy in her heart as she compared the loving bridegroom with her cool and distant Richard, she gave no indication.

At one side stood Princess Chloe, who had been bribed into good behavior by the gift of a new bliaut from Berengaria, and threatened with dire punishment by Joanna if she did not behave. On the other was Lady Innocentia de Chenevy, still radiant from her own marriage and unable to seriously believe anyone could be addressing *her* as *Comtesse*. As yet the skillful cut of her bliaut hid the thickened waist that betokened the coming babe. She had been relieved when Alouette had shown her sincere approval of her marriage to her stepbrother.

"I don't know how this happened, my lady," she had told Alouette at her first opportunity to speak to her alone. She meant the pregnancy. "I was taking the potion . . ."

Alouette had seen the anxiety shining in the liquid black Sicilian eyes that she would think Innocentia had gotten with child deliberately to try to trap Henri. It was an age-old trick, after all, though not one that often worked for peasant girls with noble lovers.

She had embraced the Sicilian girl reassuringly. "Oh, Innocentia, as if I would think such a thing! It's obvious that this babe is God's will. I wonder if he—or she—will be dark like you, or fair like Henri. I am thrilled you are now my sister-by-marriage, though you must help me find another tirewoman. Meanwhile, we shall help each other, agreed?"

Next to Innocentia sat a most unusual wedding guest, the half-wolf Zeus. The canine's ears were perked forward alertly, but his tongue lolled out in such a fashion that one could swear the animal was grinning.

Berengaria's chaplain had heartily objected to the presence of the intimidating beast. "Wolves do not belong in God's house, Your Grace," he said in a haughty tone that he hoped would hide his fear of those formidable teeth.

Berengaria was meek with priests and would have allowed herself to be dissuaded; not so Richard's sister. Joanna had the Plantagenet refusal to accept "no" as an answer.

"Was not the wolf, like all animals, created by God before men? Do not nobles often take their falcons with them into mass? Zeus helped bring this man and woman together, and I tell you, he will be present. Don't worry, he won't nip your fingers unless you missay your Latin."

As if he took her threat seriously, the priest made no protest when Zeus padded in solemnly to take his place among the rest.

Alouette and Reyner were scarcely aware of the many witnesses to their nuptial vows. They had eyes only for each other.

Their mutual absorption was easy to understand. Alouette was a vision in a blue silk bliaut the exact color of her eyes and shot through with silver. The cloth had been a wedding gift from Saladin. A pearl-studded gold circlet shone on the ebony hair that hung thick and loose, reaching nearly to her slender waist.

Reyner was dresed in a tunic of emerald green given to him by Queen Joanna, which perfectly complemented his tawny hair and dark eyes. An emerald-studded gold link belt, a gift from the king and queen of England, hung low about his waist, emphasizing the narrowness of his hips. Scarlet hose showed off his powerfully built calves. His hair, lightened by the desert sun, had been neatly trimmed and gleamed gold against his bronzed skin and white teeth. Every woman attending the wedding envied Alouette her bridegroom, just as the men sighed covetously while gazing at the lissome "Lark."

As they sat at the center of the table on the dais after the ceremony, Reyner's hot gaze over the edge of the silver goblet they shared seared Alouette with its passionate intensity. She felt alternately feverish and shivery. Was the warmth spreading through her the result of the wine she'd drunk, or the very meaningful way he gazed at her, his heart in his eyes? How delightful it was to experience love through this new sense!

At last Joanna, more perceptive than the unawakened Berengaria, brought their agony of anticipation to a close and signaled the end of the feast, despite the groans and good-natured complaints of the dedicated tipplers, who cared little about the newlyweds' impatience.

By prearrangement, there was no bedding ceremony in which Alouette would have been displayed naked to a roomful of tipsy guests. Reyner was not willing to subject her to such embarrassment, no matter how traditional it was. All the two of them must endure was the procession of joking, singing revellers they led through the streets to their house.

Once they bid the guests a patiently civil good night, however, the rest of the night was theirs. They climbed to the roof and a private bower much like the upper room they had shared in the Palace of the Kings. But this one was open to the stars and the full moon that lit the sky.

In the shimmering moonlight, Reyner removed his lady's silken garments one by one until she stood bare and beautiful before him with only the pearl-studded coronet gleaming atop her ebony hair. This she removed herself. "How beautiful this is," she said, "a perfect circle, love's own crown."

EPILOGUE

       Phillip Capet, who had taken a leisurely, circuitous route home from Outremer, stopping in Rome to visit His Holiness the Pope, reached Paris before Christmas. He would have been surprised if he had known that at the same moment as he entered Paris, the earl and countess of Hawkingham were welcoming their son and new daughter-in-law back to England. Reyner and Alouette had left much later, of course, but they were impatient to be on English soil, and had not dallied.

The French king was not so amused by the letter he found waiting for him in his chamber at the Cité Palace. It lay on his pillow, next to a bundle wrapped in oilskin. Consumed by curiosity, Phillip broke the seal on the letter and began to read.

  To Phillip Capet, King of France, greetings:

    Know you by these words that at the request of Saladin, four lives are under my protection—those of the count and countess of Chenevy and the baron and countess of New Acre (formerly known to you as Sir Reyner of Winslade and Lady Alouette de Chenevy).

    Count Henri de Chenevy, knowing nothing of the threats you once made against him, will one day return to France and serve you loyally. If you are wise and wish your days to be long upon the earth, you will treat him well. If not, you will meet your end as your lackey Fulk de Langres has, but not before I reveal to the world that you allowed the rape of your sister when it was in your power to save her. If you doubt my ability to carry out this threat, ask your servants if anyone saw this message delivered, and examine the contents of the package.

Rashid ed-Din Sinan
The Old Man of the Mountain

Phillip screamed as he unwrapped the bundle. Inside the oilskin covering was the head of Fulk de Langres.

Dear Readers,

I would love to hear from you. I enjoy knowing if you liked this book, but what is even more helpful are specific comments about *what* you liked (or didn't like) about the story! You may write me in care of Warner Books, 666 Fifth Avenue, New York, New York, 10103.

Laurie Grant
Columbus, Ohio

GET LOVESTRUCK!

AND GET STRIKING ROMANCES FROM POPULAR LIBRARY'S BELOVED AUTHORS

Watch for these exciting romances in the months to come:

June 1989
LOVE'S OWN CROWN by Laurie Grant
FAIR GAME by Doreen Owens Malek

July 1989
SHIELD'S LADY by Amanda Glass
BLAZE OF PASSION by Lisa Ann Verge

August 1989
BODY AND SOUL by Sherryl Woods
PROMISE OF SUMMER by Louisa Rawlings

September 1989
STAR STRUCK by Ann Miller
HIDDEN FIRE by Phyllis Herrm

October 1989
FAITH AND HONOR by Robin Maderich
SHADOW DANCE by Susan Andersen

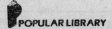